Raves for the Novels of Christine Dorsey

"*My Seaswept...*   d
read!"   s

"From the c...   -
packed tale of interesting, colorful characters and two antago-
nistic lovers who, regardless of the circumstances, can't resist one
another."   —*Rendezvous*

MY SAVAGE HEART
"*My Savage Heart* will leave readers breathless and eagerly anticipating the remaining novels in this new trilogy. Ms. Dorsey has
created another incredible hero and a wonderful love story."
                                                    —*Romantic Times*

"As always, Christine Dorsey can be counted on to give us a
tale full of adventure and romance. *My Savage Heart* is a poignantly
written, emotion-packed read that will touch your heart."
                                                    —*Affaire de Coeur*

SEA OF TEMPTATION
"In *Sea of Temptation*, the sensational conclusion to her outstanding Charleston Trilogy, Christine Dorsey demonstrates why
she is one of the most talented authors of the genre today: strong,
unforgettable characters, rousing adventures, and history com-
bine to create 'keepers.' "   —*Romantic Times*

"Ms. Dorsey's hero and heroine are both strong-willed individ-
uals and their misunderstandings add some very funny situations
to this action-packed historical. On the other hand, their fiery
passion will send your temperature rising. An outstanding conclusion to a fascinating series on the Blackstones."   —*Rendezvous*

SEA OF DESIRE
"Christine Dorsey has written a tale of passion, adventure, and
love that is impossible to put down. *Sea of Desire* is a book you
shouldn't miss and will need some space on your keeper shelf.
It is marvelous!"   —*Affaire de Coeur*

"Blazing passion, nonstop adventure, and a "be-still-my-
beating-heart" hero are just a few of the highlights of this captivating second novel in Ms. Dorsey's Charleston Trilogy. *Sea of Desire*
is not to be missed!"   —*Romantic Times*

"Let me help you," Logan said. He knelt beside her, reaching out to cover her hand with his own.

"No. You gave me this task to do and I shall do it." Her fingers were numb from the water, but somehow she didn't mind as long as his hand covered hers. "You were right to think I can't do anything."

The warmth of his hand disappeared and Rachel felt fresh tears spring to her eyes. Then he clasped her shoulders, turning her upper body around so that she was forced to look at him.

"I was wrong, Rachel. You have many talents."

"But none that are worthwhile." She sniffed and he gathered her, snuggling her against his chest. Rachel knew she should pull away, but it felt so pleasant to be there, warm and secure.

"Rachel."

She sniffed when he said her name. He really did have a pleasant way of saying it—not like when he called her Your Highness. She looked up to tell him so, but could only sniff again.

He smiled, that smile that showed his dimples, and brushed away a tear with his thumb. His face was very close to hers, his eyes very green and Rachel didn't protest at all when he curved his other hand around the back of her head. And inched her closer.

The first brush of his lips against hers was just that, a whisper of breath, the slightest pressure of warm flesh. Yet it felt like more, so much more. Rachel sighed, wondering how the mere suggestion of a kiss could feel so good . . .

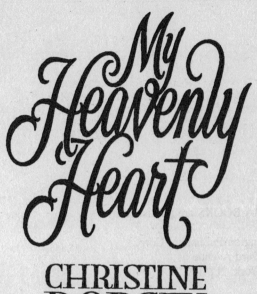

My Heavenly Heart

CHRISTINE DORSEY

ZEBRA BOOKS
KENSINGTON PUBLISHING CORP.

ZEBRA BOOKS are published by

Kensington Publishing Corp.
850 Third Avenue
New York, NY 10022

First Printing: May, 1995

Printed in the United States of America

For my father, who taught me of the "other side."
And as always for Chip.

Prologue

"Coincidence is God's way of performing a mira-
cle anonymously."

—Anonymous

Autumn 1764
Queen's House, London

"Blast Elizabeth and her confounded romantic notion of of love."

A grimace accompanied her words as evening dew
seeped through Lady Rachel Elliott's satin slippers.
They were blue, encrusted with silver lace, and they
matched her gown of silk taffeta. "All celestial blue
and star glow," Prince William, the king's brother
had said, when he saw her earlier. "You look like an
angel."

"Perhaps, but that was before I overheard Lord
Albert, Duke of Bingham, demand to know his wife's
whereabouts," Rachel grumbled to herself as she
shifted the wide skirts of her gown to avoid a flowerless
rosebush. Despite her effort a bit of lace caught on
a thorn. She gave the fabric a yank feeling more devil
than angel now. Rachel imagined she looked it, too.
Neither the shoes nor the gown were meant for tramping along overgrown garden paths and for all the
care she took while hurrying through the arbor, Ra-

chel could tell her carefully arranged and powdered
wig was askew as well.

No doubt about it, her evening was ruined. And
all because her cousin and friend, Lady Elizabeth
Bingham, insisted upon continuing her dalliance with
Sir Geoffrey . . . even though her husband was newly
arrived at court.

Rachel paused to get her bearings. Behind her,
aglow with candlelight and warmth, was Queen's
House. If she listened intently, Rachel could hear
the melodious strains of Handel played by Queen
Charlotte's band. There was laughter and fun, and
scores of swains, their lips nigh dripping with flattery,
awaiting her. The tug to return was strong.

"Oh . . ." The sound started deep in Rachel's cor-
seted chest and gritted through her clenched teeth
as she forced herself to turn away and tramp down
the grass-covered slope toward the lake. Wait till she
found Liz. She would show no mercy in reproving
her cousin. And if Sir Geoffrey spoke up . . . well, he
would feel the sharp edge of her tongue as well.
Rachel didn't care if he was broad of shoulder and
handsome of face. *She* didn't even care that his very
smile sent Liz into a swoon. There was a time and
place for such affairs. And from the expression on
Lord Bingham's face when he stormed from the ballroom, it was obvious this wasn't one of them.

There were fewer lanterns now that she'd left the
formal gardens. They offered little light and Rachel
hoped she'd be able to find Liz and Geoffrey. "Don't
let them have gone off to his lodgings," she pleaded
to no one in particular. But Rachel didn't think they'd
risk leaving the palace this evening.

"Rachel, I must go to Geoff and explain," Liz had
insisted earlier in the evening after guiding them
both into a small private alcove.

All around them music played, gaiety abounded,

and Rachel's mind was still on her flirtation with the king's brother. It took a moment for Liz's words to register. "Explain what?" Rachel asked, but Liz had simply looked at her with that dreamy expression on her face as if to say Rachel wouldn't understand.

And she didn't. If this was what love did to a person, Rachel was glad not to be afflicted with the emotion.

Rachel paused when she heard the voices over the gentle swishing of the lake lapping the shore. With a sigh she set off toward the sound. The grass was taller here, wetting the hem of her gown even though she lifted it. Why couldn't the lovers find somewhere more civilized to meet, for goodness' sake?

"There you are." Rachel marched toward the couple when she spotted them standing near the end of the pier that jutted out into the lake. It was too dark to see the expressions on Liz's and Geoffrey's faces but Rachel imagined they both were surprised when she spoke. They separated quickly, though Sir Geoffrey kept his arm about her cousin's shoulders.

"What . . . what on earth are you doing here, Rachel?" Liz sounded thoroughly flustered.

"I should think that obvious." Rachel gave an unladylike snort. "I've come to fetch you back." Rachel addressed Liz. She decided she didn't give a fig what Geoffrey thought or did. And it wasn't because he monopolized her cousin's time—time usually spent with her—since his arrival at court.

"But Rachel, I told you where I was going . . ."

"Yes, you did. And though I thought at the time it utter foolishness—"

"I fail to see why Elizabeth's and my whereabouts are your concern, Lady Rachel."

Rachel opened her mouth to tell him what she thought of men like him but before she could Liz stepped between them. "Please." She touched Geoffrey's sleeve with one hand, Rachel's with the other.

"Please don't argue. You're the two people I love most in the world."

Geoffrey seemed to think this admission called for him to step closer to his beloved.

Rachel only sighed.

"I thought you should know," Rachel began, "that your husband is looking for you."

"Albert stopped gaming long enough to realize I was gone?" Liz seemed to sink back into Geoffrey's embrace. "Do you think he suspects?"

"I haven't a clue." Rachel softened her voice and reached for her cousin's hands. They were cold. "I think we should go back to Queen's House. He seemed angry and—" Rachel paused when Liz made a low whimpering sound. "Elizabeth, it's the only way. I'll say we were together."

"You don't understand." Elizabeth's fingers linked with Rachel's. "You don't know what he's like. If he suspects something he'll—"

The rest of Elizabeth's words were cut off when a shot rang out sending a flock of ducks exploding into the night sky. It also sent Geoffrey crumbling to his knees.

Rachel's head whipped round toward shore in time to see the man standing there, a pistol in each hand. "Albert." His name escaped her on a gasp as another report sounded. Through their linked hands, Rachel felt the jolt of the ball slamming into her cousin. Then Liz fell forward, the weight of her body sending Rachel plummeting off the pier into the lake.

Panic seized Rachel the instant she hit the frigid water. The lake embraced her as surely as if it had tentaclelike arms, dragging her down. She fought, struggling in its grip till her limbs grew weak. Screams for help thundered in her ears but succeeded only in filling her mouth with the foul taste of death.

She tried to think. It was the heavy gown that caused

her to sink, the silver lace and metal hoops. If she could only rid herself of her clothing. But it had taken three maids nearly an hour to dress her and no amount of wriggling could undo their accomplishment.

She was dying. Her chest burned, the pain near unbearable. Then suddenly it was gone. So was the frigid water and the awful fear. All that remained was a slightly dizzying spin, spiraling her upward. And calm. Blessed calm.

"You've done it now. You are an idiot."

"But how was I to know she'd go after her cousin? It wasn't at all like her."

"Haven't you learned anything since you've been here? Mortals are full of surprises."

"Especially this one."

How annoying they were, Rachel thought as she tried to ignore the argument. They threatened to ruin an otherwise wonderful experience. The dark that surrounded her was soft and soothing. And up ahead a white light shone so blindingly pure and warm that it should have hurt her eyes. Except that she had no eyes, or body either.

She simply existed.

Never before had she felt so accepted, so cared for. Love surrounded her, flowed through her as she drifted about. Content, though anxious to move toward the light. At peace except—

"What are we to do?"

"Would you cease your whining? And what do you mean *we*?"

"Surely you plan to help me."

"I shall remind you again. It was your mistake."

"But I'm merely an apprentice. You were to guide me. And I only glanced away for a moment."

"Stop it!" She'd had enough of their bickering. Of them disturbing her. But Rachel hadn't meant to yell at them. Actually she hadn't yelled. It was as if she communicated with them on some plane other than the spoken word. Whatever it was, they both seemed stunned by her scolding. At least they were silent for a moment. That is until the whiner started again.

"See, I told you she was trouble."

"You didn't say trouble, merely unpredictable, and that I will readily concede." He sighed. "The question is what is to be done."

"Done about what?" Rachel decided she must help them solve their dilemma if she was to have any peace.

"About you, of course."

"Yes," the whiner agreed in an accusing tone. "It wasn't your time to die."

"Die? But I'm not d—" Rachel couldn't complete her denial. For as difficult as it was to accept—she didn't feel dead—in her heart she knew it was true. But where were the things she'd been led to expect? The host of heavenly angels? Or, God forbid, the fiery brimstone? And Rachel had another question. "What happened to Liz?"

"She's gone on, as has her soul mate Geoffrey."

Rachel knew instinctively the spirit meant gone on toward the light. The radiant light that shimmered just out of reach. "Then send me on," Rachel insisted. "I'm ready to go."

"If only it were that simple."

For the first time Rachel felt an inkling of fear. "You can't mean I'm destined for . . . for hell?" At that moment her soul seemed awash with memories of her life. And to Rachel's discomfort, some shone less than sterling in the pure light of the afterworld. There was the time she lied to her mother about the reason for her scrapped knees and torn dress. Then there was the gossip. She was quite fond of court intrigue and never hesitated to pass any crumb of information along to Liz. And she wasn't very pious. Or charitable. Just last week she passed by an alms seeker pretending not to see the wretched man. And then there was—

"Oh, do stop your reminiscing. I don't care to review all your misdeeds. Besides, you're not destined to eternal damnation."

"Thank God," Rachel thought with a sigh of relief.

"Precisely. But never mind that now. Didn't you hear what Ebenezer said? It wasn't your time to die."

Ebenezer? The spirits had names? Rachel pushed that thought aside. The answer to the problem seemed simple enough. It wasn't her time to die, so . . . "Send me back to my life."

"It isn't that easy."

Ebenezer agreed. "You've passed over."

"But it was a mistake. You said so yourself. *Your* mistake." Her temper—another of her faults if she were honest—was upon her.

"I'm only an apprentice."

Rachel was preparing her next argument, after all, none of this was *her* fault, when the other spirit interrupted.

"There is something we might do." He paused just long enough to garner Rachel's and Ebenezer's attention. "Perhaps if she earned her way back."

"Of course." Ebenezer sounded relieved. But then the whiny edge returned to his thoughts. "Do you think He will agree to it?"

"We shall see. There are precedents, of course. We must speak with Him straightaway."

Rachel felt the force of the two spirits leaving her. "Wait!" She wasn't sure she liked this turn of events

any more than she liked the ones that brought her
here. ''What do you mean precedents? What must I
do to earn my way back?''

Off in the distance near the light she felt the spirits
pause. Then the one who seemed to be in charge
answered. ''It's very simple, actually. You need only
save the life of a lost soul.''

Chapter One

"Sometimes accidents happen in life from which
we have need of a little madness to extricate
ourselves successfully."

—La Rochefoucauld
Maxims

"Don't jump, for heaven's sake!"

The sound of another human voice would have
shocked Logan MacQuaid even if the words weren't
screamed in his ear. Gravel slid beneath his moccasined feet as his body jerked. He scrambled, catching
himself as he teetered precariously on the edge of
the rocky summit that looked out over the gap below.
His heart pounding he twisted around, catching a
glimpse of silvery blue from the corner of his eye.
Then something . . . or someone touched his arm.
He recoiled instinctively and this time no amount of
scrambling kept his feet from sliding over the edge.

"Shit!" Logan wrenched around, clawing at the
granite, clutching at the rock face with his hands and
feet, knees, anything to stop his descent. Knowing
what lay below.

A sudden and painful trip to eternity. Pebbles torn
loose by his thrashing rained around him, clattering
down the side of the mountain. He grabbed hold of

an outcrop of moss-covered rock, jolting to a stop a good rod from the top.

Sweat slicked his palms. *Pull yourself up. Pull yourself up, damnit*! Logan wasn't sure if he said the words aloud or not. He was trying to control the panic swelling inside him. He hated the thought of having nothing beneath his feet. Nothing. The sound of his ragged breathing roared in his ears and Logan forced himself to inhale slowly. But he didn't look down.

Around him the wind whistled, chill with the promise of winter. And he just hung there, doing his best to hug the rock, feeling his fragile hold slowly slipping away.

Then he heard the voice again.

He must be hallucinating. No one knew better than he how pain and loneliness could do that to a body. But the more he tried to ignore the shouts, the more insistent they became. Finally he had no choice but to look up. More loose pebbles skittered down the cliff when he shifted.

"Are you all right?"

Logan squinted. The sun had started its afternoon dip toward the west, the last rays glinting at him from atop the mountain. They formed an aurora of light behind what appeared to be a woman. A woman with a huge pile of white hair curled crookedly on her head. But that was ridiculous. Yet he could see her head as she leaned over the edge of the cliff. Logan blinked, squeezing his eyes shut before he allowed himself to peek again. The idea that a woman would find her way to this remote mountaintop was so absurd he was convinced she was his imagination . . . except she was still there. And still frantically calling to him. The same idiotic question over and over.

"Are you all right? Are you all right?"

"Hell no, I'm not all right," Logan yelled. If she were an apparition only the solitary eagle circling overhead would hear him talking to himself. And in a few more moments, after he plummeted to his death, what in the hell did it matter anyway?

"What shall I do?" Her head disappeared a moment, then popped back into view. "I don't know how to help you."

Logan could swear he saw a hand reach down toward him, a hand nearly dripping with silver lace. But it didn't come within fifteen feet of reaching him and was quickly withdrawn. He must be losing his mind. His half-brother Wolf said it would happen sooner or later if Logan kept to himself . . . and the drink.

Christ, he didn't want to die like this, despite what he'd thought in the past. He had to fight this foolishness. Logan concentrated on sliding his left foot up slowly till his toes found a small niche in the rock.

"Tell me what to do."

The voice was pleading now and taking Logan's attention away from working his other foot into a toehold. "Get the hell away from me!" He was in a life-or-death struggle. He didn't have time for distracting daydreams.

"I can't." His imagination sounded incensed. "I've been sent to save you."

"Then for God's sake get a rope."

Then she just vanished, leaving Logan convinced he'd imagined the entire thing, as he tried to make himself loosen his grip on the slippery ledge to feel for something higher up to grab hold of. He couldn't let panic overpower him. He couldn't.

Sweat ran rivulets down his back. It streamed into the creases across his forehead and stung his eyes. But it didn't keep him from noticing the rope that flopped down not two feet to his left. It was his. He recognized it as one he'd traded skins for at Seven Pines. But what was an apparition doing with his—?

"I tied it to a tree," she yelled. "I think it's strong enough to hold you."

Damn, this imagination thing was getting out of hand.

"Well, aren't you going to grab hold of it?"

Logan swallowed, the natural function painful because of the tightness of his throat. He had lost what was left of his mind. There was no woman. No rope. Except he could feel it bumping against his arm as she jiggled it.

Whomp!

It hit him again.

"What are you waiting for?"

She sounded impatient and it was all Logan could do to keep himself from laughing out loud. He glanced toward the rope, then squinted up, unable to see anything distinctly.

"What the hell." There was no place above him to grip the side of the mountain. He might as well die hanging to a nonexistent rope. If he could only make himself let go and try. Logan clamped his teeth down on his bottom lip and tasted blood. As many times as he'd thought about death—thought about taking the extra step off the cliff necessary to end it all—this should have been easy. But it wasn't.

The vast emptiness below him seemed to beckon, to laugh at him, a mocking laugh, a victorious laugh. And even though Logan knew it was only the wind rattling through the pines, he couldn't make himself let go. *Concentrate on breathing. Pretend you're simply reaching for a rope.* "No! Don't look down. Won't do any good to look down. Pretend you're somewhere with solid ground beneath your feet. Anywhere. Seven Pines. Aye. You're at Seven Pines and someone . . . Raff asks you to hold this rope for him and you . . ." Logan jerked his hand off the rock ledge and grabbed for the rope.

Twisted hemp bit into his palm as his long fingers clutched for purchase. At first relief that he defeated his paralyzing fear overshadowed his surprise that the rope was real.

It was easier to let loose his death-grip on the rock with his other hand. Now both fists clung to the rope. And though it swayed and groaned with his weight, the rope held. At least he didn't go swinging down into oblivion.

"Climb up, can't you?"

Damn, she was a nag, her voice sharp and edged with impatience. If he had to conjure up a female, why couldn't she be soft-spoken? Logan took a deep breath and inched his right hand up. Then his left. Right. Left. The muscles in his arms bulged as he pulled his weight up the rope, inch by inch.

The rope hummed, taut and straining, as Rachel clasped her hands and glanced back toward where she'd tied it about the tree. It appeared to be holding, though she couldn't be certain. Tying ropes . . . tying anything was not a skill where she excelled. Why even her petticoat tapes were fastened by her lady's maid. But she'd done her best. Now why didn't the foolish man come along? There was more than his life at stake . . . a lot more.

Rachel hurried toward the side of the precipice when she heard a string of mumbled curses. Then a hand appeared groping its way over the edge. She stepped back as he hauled himself straining and puffing onto the gravely ground. He lay there sprawled out at her feet, his face pressed into the dirt, his feet dangling over the cliff. She could see little of him other than he was large, garbed in buckskin, and had long, tangled black hair. And that his breathing swelled the side of his chest like a bellows.

"Are you all right?" Her question was tentative . . . and went unanswered. Rachel stepped closer. "Ex-

cuse me," she began, only to have something latch
on to her foot. Before she could do more than squeal
in dismay her ankle was jerked and she landed hard
on the ground, amid blue silver silk and petticoats.
The creature bounded up pressing her down till the
pebbles dug into her shoulders and plopped on top
of her.

"Who are you?" His voice was a low growl, demanding in her ear, and Rachel tried to answer. But
the brute had knocked the air from her lungs and
his weight kept her from taking a breath. Which
shouldn't really matter since she was already dead,
but for some reason it did. Rachel wriggled against
his strength, tearing at his clothing with her fingers.
When he shifted, she sucked in air, now breathing
near as hard as he.

"You heard me, wench. What's your name?"

He was so close she could see the tiny flecks of gold
that starred from the center of his green eyes. For a
moment she just stared, fascinated. But then his rough
hand wrapped around her chin, and the reality of her
circumstances flooded about her. With a twist of her
aristocratic head, Rachel dislodged his hold.

"I," she said in her haughtiest voice—the one she
reserved for servants who dared not anticipate her
every whim—"am Lady Rachel Elliott. And you will
kindly remove yourself from my person."

Her words seemed to startle him, for he blinked,
and for a moment she thought he would comply with
her command. But instead he settled his long body
more securely on top of her, his legs sliding between
hers.

"First you will tell me what demon possessed you
to near kill me."

"Kill you?" It was disgraceful the way he lay there
looking at her. But Rachel refused to enter into a
contest of strength with him. For one thing she would

most certainly lose. For another, as uncomfortable as she was, none of this really mattered. She saved his wretched life, though by the looks of him she couldn't understand why anyone cared that she should. She would soon be gone, back to where she belonged. "It was I who saved you from leaping into the abyss. And I assure you, t'was no demon that possessed me."

"Mortal man then?" He pushed up on his elbows enough to glance around the clearing. "Who's with you?"

Rachel's eyes were focused on his taut, sun-darkened neck. "No one." She tried to sigh—this was all becoming very tedious—but his chest was in the way. "I came alone. Now would you kindly—"

But she never was able to finish her request for before she knew what he was about there was a knife near as long as Prince William's sword poised beside her cheek.

"Don't be lying to me wench."

"I am *not* lying."

The blade inched closer. "You think I don't know how steep the path to get up here is? How out of the way it be?"

Rachel admitted to a moment of fear. The kiss of steel along her face seemed very real. But she didn't imagine a person died more than once, at least not two times in as many days. She looked him straight in his strange light eyes. "It matters naught what you do to me."

"Oh?" He lifted a dark brow. "And why might that be?"

Rachel pursed her lips. Should she bother explaining herself to the brute? The slight pressure of the blade skimming her skin decided it. "I'm not . . . well, I'm not what I appear to be."

He pushed further up on his elbows, giving her an insolent stare. "You appear to be a woman."

Heated blood rushed to her face and Rachel's lips thinned. Blushes were something she could prettily fake. They were not something caused by men garbed in animal skins. "I am not real," she managed to say between clenched teeth. But the last word was cut off as she sucked in her breath. He'd covered the exposed curve of her breast with his free hand. His palm was rough and hot, heating her flesh.

"You feel real enough." His fingers dipped beneath the lace-trimmed bodice.

Rachel could only sputter. Which wasn't like her at all, she who was known for her sparkling wit and clever conversation. She who was rumored to have captured the heart of the king's brother. "Stop it this instant," she finally managed, but could have saved her breath. He seemed to have tired of the diversion and with a swiftness and grace she never expected pushed to his feet. His hand manacled her wrist, dragging her up with him.

He glanced about the clearing again as if he expected someone to come leaping out at him, then seemingly satisfied, sheathed the knife down the side of his soft boots. "I'll have an honest answer from you now, woman," he said, his grip tightening around her arm. Without waiting for her to speak he pulled her toward a rough log dwelling.

She'd barely noticed it before when she was looking for the rope. At the time her mind was filled with what might happen to her if she failed to save him. Now she studied the structure with a somewhat detached interest.

The building was small and crude, the wood not even planed but still covered by thick bark. These logs were piled one atop the other to form the walls, though one side was almost entirely covered by a stone chimney. Facing the cliff was a door made of naught but a few planks of wood. It stood ajar.

Without ceremony he yanked her through the portal, giving her a shove that sent her sprawling onto a thick pile of furs. Dust puffed into the air and Rachel sneezed delicately.

The creature didn't seem to notice. He was too busy checking the charge in the flintlock rifle he grabbed up from beside the door. He turned toward her and Rachel almost laughed. Did he honestly think to frighten her with a gun? She who had already drowned in the lake behind Queen's House? It was Liz who'd been shot, Liz and Geoffrey. The smile that played at the corners of her mouth disappeared as the explosive sounds echoed through her memory.

"What the hell is wrong with you?"

The sharp edge to his question filtered through to Rachel and she blinked, taken aback by his nearness. For now he squatted in front of her, close enough for her to notice his eyes again, to feel the warmth of his rum-laced breath. The rifle lay at an angle across the buckskin molded over his thighs. His hands clasped her shoulders and though they were still now, Rachel had a feeling they'd been shaking her moments ago.

She reached up to straighten her wig and her fingers brushed the slope of her cheek. It surprised her to find the smooth skin wet with tears. Rachel took a deep breath. "There's nothing amiss with me that leaving your odious company wouldn't cure."

He studied her a few moments, eyes narrowed, jaw clenched beneath a layer of dark whiskers. Pushing himself up, he strode toward the door, glancing back only long enough to say, "I don't recall inviting you for a visit." Then he peered outside, cradling the rifle loosely in the crook of his arm. But Rachel didn't doubt he could bring the weapon to his shoulder and pull the trigger faster than she could snap open a fan. At least he wasn't aiming her way. He seemed intent upon watching for someone outside.

Foolish man.

If there was anyone out and about, they had nothing to do with her. She'd arrived here . . . Rachel tried to remember exactly how she did get here, wherever here was. She could recall the light and the angels telling her to save a lost soul, then a whirling vortex of sound and colors. There was never any doubt in her mind that the man by the door was the one she was to rescue.

Though to be sure, she couldn't imagine why he was worth the bother. He was hardly a prince or even a man of any consequence. His manner of dress was strange to her, animal skins wrapped tightly about his feet and legs, more skins forming a loosely draped shirt. Certainly not the trappings of a gentleman.

Nor did his manners show signs of breeding. His voice had neither the soft melodic cadence nor the ease of speech she was used to. He was gruff and unappreciative of her sacrifice for him.

Rachel took a deep breath and wrapped her arms about her waist. She was cold and uncomfortable. The low burning fire in the hearth gave off more smoke than heat, filling the small cabin with a haze that burned her eyes. She was more than ready to leave.

But how?

She had saved his miserable life. Why wasn't she gone from this place? Rachel sucked in her cheeks and looked up toward the ceiling. Ignoring the blackened rafters hung with more animal skins, she whispered under her breath. "Take me back . . . please."

"What be you mumbling about?"

Rachel's head snapped down, her eyes locking with his. "I don't mumble."

"Nay, of course you don't."

"I don't." Rachel turned her face away, then looked back quickly. "Where are you going?" He opened the door wider and stepped through, still carrying the rifle.

"I'll be taking a look about for your friends," he said, ignoring her assurance that she came alone.

At least he was gone.

Rachel took a deep breath and, gathering her skirts, stood. Now all she had to do was . . . Hugging herself, Rachel pursed her lips. Whatever was she supposed to do? Certainly God knew her task was complete. He knew all, didn't He? Then why wasn't He putting her back in her real life? Or at least returning her to those two meddlesome spirits?

The cabin was small. No more than ten paces took her from end to end, from hearth to window. She measured the dwelling several times before inspiration struck her. "Of course." With a sigh of relief Rachel returned to the disheveled pile of furs and dropped to her knees. She took a moment to spread her silver and blue skirt about her.

How could she be so foolish . . . so irreverent to think she could speak with God or His angels standing up. Piously she folded her hands. Her wig cocked forward over one brow as she bowed her head.

"Blast this—" Rachel bit off her blasphemous words, glancing nervously toward the crude ceiling before impatiently setting her hairpiece to rights. Then she lowered her head, squeezed her eyes shut, and tried to clear her mind of all but the purest thoughts.

"God in Heaven, hear my humble prayer." She paused, waiting for the Heavenly Spirit to flow through her. It didn't. Perhaps it wasn't necessary. After all, she was one of God's instruments. An angel herself. An angel returned to earth to do God's work. Buoyed by that thought, Rachel continued. "I have done what you asked of me." And not without considerable hardship and—Perhaps she shouldn't complain of the inconvenience. "I have rescued your . . . your . . . lamb." Somehow she found it difficult to describe the man she saved as a lamb. A bull, perhaps. Or a bear. Rachel choked down a giggle, deciding it didn't matter how she referred to him. The Lord knew whom she meant.

"As you can tell, I have completed the task described to me and wish to return home." She paused. "To Queen's House, if you please." A smile curved her lips. That appeared to be everything. But her "amen" was drowned out when the aforementioned lamb burst through the door.

"Where in the hell did you come from?" Logan slammed the door behind him. "You heard me wench, I want an answer." This last was spoken in a more subdued voice as he realized what she was doing. Though certainly no saint, he drew the line at interrupting someone's prayers. Except that he wanted some answers and he wanted them now.

She seemed to be finished anyway, for she stood, facing him, her chin raised in that haughty way she had as if she did him the most wondrous favor deigning to receive him. Except crude and primitive as it was, this cabin was his. She'd shown up on his mountain, *his* mountain, without so much as a by your leave, and he couldn't find a footprint or a broken twig to indicate how she got here.

And now she looked at him as if to say he could die and shrivel up before she would answer him. All from a slip of a woman with a skirt full enough to

hide a scalping party. And hair that would do any
warrior proud . . . if he displayed it on his scalp pole.

Logan took a deep breath and tried again. "I've
done a wee bit of tracking in my time and I can't
find any sign that you came by way of the path."

"I didn't."

"There be not so much as a crushed leaf or a
disturbed spiderweb in the forest."

She merely shrugged shoulders that shone pearly
white even in the dim light from the smoldering fire.

"Well now if you didn't come up the path nor
through the forest, that leaves but the face of the cliff
out yonder, and we know since you pushed me—"

"I did not push you." Rachel folded her arms. "I
saved you."

"So you keep saying."

"Because 'tis true. You were going to jump off the
edge." Why else was she sent?

He only shook his head while he rested the rifle
back against the wall, and crossed his arms in a masculine mimicry of her stance. "I was but standing there
admiring the view before you came."

Rachel paused. "I don't believe you."

He shrugged as if what she believed or did not
believe was of little concern to him. "Now, how did
you get here?"

"You tell me." Rachel stuck out her chin. "What
way is left?"

"Well, as far as I can tell there's but to come flying
down from the sky like a . . . ." A strange light shone
in her eyes and Logan could barely get the word
"bird" past his lips. Then she looked away and he
let out his breath on a ragged laugh. "Now you'll not
have me crediting that, wench."

"Credit what you like." She turned her back to
him. " 'Tis all the same to me." Two could play at

this game, Rachel thought with a smirk. Then she remembered where she was. Why was she still here? Why?

"Who are you?" Logan realized there was more puzzlement than command in his question, but he couldn't help himself. He saw something. In her eyes. In the expression on her face, that made him question his own judgment.

But then that was hardly a new predicament. Still . . .

She glanced at him over her shoulder, the tilt of her rounded chin still arrogant. "I told you, did I not? I'm Lady Rachel Elliott. A ward of the king. One of the queen's ladies in waiting."

"And that would be Queen . . . ?"

Rachel whirled around on a sigh of exasperation. "Her Royal Majesty Queen Charlotte, of course." Was the man such a pudding head not to know his own sovereign?

"Ah," he said, leaning his brawny shoulder against the wall and crossing one ankle over the other. "Of course."

She didn't like his tone. Rachel's body tensed and she stared at him through narrowed eyes. He was mocking her and nobody, *nobody*, did such a thing without chastisement. Yet there didn't seem to be anyone about to mete out her punishment. And she certainly couldn't do it. He loomed over her and he obviously had no respect for her station.

It was nigh time she returned to her own world.

Rachel sucked in her cheeks. Perhaps she was to find her own way home. Of course. How silly of her not to realize that before. She would have this creature take her to the Queen's residence and all would be as it should be. His eyes widened when she gave him her most gracious smile. "If you would be so kind as to escort me to Queen's House, I will—"

"I'll not be going anywhere till spring, Your Highness."

"Till spring. But . . . but 'tis barely autumn." His response to that was a mere shrug. "I must return to my home."

With a lazy motion he shifted away from the door, offering her an unobstructed exit. Rachel hesitated before pride lifted her chin. Fine. She would go alone. Her gaze drifted to the wild, untamed land framed by the open doorway. After taking a hesitant step she paused. "Would you be so kind as to direct me toward London." She heard him laugh, a deep, booming sound, but when her eyes found his face it was sober.

"Head east," he began, "once you cross the mountains you shouldn't have too difficult a time . . . till you reach the sea."

"The sea?"

"Aye, the Atlantic Ocean stands between you and London but—"

"That's impossible." Rachel clenched her hands together and twirled away, her skirts floating out about her ankles. But it only took a moment before she twisted back. "Where am I?" When he didn't answer immediately Rachel lurched forward, catching the front of his buckskin shirt in her fists. Shaking did more to dislodge herself than him, but that didn't stop her. "Tell me where I am." But though she demanded to know, the knowledge seemed to fill her with despair.

"The colony of South Carolina . . ." she repeated his answer. As her voice trailed off she let loose of his shirt. She paced the cabin again before facing him. "Then I was obviously mistaken about finding my own way home. They will come for me."

"They?"

Rachel expelled her breath in an unladylike sigh. Discussing this with him was becoming a bore. She would just tell him and be done with it. Mayhaps then he would leave her alone to await ... She wasn't certain what would happen, or when. But she did know *something* must. No fate could be as cruel as leaving her here.

"I was sent to save you," she said, straightening her shoulders. "By angels."

If she expected him to be awestruck by her announcement, she was sadly disappointed. His first reaction was a booming laugh that tightened her lips. The next was to grab her shoulders in his crushing grip.

"I've had enough of your lies, wench. It will be the truth you'll be telling me."

"You doubt heaven exists?" For the first time she was frightened of him. His anger seemed a palatable thing.

"Nay. I've no doubt there be a heaven ... and a hell."

"Then why must you mistrust me?"

He yanked her up against his hard chest. "An angel you might resemble, but I know better. For if someone sent you to me 'twould be no messenger from God. Twould be the devil himself."

Rachel stared into the hard green eyes and nearly believed him.

Chapter Two

"What is madness? To have erroneous percep-
tions and to reason correctly from them."
—Voltaire
Philosophical Dictionary

No amount of drink made her disappear.

Logan lowered the jug from his lips, and swallowed
before backhanding his mouth. He sat in the corner
where the stones of the hearth met the south wall,
his long legs stretched out on the earthen floor. And
he watched the woman as she slept.

Last evening after she insisted she was tired and
he offered her the only bed in the cabin—the one
where she now lay—he walked outside. Though night
was upon them, the sky was clear and bright beneath
a canopy of moon and stars. The kind of cool, crisp
night that Logan relished. But it wasn't the heavens
that was on his mind. At least not that bit of it he
could see overhead.

What in the hell was going on? He didn't believe
her for one minute. She was no angel. Hell, he didn't
even credit that she was Lady what's-her-name. Despite the diamonds. Logan kicked at a clump of winter
dry grass. As if some high and mighty member of
King George's court would show up on the Carolina
frontier.

"As if I'd be wanting them here," he mumbled. He might not have been old enough to fight for the Bonnie Prince like his brother, James, but he never forgave the British crown their role at Culloden.

All of which was irrelevant anyway. For there was obviously not a parcel of truth in anything she'd said. Either she was mad. Or he was. And since he'd been told as much before, not to mention wondering often enough himself, Logan was willing to admit he'd imagined the entire incident.

Until he wandered back into the smoky cabin and saw her sound asleep on a pallet of furs. She lay on her side, fully dressed, her cheek pillowed on curled fingers like a child. But it was not a child's body clad in that riotously adorned gown. Logan stared a moment at the breasts nearly tumbling from the lacy décolletage, then swallowed and reached for the nearest jug.

If he wasn't mad, then she was.

The caress was continuous. Rachel smiled, though she did her best to remain in the netherlands of slumber. But she couldn't ignore the touch. It was warm and . . . and wet! Rachel's eyes popped open, only to meet the droopy gaze staring at her from both sides of a black, moist nose.

"Oh, for heaven's sake." She skittered up and back, knocking her wig further askew in the process. She didn't care for dogs . . . animals in general for that matter. And this one was practically plastered against her side, its big pink tongue dangling out of an open mouth.

"Shoo. Go away," she implored while glancing about. Memory and realization that she was still someplace in the wilds of the New World assaulted her simultaneously. She nearly groaned. Last night she was so sure as she fell asleep on the disgusting pile of animal pelts that she'd awaken in her own luxurious bed beneath a canopy of gilt and brocaded silk. Yet here she was . . . still.

And now to make matters worse, there was this dog. A large black-and-white spaniel. And he seemed unable to understand the simplest of directions.

Keeping her eye on it Rachel gingerly pushed to her feet. Her gown was intolerably wrinkled, the silver tarnished in spots and the hemline ragged. And it had been such a beautiful gown.

Rachel sighed and caught the spaniel's eye again. "Where is he?" she demanded before crossing her arms and tramping across the furs, kicking at one that tangled with her foot. The fire was long cold, which accounted for the gooseflesh covering her arms. But she glanced hopefully in the hanging iron pot anyway.

"He's gone hunting, has he," Rachel said, toeing a puff of dirt toward the burned-out ashes in the hearth. " 'Tis a good thing, for I am hungry." The glance she tossed the dog over her shoulder showed her indifference. "What does it matter how hungry you are? You're nothing but a—"

The rest of her words along with the sudden realization that she was having a conversation—of sorts—with a dog were interrupted as the man pounded into the cabin. He was dressed as yesterday in a buckskin jacket, long dark hair tangled about his shoulders, and an extra day's worth of whiskers shadowing his lower face.

" 'Tis awake ye are." When Rachel said nothing he glanced from her to the gray ashes in the hearth and back. "I'd of thought ye might start a fire while I was gone."

Start a fire? Was the creature mad? "I, sir, do not start fires. Servants start fires."

"Ah." He lifted a straight dark brow and stared at her a moment longer before tossing something her way. Reflexes had Rachel catching the furry bundle. He turned toward the stack of wood piled to the side of the fireplace. "We seem to have misplaced all the servants for the moment."

Rachel raised her chin. "Then I suppose you will have to do it."

"This time," was all he said before bending over and exposing a few smoldering coals beneath the ashes. He added a bit of kindling, then blew on it gently, coaxing a tiny flame to life. Rachel watched until she grew bored, but it wasn't until she decided to cross her arms to ward off the chill that she realized what she held.

Her squeal caused the man to jerk around and the dog to bark.

"What the hell did you do that for?" Logan settled hands on knees and pushed to his feet. "Down, Dog," he yelled as he scooped up the rabbit she'd dropped to the floor.

" 'Tis dead."

He gave her a look out of sea-green eyes that seemed to say he found her amazingly stupid. But all he did was yell at the dog who ran around the tiny cabin, yelping with excitement. With a sigh Rachel turned her back on the scene. But when his owner's shouted commands had no effect on the spaniel, Rachel caught the dog's eye as he bounded past her.

"Oh, do be quiet," was all she said, but it seemed to calm the animal. The spaniel stopped in its tracks, then, as if deciding it had enough activity for one day, pranced to the center of the furs spread over the floor and plopped down.

"Lazy bag 'a bones."

The man's words brought her attention back to

him as he strode through the open door. Rachel
watched as he placed the rabbit on a stump, then
arced a small ax down, severing the rabbit's head
from his body. Rachel found it difficult to swallow.
He quickly skinned the small animal, removing its
entrails. Then he reentered the cabin and tossed the
rest into the pot. He splashed water from a rope-
handled pail over the meat, before swinging the iron
pot over the now crackling fire.

Then he turned to face her.

At first he said nothing, and Rachel had to force
herself not to squirm under his steady gaze. Which
was ridiculous. She was an intimate of the queen,
enamored by the king's brother. There was no reason
to be intimidated by a man more beast than human.
Yet she was the first to glance away.

It was then that he spoke. "I don't know who you
are or how you came to be here—"

"I thought I made myself clear—" Rachel began
but he lifted his hand, palm out, and she clamped
her mouth shut.

"Since you chose to be here for the winter—"

Now it was her turn to interrupt. "I did not *choose*
any such thing. I was . . ." Rachel paused. It didn't
seem worth the effort to repeat the circumstances
surrounding her arrival. He did not believe her last
night, nor did it seem as if the morning made him
more receptive. He should know one thing however.
"I shall not be remaining here for the winter."

He continued on as if she hadn't spoken. "There
are a few things I'm believing should be made clear.
First being that be my bed." His chin jerked toward
the pile of skins where the dog lay sleeping. "If you
be wanting to share it with me, I'm willing but—"

"Share it!" Rachel could hardly believe her ears.
"Are you daft?"

"More than likely," he admitted. "But that 'tis not the issue. Sleeping arrangements are. And I would like my bed back."

"Well you may have it." Rachel whirled around, eager to leave this man's odious company only to realize there was no place for her to go. The cabin was so small. All she could do was stand there, impotent anger welling up like an underground spring. But it seemed he wasn't finished.

"Since we'll be sharing the food and lodging—"

"I shan't be staying," Rachel threw over her shoulder, though, in truth she had no idea when she would leave or how.

He seemed to have the same misgivings for he paid her interruption no mind. "I think 'tis fair you do the cooking."

Cooking! Rachel twisted back around. Who did he think he was? And more importantly didn't he realize who *she* was? Rachel opened her mouth to tell him . . . again, but he had already gathered up his rifle and was striding through the door. All she managed to do was yell at his retreating form. "I do not cook. Servants cook." He ignored her, walking with a steady gait toward the woods.

Rachel slammed the door only to jerk it open again. "Wait." Whether it was the word itself or her frantic tone, Rachel wasn't sure. But he did stop, glancing back, his brow raised.

"Where are you going?"

"I've some traps to see to."

"Oh." Rachel's hand tightened on the latch. "I have need of . . ." She took a deep breath and tried again. "Where is your necessary?" She thought she noticed the ghost of a smile curve his lips, but before she could become indignant it was gone.

He simply made a sweeping motion with his hand. " 'Tis all about you, Your Highness."

"Your Highness, indeed!" Rachel gave the door a push, then kicked it for good measure. "And what does he mean, all about you?" Rachel asked the question, yet she feared the answer was obvious. "Oh, I know what he means," she said as the dog lifted his head, opening sleepy eyes to her. "I've . . . well, I've relieved myself in the woods before . . . as a child. It's just that civilized people . . . never mind."

She paced the length of the cabin twice before grabbing hold of the latch and yanking open the door. Once outside she hurried on her way, shivering from the morning chill. Had it been this cold yesterday? Rachel couldn't remember. But by the time she rushed back into the cabin her teeth were chattering.

Maneuvering the only chair in the cabin closer to the fire took more effort than Rachel wished to expend, but for the sake of warmth, she did it. Then she settled down, spreading her skirts, and waited. She couldn't exactly call the aroma wafting from the iron pot pleasant, but it did remind her that she was hungry. How long had it been since she ate? Rachel tried to recall but the memory became all tangled with Liz's and Geoffrey's deaths and the reason she was here.

To save this worthless creature's life.

Which she had done . . . and not without considerable sacrifice, so why wasn't she—

Her question came to a sudden halt when the object of her lament pushed open the door. He glanced at her once, almost as if he were checking to see if she was still there, before leaning his rifle in its usual spot. He crossed to the hearth and gingerly picked up a metal plate that had grown hot from the fire. With a spoon he scooped some of the rabbit out of the pot. To his credit he looked up, silently offering her the plate.

Rachel shook her head. "I'm not hungry."

It was an obvious lie, but he simply shrugged and began to eat. She expected his manners to be deplorable . . . after all, he was, but he ate with some decorum, though he stood the entire time. It wasn't until he was nearly finished that Rachel realized the reason. She sat in his chair.

So be it. He was well served, having but one chair to his name. Rachel folded her arms and tried not to watch him scoop the last bit into his mouth. It wasn't the fare she usually ate, but perhaps she could force herself to partake of a bite or two.

He spooned more onto the plate and Rachel smiled, ready to ask for it. But before she could, he set the dish on the dirt floor. "Dog." It only took that one word for the animal to lift his head, black nose sniffing the air. Before Rachel's startled eyes the dog stretched, stood, loped over, and wolfed down her meal.

Rachel jumped to her feet, but it went unnoticed. The man was already back through the door taking his gun and an axe with him. "How could you?" Rachel mumbled, fighting back tears for the first time since she'd . . . died.

"Yes, yes, I know you are hungry," she sniffed, "but so am I. And cold and . . ." Her brimming eyes glanced down at her gown. "And dirty. And I don't know where I am, or why I'm here." She sucked in her breath on a sob. "Or why I'm talking to a dog, for heaven's sake."

But this time she received no response. The brutish animal just continued to push the pewter plate about with his nose and tongue, savoring every last bit of meat.

Rachel plopped back into the chair, exasperated. She stayed there until a steady thumping from outside tore her attention away from her empty stomach. At first she tried to ignore the sound, but finally she stood, straightened her wig, and moved across the room to peek through the small window of what appeared to be oiled skin. She couldn't see anything. In annoyance she turned to the door.

The air was warmer now, though still chilly enough for Rachel to hug her arms. But then she wasn't doing labor. The man was. He stood near the side of the cabin, his back to her, chopping wood.

And he was naked to the waist.

Rachel had thought him stout or at least prone to fleshiness. Now she realized it was the padding of skins that made him seem so. Without them he was not the least fleshy. He had broad shoulders and thick upper arms, especially when he hefted the axe, but his waist was trim, as were his hips. He didn't look like any man she'd ever seen before, and not just because of his hair and manner of dress.

He paused, swiping his arm across his brow and just as quickly turned. As if he'd felt her looking at him. His eyes locked with hers and Rachel had an uncomfortable feeling her face was turning a bright pink.

"I wondered what you were doing," was all she could think to say.

He said nothing, just looked at her with those green eyes till she turned away and reentered the cabin.

She'd never spent a longer, more uncomfortable day. Rachel divided her time between pacing the tiny cabin and sitting in the chair. She was bored beyond measure. Back at Queen's House there were friends to talk to. Liz. No, not Liz, anymore, Rachel reminded herself, and stopped. She didn't want to think about what her life was . . . what it would be again.

For now she was stuck in the backwoods of nowhere. With a man who seemed unable to utter more than a few words. At least that's all he'd spoken to her today. The few times he entered the cabin today— once to call for his dog and two times carrying armfuls of chopped wood—he merely looked at her as if he wished she'd disappear.

And in that they were of like minds.

Except that she couldn't.

And she couldn't imagine why that was.

Actually, by the time the feeble bit of light filtering through the window was gone, Rachel had tired of thinking on it. She was dozing in the chair when a sudden burst of cold awoke her. He was standing in the open doorway, his form backdropped by twilight, and he was staring at her. Though she couldn't clearly see his face, Rachel had no doubt of that. She also had no doubt that his expression was one of annoyance.

She straightened the crick in her neck as he strode into the room, kicking the door shut as he moved. She wasn't used to falling asleep in chairs. When he stood between her and the hearth he stopped.

"You're wet." Rachel hastened to draw back the hem of her gown which already bore bleeding spots of dampness where he dripped on her. But he didn't seem concerned by the fact that he was soaking her clothes . . . her. He leaned forward, grasping the arms of the roughly made chair with his large hands.

Imprisoning her.

Water streamed from his dark hair, dropping in fat, cold plops onto her bodice as Rachel arched back as far as she could. "What do you think you're doing? I am Lady Rachel—"

"And I don't give a damn who you thinks you are, or what for that matter."

It was nearly dark but he was close enough for Rachel to see the moisture beading on his long, dark lashes. To feel the warmth of his breath. His eyes bore into hers as his presence continued to soak her.

"I don't even care how you came to be here. The truth is you are, for I'm fully sober now and you still be here. So—"

"I am not some drunken fantasy, sir!" Rachel's chin shot up, bringing her face closer to his.

"As I've finally concluded. But whatever you're doing here, this be my house and—"

"Such as it is."

"And you be here out of the goodness of me heart."

She said nothing to that, but the roll of her eyes heavenward conveyed what she thought the odds were that he even had a heart.

"So if you be staying here, you'll be doing your share."

The nerve of the man. "Share of what?"

"Chores for one."

"Chores? I never heard of anything so ridiculous. Queen Charlotte's ladies do not do chores. We . . . Are you listening to me?" But he wasn't. She could tell that by the set of his broad shoulders. He now bent over the hearth, trying to coax the few remaining embers back to life. He'd jerked away from her, leaving Rachel wet and chilled.

Pushing to her feet Rachel took the few steps necessary to put her beside him. "Would you look at what you've done to me." She brushed at the gown with her palms. "I'm cold."

He said nothing, only continued to feed chips of wood into the fire. "Did you hear what I said?" She hovered over him as he squatted in front of the fireplace. "Answer me." Rachel's voice shrilled higher. She wanted to take him by his naked shoulders and shake him. She wanted to grab his head and box his ears. She wanted to—

Before Rachel could even think of the consequences she jerked her leg back and kicked him. It hurt her toes as much as it did his leg, she imagined . . . possibly more. But that didn't seem to be the point.

She had a fleeting image of his face looking up at her in shock before something circled her ankle and she was sprawled on the hard, dirt floor, his damp body on top of her.

Her palms flattened against his chest, pale against sun-darkened skin, trying to push him off. But he did not budge. If anything he settled more firmly.

"I will not put up with this from you. Not in me own house. Not when I neither asked or want you here."

If her tongue were given free rein she would tell him exactly what she thought of him. But something in his expression warned her against it.

She lay there, staring at him, feeling the pull of his eyes to the tips of her toes. Her heart pounded and her breathing became shallow as he came closer. She could feel the heat of his breath on her mouth. And he was right. There was no scent of rum to sicken her stomach.

Rachel wasn't certain when she realized he planned to kiss her. She only knew she should be enraged. And that for some reason she wasn't.

And then he was pushing to his feet, pulling her up with him. Rachel grabbed for her wig but it toppled off her head, landing on the floor in a shower of white powder. They both stared at it a moment before Rachel shoved away from him and scooped it up with a flourish.

He let her go, acting as if the entire incident hadn't happened as he tossed a log onto the revived fire. But Rachel couldn't forget what he'd done. She slapped at the dirt on her gown with one hand, holding the wig with the other, sniffing the entire time trying to keep tears of frustration from showing. She wouldn't let him know how much he upset her. She wouldn't.

After all, she was here to save him. *Had* saved him. He should be thanking the heavens that she came when she did, rather than treating her as if she were some sort of pariah.

But he didn't seem to care at all. Once he turned away from her, back toward the hearth, it was almost as if he forgot her existence. With his hands he scooped some manner of crushed grain from a nearby sack, dumping it into the pot. To this he added water, gave it a stir, and swung the whole over the now blazing fire.

It was warmer now. Rachel stood, holding the obscenely disheveled wig. Not knowing exactly what she should do. Which in itself was a frustration. She always knew what was expected of her. And she always managed very nicely. But now she had no idea what to do. So she did nothing. Only stood watching as the man retrieved a loose-fitting shirt of coarse material from a peg on the wall and yanked it over his head.

At least he was covered, though by no means suitably garbed. But he *was* covered. She found his nakedness disconcerting.

"How did you become so wet?" The heavy length of dark hair dampened the shirt.

" 'Tis my habit to bathe when the need arises." The look he slanted over his shoulder suggested she might consider the possibility.

The idea of soaking in hot, fragrant water was so appealing Rachel failed to take offense. "A bath would be heavenly. If you'd prepare the tub, I think I can manage the rest on my own." At least she assumed she could. Of course she was used to being pampered and waited on, but she certainly didn't want *him* assisting her.

Rachel was so enthralled with the idea of being

clean she didn't notice his reaction till he loomed over her. "You spend your day doing naught but warming your backside on my chair . . . *my* chair. You fail to fix even the basest of suppers. You allow the fire to die out so 'tis freezing when I come back from a soaking in the creek, and you think 'tis my duty to prepare your bath?"

It obviously wasn't a question he expected her to answer, for with an expression of contempt he turned back toward the fire. And Rachel decided a bath was not in the offing. Not that she wished for a "soaking in the creek" as he put it. She would simply wait until she returned to Queen's House.

If only she could wait till then to eat. Unfortunately Rachel was near faint from hunger. It had been so long since she'd eaten, she couldn't remember what her last bite of earthly food was. But she knew it must have smelled a bit more tempting than the odors coming from the pot. Still, she wanted nothing more than to behave like a charwoman and devour every last bite.

She watched, her mouth watering as he spooned the cooked meal into a shallow wooden bowl. And waited for him to hand it to her. Then watched in shock as he settled himself on the floor, crossing his legs and using a spoon to shovel the food into his mouth. It was only after several bites—bites that Rachel could almost taste—that he glanced up.

"Help yourself," he said, inclining his head toward the pot.

Help herself? She'd never helped herself in her life. The very thought. But it seemed unlikely that he would wait upon her. And memories of her earlier fare being fed to the dog were still vivid.

Rachel's sigh of resignation was heartfelt. There were several shallow scooped bowls stacked on a crude shelf, along with a few bent and dented spoons. Rachel chose one of each, then moved with as much dignity as she could toward the caldron of bubbling gruel. The pot was hot, which she should have known, of course, but she could tell he watched her and that made her nervous. Leaning forward she managed to scoop several spoonfuls into her bowl without touching the pot before a new odor struck her.

At nearly the same instant she was knocked from the side and tumbled onto the floor in what was becoming an all too familiar way.

But this time he was rolling her and slapping at her legs, and Rachel couldn't keep from screaming. When he stopped her cheek was pressed to the dirt, her nose inches from her spilled bowl of gruel, and she could not suppress her anger. Jerking around, she pushed up on her elbows, her eyes blazing.

"What do you think you're—"

Rachel's mouth clamped shut, then opened on a shriek. "I'm on fire!" Smoke curled up from her skirt hem and she realized it was burning silk that she smelled. "Help me!"

But even Rachel realized her pleas were unnecessary. He'd already smothered the flames and was plucking at the scorched fabric, mumbling a string of curses under his breath.

"For God's sake, woman, don't you know enough not to catch yourself afire?"

"Of course, I do. It's just that I never—What are you doing?" Rachel struggled to shove what was left of her overpetticoat down as he flipped it up.

"Would you stop?" With one hand he pinioned her ankles, stopping her from kicking at him. "I'm only checking to see if you're burned." His eyes met hers. "Hold yourself still."

His tone was low, almost gentle, and seemed to brook no argument. At least Rachel couldn't seem to form one as his hands and gaze roamed over her legs. He removed her shoes, her dainty silver and blue shoes that were now dirt-caked and singed. Then his long fingers felt beneath her skirts, untying her garters. Her stockings were silk, white, with decorative clockwork of pale blue. At least they had been before . . . before everything that had happened to her. Now they were dirt smudged and scorched, with holes the size of half crowns burned through revealing reddened skin.

Rachel held her breath as he rolled the stockings down her leg.

"Am I hurting you?" His gaze met hers again, the green now as dark as a holly leaf.

"No." There was some pain to be sure. Now that the initial fright was gone, she was aware that several areas on her skin felt hot. But that wasn't what made her throat tight.

He lowered his gaze, and Rachel watched the shadow of his lashes as he examined her legs. She expected his touch to be rough, but it wasn't, and when he placed hands on knees to push to his feet, she wondered at the lack of warmth his departure brought.

"What are you doing?" Rachel twisted, shifting about to see him pull a few dried leaves from a sack. These he crumbled into a small earthen bowl. He added a glob of a whitish-gray substance and stirred with the tip of his finger. "What is that?" Rachel tried to scoot back as he knelt again in front of her.

" 'Tis naught but a bit of bear fat." His palm cupped and lifted one of her legs.

"What did you put in it?"

"Something that will make your burns feel better." That green stare seemed to bore into her. "I won't hurt you."

With two fingers he rubbed the mixture onto her flesh, making sure to cover all the areas reddened by the flames. Rachel couldn't tell if it lessened the pain or not. She was too entranced by the circular motion of his fingers, long and dark from the sun, and seeming more so when juxtaposed on her pale skin.

After he finished Rachel expected he would stand, but he only leaned back on his heels, his hands hanging loosely between his knees, his stare still on her exposed legs. Then he lifted his gaze. It met hers. And time seemed to stop. It was almost as if they shared a trance.

Which was foolish for in the next instant he grabbed up the bowl and pushed to his feet. "In the future try not to be catching yourself afire." He paused on his way to put the bowl back on the shelf. "Wearing something with a few less ruffles might help."

"The king found no fault with my gown." How dare this . . . this man criticize her clothing. He who wore either animal skins or nearly nothing at all.

"The king."

Rachel couldn't tell if the contempt in his voice came from a dislike of his sovereign, or that he didn't believe her. Whichever, he simply shook his head, then called for his dog. "Get yourself up you lazy mongrel."

Despite the order, the dog seemed in no hurry to comply. Yawning, it stretched and shook. By the time it headed for the door, the man had shrugged into his jacket and grabbed up his gun.

"There should be a serving or two left in the pot." He glanced over his shoulder. "If you think you can manage."

Rachel stood as gracefully as she could, turning on him with her head held high and her dignity intact . . . despite her appearance. "I shall be quite all right."

He inclined his head, a motion that made his dark

hair tumble forward. "I'll be back in a bit. Oh, and there be some furs in the corner you can use to make a pallet."

With that he turned and followed the dog out the door.

It hurt her legs to walk, but then she didn't have a choice. Ever mindful of the flames Rachel scraped what food was left in the pot into a bowl. The mixture was lumpy and scorched and Rachel was glad the man wasn't here to see her stoop so low as to eat it. But she was hungrier than she'd ever been, and it didn't taste *that* bad.

After she filled her stomach all she could think of was lying down to rest. But she was afraid of what he might do if he came back to find her in his bed. She glanced at the bed of furs which, despite being on a dirt floor in this hovel, looked inviting, then toward the pile in the corner.

Clenching her teeth she stepped gingerly toward the heap. "Why can't he make another bed?" she mumbled. "After all, this is his house." She held one of the furs up and examined it contemptuously. "And his bedding. I don't see why I—"

The cold draft sent gooseflesh across her skin. She turned to see why he didn't close the door, a sharp retort on her lips.

But it was the echo of her scream that rang through the cabin.

Chapter Three

"Of all the passions, fear weakens judgment most."
—Cardinal de Retz
Mémoires

It hit her like a bolt of lightning. Why she hadn't returned to her own life. What she had to do.

She wasn't sent just to save the man from jumping off the cliff. She was sent to save him from the painted heathen standing in the doorway.

But how?

The revelation left her speechless. All she seemed able to do was stare at the savage. Her heart pounded and she found it difficult to swallow. Especially when he took a step toward her, and then another.

Rachel's eyes darted about the small cabin looking for something to use against him. He carried a rifle, cradled in one arm, the same way the other man did. There was also a small axe and a knife hanging from his belt. She wouldn't have a chance against him. But more importantly, Rachel feared the man she was sent to save wouldn't either.

The savage moved closer and the light from the fire reflected off his coppery skin, the evil darkness of his eyes. His voice was harsh, the words gutteral and incomprehensible, and he was almost upon her.

He reached out a hand to touch a lock of Rachel's hair that had escaped from its pins at the same moment her man—the lost soul whose life she was to save—appeared in the doorway.

Rachel hurled herself at the savage, knocking him backward, and yelling to the man at the same time. "Run! Save yourself!" She clawed and kicked with her bare feet, and tried to do all she could to save the man's life.

The savage was yelling, too. Nothing she could understand, but she didn't care. She hit and scratched and might have actually drawn blood had not something grabbed her from behind. Without warning she was hauled off the savage by a steel-like arm around her waist.

"What are you doing?" she demanded. She wriggled in the man's clutches, trying to free herself. Couldn't he see the danger? Was he sightless as well as stupid?

" 'Tis I who should be asking you that question." His free arm dropped down over hers, pinioning them to her sides. He held her off the floor and when she continued kicking he squeezed, pressing against her breasts. "Behave yourself," he growled in her ear.

And all the time the savage just stood there, his face looking as if it were cast of bronze, staring at them.

The fight was gone from her. Rachel went limp in the man's arms. Then he lowered her feet to the floor. She tried to calm her breathing, tried not to notice the way his rough shirt rubbed against the curve of her breast.

Then to Rachel's surprise the man spoke, but it was nothing she understood, though the painted savage seemed to. He pressed his lips together and folded his arms, regarding her through eyes that glittered like jet.

"This is your woman?" he asked in broken English, each word barely more than a grunt.

"Nay." Rachel was released from his hold, though he did rest his hands on her shoulders. "She is not my woman, but she is my responsibility."

"Your responsibility?" Rachel squirmed around till she could see the square, whiskered jaw. "You don't seem to understand, you are my res—" The tightening of his fingers on her silk-clad shoulders brought her protest to an abrupt end. Rachel listened in silence, slowly turning back to the savage.

"I welcome my friend, Swift Fox, to my home. Please sit and we will make talk."

The expression on the savage's face softened, though he still glanced at Rachel with apprehension. Apparently her man noticed this, too, for he turned her toward the corner, giving her a slight push, while whispering in her ear. "Off with you and sit." He paused before adding, "And for once do as you're told."

"I always do," Rachel began, only to realize he wasn't listening to her. He and his *friend* were settling down by the fire. A jug was passed from one to the other, as was a pipe. Rachel stood watching as they spoke to each other in that strange, guttural language, finally accepting the fact that the savage was no threat. At least not to the man whose life she was to save.

Finally, tired and sore—the burns on her legs hurt—she huddled down on the pile of skins. They didn't seem to notice. Actually since they began, neither had so much as glanced her way. They seemed content to take frequent swallows of whatever was in the jug. She felt ignored and cold as drafts crept through the holes between the logs. Even though she thought she should keep watch, Rachel was just as glad when sleep overcame her.

What was he to make of her? Logan stood, staring down at her curled-up form. The night was late and Swift Fox had just fallen asleep, or passed out, on Logan's pallet. His Cherokee friend didn't hold his liquor too well, unlike himself, Logan thought. He had as much to drink as Swift Fox and the last thing he felt like doing was sleeping. Too great a chance he'd dream.

Logan shook his head. He didn't want to dwell on the nightmares. The woman was a safer subject to ponder . . . though on second thought he wouldn't call her safe at all.

She'd gone at Swift Fox like a bear protecting her cub, all sharp claws and emotion. She shocked the Cherokee for certain. He repeated the story often as the evening progressed and the jug grew lighter.

"She did not come after me until you arrived," he'd said, after taking a puff off the pipe. "She was not afraid for herself."

Logan squatted down near the pile of furs. "Who are you?" he whispered. Lady Rachel Elliott she'd said, but that just didn't make sense. Not that he didn't think an English Lady could live on the frontier. His half brother Wolf had married Lady Caroline Simmons and they made their home at Seven Pines. But Caroline hadn't just appeared one day by Wolf's side insisting she was there to save him.

Leaning forward, Logan studied her with narrowed eyes. He sure never saw Caroline decked out like this either. Logan's gaze swept over the silvery gown and diamonds twinkling at her neck and ears. There was a beauty patch on her cheek, its edges curled from wear. With his finger he brushed it off, wondering why anyone as lovely as she would paste something false on her face.

But then the same could be said for the powdered wig. Her own hair was a shimmering pale blond. She was no angel, of that he was certain, but she did look like one.

Which made absolutely no difference, Logan assured himself as he pushed to his feet. She was a problem he didn't need. But one he didn't quite know how to rid himself of.

For now she looked damned uncomfortable. Cursing under his breath, Logan spread several layers of skins on the floor. Then nudging Dog aside he scooped his unwelcome guest into his arms. She nestled closer, her breath fanning his neck. Logan allowed himself to savor the feel of her only a moment before stretching her out on the pallet.

When he lay the bearskin over her she rolled her head from side to side. She was mumbling, something unintelligible at first, but when he leaned closer he could make out what she said. "I have to save him. I have to."

Logan backed up. This whole thing was insane. *She* was insane. And he was just as insane for listening to her for one second.

He strode to the door, grabbing his coat off the peg as he reached for the latch. He felt restless. There was no reason to attempt sleep. Perhaps a bit of night air would help. After he opened the door he gave a low whistle. The dog always enjoyed these night forays.

But obviously that was before the woman arrived. For he was already cuddled up close, his canine head wedged against her side.

"The hell with you both," Logan said under his breath before stomping into the clear, cold night.

*   *   *

The cabin was empty when Rachel woke the next morning, but someone had built up the fire and a delicious scent wafted up from the pot. She stretched, lifting her arms high above her head and wondered how she'd come to be lying flat on a bed of furs. Oh, what did it matter? She slept well, was rested, and despite the reddened areas on her legs felt better than she had since . . . since her death.

Though she told herself there was nothing humorous about her situation, Rachel couldn't help laughing. Which was what she was doing when the man pushed through the door. He was wet again, clad only in some sort of short apron that covered him from waist to mid thigh, front and back. But despite his near nakedness, it was his expression that held Rachel's attention. He looked as if he'd eaten a lemon. Rachel's countenance sobered.

He stomped to the hearth, his back to the flames and stared at her a moment. " 'Tis glad I am that you find time for levity . . . and sleeping. Though most would think the time of day for being about was long past."

Rachel elbowed her way to sitting. Her pleasant mood was a thing of the past. "Are you saying I slept too late?" Why, she could swear it was still morning. What did the man want?

He only grunted in that way Rachel found very annoying.

She brushed a tangle of curls from her face, wondering what had become of the pins that held it up. "I'll have you know I've been called an early riser, by some. Even if I attend an especially late entertainment I ring for my chocolate by half past ten."

He lifted a brow before turning to warm his front side. "That early?"

His sarcasm was no more appreciated than his monosyllable grunts, Rachel decided, and told him so. This elicited no response at all.

"Who are you?" Rachel folded her arms when he glanced around. "You do have a name, don't you?"

"Logan MacQuaid."

"Ah, I thought I detected a Scottish brogue." He said nothing to that but then she supposed she should be growing use to his reticence. "From where in Scotland do you hail?"

"Alloway near Ayr."

Rachel folded her hands, resting them on the fur blanket covering her lap. "And how long have you been in the colonies?"

"Since forty-seven." Logan reached for the shirt he'd taken off earlier and pulled it over his head.

Rachel found it a bit easier to concentrate with his chest covered. She sighed. "What of your friend?" She glanced around. "Where is he?"

"Swift Fox left early for his village. Now, if there be no more questions for me Your Highness, I suggest you rise from your royal bed."

Royal bed indeed. He was so annoying. Rachel lifted her chin. "I can't for the life of me imagine why."

He wasn't going to ask, Logan assured himself as he dished out his portion of stew. He didn't care what she was talking about. He didn't care anything about her. But he found himself glancing back as she pushed aside the heavy bearskin. "Why what?" It was more command than request and Logan noticed the sharp lift of her head when he spoke.

She stood, smoothing down the torn and ragged skirt as best she could before facing him, her shoulders back, her stare haughty. "Why anyone should care what becomes of you."

Logan's hand paused, the spoon carrying a bite of

stew forgotten. "For once we are in complete agreement, Your Highness. 'Tis not a soul who does . . . myself included." He stared at her, his green eyes hard, before adding, "And 'tis the way I like it." He lowered the spoon and the bowl without eating. Not bothering to retrieve his jacket he stomped out of the cabin, and was immediately sorry.

The weather had turned cold with a northern wind that tore through his homespun shirt. He looked back at the cabin door and imagined himself opening it. Imagined her haughty expression. If only he hadn't made such a dramatic exit.

But then this wasn't the first time.

There was the time he stormed out on his half-brother Wolf, vowing to kill every Cherokee he could find. It was a stupid thing to do. Even if he'd just discovered his wife and daughter were dead . . . massacred by Cherokee.

Logan turned away from the cabin and stalked to the edge of the cliff that looked down over the valley below. Damn it all, Mary died years ago. He should be at least able to think about it without this terrible feeling of . . . Logan squeezed his eyes shut and swallowed.

God, what he wouldn't give for it to be grief that consumed him. That's what it should be. Grief for his wife. Grief for the child, the infant, that he'd never seen. And oh, Lord, he was sorry, sorrier than he could ever say, that they were gone.

But it was guilt that overpowered him. Guilt that kept him on this mountain and forced him to stand on the edge when fear of the heights made him dizzy.

For it was his fault they were dead.

His fault.

*   *   *

She managed to fix herself some of the stew without catching herself on fire. Logan noticed the dirty bowl on the table beside the chair when he finally returned to the cabin. Actually two dirty bowls. The second— the one he'd abandoned when he left—was on the floor. The dog in his usual spot on Logan's bed appeared satiated.

He supposed he had that coming after feeding *her* meal to the dog the day before. Except that this was *his* cabin and *his* food and as far as he could tell Her Highness hadn't lifted one of her delicate little fingers since she arrived uninvited on his doorstep.

And damnation the cabin was cold. She'd sat right in front of it and let the fire die down. Again.

"There's a settlement at the other end of the valley." Logan tossed a chunk of wood onto the waning fire. " 'Tis but a day from here." He glanced at her, mentally calculating how inept she would be traveling in the wilderness. "Maybe more."

She didn't say a thing, only sat in his chair, *his chair*, and stared at him with her big blue eyes. "We'll be leaving at first light."

"For where?"

Didn't she ever listen? "For the settlement. For McLaughlin's Mill." The log caught and crackled behind him. The flames threw dancing flickers of light across her face as she pursed her lips.

"How long will we be staying?"

"There be no 'we.' " Logan leaned against the stones surrounding the fireplace. "I'll be taking you there and returning. The Mill 'tisn't London but you'll find it—"

"I can't go there. I won't."

His fists clenched and Logan forced himself to relax his fingers. "Ye don't have a choice."

"But you said you weren't leaving. You said—"

"I changed my mind."

"Was it because I fed your share of food to the dog? For if it is—"

"That's not the reason." Though it certainly was a factor. But Logan had decided when he was outside that he couldn't have her staying here all winter. He didn't want her here. Or perhaps it was he wanted her too much.

Logan folded his arms, forcing his thoughts away from how long it was since he had a woman, and how comely he found this particular one. Despite her disheveled appearance. Despite the haughty tilt to her head. Despite the fact that she was mad.

"You don't seem to understand, I—"

"Aye, 'tis true, I don't. I don't know how you got here. Or what you want with me. But I do know we're setting out for the Mill come morning."

Except by morning she was burning up with fever.

Logan awoke before dawn to ready for the trip. At first he thought her tossing and moaning the result of a dream, perhaps it was this place that forged the nightmares that haunted her. But as soon as he built up the fire and was able to see her he knew what the flushed tone of her skin meant.

He knelt beside Dog on the pallet—his pallet— and touched her shoulder. When her eyes opened they were large and glassy. She smiled slightly. "I . . . don't feel very well," she whispered.

He started to rise only to have her hand clamp over his. Her heat scorched his skin.

"Don't leave me . . . please."

He touched her cheek. " "I'll be gone but a moment. To fetch some medicine and water."

She seemed to accept that, for her fingers loosened their grip and she shut her eyes.

* * *

Her thoughts were a jumble, and as hard as she tried, Rachel couldn't straighten them out. Sometimes she could swear she was home at Queen's House sharing a bit of gossip with Liz. Other times she was swallowed by water as cold and green as Logan Mac-Quaid's eyes. Those eyes seemed to haunt her. She told Liz of them, of the tall, silent man with the gentle touch. The man she couldn't seem to save.

And then there was the light.

Rachel blinked against the glare. This wasn't like the other time when she met the angels. Then, she felt calm and at peace. Now she ached.

"How are you feeling?"

Rachel turned toward the voice, the one thing she remembered as constant through all her dreams. "What happened to me?"

"You had a fever. It came upon you quickly. But I think the worst is over." He moved the light, which Rachel could see now was a candle. "Can you drink something?"

"It tastes horrible, doesn't it?" She remembered that too. He kept coaxing foul liquid down her throat.

"Aye," he said and laughed. "But I'll add a bit of honey to it."

"You don't laugh very much, or smile either. I like it." She must still be feverish to be saying such things. He didn't seem to take her words as a compliment. He merely stood as if she said nothing. In a few minutes he was back, lifting her shoulders and placing a metal cup to her lips.

That's when Rachel discovered she was naked beneath the fur blanket.

She knew she should be outraged. But for some

reason as she sipped the liquid, tasted the honey, she wasn't.

However by the next morning when she woke, her thoughts weren't nearly so charitable. She raised her head enough to glance around the cabin. *He* was there, by the hearth, stirring something in the pot. He straightened, turning toward her as if he knew she stared at him. For a long time they said nothing and Rachel felt the strong pull of those green eyes. Like in her dreams.

But this was no dream. Her life . . . or nonlife . . . was more a nightmare. A nightmare from which she seemed unable to escape.

"Where are my clothes?"

His brows lifted. " 'Tis obvious Her Highness is feeling better."

"And 'tis just as obvious you are a scoundrel, taking advantage of me while I was sick, and—"

"First let me assure you that I am what you say." He inclined his head in a mocking bow. "A scoundrel through and through."

"I knew it." Rachel clutched the bearskin to her chin.

"Aye, it must be reassuring to know you needn't alter your opinion of me."

Rachel simply glared.

"But on the other hand, there was no advantage taken of you while you lay feverish. I hardly find your *charms* irresistible."

Rachel felt his comment like a blow . . . well, at least a blow to her pride. "I wouldn't expect you to have discriminating enough taste to appreciate me. Why the king's brother is just waiting for me to—"

"Aye, I'm certain he's madly in love with you, and pressing for your hand so he can make you his princess," Logan said as he grabbed up a bowl, ladling some broth into it.

Madly in love was a bit strong. But he had sought her company and, was rumored, her hand. Rachel wondered briefly if he'd been saddened by her death. She couldn't imagine Prince William being more than mildly sorry that she couldn't partner him in a quadrille again. With a shake of her head she brought her thoughts back to the present. Mr. MacQuaid was approaching, a bowl of steaming liquid in his hands. But though her stomach growled from hunger she wanted, needed, some answers first.

"Then why did you uncloth me?" Rachel knew color stained her cheeks so she raised her chin a notch to counter it. She didn't think he would answer her at first. He'd squatted beside her, bowl in hand.

"I expect since your voice is back in good form, you're also able to feed yourself."

"I am."

With a shrug he set the bowl on the floor, giving the dog a meaningful stare before rising to fix himself some of the food. "You were uncomfortable," he finally said.

"That hardly gives you the right to—"

"Treat your fever?" His head shot around and Rachel noticed he spilled some of the hot liquid on his hand. But he took no heed. "Be that what I've no right to do?"

"No, but—"

"I did not ask you here *Lady* Rachel. I did not ask you to try and push me down a mountain, or catch yourself on fire, or attack my friend. And I most certainly did not ask you to come down with a fever and take three days of my time, nursing you back."

"Three days?" Rachel took a deep breath, then her gaze sought his. "I was sick for three days?"

"Aye. But I wasn't going to let ye die."

"Little chance of that."

"What?"

"Oh, nothing. I just didn't realize I could become so ill."

"No one is immune to fevers."

"So it would seem." Since she was already dead, or at least had died once, Rachel assumed this stint on earth would be . . . well, charmed. That she would be like an angel, floating down to do her good deed, then floating back to the heavens accompanied by a crescendo from a celestial chorus.

Obviously, that wasn't the way of it. She had no golden wings, and though she hadn't tried, Rachel seriously questioned her ability to fly. She was like a real person . . . like she was before. Able to smell and taste and feel. Capable of burning herself and becoming ill. She appeared to have no special powers, nothing to help her with her task of saving Logan MacQuaid's life.

And if truth be known, he seemed better able to take care of himself than she was. He was certainly large enough, and strong enough to do it.

"The broth will taste a might better if you eat it warm."

"What . . . oh, yes, thank you." Rachel glanced up to see he'd finished his meal and was heading for the door.

"I'll leave you alone for a bit." His eyes darted to the pile of silver-blue silk. "If ye need any help—"

"I'm sure I can manage." Rachel bid him leave with a wave of her hand. She waited till he shut the door before pushing aside the fur and trying to stand up. She was weaker than she thought, but she wasn't going to allow that to keep her unclothed one moment longer than necessary.

She got her arm tangled in the sleeve of her shift. And there was the unmistakable sound of tearing threads before she managed to smooth it down over her hips. And she thought this would be the easiest of her garments to put on. Oh, where was her maid when she needed her?

Rachel sank into the chair, dropping her head in the cradle of her hands. That's the way Logan found her when he came back in the cabin. He helped her back to the fur pallet, let her lean against him as she ate her broth, and didn't say anything about her earlier false bravado. All of which made her very grateful.

Rachel was more cautious the next time she got up. She asked Mr. MacQuaid for a bucket of water . . . warmed, and though he grumbled a bit, he complied. She at first requested a tub, of course, but quickly learned one was not available.

Which no doubt explained why he chose to bathe in the creek. She however did not.

He lent her a comb and brush, and Rachel was surprised by them. The set was not as ornate as the one she had in London, but it was silver.

Rachel washed her hair, using the soft soap he gave her, then standing by the fire quickly washed her skin. When she was finished she pulled the shift on again and began combing the tangles from her hair. Which was not an easy task. It seemed to take forever and her arms were tired when she finished, but she was determined to finish dressing. How could she possibly save him if she were bedridden?

The corset proved a problem.

Rachel slipped her arms through the straps and held the boned silk to her breast. But the ties were in the back and despite several tries she could not lace it up. Rachel glanced at her gown . . . her only gown, then toward the closed door. Though she was naturally slender, had grown thinner still since her death, her ball gown would not fit about her waist unless she wore the corset.

Her gaze strayed to the door again. She could hear

him outside. The steady *thump, thump* of his axe. What to do. She'd never dressed herself before, and it appeared she could not now.

With a determined step she marched to the door and pulled the latch. "Mr. MacQuaid." He didn't respond the first time she called, though the dog who was sleeping in a puddle of sunshine lifted his head. "Mr. MacQuaid!"

The axe bit into the chopping block with enough force to make Rachel think he'd heard her quite well the first time.

He turned, backhanding the sweat from his forehead as he did. "What do you want now?"

Rachel's lips thinned. He could be so . . . She couldn't even think of a word to describe him. Did she have to ask? Couldn't he tell what the problem was? But no, he just stood there his legs spread, hands on narrow hips and glared at her. He didn't even have the decency to pull his shirt back on. His chest was broad and covered by a wedge of curly black hair and Rachel jerked her gaze away when she realized she was staring.

"I can't lace my corset."

He reached for the axe handle, giving it a hard tug. "Don't wear the tortuous thing."

"I must. Without it my gown won't fit."

"Hell and damnation," he growled before swinging the axe back into the wood. "Turn around." Logan grabbed the laces none too gently and studied the double row of silk-edged holes.

"I believe the thread is to be laced through in a crisscross manner, though I must admit I've never done it."

"I can see what needs doing. Just stand still."

"As you wish, sir." Rachel reached out to steady herself against the log wall. She tried to do as he said, but each time his knuckles skimmed across her thin shift her body gave a little jerk. She couldn't seem to help herself. She could smell his musky scent, feel the heat from his body. Gooseflesh crept down her arms and she had to concentrate on breathing.

For his part Logan could hardly keep himself from reaching around and cupping the breasts that pushed up from under the corset. His fingers felt thick and inept as he forced the ribband through a tiny hole. His hand brushed her skin and for a heartbeat he paused, only to begin again, jerking the laces through the eyelets with a vengeance.

"Don't break the thread. It's the only one I have."

"Excuse me Your Highness. I've had sore little practice playing the lady's maid."

"You needn't snap at me."

That's where she was wrong. It was either snap or throw her down on the ground and bury himself inside her royal body. And wouldn't the high and mighty Princess just love that? Of course she wasn't the only one who'd deplore his actions. Once his seed was spilled Logan knew he would regret having touched her. No, better to concentrate on what the hell he was doing and get it done.

"Tie it off. No, pull it tighter first."

"Would you make up your mind!"

"Pull." Rachel sucked in her breath. "Yes, that's it. No, why did you let it go?" When she received no answer, Rachel turned. Standing in the clearing was the savage who'd visited earlier. Beside him stood an old man with long white hair. She glanced up at Logan MacQuaid and could swear he blushed beneath his heavy growth of whiskers.

Chapter Four

"The soul is unwillingly deprived of truth."
—Epictetus
Discourses

"Lone Dove." Logan realized he still held the laces of Rachel's corset and let them slip through his fingers. At the same time he stepped in front of her, though he knew both Swift Fox and the Cherokee Adawehis had seen her . . . had seen what he was doing. "I am honored you have visited my home."

Hell, Lone Dove must be near four score. Logan assumed this Adawehis never left the Cherokee town of Cheoah. Lone Dove was their conjurer, a holy man to his people. Logan had never seen him outside the dark confines of the Council House. Yet here he was after climbing the west trail not even breathing hard and staring at a point near Logan's left shoulder.

A glance behind him confirmed Logan's fear. She no longer stood behind him, but had moved to his side. And she seemed either unaware, or unconcerned that the corset, though untied at her waist, pushed her breasts up enticingly. She paid no heed to his glare.

"I've come to make talk with your woman," Lone Dove raised his arms, lifting the feather-adorned cape like wings.

"She's not my wom—"

"You may present your friend to me, Mr. Mac-Quaid."

She stepped forward and lifted her hand as if she expected the chief to drop to his knees and kiss it. For all that she wore only a silky shift and corset, she held her head high and her shoulders straight. Logan watched the breeze shift the golden curls along her narrow back a moment before letting out his breath. She didn't seem the least concerned by the old man's birdlike mask.

"Lone Dove this is Rachel Elliott."

"Lady Rachel Elliott," she corrected. "I'm one of Queen Charlotte's ladies-in-waiting. She's King George's wife, you know."

Logan tried to catch the holy man's eye but he stared only at Rachel, which probably wasn't that difficult to do. Logan had been hard pressed not to look at her when she came out of the cabin. Yet he wanted to do something, give some sort of signal to let Lone Dove know that she was not to be believed.

But the Adawehis had taken her hand, and though he didn't kiss it, he did envelope her dainty fingers in his. "I have not met your King George, but my mother's brother traveled across the big water to his home."

"Oh, of course, I remember, the king met with several of your people at St. James Palace last summer. Your relative was all the rage."

"He enjoyed seeing for himself the things told to him by the Little Carpenter and other of our brothers who visited your land before. The large tower where enemies are imprisoned, the large stretches of land used for riding and visiting."

"Ah, yes I do believe they strolled through St. James Park. London is so lovely." Rachel sighed. "Sometimes I miss it terribly. Perhaps you can visit me there.

I could show you the Queen's House. The park there is so beautiful. Her Majesty had a charming pavilion for the king's birthday. And I could introduce you to King George. I'm sure he would—''

"For God's sake, Rachel." Logan had heard enough of this. What if Lone Dove believed what she told him?

"I beg your pardon." She fixed a look on him that would make a lesser man, or one who didn't know she was making the entire tale up, quake in his boots. Logan simply returned it.

"I am old and fear it is too late for me to make such a journey. But I have come to talk with you. Come, we shall go inside."

Logan watched as she smiled up at the old man, a dazzling smile that lit up her face. Then together they entered his cabin and shut the door, leaving Swift Fox and him outside.

He stood there a moment scratching his chin, then his eyes sought Swift Fox. "What the devil is going on here?"

His friend only shrugged. "Lone Dove insisted he must come to this place to see her."

"Who? Rachel? But why?"

"That I do not know." Swift Fox squatted and reached out to scratch the dog's head. True to form the animal rolled over, offering up his speckled stomach to be rubbed.

Logan rolled his eyes heavenward before bending to retrieve his shirt. He yanked it over his head, pulling his hair from the collar and prying the axe from its nitch in the block before turning to the young Indian. "What did you tell Lone Dove about her?"

"Very little." An insistent whine reminded him he'd stopped his petting. "I said the woman had appeared from nowhere."

"Ah, shit, Swift Fox." Logan swung the axe, cleaving a log in two. "Why in the hell did you tell him that?"

"It is what you told me."

"I said I didn't know where she came from. And I don't. But she came from *somewhere*. She had to. And it wasn't King George's court."

"You believe me, then?"

Rachel leaned forward and touched the old man's hand. He looked up at her with eyes as black as the darkest night. Eyes that seemed to know more than a mere man.

"I have no reason to doubt you and every reason to trust what you say."

"Thank you." Rachel took a deep breath. They were seated on furs drawn before the hearth. Their legs were crossed much as she'd seen Logan Mac-Quaid sit when he visited with Swift Fox. Though at first she felt awkward on the ground, her reaction disappeared as she and the Adawehis conversed. And now to know that he didn't think her tale ridiculous . . . to find he truly accepted what she said, was such a relief. "I never knew how difficult it could be to have someone not credit what you say."

"You speak of Logan MacQuaid."

Rachel nodded. "He believes none of it."

"You have told him?"

"Not everything. But you saw the way he was when I spoke of home, of the king and Queen Charlotte. His response was the same when I explained I was sent to save him."

"Perhaps he feels he needs no saving."

"I don't doubt that." Rachel sighed, leaning forward to rest her chin in the cup of her palm. "He thinks I nearly startled him to death." Her tone grew softer. "He fell off the cliff when I yelled at him, but 'twas not my fault. I thought ... think ... he was about to jump." Another sigh. "And I imagine Swift Fox told you of my attempt to save Mr. MacQuaid from him."

"He told me."

Rachel looked up through her lashes. "You're very much the gentleman not to laugh." Her smile was sad. "I think ..." She bit her bottom lip. "I think a mistake was made. The only way I can return to my own life is to save Mr. MacQuaid's. And I fear I can't do that."

"You believe the spirits misjudged you?"

"Yes." She spoke the single word softly. When he made no response, Rachel glanced up at him. His walnut-brown face was wrinkled more than usual as he pursed his lips.

"I do not think the spirits are confused. They do not err as we do. You will find the way to do what you must."

"I wish I were as certain as you." She spread her fingers on the bear fur. "I don't even know how to live here." She glanced up quickly. "It is so hard to know what to do."

"The Adanti, my people, believe there was once only water and all the animals lived together in the sky." As Lone Dove spoke his arms gestured to embrace the heavens. "It was very crowded so Sayunisi, the Water Beetle, dove into the water and found mud. He brought it to the surface and it grew to what is now the earth. Someone long ago," his eyes met Rachel's, "attached the earth to the heavens with four cords. That is our link," he said. "Most of us only travel up. But I believe you have made the voyage back to earth. And I believe you will know what to do when the time is right."

"I want to accept what you say. What I was told."

His hands touched her shoulders. "I shall talk to the spirits. Ask them to guide you. But you must listen to your heart. To your own spirit, too . . . the spirit within you."

Rachel nodded. She would do as he suggested, but she feared . . . nay, knew, there was no spirit within her.

"What the hell are they doing in there?" Logan tossed another chunk of wood onto the growing pile by the door. He'd been chopping nonstop for hours. At this rate he wouldn't need to repeat the task for a fortnight.

"I have said, I do not know." Swift Fox lifted the cane flute to his lips and continued playing a series of notes that sounded like the call of a tanager.

Logan was tired of hearing it. Or perhaps he was simply tired of wondering what went on behind the closed door of his cabin. He leaned on the axe handle a moment, then straightened. "I'm thinking I should go in there."

He'd taken only a few steps before he felt the hand on his shoulder. "The Adawehis will not like it."

"Nay? Well, I'm not liking it that she's in there filling his head with nonsense."

"Lone Dove knows what is true and what is false."

Logan scowled, but he turned back, grabbing up the axe handle again with a vengeance. The Cherokee put great store in their Adawehis. Great faith in their powers.

He'd seen these holy men interpret dreams and change the course of a man's life. They sat at all the Councils, guarding against evil spirits, and they advised the chiefs during peace and war.

It was not for him to tell Lone Dove who he could listen to. At least he didn't plan to get in a wrangle

with the holy man over it. Or over the woman. As
soon as she was strong enough they would head down
the valley. Let the good people of MacLaughlin's Mill
take care of her and her lively imagination . . . or her
madness.

Long shadows cast by the loblolly pines speared
across the clearing by the time the door opened.
Earlier the dog had opened his droopy eyes, stretched
and trotted off into the trees to hunt something for
his dinner. Logan could hear his excited yelp over
the growling of his own stomach. His shoulders and
back ached from all his chopping. And he wished
he'd thought to bring a jug outside with him this
morning.

As the Adawehis and Her Highness stepped into
the fading light Logan glanced down at his friend.
Swift Fox had long since given up imitating birds to
fall asleep, his head pillowed by a tuft of dried grass.
So he missed the golden aura of light that seemed
to drift above her head.

It glittered and shone brighter than the diamonds
at her throat. Logan blinked, opening his eyes slowly
and it was gone. And she was staring at him with
that expression. The one that seemed to imply she
considered him no more than a peasant to do her
beck and call. " 'Twas a trick of the setting sun," he
mumbled, only to shake his head when Lone Dove
asked what he'd said.

The old man seemed very pleased with himself if
the smile on his wrinkled face spoke true. "I have
invited your woman to join us for the festival of *Ah,
tawh, hung, nah.*"

Logan's eyes widened. "You've what?"

"You are to come with her. To be her guide."

"I am honored of course. But I'm afraid 'twill
not be possible. Perhaps *Lady* Rachel did not men-

tion this, but she is leaving soon to return to her palace.''

She did not find his sarcasm amusing. Rachel allowed her disdain to show for an instant before flashing Mr. MacQuaid a brilliant smile. "I've assured Lone Dove that I shall be here at the time of the festival and would be most pleased to attend.''

Their eyes met and held: his not bothering to conceal their anger, hers unbrightened by the upward turn of her lips. It was the Adawehis who broke the deadlock of their stare. He stepped between them, drawing first her hand, then his into his own. When he spread his fingers their hands were linked.

"Listen to your heart, Logan MacQuaid. It will not lead you astray.'' Then he motioned to Swift Fox who was just now pushing to his feet and together they headed toward the path down the mountain.

Rachel and Logan watched them leave, each deep in their own thoughts before suddenly realizing their hands were still entwined. As one they let go, pulling away till they stood more than a rod apart.

Logan was the first to speak. "And what was that all about?''

Rachel, who'd suddenly grown very interested in the lace cascading down her shift sleeve, glanced over her shoulder. "Whatever do you mean, Mr. MacQuaid?''

"The invitation. How did you manage that, and why did you accept?''

"I accepted because I'd like to go, of course. There rarely is another reason for me to endure anyone's company.''

Except for him. Perhaps she hadn't come out and said it, but Logan knew what she meant. And he didn't give a damn. He was more than tired of having her around ... would be well rid of her. Unfortunately that glorious day didn't seem close now.

"I still want to know what you said to make him invite you. Whites are rarely included in the cementation ceremony."

"You've been before." Rachel bent down as the dog bounded into the clearing.

"How did ye know that?"

"Well . . ." Rachel started to say that Lone Dove told her, but he hadn't. At least she didn't remember him saying it. But how else *could* she know? Rachel patted the dog absently on top his furry head. "The Adawehis told me, of course. Your dog caught a rabbit," she added as much to change the subject as to explain the excited way the animal was prancing about.

"How do ye know that?" Logan assumed the dog had tried, but was also fairly sure he hadn't succeeded. After all, he very seldom did. And there wasn't a scrap of rabbit hair to prove otherwise.

He told me, didn't seem an acceptable response, yet Rachel knew the dog had. But Mr. MacQuaid already thought her mad. Imagine what he'd make of a revelation that she could communicate with a dog.

The dog already was sprawled in one of his favorite poses, on his back, his legs in the air, tongue lolling from his open mouth. If he did have anything to say to her, Rachel was certain she'd rather not hear it.

With a shake of her head, which sent golden curls spilling over her bare shoulders, Rachel dismissed the entire thing. Yet she couldn't help asking, "What is his name? I've never heard you call him anything but Dog."

Logan paused before stepping into his cabin. When he glanced back he was again struck by how beautiful she was . . . and how annoying. "There be nothing else."

"Nothing but 'dog'?" Without realizing what she

was about, Rachel stepped closer to the sleeping span-iel. "But that's unheard of. One always gives pets a name."

Logan turned to face her, his jaw clenched. "He is not my pet. And he has no name."

There was more to his words than what he said. Rachel realized that on some plane she couldn't com-prehend, and at the moment didn't wish to try. He was such an exasperating man. Certainly the animal sprawled at her feet was no prize. He was lazy and hardly a watchdog. But he deserved a name.

Rachel met his obstinate stare with one of her own. "Then I shall name him." His dark scowl nearly brought a smile to her lips. "Henry, I think." Rachel sank down to tickle the ruff under his chin. "What think you of that, brave hunter of rabbits? Do you like the name Henry? 'Tis the moniker of several great kings."

"And no damn dog of mine shall wear it."

"Oh, really?" Rachel tilted her head to look up at him. "Well, it appears to be too late. He's already named."

His jaw hurt from clenching it, Logan realized, and immediately tried to make himself relax. What in the hell did he care what she called the scruffy mutt? She was a temporary nuisance, a temporary annoyance he had to suffer. He almost laughed at that thought. Perhaps she had been sent . . . sent to punish him further. Well, if that was the case, she was damn good at her task.

Logan turned on his heel and slammed into the cabin with a mumbled, "Call him whatere you like." Logan knew it would make no difference. The animal did as he chose.

Except that in the days that followed that didn't seem to be the case.

She was still weak from the fever. Logan couldn't

help but notice. And though he wanted nothing more than to let her fend for herself—to put a stop to the infernal waiting upon her he seemed to do—he couldn't. At least not yet.

So she sat in his chair, what he'd come to think of as her throne, and accepted a cup of tea, or bowl of stew. For the most part she was gracious, so damn gracious Logan felt like a servant in his own home.

And she continued to call the dog Henry.

He was sure she did it to annoy him at first. She'd look down that freckle-dusted short nose of hers and sigh as the animal lay sleeping, its legs sticking straight in the air. "Doesn't Henry look adorable? I've never seen a dog sleep quite like that before."

To which Logan would grunt something unintelligible. He wasn't going to give her the satisfaction of a discussion.

"I once had a dog, you know."

It was three days after the Adawehis's visit and Logan had just returned from his morning bath in the creek. The last thing he wanted to discuss as he stood by the fire drying off, was dogs. His own had opted to stay sitting by her chair rather than bound outside with him. But his lack of comment seemed to make no difference. She continued as if he'd shown a keen interest in her statement.

"I was much younger. And my father didn't know of it, of course."

She paused and something in her tone made Logan stop as he pulled the shirt down over his head. "Why would you say 'of course'?"

"What?" She glanced up as if only now realizing he stood before her. "Oh, dogs reminded him of my mother. She apparently had several that she kept with her nearly all the time, or so the cook's helper told me once."

"Your mother died, then, when you were young?"

"No." Her eyes met his. "She left. It was all quite scandalous. She ran away with a younger son of my father's friend, Lord Bathoon. No one knows what became of them. Some say they committed suicide by leaping into the sea, their hands joined. Others, that there was an accident as they rode in their carriage along the cliff road. Or, perhaps they're still alive, living together in some hovel in the south of Wales."

When she ended her speech her voice was unusually bright as were her eyes. And Logan stood still, the sound of the cracking fire and the dog's snoring all that broke the silence.

"Gracious." She wiped her palms down across her silvery blue skirt. "I can't imagine why I started telling you of my past like that."

"How old were you?"

"When she left, you mean? Hardly more than a babe. I remember very little about her." She took a breath, placing her hands on the chair arms and stood. "I don't wish to discuss this further."

With a mere mention of the name, "Henry," the traitorous dog bounded to his feet and followed close by her skirts as she headed for the door. "I believe I shall take a stroll while you prepare our morning repast."

And to think he'd had a moment of sympathy for her . . . even liking. He who knew what it was like to live with memories he'd as soon forget. Well, he'd be damned before he turned into her personal lackey. If she was strong enough to "stroll about" she was strong enough to "prepare her own repast." His too, for that matter.

It really was lovely here. There was none of the controlled beauty of the parks around Queen's

House, but Rachel loved the mist-shrouded mountains and the scarlet and gold valley. Each morning the vapors drifted up, dancing through the fir and spruce. *Sha-cona-ga* Lone Dove had called it . . . blue like smoke.

Rachel stood on the edge of the precipice looking out over it all. Henry lay by her feet, already asleep. She wished she hadn't thought about her mother . . . wished she hadn't told Logan. She was here for one reason and one reason only. And it had nothing to do with dredging up unpleasantness from her past. From the moment her father died, leaving her orphaned, and she'd gone to live with her closest living relative, Queen Charlotte, Rachel decided to put thoughts of her mother behind her.

She'd only shown the slightest interest when Liz showed her a portrait of Lady Anne in the gallery at St. James Castle. Of course she'd wondered what her mother looked like . . . all paintings of her mother at her home in Devonshire had been destroyed when she left.

And to be sure, she'd been astonished at the resemblance between herself and her mother. "At first I thought I'd come across a portrait of you," Liz had said, while Rachel stared at the gilt framed canvas. Then she turned, without saying a word and walked away. She never went back for a second look. She never discussed the incident with Liz. Her closest friend Liz.

So why, when there was no need of it, did she bring the issue up with a man she didn't even like?

Rachel shut her eyes and took a deep breath, opening them again to stare unseeing over the landscape. What was she doing here? Logan MacQuaid seemed in no danger of having his life snuffed out. She'd seldom seen a man more capable of protecting himself.

Yet Lone Dove was not surprised by her assigned task. He accepted her words with no qualms . . . accepted them perhaps more easily than she did herself. For the more time that went by, the more impossible her assignment seemed. And she did long to return to Queen's House. For the peace and pleasure she'd known there. For the chance to avenge her friend's life.

What was Lord Bingham doing right now? Did he consider himself a fortunate man, well rid of an unfaithful wife and her lover and friend? No one to point a finger toward his guilty heart and reveal his sin. But she would do it. When she returned, she would tell the Queen and Lord Bingham would bear the punishment for his crime.

But first she must finish here. And patience was something Rachel never held dear. "Listen to your spirit," the Adawehis had told her. "You will find the way." But her spirit told her nothing and her mind only screamed that she must hurry.

She was an angel. Surely she could control things about her if she tried. Could summon a chorus of hosannas. Could fly. Rachel paused, a slight smile tilting the corners of her lips. Of course, angels could fly. Any painting she'd ever seen showed them hovering, their wings outstretched. Granted, she had no wings, least none she could see, but she must possess them all the same. She must be able to fly.

She stepped forward, not sure she actually planned to try it—not ever getting the chance.

Strong arms wrapped about her waist, moments before the thrust of his body knocked her to the side. He rolled before they hit the ground, absorbing most although not all of the shock. Rachel barely had time for her breath to return before he had rolled again, this time on top her.

"What in the hell were you about to do?"

His face was above hers, dark and angry, his green eyes narrowed.

"I was . . ." Rachel bit her lip. At the moment it seemed perfectly ridiculous to say what she thought of doing. Testing one's ability to fly by leaping from the side of the mountain was madness. At least he would think so. "Nothing. Now please get off me." But he didn't obey. She could feel the pebbly hardness of the ground beneath her back as he settled on her more firmly.

"I saw you with me own eyes, Rachel."

"You saw nothing." She was angry now, and only partly because she wasn't sure he hadn't seen the truth. "Get off I say. Get—"

But the rest of her words were cut off when his mouth covered hers. His kiss was rough, as she expected from him, hard and uncompromising. Not like the few kisses she'd shared with William.

Beneath her gravel and dirt ground into her clothing and hair, and above her his weight was oppressive. But his tongue pressed into her mouth, stirring to life sensations that filled her with longing. Which was folly, if not completely impossible. How could someone who wasn't even alive feel as she did?

Rachel tried to focus her mind on that as well as the fact that she could barely tolerate the man. But none of that seemed to matter as his lips pressed into hers. Of their own volition her arms wrapped around his neck, her fingers tangling in the long strands of obsidian hair. Her breathing grew shallow and quick, her heart thumped painfully in her chest, and she could only hold on to him, pull him closer.

He shifted, sending his tongue and a salvo of shivers down the side of her neck. Rachel gasped in air, moaning when his hand covered her breast, pushing it up free from the binding confines of her stays. The pads of his fingers were work-roughened and none too gentle as they massaged her flesh. But that did nothing to impede the dizzying excitement that grew within her. If anything his touch fanned the flames as surely as a quickening wind would.

Her nipple grew painfully taut, and only the moist heat of his mouth assuaged the ache. She was swirling in a vortex, her body arching toward his, her hands restlessly exploring the ridges and valleys of his back.

And then it was gone.

Her body still sang. But his weight was gone. The delicious things he did with his hands and mouth were gone. The transition was so quickly made that at first Rachel wondered if some invisible force had plucked him off her.

But then she opened her eyes and saw he'd merely rolled to the side and now sat knees spread, bent head in hands. His face was hidden to her by the loose fall of dark hair, but Rachel could see the ragged rise and fall of his chest as he gulped air into his lungs. His breathing matched her own.

He turned his head, staring at her a moment with those green eyes before he spoke. When he did his voice was husky and low. "Now do you know why I want you to leave?"

Chapter Five

"He who considers his work beneath him will be above doing it well."

—Alexander Chase
Perspectives

"You drink too much."

Rachel stood in the open doorway, looking into the small cabin. He sat, or more correctly, *sprawled*, on the chair, a jug perched precariously on one knee. At the sound of her voice he glanced up, not quite meeting her stare.

"And what if I do? 'Tis naught to you."

She wished what he said were true. Oh, how she wished it. But nothing could change what she was sent to do. Nothing.

Rachel had lain on the ground, her legs spread beneath a twisted skirt, her mouth wet and tingling, wondering what to do. He was no longer there to befuddle her thoughts. After his initial comment about wanting her gone he'd pushed to his feet. "Don't go near the edge again," was all he'd said before striding hurriedly toward the cabin.

As if she would dare.

No, her encounter with Logan MacQuaid had left her quite dizzy enough without needing to step off the edge of a cliff to test her ability to fly. It also left her feeling very human. And confused. And embarrassed. And heaven only knew how many other emotions rattled about in her brain, like so many bees buzzing about a rose.

"Listen to the spirit within you."

Lone Dove's words came back to her again. Listen to her spirit rather than her mind. But how? She lay there on the ground until the discomfort of the terrain finally forced her to rise and brush the dirt and pebbly stones from her clothes.

Rachel had still been wondering what to say to him when she opened the door to find a cup pressed to his lips. He took another swig now almost in defiance of her remark.

"Mary forgave you long ago."

Rum splashed down the front of his open-necked shirt, wetting the tangle of dark curls on his chest. He yanked the dented pewter from his mouth. "What the hell are you prattling on about?"

She didn't know. Rachel blinked and searched her mind, trying to remember where that thought came from. Nothing. Yet it was there. The very strong conviction that he'd been forgiven. By a woman. Mary.

And it was clear Logan MacQuaid knew of whom she spoke.

He set the cup on the floor and turned in the chair to face her. His speech was only slightly slurred. "I want to know what you meant by that remark."

"She wouldn't want you to carry on like this. To drink yourself into oblivion." Rachel took a step forward, inwardly cringing when he recoiled. It was the slightest of movements and he quickly caught himself, straightening his shoulders and pushing to his feet.

His step was surprisingly steady as he moved toward the door. He grabbed up his musket, glancing back only once to call for the dog to follow. The spaniel sat by Rachel, having awakened and meandered into the cabin when she did. He was hunched down, licking his paw almost as a cat would, and he ignored his master's grumbled, "Come on with you, Dog." It wasn't until Rachel urged him on with a "Go with him, Henry," that the animal stood and loped along.

Rachel sighed as they disappeared behind a screen of holly and pines. How could she protect him if he rushed off into the woods without her? And how could he keep from rushing away from her when she spoke of a mysterious woman and forgiveness?

She shut the door, crossing to the chair and settling in, her chin resting in the cup of her palm. Who was this woman and what did Logan do that needed her forgiveness? Rachel tried to concentrate, hoping the answer would come to her, but it didn't. She was only left with a headache and the decision that he must have loved her very much to act as he did.

For some reason she couldn't begin to fathom, Rachel wasn't pleased by her conclusion.

He'd made a fool of himself.

Logan stood outside, steeling himself to enter the cabin. His own cabin for God's sake. As if he should have to worry about what he said or did in his own home.

God, what demon had sent her to plague him?

If he wasn't lusting after her she was reminding him of things he'd worked hard to forget.

Mary forgives you, indeed.

Where had she come up with that? Logan took a deep breath and shut his eyes. For a moment, when she first said it, he could have sworn it was Mary forgiving him. Which was ridiculous. It had to be ridiculous.

Any further attempt to delay going inside was sabotaged by the dog's insistent scratching on the door. "Can't bear to be away from her, can you, you lazy mongrel?" Neither his tone nor the sad shake of his head matched his words as Logan lifted the latch.

It was dark inside with only the glowing coals of a long untended fire to battle the gathering night. "Damnation," Logan mumbled under his breath. The woman truly was worthless. He didn't know what made him expect to be greeted by the aroma of dinner cooking, or the pleasant flicker of a lit candle. But there was none. And he should have known better.

Anger welled up, only to sputter and die when he caught sight of her. She was asleep, her golden hair a halo about her head, her chin tucked down in the fur blanket. She'd been ill, he reminded himself. And she was weak still from the fever. For tonight he would let her sleep. But starting tomorrow he would instruct her in some basic rules of frontier living. If she intended to reside with him until the festival of *Ah, tawg, hung, nah,* she would start earning her keep.

"I'm not at all certain what it is you wish me to do."

Rachel stood on the shore of the swiftly churning river. Logan MacQuaid was a rod over from her, squatting on a flat, moss-covered rock, holding out his hand toward her.

"I told you, 'twas easier to reach the water from here."

"Yes, I know that's what you said." She pretended not to see his beckoning fingers. "I just don't think I've any desire to reach the water."

"How else do you intend to do the laundry?"

Which was the crux of the dilemma. She had no desire to do the laundry. However, he seemed to think it an excellent idea.

"I don't do laundry. Servants do laundry."

"So you've said. Repeatedly." Logan stood, hands on hips, tired of waiting to help her across the trickle of water that splashed around the rock.

"And I really don't think it necessary that I learn. When I return to England the washerwoman will take care of my dirty linens."

"Well Your Highness isn't in England. And from where I stand you're the closest thing to a washerwoman we have. Now give me your hand."

She didn't seem to have a choice. Rachel took a deep breath and reached out her hand. It was immediately grabbed by his and she was yanked toward the flat rock. Water swirled around her, splashing her beautiful blue-and-silver shoes, which weren't really beautiful anymore.

It surprised Rachel that the creek didn't scare her—after all, she had drowned. But it didn't seem to affect her at all.

"Now I'll show you how 'tis done," he said, taking one of the shirts from the pile by his side. "You dip it in the water, like so." He dredged it through the current a few times till it was dripping wet. "Then you work some of this soap into the fabric." He matched action to words, scooping several fingers full of soft soap from a crock and squeezing it into the rough material till gray bubbles formed. "Rinse it and drape it over a branch to dry," he said, handing the sodden shirt to her before leaping back into the long grass on the shore.

"That doesn't look too hard for you, does it?"

"Of course not." She wasn't an imbecile. Perhaps she never did anything like this before, but that certainly didn't mean she couldn't. She'd always been a quick learner. Master Howard, the dancing instructor commented that she mastered the quadrille before

any other young lady. She even enjoyed her lessons
. . . sometimes. And her needlework was neat and
precise if not inspired.

Of course she could perform this simple task. Yet
looking down at the pile of soiled laundry, then the
icy water, did not exactly make one long to begin.
"Why am I washing your clothes, again?"

He grinned at her, which took Rachel completely
by surprise. She was accustomed to growls from him,
and scowls and even the occasional guffaw of laughter, but never a grin. His teeth looked very white
against his sun-darkened skin and black whiskers. And
despite his rather disheveled and straggly appearance, she had to admit his smile was captivating.

"Ah . . . what did you say?" Had she actually been
concentrating so much on his momentary slip into
good nature that she missed his response?

"I said my clothes are dirty. If you wish to scrub
yours too, I won't object."

"That's hardly the point," Rachel called after
him as he began striding away. He paused to look
over his broad shoulder and she continued. "Since
they're your soiled linens, I think you should wash
them."

"Then who would hunt for dinner?" He arched a
dark brow. "You, perhaps?"

Rachel's lips thinned. Of course he knew she
couldn't hunt. By the looks of the long rifle she
couldn't even lift it. "I wasn't aware one prevented
the other."

"In other words you're of the opinion I should do
both?"

"I assume you have before. Certainly you laundered your clothing before I came."

"Occasionally. However, I wasn't obliged to provide supper for two as I am now." That said he lifted

the rifle, cradling it in his arms and started toward the path behind the cabin, only stopping when she called out again.

"Do you think perhaps I should go with you?"

He glanced back over his shoulder, his expression questioning.

"In case I'm needed to . . . " She bit her bottom lip.

"Save me?"

It did seem ridiculous, now that she heard him say it aloud. Rachel squatted, plunging the soapy shirt into the water. "Never mind."

But she couldn't help glancing around as he disappeared behind a copse of trees. Then she stared back at the pile of dirty laundry. How had she . . . *she* managed to get herself into a situation where she was expected to clean a man's dirty linens? Her mind wandered back to England for a moment, to Queen's House and the bevy of servants at call. How she'd taken for granted that her gowns were always clean, her underthings, fresh. Did someone take them to a river and pound them on a flat rock for her? Rachel laughed at the thought. The palace had a laundry . . . somewhere.

Rachel sighed and when she did her eyes met Henry's. Logan left him when he went hunting and the dog sat now on his haunches, his mouth open, his dripping tongue hanging out, as if amused by her predicament.

"If you continue to laugh at me like that I shall . . . shall toss you into the river. We shall see how you enjoy that, Henry."

In response the dog leaped up, bounding forward and nearly knocking Rachel over in his exuberance to dive into the water. A splashing array of sun-sparkling droplets cascaded over her as the animal dove headlong into the current.

"Oh, my!" The chilly spray took Rachel's breath away. Her eyes popped open and she wiped water from her face as she watched Henry frolic about. "I shall pay you in kind for that, Henry. Don't think I won't." But, of course there was nothing she could do now. The dog obviously loved being in the water. Which made one of them, Rachel thought as she leaned down and picked up another shirt.

It smelled of Logan.

Not heady with perfume as the men of her aquaintance in London. But of the outdoors and sweat, and a certain fragrance that seemed to be his alone. She was smiling when she brought the shirt to her face and inhaled; frowning when she realized what she was doing.

"For heaven's sake," she squealed, bending over and splashing the linen into the water. It was barely wet when she scooped a handful of soft soap and spread it over the shirt. The water was frigid. The lye in the soap burned her hands. She couldn't seem to work up any suds. And she didn't much care.

Holding the shirt between her finger and thumb she swirled it once through the water, then leaped onto shore and carried it dripping wet and soapy to toss over a bramble of rhododendron branches. The next shirt she washed much the same way, and the next. By the time she was down to her last piece of dirty laundry, Rachel was nearly as soaked as her wash.

Henry had long since climbed from the river and lay drying himself in a patch of golden sunshine. Rachel scowled at the animal. Straightening, Rachel spread her palms on the small of her back, stretching. "Perhaps I should let him call you simply dog.

"Oh, I know this isn't your fault," she admitted but her voice sounded peevish. "He *is* the one I blame, believe me. But you could at least be sympathetic, you know." She scooped up the final shirt, bending forward and grumbling at the same time. "This water is so cold. And I hate this—"

The word soap never crossed her lips for as she reached around for the crock her feet slipped on the wet and sudsy surface. With a windmilling of arms that did nothing to stop her fall Rachel splashed into the bone-chilling water. Her scream ended with a gulp of icy liquid and Rachel was living her death again.

Logan held his breath, as his finger slowly squeezed back the trigger. He'd caught sight of the buck's tracks over the ridge and trailed him for over a mile, finally catching sight of the fine animal after it had circled back toward the cabin. His mouth watered at the prospect of venison steaks as he drew a bead on the buck. In just a moment he would fire and—

"What the hell?" Logan and the deer heard the scream simultaneously. The buck reacted instantly, lifting his antlered head and galloping off into the woods. Logan raced toward his cabin just as quickly.

My God, what had she done now? Logan leaped across a trickling stream, his feet trampling the undergrowth of moss on the other side. She could hardly catch herself on fire while washing his clothes, and she knew better than to approach the edge of the ravine. Didn't she?

Damn! He climbed over a boulder and thought of Ostenaco. Swift Fox had said he was far away in Kaintukee, but perhaps he'd returned. Perhaps he had come, looking for Logan and finding Rachel.

Logan's lungs burned as he burst into the clearing. The dog was at the edge of the river, barking his fool head off and Logan headed there on the run. It wasn't till he passed the border of hollies that he saw what the commotion was about.

He waded into the water, mentally bracing himself against the cold and reached down, yanking her up by her shoulders. She was soaked and sputtering and nearly blue from the cold. "What the hell are you doing, Rachel?" Logan scooped her up without waiting for an answer. He strode toward the cabin, kicking open the door and settling his shivering bundle by the hearth.

It was stone cold.

Logan muttered an oath hot enough to sear Rachel's ears, but that was the only part of her that was warm. "I told you to toss some logs on the fire before you came out."

He had, too. Rachel could clearly remember sitting in the chair earlier today as he spoke to her. He stood leaning against the door, one foot resting on a keg and he was telling her that he no longer intended to play her servant. "As long as you're to be living here for a while you will earn your keep," he'd said and Rachel had visions of him lying atop her, kissing her.

But he quickly dispelled that notion before she could conjure up a decent degree of indignation. He wanted her to work ... to do her share. She sat listening to him in disbelief, wondering just who he thought he was talking to as he listed several chores that were to be hers.

"Keeping the fire going is partly your concern. I shall chop the wood, but you're to throw logs on the flames when need be."

She said nothing.

"And I think you can do the wash, too."

"I'm to be your servant then?" she asked with a lift of her chin.

"Nay. We'll work together. Now I'll be in the barn. Make sure the fire's going strong before you come out."

But of course she hadn't and now she was freezing

to death and all because the awful man made her wash his shirts. Rachel stood on the dirt floor, dripping wet and watched as he coaxed what was left of that morning's fire back to life.

"Grab up a fur and wrap it about you," he said, glancing over his shoulder. "And I'd get out of those wet clothes if I were you. You'll be coming down with a fever again."

He acted as if this were her fault, Rachel thought. She still stood where he put her, too taken with shivers to follow any of his directives. It wasn't until he had flames licking around several logs that he glanced back again and then it was with a scowl on his face.

"Can you do nothing for yourself then?" He pushed to his feet and approached, looking as if he did plan to play the part of lady's maid again. Thoughts of him helping her out of her gown were enough to spur Rachel to action. She twisted away, scurrying behind the curtain he'd hung for her privacy. Her fingers felt like shards of ice as she tried to unfasten the hooks on her bodice.

"I could have drowned, you know." She had thought she was drowning . . . again.

She could hear him moving about in the room. Could hear his amused chuckle. "I seriously doubt that Your Highness."

"I don't swim." Rachel managed to untie the tabs of her petticoat.

"But I assume you can stand."

"Stand?"

"Aye. Which is all 'twas necessary to rise above the water."

Rachel felt the heat of embarrassment seep up her neck. She was so agitated when the water closed in over her head, remembering the other time . . . the time she died . . . that she'd panicked. She stepped from behind the curtain wrapped from chin to toes in a fur blanket. She still shivered, but could feel a bit of warmth permeating the cabin.

That is until she met his stare and noticed the chill of his light green eyes.

He didn't say anything but she could feel what he was thinking. Disappointment. In her. And a very real regret that he was forced to offer her hospitality until they visited the Cherokee town.

Rachel took a deep breath and stepped closer to the flames. "I will attempt to be more diligent with the fire." She slanted him a look up through her lashes, hoping to see an expression of belief on his face. She glanced down quickly. The devil take him. She didn't give a fig what he thought.

The afternoon brought a new revelation. He expected her to milk the cow.

Rachel stood in the doorway of the barn, staring at the cud-chewing cow. This really was more than she could tolerate. Dust motes danced in the slant of late afternoon sun that shone through the slit of a window. The air smelled strongly of straw and animals, and for an instant she seemed carried back to the stables at Queen's House.

She always enjoyed riding.

Rachel sighed. There was no horse to have saddled. Nothing but a pie-eyed cow. She could refuse to do it, of course. Rachel didn't think Logan MacQuaid would hurt her, or even try to force her. But she couldn't help recalling his face when he noticed the fire was out. And the memory of how cold she was wouldn't go away either.

"Well, Mistress Ellen it is but you and me." Rachel wasn't sure what made her call the cow that, but the creature seemed pleased. She shifted her head around, staring at Rachel with large, liquid brown eyes. Patting her neck seemed as natural as flirting over the fringe of her fan. "I really don't know how to do this. Oh, I realize *he* showed me this morning, but . . . " Rachel let the rest of her sentence drift off as she reached for the small three-legged stool.

She settled down as Logan did this morning, between the cow's front and back legs, prepared to be repulsed—surprised when she wasn't. Rachel edged the pail beneath the swollen udder and took a deep breath. "You do realize I've never done this before, don't you, Mistress Ellen? Yes, I imagine it is rather simple, however . . . Oh, for heaven's sake." She reached out, tentatively touching, then squeezing the cow's teats. She was rewarded with a squirt of sweet-smelling milk splashing into the bucket.

She couldn't help laughing. "What a wonderful creature you are, Mistress Ellen." Her fingers tightened again. By the time she'd found a rhythm of sorts the pail was full of frothy liquid with a canopy of steam rising above it, and Rachel's forehead was pressed against the cow's hide.

"This is one of Logan MaQuaid's chores I shall gladly do," Rachel said as she lifted the rope handle, placing the milk near the door. Before she left she gave the cow a small curtsey. "It was my pleasure to meet you, Mistress Ellen.

"And I do appreciate your flattery about my hands." Rachel examined her palms. "I do imagine they are smoother than Mr. MacQuaid's."

There was no imagining about it. She knew exactly how Logan MacQuaid's hands felt. Each time he touched her it was obvious they were work-rough. And strong. And gentle. Rachel pushed that thought from her mind. "I'll return tomorrow morning, Mistress Ellen."

As she walked back to the cabin, Rachel realized she was beginning to hate her gown.

She kicked at a piece of torn silver lace tangling about her foot. And spilled some milk in the process. Why wasn't she wearing something a bit more sensible when she drowned? Something that would hold up a bit better. Her gown was in tatters—her dip into the lake certainly hadn't helped its appearance.

Oh well, as soon as she returned to Queen's House, she would be able to choose from her large collection of gowns. First she'd immerse herself in a tub, with lots of delicious hot water and soap that smelled of flowers and left her skin feeling soft and smooth. She'd have her maid wash her hair and brush it dry, then dress it in the most fashionable of styles. Rachel closed her eyes reminiscing about the life she used to take for granted. Remembering also that Liz had no chance of returning to it.

No, as much as she would like a bath and clean clothes, her first duty when she returned would be to speak out against Lord Bingham. Her first duty, and her first pleasure.

Rachel started back toward the cabin with a more determined step, only to stop abruptly when the door opened and Logan appeared.

"Have a care for the milk you're spilling Your Highness."

Rachel righted the pail, but she couldn't take her eyes off him. "You look . . . different."

He seemed not to understand her statement for a moment, then grinned rather self-deprecatingly. That's when she first noticed his dimples. Two of them on either side of his mouth. At first they seemed out of place on such a solemn man. But the more she looked, the more taken she was by this new discovery. He was far more handsome than she'd originally thought. His beauty was as rugged as the land.

"I thought it best to rid myself of the beard before the ceremony of *Ah, tawh, hung, nah.*"

"Oh." Hardly a witty comment, but Rachel couldn't think of a thing to say. It occurred to her that she was staring rather unabashedly and quickly averted her eyes. "I've milked Mistress Ellen," she said for lack of anything better to say.

He arched a brow but made no comment about her naming his cow. He did step forward looking at the pail with some interest. Rachel thought him about to chastise her for spilling so much but instead appeared pleasantly surprised. "I see the cow tried a bit harder today."

"What? Oh, yes."

"I started supper. There's bacon frying in the skillet. Pray, see that it doesn't burn."

Rachel nodded. She was staring at him again, wondering how it was she'd never noticed how handsome he was. He'd tied back his hair with a bit of leather and between that and the missing whiskers she could actually see his face for the first time. The wide forehead. The straight blade of nose and the full sensual lips. Combined with the startling green eyes that she'd always thought attractive, he was really very appealing to look upon.

Not like the gentlemen at court Rachel assured herself quickly as she turned and hurried into the cabin. With their silk waistcoats and powdered wigs, they were by far the better looking. Yet she couldn't keep from peeking around the door as she went to close it.

He was going to chop more wood. He always took his shirt off to do that. Such a ghastly uncivilized habit, Rachel told herself as she lingered in the doorway. Who wanted to look on a man's bare chest and muscled back? He yanked the linen over his head and Rachel bit her bottom lip. She tried to swallow but her mouth was dry.

He hefted the axe and sent it forging down, cleaving the block of wood and Rachel's fingers tightened on the door. He really did have a very appealing body. She'd long suspected Prince William of using pads under his clothes and stockings to enhance his appearance. It was obvious Logan MacQuaid would not have to resort to such practices.

Rachel wasn't certain how long she watched him at his task. Every time two chunks of wood split from one she told herself she didn't care what he looked like. She was sent to save him and the sooner she could accomplish that, the sooner she could return to her real life. But she still stayed to let out her breath when his arms lifted high over his head.

It wasn't till she saw him pause, the axe poised in midair, that she noticed the smell. Unfortunately, that seemed to be what caused him to stop also. He twisted around, his eyes meeting hers for an instant before she squealed and slammed the door.

The bacon was ruined, burned to a crisp.

Chapter Six

"Every living thing in this world is put in the charge of an angel."

—Saint Augustine
Eight Questions

"When are we leaving for the Cherokee town, Cheoah is it?"

"Soon."

"Yes, but when? Would you look at me please when I speak to you."

There it was again, that haughty tone, and Logan knew what her expression would be—a sharp-eyed stare down the length of her delicate nose—before he glanced up. And he lifted his head with reluctance. Not only did he tire of her orders and wish to show her he would tolerate them no more, but he would just as soon not notice the sweet curve of her breast, above the ragged neckline of her gown. Or the face that could only be described as beautiful despite her superior attitude.

He settled back against the log wall, marking his place in a large book with one finger before deigning to glance her way. And Rachel came to a startling conclusion.

She hated to be ignored.

Perhaps not so startling when she thought on it. Her father had ignored her and she'd hated it. But that had been long ago. Ever since she moved to London, to Queen's House, no one had dared overlook her. Not that anyone would, she assured herself. She was usually the center of attention with friends and admirers never far away.

Everyone thought her pretty, too.

Except Logan MacQuaid.

"You have my complete attention, Your Highness."

He sounded annoyed and sarcastic and Rachel lifted her chin a notch higher. Which made it more difficult for her to see him sitting there on the floor. Didn't he realize how barbaric that was? He sat with one long buckskin-clad leg spread out in front of him, the other bent at the knee. A book rested in the V made by his thigh and body.

"I asked you when we are leaving for the Cherokee village." She knew he didn't want to take her there . . . it was only because the Adawehis had insisted. In some perverse deep corner of her soul, that made Rachel all the more determined to go . . . even if she didn't feel he might need her to save him.

"We'll start out day after next. How are you coming with your cloak?"

Rachel glanced down at the animal skins in her lap, then twirled the bone needle between her fingers. "Fine," she said while trying to push the point through the tough hide. When it didn't go easily she gave up and tried to recapture his eye. He was back reading, his head bent forward, a stray lock of dark hair falling across his cheek.

She had to admit his reading surprised her.

When first they met, after she had a good look at him, Rachel would have wagered he hardly knew what a book was, let alone had the capacity to read one. But he had several leather-bound volumes, and though it was nothing compared to King George's library, she couldn't help being impressed.

"When does the festival begin?" She watched him take a deep breath, watched his chest expand beneath the loose-fitting shirt before he lowered the book.

"In five days."

"How do you know? Did Lone Dove tell you or is it always the same day such as Christmas?"

"Ah, tawh, hung, nah is the ceremony of cementation. It is the tribe's chance to begin anew. And it is celebrated ten days after *Nung, tah, -tay-quah."* He paused. "The first new moon of autumn."

"I see." She caught the telltale shifting of his hands as he began to reopen the book . . . to shut her out. "What are you reading?" She'd glanced at his books several times when she was bored but couldn't understand even the titles on most of them.

"Miscellaneous Observations in the Practice of Physick, Anatomy and Surgery."

"A book on medicine?" When he nodded she rushed on. "Are you a physician?" Except for the fact that he looked as he did and lived in a small hidden corner of nowhere, it seemed to make sense. He'd mixed medicines and nursed her to health when she had the fever. But he quickly dispelled that notion.

"Nay, I'm no doctor."

"But the books. And you appear to know so much."

" 'Tis an interest, nothing more. At one point I'd thought to pursue . . ." Logan clamped his mouth shut. Why was he telling her these things about himself?

"Why didn't you?" He obviously enjoyed studying.

He shrugged as if whatever the cause it mattered naught to him. But Rachel wasn't fooled. "My father brought me to the new world."

"Couldn't you have stayed in Scotland? Surely there was a way."

"Have you not heard of Culloden, Your Highness?"

"Of course." She was no student . . . of history or anything else for that matter. But who hadn't heard of the battle between the Duke of Cumberland's forces and Prince Charles. "It was a glorious victory."

His dark brow arched. "That interpretation would depend upon whose side you were on."

"But surely you weren't—" Rachel stopped and bit her lip as he cocked his head to one side and stared at her. "You're Scottish. I'd forgotten." She'd never been around anyone whose beliefs differed markedly from hers. Oh, perhaps there was a disagreement about whose music, Handel's or Bach's, was the most melodic. Or who painted the most passionate portraits. But not something as profound as who should be king of England.

"Though you couldn't have fought for the Pretender, could you? Certainly you are too young, sir." Rachel leaned forward. "The battle was so very long ago."

"Nineteen years is not so very long, Your Highness. But you're quite right, I didn't go to battle for the Prince. But my brother did. He was captured and hanged."

"Hanged?"

"Aye." Logan smoothed his hand over the worn leather binding of the book. "He was hardly more than a lad. Seventeen. Five years my senior."

"And they hanged him?"

He said nothing but then he didn't have to. Suddenly she could feel his pain, knew the horror of having someone he admired, nearly worshiped, taken in such a way. "You loved him very much," she said and held his gaze when he looked up.

"He was my brother though we shared but a father."

His eyes hardened, the dreamy shades of the sea turning to the glitter of glass, and Rachel clutched the chair arms, her nails digging into the hard wood. A thought—nay more a feeling—swept over her, of hatred, of betrayal. She wet her suddenly dry lips. "Your father," she began, not knowing exactly how to word her question.

"Was a true bastard." Those intense eyes met hers, held.

"Is he dead?" Rachel's voice was but a whisper.

"Aye." He looked away and Rachel let out a breath she didn't realize she held. It was as if the spell was broken.

"But I don't understand." And she didn't. A moment ago it had all seemed within her grasp. She didn't know just what *it* was, but somehow she thought it held the key to her stay here . . . to saving his life. But that was ridiculous. His father was no threat to him. By his own account his father was dead.

And Logan didn't seem willing to explain anything to her. He ignored her remark, instead studying with furrowed brow the pile of skins in her lap. "Are you sure you can sew?"

"Of course I can." Rachel loosened her grip on the chair and felt about for the needle, unfortunately finding the point first. "Ouch." She stuck the tip of her finger in her mouth and glared at him, almost as if it were his fault that she pricked herself. It *was* his fault.

If not for him she wouldn't even attempt this horrid task of making herself a coat of animal skins. When he first suggested she might like something warm to wear on their trip to the Cherokee town, she thought it an excellent idea. She was tired of either being cold or draping a heavy fur about her shoulders.

But that was before she learned she was expected to make the garment. She did have some experience with needle and thread. What lady didn't? She embroidered, and worked tapestries, and was generally known to have a fine, delicate stitch.

Except that fine and delicate did not work with this.

She had no idea how to construct a sleeve or form the body of a jacket . . . which was why she was making a cloak. But even with that she could barely manage to push the sharpened bone needle through the thick hide.

Yet she had her pride.

So she continued to try.

"Would you like me to help you?"

Rachel lifted her lashes and slowly let her finger slip from between her lips. There was something in his tone she hadn't heard since she was ill and even then she'd wondered if the fever made her hear things that weren't truly there. Something burned behind her eyelids and she blinked several times before forcing a smile.

"I've decided to make a cape instead of a jacket," she finally said. "I think 'twould be more stylish, don't you?" Before he could answer she hurried on. "I had a cape when I went to the lake after Liz. A fine one of deep blue velvet with silver lining. It matched my gown. But I must have lost it somehow. Perhaps when I fell into the water."

Rachel glanced up to find him staring at her intently. She had the uncomfortable feeling that he thought she was mad. She cleared her throat. "Don't you think a cape would be nice?"

"I suppose." Logan leaned back against the wall. "If that be what you prefer."

But that didn't help her push the needle through.

* * *

Which was what she was trying to do the next morning.

She'd risen near dawn as best she could figure. Hours before she ever awakened in England, even though Queen Charlotte did wish her ladies to attend morning prayers. But it appeared that Mr. MacQuaid expected her to cease sleeping when he did. He made no attempt to be quiet as he tossed wood on the fire. Then he whistled for the dog to come with him.

Henry, of course, had stayed where he was, draped over Rachel's feet.

"Come on with you, Dog," he'd growled after yanking open the door, allowing a blast of cold air to sweep through the cabin.

"Oh for heaven's sake Henry, do go with him. You know you enjoy your morning swim. You're just being stubborn." That said, Rachel pulled the bearskin over her face. But she didn't miss Logan's muttered curse as the dog pushed to his feet and trotted through the open doorway. Or the peace-shattering slam as the door shut behind him.

She snapped the fur down, sat up, and finger-combed the tangled curls from her face. Before wandering outside to nature's privy she laced up her corset. She'd long since given up trying to mold her body as rigidly as before. Then she carefully slipped on the tattered remains of her once lovely gown.

Back inside she spread her cape, at least the skins that were to become her cape, on the floor. She managed two uneven stitches before the burst of cold air heralded his return. Rachel didn't turn around, but she knew what she'd see if she did.

Every morning, no matter how chilled the air, he bathed in the creek. She didn't know if he wore the leather breach cloth when he dove into the water, but he always had it firmly secured about his narrow waist when he returned to the cabin.

That was all he wore.

Rachel tried to concentrate on shoving the needle through the hide as she heard him take a strip of linen and rub it over his hair-roughened skin. Every day he dried himself briskly in front of the fire. Then he wrapped on his leggings, and soft boots. Rachel forced the vision of his long muscular legs from her mind.

Soon he would reach for a clean shirt from the pile she washed. He'd shrug it over his head and—

"What the hell did you do to my shirt?"

Despite her resolve not to look at him, Rachel twisted around. He was as she imagined him, covered from the waist down, broad chest bare. Black hair, wet from his recent dunking, dripped, the water running in rivulets down across his shoulders. Rachel swallowed as she watched a drop weave through the curls surrounding one of his nipples. The cold had made it hard and pebbly. Rachel tore her eyes away only when he spoke again.

"Didn't you rinse the soap from it?"

"Well, yes . . . of course, I did." But obviously not very well, for the shirt was so stiff it nearly kept its shape. She'd thought it seemed unusually hard when she gathered it off the branches, but hadn't thought too much about it. His shirts were made of the coarsest fabric and she simply assumed that was the way they became when clean. But it was obvious from the expression on his face that wasn't the case.

She wished he only looked at her with anger. She could handle that and give him back more than she received. After all, she wasn't meant to do such menial tasks as laundry. But his scowl was softened by the disappointment in his eyes.

Rachel pushed to her feet, grabbing the shirt from

his hand, scooping up the others that were equally soap-stiff, and ran toward the door. She slammed it and hurried to the creek before Henry could roust himself to follow. Which was why she was surprised to feel his wet nose on her arm as she swished a shirt through the frigid water.

"You really never laundered *anything* before, did you?"

The sound of his voice coming from so close behind her made Rachel's back stiffen. She quickly brushed away a tear that had escaped her lashes. "Of course not. Do you honestly suppose it is something the queen has me do for her?"

He could tell she was trying to sound cavalier, but the slight quiver in her voice ruined the effect. Logan knelt beside her, reaching out to cover her hand with his own. She tried to wriggle from beneath him, but he held firm. "It doesn't matter that much, you know."

"Don't be silly. No one can wear something this full of soap." Rachel glanced down to where the shirt still floated in the water, surrounded by a thick scum of gray.

"Let me help you, then."

"No. You gave me this task to do and I shall do it." Her fingers were numb from the water but somehow she didn't mind as long as his hand covered hers. "You were right to think I can't do anything."

"Nay."

The warmth of his hand disappeared and Rachel felt fresh tears spring to her eyes. Then he clasped her shoulders, turning her upper body around so that she was forced to look at him.

"I was wrong, Rachel. You have many talents."

"But none that are worthwhile." She sniffed and he gathered her, snuggling her against his chest. Rachel knew she should pull away, but it felt so pleasant to be there, warm and secure, inhaling his smell and crying against his hair-roughened flesh. For now that he held her, she seemed incapable of stopping the tears.

His arms wrapped tightly about her body and she tried to burrow more deeply against him. She never cried. Never. At least not since the day years ago when her mother left. But now she couldn't seem to stop. And all because of not being able to wash some stupid shirts.

"Rachel."

She sniffed when he said her name. He really did have a pleasant way of saying it—not like when he called her Your Highness. She looked up to tell him so, but could only sniff again.

He smiled, that smile that showed his dimples, and brushed away a tear with his thumb. His face was very close to hers, his eyes very green and Rachel didn't protest at all when he curved his other hand around the back of her head. And inched her closer.

The first brush of his lips against hers was just that, a whisper of breath, the slightest pressure of warm flesh. Yet it felt like more, so much more. Rachel sighed, wondering how the mere suggestion of a kiss could feel so good, wondering what it would be like to have that mouth pressed firmly to hers.

And then she had to wonder no more.

As if they were caught in the vortex of the waterfall whirling beneath the falls he swept her against his body. From knees to chest there was not a sliver of space between them. His open mouth devoured hers.

Rachel's fingers twined with the damp hair at his neck. Her heart pounded and she thought she could hear the echo of his in reply. The kiss deepened, his tongue filled her mouth as if searching for some

mythical part of her he couldn't quite understand.
And Rachel could only cling to him, absorbing the
sensations that exploded within her.

She'd been kissed before. Somewhere in the back
of her mind she remembered a stolen moment with
the prince. His thumb lifting her chin. Her lack of
any genuine response. And she cared for the king's
brother; hoped to wed him when she returned.

Rachel squeezed her eyes shut, wishing she hadn't
thought of that. Wishing she could just go on floating
in the sensual haze Logan MacQuaid inspired. But
it was no use.

She couldn't forget who she was . . . what she was.
And why she was here. She wasn't sent here to suc-
cumb to this man's kisses. She was here to save his
life. And though she wished to believe otherwise,
Rachel knew this wasn't the way.

It took him a moment to realize she was pushing
away. At first when she twisted her head to the side
he took it as an invitation to ravish her neck. And
the shivers that his tongue and teeth sent rippling
across her skin came close to making her forget her
resolve.

"Please, Mr. MacQuaid."

He nibbled. "Please what?"

It was a logical question and one Rachel had to
force herself to answer. "You . . . we must stop this
insanity."

Insanity.

Logan let his arms drop to his side, not even bothering to steady her as she swayed toward him. Insanity
she called it. For a moment he'd thought this the
only sane thing he'd done since she arrived, unex-
pected and unwanted, on his mountain. He was a
man with needs. Needs he hadn't addressed in some
time. And she was a woman, attractive and desirable
despite her haughty and aggravating ways.

Why shouldn't they . . . ? He couldn't quite put a name to what they had come close to doing. What he was still willing and, if the ache in his groin was any indication, able to do.

At first when she protested he thought she might be opposed to the spot, for he'd come close to taking her right there on the ground. But he could tell by the look in her eyes, though she wouldn't quite meet his own, that wasn't the problem.

She pushed to her feet, gathering the tattered remains of her skirt about her, smoothing out the folds as if the silk weren't burned and torn. Then while staring down her nose at a point over his left shoulder, she mumbled a few words about retiring to the cottage. Her hair whirled out in a billowing cloud of gold as she turned abruptly and marched inside.

Leaving him with the damn shirts to rinse out.

Logan grabbed them up and without any thought to his actions strode into the water. He didn't stop until the cold water lapped around his waist, cooling that part of him she'd set aflame.

This wasn't working out at all as she planned.

Somehow when she met Lone Dove and he suggested she come with Logan to the Cherokee village it seemed so logical. The Adawehis believed in her. Believed *her*.

She even suspected that somehow he would help her.

Which was why she was so eager to go, even though she knew Logan MacQuaid wasn't. But that was before she realized how much walking was involved.

Now she understood why Logan was so shocked to see her when she first arrived on the mountain. On her own she would never have found this place.

"Do you suppose we might rest a bit?" Rachel

dragged the back of her hand across her forehead, grimacing when she noticed the perspiration. The sun was warm and for all the work she had done on her cloak it was flung over her arm.

"We just started," he growled as he climbed over an outcrop of moss-covered rocks. He did reach up to help her over the obstacle for which Rachel supposed she should be grateful.

She wished more than ever that she could fly.

And that she'd never kissed him.

He'd barely spoken a score of words to her since the encounter by the creek. She was too flustered to remember the shirts until he returned, soaking wet. He'd taken one look at her sitting on her haunches before the cape and yanked out his knife. For one horrible second Rachel thought he was going to test her claim that she was an angel.

But he only squatted down and stabbed a string of holes where the skins overlapped. Then with some rawhide twine he laced the two pieces together. When he finished he looked up and Rachel glanced down quickly. She'd been staring at him wondering why he was soaking wet again when he already took his ritual morning bath, and wishing she knew what to say to him.

Except that it seemed there was nothing to say. He showed her how to sew her cape without words and he spent the next few days existing beside her in much the same way.

When she asked questions such as how far away the village was, or how long it would take them to reach it, he gave noncommittal grunts and left the cabin.

His response to her request for a rest was the most he'd said to her in two days. And it wasn't very satisfactory.

"Perhaps you feel as if the journey is just begun, however I am tired."

He knocked away a pine branch and looked over his shoulder. "We need to make MacLaughlin's Mill by late afternoon."

MacLaughlin's Mill? Rachel hurried to catch up with him, stepping in her haste on a stone and sucking in her breath. She ignored the pain as best she could and grabbed for his arm. He swung around as if she burned him.

"What in the hell are you doing rushing up on me like that? I'd have thought you learned your lesson the first time you did."

"Never mind that." She stepped in front of him on the narrow path. "I told you I wasn't going to MacLaughlin's Mill. That is the settlement you told me about, isn't it?"

"It is." His stance mimicked hers.

"I told you I wasn't leaving you. Not until I save your life. Though why I should even bother I don't know. You lied to me, making me think you were taking me to the Cherokee town when all along this was your plan. Well, I won't do it. I won't go." She crossed her arms and glared at him, showing her resolve. Pretending it wasn't possible for him to pick her up and toss her across his shoulder to take her to MacLaughlin's Mill without her consent.

"Are you finished yet, or is there more venom to come pouring forth from your mouth?"

She raised her chin. "I won't go to MacLaughlin's Mill."

"Fine." He lifted her by her elbows, depositing her behind him on the path without so much as a by your leave. "Then the cow's discomfort shall be on your conscience, not mine."

The cow? Mistress Ellen? What in heaven's name

was he talking about? Rachel pressed forward, past Henry who didn't seem in a communicative mood, to latch on to Logan's arm again. This time he didn't appear surprised when he turned toward her.

"What are you talking about? How will my refusing to go to MacLaughlin's Mill harm Mistress Ellen?"

She didn't think he would answer her at first. He simply stared, something in the depths of his green eyes reminding her of when he kissed her beside the creek. But she didn't think for an instant that he planned to repeat that. No, he was angry. The slight indentation of his dimples caused by the hard, straight line of his mouth told her that.

"First of all, I'm not *taking* you to MacLaughlin's Mill. We are traveling through. And secondly unless I can persuade young Angus Campbell to make his way up the mountain and care for the cow, she'll be getting mighty heavy with milk."

"Oh." Rachel bit her lower lip. Her hand still rested on his arm and she made no attempt to remove it. "We didn't discuss that."

"What are you talking about?"

"Nothing." Rachel shook her head and finally let her fingers slide off his sleeve. She had had a lovely conversation with the cow this morning but it hadn't included what the animal would do while she and Logan were away. "Of course we shall have to see to Mistress Ellen's needs." She glanced up. "As long as you have no intention of leaving me behind in MacLaughlin's Mill."

"I said I'd take you to Cheoah and I will." Though he was as daft as she to do it, Logan finished to himself. And he did plan to leave her at the Mill on his way back home. There was no way he could spend the winter holed up in the small cabin with her.

After their discussion she made no more attempts to make him stop for a rest, which is why he suggested it himself when they reached the shores of the swiftly running White River.

"I can go on," she said, though her feet were sore and her legs were tired.

"There be no need. I'd always planned to rest here."

"So then Mistress Ellen will be all right?"

"She'll be fine." Logan felt a bit guilty now that he saw her expression of concern for the cow. He had an arrangement with Angus about taking care of his animals, including the dog. There never was any real danger to the cow, except, of course, he had to let Angus know to head out for his place.

He just hadn't liked her accusing him of taking her to the Mill and leaving her. Hadn't he said he'd take her to the Cherokee town? Did she think he wasn't a man of his word? There were few things he had going for him to be sure, but his word was one of them, damnit. And he didn't appreciate her acting as if it wasn't.

"You can sit down, you know." She was just standing, leaning against a hemlock and Logan had an uncomfortable feeling he'd pushed her too far and too long. Especially when she looked up at him, a half smile curving her lips.

"I fear if I do, there will be no getting me up again."

Logan glanced down at her feet, clad in those ridiculous blue and silver shoes. The heel of one was broken off and he knew they must be uncomfortable. "Rachel . . ." he began, only to stop when raucous barking pierced the afternoon silence. Logan twisted around. "What the hell is the dog up to now?"

"Henry?" Rachel took a tentative step along the path.

"Stay here. I'll fetch him. Most likely he's treed himself a squirrel and won't let up." Except Logan never heard the animal sound this excited about a squirrel.

Rachel watched as he jogged off the path toward the sound of the yelping. She waited only a heartbeat before following. She knew. She just knew Henry was in trouble.

Twigs and brambles caught on her clothing as she pushed through the woods, but she didn't let that stop her. The closer she got to the sound the more concerned she became and the faster she pushed . . . regardless of her fatigue.

And then she burst into an opening and knew what the problem was.

Her scream had no effect on Henry or the giant bear he faced.

Chapter Seven

"Do not forget to entertain strangers, for by
so doing some people have entertained angels
without knowing it."
                                            —*Hebrews* 13:2

"Get the hell out of here!"

Logan flung the command over his shoulder as he
raced into the clearing. The air seemed to vibrate
with the dog's yelping and the guttural snarls as the
black bear reared up on his back legs.

"Dog!" Logan yelled several times for the spaniel
but to no avail. He still danced around in front of
the enraged bear, hind quarters raised and teeth
bared. But those teeth were no match for his adversary's huge fangs or the claws that swiped through
the air.

The dog yiped and backed away only to foolishly
attack again, more aggressively than ever. "Damn you,
Dog!" Logan shouldered his musket and drew a bead
on the bear's black shaggy head. His finger tightened
on the trigger just as the giant beast turned toward
him. He sniffed, letting out an angry bellow and,
ignoring the dog, began plodding toward Logan.

At the same moment, from the corner of his eye,
Logan caught a flash of silvery blue. She was racing

forward, yelling something to the dog, ignoring the fact that the bear was no more than two rods away. "Rachel!" The break in his concentration was no more than a second, but that's all the time it took the bear to lunge forward. The musket was torn from his grip.

"Rachel! Rachel, get out of here!" Logan jumped back, barely missing a deadly pounding by a huge paw. In one fluid motion he unsheathed the knife from his leggings and leaped between her and the bear. "Rachel!" My God, she was coming right toward him, toward the angry, growling bear as if she were as mad as he thought her.

"For God's sake." Logan sprang up from his crouch, pushing her away just as the hairy black beast pounced. He thrust forward, aiming the blade upward toward the bear's chest, but something or someone grabbed his arm. He swung his head to see what in the hell she was doing when something hard exploded down over his head.

"Rachel . . ." He tried to fight the darkness that closed in around him. She was going to be killed, torn to shreds by the vicious claws. "Rachel." Just before blackness overwhelmed him he thought he heard her talking. But he must have been dreaming. She couldn't be fussing at the bear telling him to settle himself down this instant . . . could she?

"Logan. Oh Logan, please don't be dead."

Her voice drifted to him from the soft netherlands of unconsciousness. He felt her hands on him, soft and warm, and the sensation was almost enough to make him ignore the throbbing pain at the side of his skull. He imagined her there looking like an angel and he realized he must have died. For she was dead surely. So was the dog.

Logan's eyes popped open when something wet and cold flopped onto his face. "What the hell . . . ?"

"Oh, thank heaven, you are alive." She grasped his shoulders with two hands, leaning down and kissing him soundly on the lips before rocking back on her heels. "I'm so glad."

He wasn't dead. He was alive and so was she. And he'd be damned if the stupid dog wasn't sprawled by his side busily licking at the drops of water dripping from the cloth she'd slapped onto his forehead.

Logan pushed up on his elbows, grabbing at the wet rag and tossing it aside. He jerked his head around—grimacing at the pain that caused, searching for any sign of the bear. There was none. The clearing was calm. Birds sang in the poplar trees and he could hear the bubbling harmony of the river.

"What happened?"

"I fear you hit your head. Actually, it was the bear that hit it."

Logan forced himself to focus on her face. "And after that . . . ?" he demanded.

She shrugged. She actually shrugged as if the rest was hardly worth mentioning. "You fell and were unconscious for some time. How do you feel?"

"Fine." Logan dragged his hand down over his face. His first attempt to struggle to standing met with failure. It wasn't until she linked her arm with his that he managed to gain his feet.

"Are you quite sure you are all right? You took a nasty blow. And even though I realize you wish to reach MacLaughlin's Mill as quickly as possible I think perhaps you should—"

"Damnit, Rachel." He pushed away from her clutches and scooped up the musket. "Where is that damn bear?"

"He's gone."

"Gone?" Logan glanced down at the dog who was busy growling and shaking the piece of cloth as ferociously as the bear might have shook him. And Rachel.

"Where did he go, Rachel?" Trying to figure out what happened was making his head hurt worse.

"Into the woods." She pointed. "That way I think. But there's nothing to worry about. He won't be back." She had hold of his arm again and this time Logan let her lead him to a fallen log. "I really think you should sit awhile. You have a rather large lump on the side of your head."

Logan reached up with tentative fingers, sucking in his breath when he touched the wound.

"There, you see." She whirled around, tapping her silver-toed shoe on the ground when she noticed the dog. "Henry, bring that here this instant. You know it's for Mr. MacQuaid's head. And I should think you'd be a bit more contrite. Your mischief caused a bit of trouble today."

While Logan watched in disbelief his dog stopped playing and trotted toward her, the scrap of fabric in his mouth. And he'd be damned if the lazy mutt didn't appear remorseful. Logan blinked, shaking his head, only to call out when she slapped the newly dampened rag on his sore head.

"Henry did not mean to cause so much trouble."

"And I suppose the bear did not mean to thump me on the head."

Rachel dabbed at his lump, wincing whenever he did. "Actually, I think he did." She stepped back, tilting her head, regarding him. "Are you feeling any better?"

"I suppose so." Logan stood, pleased to see that his legs didn't feel as if he were on board a ship. "We better be off."

His original intent was not to stay in MacLaughlin's Mill for the night. But then he hadn't planned on having a run-in with a bear either. And he still hadn't figured out why Rachel and he and the dog too weren't torn to shreds. Not that he was complaining, but he'd seen what an angry bear could do. And he'd have wagered a goodly sum that bear was angry.

"This is it? This is MacLaughlin's Mill?" Rachel stepped around him and stared at the few buildings that made up the village. There were several cabins, similar to his own, though generally larger, and the mill for which the place was named. It sat squat beside the river, its paddled wheel turning with the current.

"The Campbells' place is over there." Logan pointed toward one of the crude, log cabins before starting toward it.

Rachel had no choice but to follow. She kept her gaze forward but she knew several people watched her as she walked across the cleared area. Most of them called out a greeting to Mr. MacQuaid to which he responded in a much friendlier tone than he typically used with her.

He raised his hand to the planked door, but before he rapped his knuckles against the splintered wood, he leveled a look at her. "These are good people. Decent hardworking people. I'd appreciate it if you'd mind yourself."

Rachel's chin shot up. "Are you implying that I don't know how to behave in society?" The very idea. She was known for her charming wit and gracious manner. Well, perhaps not known exactly, however she certainly got along with people. Unlike her accuser who lived by himself on a mountaintop and rarely spoke more than two adjoining sentences.

"I am saying they won't appreciate stories about being the queen's lady and knowing the king."

"But I *am* one of her highness's ladies in waiting. And as for the—"

"Just keep it to yourself then, if you insist upon

believing it." Logan refused to be intimidated by her
stare even though it had turned haughty with that
certain tilt of her head that made it appear she stared
down her nose at him.

"Are there any other orders, Mr. MacQuaid?"

"Nay." He turned back and knocked, forgetting
too late that he should have demanded she stop pretending to converse with the dog. But the door was
swept open and Penny Campbell's broad face was
beaming at him, her work-roughened hands pulling
him into the cabin.

"Glad I am to see you Logan lad. It's been too
long. Malcolm will be glad you've come."

"We can only stay for the night, Penny," Logan
said, bussing her soundly on her cheek and watching
the apples brighten in them.

"Well 'tis grateful we are to have you for however
long." She paused as if realizing what he'd said and
glanced around his shoulder toward the woman still
standing in the doorway. The surprise that darkened
Penny's blue eyes was quickly blinked away and those
same eyes crinkled as she smiled. "Oh, you've
brought a guest."

Logan nodded, wondering what the older woman
would think of his "guest's" appearance. Rachel's
hair was a tangle of curls that brushing only seemed to
make bushier. And her clothes . . . He hadn't realized
himself just how tattered and torn, not to mentioned
burned, her gown was.

But she held her chin high and curtsied when he
presented her to Penny. Curtsied in a way that made
him wonder if she had indeed practiced in the court
of King George. Which was absurd. She glanced at
him when he introduced her simply as Rachel Elliott
and he wondered if she would insist upon keeping
up her charade of being a Lady.

He never knew if she planned to point out his

omission for right then Angus came barreling through the doorway.

"I thought that was you I saw from the fields." He glanced apologetically toward his mother. "I have Papa's permission to come check." He grinned when she dismissed his statement with a wave of her hand. With the other she lifted a heavy iron kettle hung from a hook over the fire.

"I've no doubt your papa will be here soon himself." She set the kettle on a trivet and turned back. "Sit. Sit," she said with another wave of her hands. "You must be tired from your journey."

Though the furnishings were crude, they were more plentiful than in Logan's cabin. Rachel settled quickly into a chair near the homemade table. Logan, she noticed, did not. He was reaching up to a shelf above the hearth following Mistress Campbell's instructions to lift down a china teapot. It was delicately shaped with gold scrollwork and it seemed so out of place in this cabin with its heavy wood furnishings and sturdy occupants.

The teapot didn't seem out of place in Logan MacQuaid's large hands. Rachel watched as he passed the porcelain to the woman who quickly pressed it to her ample breast. Rachel thought him crude when first she saw him, large and coarse. But now Rachel knew different. He was tall and broad-shouldered true, but any bulk was muscle. And his hands beneath the work-rough calluses and scarred knuckles were those of a gentleman, long fingered and tapered.

"Do you not like tea, then?"

The silence clued her that something was amiss. Rachel's gaze flew to Mistress Campbell's face and she realized the woman had asked her a question . . . perhaps more than one. She also realized she was staring at Logan MacQuaid's hands, and remembering what they felt like on her body.

She felt herself flush. "Tea? Oh yes, I love tea. I haven't had any in so long." That was one of the myriad things not available on the mountain. "And I simply adore it. At home we take tea with the queen nearly every afternoon and it's such a delightful—"

"Would you like me to help you with that, Penny?"

That was carrying the small teapot to the table. A chore the mistress of the house was more than capable of handling on her on. She shook her mobcapped head and continued to stare at Rachel, a bewildered expression on her round face.

Logan's glare was not difficult to understand.

Rachel felt the heat of it to the soles of her blistered feet. So what if he didn't want her to talk about her life . . . her real life. He didn't believe her so he assumed no one else would. Rachel sighed. Chances that anyone would credit such a phenomenal happening were remote.

For heaven's sake, she knew it true . . . had lived it . . . and the more time that went by, the more she began to doubt it herself. If it weren't for the memories of Liz, of the way she was murdered, Rachel might wonder if Logan was right to think her mad.

At any rate, what would be accomplished by speaking of the past? So Rachel smiled sweetly, accepted a chipped pottery cup filled to the brim with fragrant, steaming tea, and held her tongue.

"The teapot was all we were able to save when we made the trek here," the woman said in way of explanation, or apology, for the crude mug.

Her words seemed so heartfelt and sad that Rachel felt a strange empathy for her. It seemed they had both endured a journey to this wild land . . . that they both had regrets.

Rachel held the cup as if it were the royal china and took a delicate sip. Her smile was angelic. "I do believe this is the finest tea I have ever tasted." Her reward was the look of gratitude on Mistress Campbell's round face. And the softening of Logan's scowl.

The son, Angus, after his initial burst of words, was a quiet sort who still stood in the corner by the door. Rachel had glanced around at him once only to notice the way the lad looked at Logan. As if he admired him above all of God's creatures.

Poor, misguided youth, Rachel thought at the time.

She was reminded of her earlier thoughts when Logan motioned the boy closer. "How have ye been doing, Angus? I've a favor to be asking, if you don't mind."

"Do you want me to see to your place?" he asked as if he was being offered a dukedom.

"Aye. There's a cow up there who would be as grateful as I if you milked her."

"I'll leave straightaway . . . may I, Mother?"

"Wait a moment," Logan laughed. "I think there's time to eat a bite first."

His mother agreed and it was when the boy stepped up to the table to reach for the hunk of bread Penny sliced from a still warm loaf that Rachel saw he had only one arm. The other was no more than a stub, ending above the elbow, the skin rough and puckered.

As soon as Rachel realized she stared her gaze jerked down to watch the steam rising from her tea. What could have happened to him? He wasn't much more than a boy. Fourteen at most. She drank too deeply, burning her tongue in the process.

Angus ate two more slices of bread and a bowl of stew, joking and talking with Logan the entire time before pushing to his feet and grabbing up his jacket.

"We should be back in less than a fortnight." Logan turned to the woman. "I'm sorry to be taking your boy away from you for so long."

"You know he would do anything for you." Penny paused. "Malcolm and I would as well."

Do anything for Logan MacQuaid? Rachel could hardly believe her ears. She, of course, was stuck with him, trying to save his life, but these people were under no such obligation. Why should they care so much for this silent, moody man? Perhaps she would ask the woman if she ever got the chance.

"I'll stop and say my goodbyes to Papa," the boy said as he bent down to kiss his mother's rosy cheek.

And then Logan stood, announcing his intention to go to the fields with Angus and give Malcolm a hand, and Rachel found herself alone with Mistress Campbell, who appeared as curious about Rachel as Rachel was about their relationship with Logan.

"Would you like some more tea?" The older woman stepped toward Rachel. "Or something to eat? I was planning on waiting until they came in from the fields but if you're hungry . . ."

"No." Rachel held up her hand. "I'm fine, really." She glanced around the cabin. It was larger than Logan's and, crude though it was, showed signs of a woman's touch. There were curtains of striped fabric hanging by the windows. And a door leading to another room. Rachel imagined it was a bedroom. Probably with a real bed, unlike the pallet of furs Logan MacQuaid slept on.

There was also a room or some sort of loft reached by a ladder. Rachel didn't realize she stared at it until Mistress Campbell asked if she wished to rest. "You can have Angus's bed since he won't be needing it tonight."

"Thank you but I'm not tired." Which wasn't exactly a lie. Now that she was off her feet, Rachel found herself much more comfortable. "Your son," she began before she lost her nerve. "He isn't afraid to go up on the mountain by himself?"

The woman looked up from peeling potatoes and smiled. "Angus fears very little."

"That's good, I suppose. Yet I would think . . ."

"If your meaning because of his arm that he should fear more, it seems to be just the opposite."

"I didn't mean . . ." But of course she had. Rachel glanced down at her lap. "What happened to him?" And why do you all adore Logan MacQuaid so, she wanted to add but didn't.

"His arm had to be cut off, amputated, it was. By Logan MacQuaid."

Rachel was certain her eyes were large as saucers.

" 'Twas during the wars."

"The wars?"

Mistress Campbell looked at her as if she were quite ignorant. "With the Cherokee."

"Oh."

"We were on our way to Fort Prince George, because of the trouble, and we were spending the night at Sutter's Ford when the Cherokee attacked. It was a small war party and the men, including my Malcolm, were well armed. The children and I were huddled, standing on a table inside the hearth. But then Malcolm called out for me to bring him a powder horn. Before I could move, Angus had scrambled off the table and was racing across the cabin." She paused and Rachel wasn't certain she would continue. But she picked out another potato, examining it a moment, then spoke again.

"It's strange, isn't it, when one moment in time seems to change everything. When if you had all your prayers answered, it would only be for that one instant to be given back to you." She looked up, her gaze locking with Rachel's, the knife and half-peeled potato forgotten. "You see, I hesitated when Malcolm called. The musket fire and screams paralyzed me into letting my son almost die."

She shook her head, as if trying to dislodge the memory. "The savages were repelled, but Angus was shot . . . he was in a bad way. Burning up with fever and the arm was festered." She looked up and smiled. "And that's when Logan MacQuaid happened by. On his way to kill the heathens, he told us, when Sutter invited him to sit a spell. He'd had his own losses and was out for revenge. But he took one look at Angus and stayed a fortnight."

"And that's when he amputated your son's arm?" Rachel realized she gripped the chair arms and forced her fingers to loosen.

"Had to. If he wouldn't have the lad would be dead singing with the angels right now."

Rachel wondered if people had the right idea about angels. She'd seen no heavenly chorus. But this wasn't the time to debate the issue. Besides, there were other things she wished to know. "Didn't you ever . . . I mean, his arm. Was there no other way?"

"You would have had to see him. To see the boy. To see Logan when he did it." The knife sliced through the potato. "There was no other way to save my boy."

She chopped another potato before she glanced up. "I don't know what got into me, talking your ear off the way I did. It's not like me at all." She smiled. "Truth is some of what I said, I've never told another person. Malcolm and I never even talked about the day it happened." Gathering up the quartered potatoes, she dumped them into a pot and swung it back over the stove. With a sigh she wiped her hands down the front of her apron. "I think we each blame ourselves for what happened."

"It's no one's fault. Not really." Rachel pushed

out of the chair and wrapped both arms around the woman's ample shoulders. "Sometimes things happen. We don't know why. But there is a reason." She held her close. "There's always a reason."

"Looks like it'll be an early winter."

Logan knelt beside the river, splashing water over his face and chest and grunted his agreement to Malcolm. It was nearly dusk and they'd been chopping corn husks for fodder for several hours. And he couldn't help worrying what kind of mischief Rachel had accomplished while he was gone.

"It be none of my business, Logan, but—"

"She's just a woman who wandered upon my cabin," Logan supplied, knowing exactly what his friend was going to ask. Saving him the effort. "I don't know how she got there. One minute I was alone. The next . . ." He shrugged into his shirt, smiling at Malcolm's expression. "I'll be the first to admit it sounds strange."

The older man scratched his nearly bald head, then stuffed a battered felt hat back over the remaining red curls. "You planning to take her to Charles Town?"

"Nay." Logan fell in step beside him. "I was thinking to bring her here, but then Lone Dove paid a visit and invited her to the cementation festival."

"The Adawehis asked *her to* the *Ah, tawh, hung, nah?*"

"Unbelievable, isn't it." Logan stopped and turned to face Malcolm. He'd been a friend since the fall of '59 and was probably the only one Logan had who wasn't Cherokee. Except of course for his half-brother Wolf. But then Wolf was part Cherokee himself. "I'm afraid she says some rather strange things sometimes."

"How do you mean?"

Logan finger-combed his damp hair, taking a

leather thong from his pocket and tying it back before figuring out exactly how to answer that question. He wished now he hadn't spoken, friend or no friend. Anything he would say made her sound madder than a rabid dog.

But Malcolm was looking at him, and Lord knew the woman *was* madder than a rabid dog. "She has this . . . fantasy, I suppose you'd call it, that she used to live with the queen."

"Of England?"

"Aye."

"Then perhaps she's saner than you or I. She left that hellhole, didn't she?"

Logan chuckled and slapped Malcolm's rounded shoulder. "Do you think Penny made scones for supper? It's been awhile since I've had something decent to eat."

"I thought since you'd gotten yourself a woman you might be faring better."

Logan just slanted him a wry look before lifting the latch. He'd hardly say Rachel Elliott, or who ever the hell she really was, had improved his life.

When they reached the cabin, he noticed she'd braided her hair and twisted it around her head. The effect made her appear a bit neater, though as he sat down at the table Logan found himself missing the wild riot of golden curls. And then he discovered it wasn't she who had dressed her hair but Penny. The older woman mentioned during supper how much she'd enjoyed playing lady's maid to Rachel and Logan's eyes jerked toward his companion. She wouldn't meet his gaze.

As soon as the table was cleared he grabbed her wrist. "If you'd be kind enough to join me for a short walk," he said, never giving her a chance to decline. It wasn't until they were outside that she pulled her hand away.

"What do you think you're about?" she demanded.

"I was going to ask you the same thing, Your Highness. What's the idea of treating Penny as if she were your servant?"

"I did no such thing." Rachel stopped walking along the split-rail fence and turned to face him. "Penny is a sweet woman."

"So sweet you can take advantage of her." He came to a halt also and stood looming over her. Behind them the sun illuminated the sky with its swan song of color. The passionate fire reflected in Rachel's eyes.

"I never—"

"Then explain this." Logan's fingers toyed with a lock of golden hair that had come loose from the pins.

"Penny braided it for me."

"Like a lady's maid?"

Rachel's chin lifted. "Like a friend." She tried to turn but his fingers opened, catching her chin and jaw, keeping her eyes fixed on his. She swallowed, wishing it didn't feel as if the breath was sucked from her body.

"You forget, I know you."

"You don't know me at all," came her reply. But the vehemence of her words lost its sting as his mouth descended to capture hers.

He hadn't meant to kiss her. Hell, he was angry with her and had been since Penny made that comment about a lady's maid. The kiss deepened. Make that ever since she stumbled into his life, disrupting his peace and solitude. But he couldn't seem to stop touching her and now she was in his arms and he could taste his anger blended with hers. And her arms were twined around his neck.

His tongue thrust deep, attacking, retreating, making her knees weak. How could she allow this to happen again? Moments ago she hated him and his insolent comments. *I know you*, he said. But he didn't. No one knew anything about her, yet he could dissolve her anger with a look, a touch.

His lips tore from hers and for breadth of a heartbeat they stared into each other's eyes, each with the same expression of bewilderment and desire. And then he was reaching for her again, his mouth hungry.

It was the barking that made them jerk apart.

Rachel turned guiltily, wiping her hand across her tingling lips, then reaching down to brush wrinkles from an overskirt too torn and frayed to hold a crease.

Logan stepped forward calling toward Penny who was tossing a bucket of soapy water out the door. She looked up and waved, but Logan wasn't foolish enough to think she hadn't noticed them before . . . or that his voice was unusually husky. He scowled and headed for the cabin only stopping when he felt her hand on his arm.

"I asked her to show me how."

Logan glanced around, his expression puzzled.

"To braid my hair." Rachel shrugged. "I'd never done it before." There was no reason to tell him that she usually *did* have servants to do such tasks for her. He wouldn't believe her. But she didn't want him to think it was in her nature to take advantage of a sweet person like Penny.

He looked at her long enough to make her wish she hadn't spoken, then nodded. "It looks pretty," was all he said before leading the way back to the cabin.

Malcolm sat next to the fire, a clay pipe cupped in his palm. He motioned for Logan to join him. Rachel settled on the other side of the hearth, beside Penny. She held the yarn as the older woman wound it into skeins. They talked of the frontier, of the hardships and pleasures, and her dreams for her son. It was

warm and cozy and an evening like none Rachel had
ever spent.

She felt comfortable and relaxed except for the
times she could feel Logan's eyes on her. She tried
to ignore him, not to meet his stare, and succeeded
until she heard Penny say that she and Logan could
sleep in the loft.

Then their eyes flew to one another.

"I don't think . . . I mean—"

"I'll just make myself a pallet by the fire, if you
don't mind."

Both Penny and her husband had risen and were
on the way toward the door that led to their bedroom.
They paused and turned as one, looking first at Rachel, then Logan.

They shrugged in unison. "If that be what you
want."

Of course it was what *she* wanted. Rachel lay on the
cornhusk mattress sometime later. She couldn't seem
to fall asleep even though she was tired. She wondered
if Logan was awake on his pallet by the fire.

It was a silly notion to think they would want to
sleep together, no matter if Penny had seen that kiss.
She was only here to save his life. It was not as if she
cared for him. Yet as she lay there in the darkness
with the slivers of moonlight slanting through the
cracks between the logs, she couldn't help thinking
about what he said about her hair.

He thought it pretty. Somehow that meant more
to her than all the compliments she'd received from
the accomplished gentlemen of her acquaintance.

Chapter Eight

"Angels and ministers of grace defend us."
—William Shakespeare
Hamlet

"She did not say for you to follow her."

Logan turned, blocking the doorway to the Cherokee house he and Rachel were to share and folded his arms across his chest. The old woman who'd shown them to their lodging also gave Logan the Adawehis's summons to come to the Town House. And she had clearly mentioned only his name. But as usual that didn't seem to stop Rachel.

"But certainly the Adawehis wishes to see me also." Rachel took a step forward, sighing when Logan didn't move, only stood there, his jaw jutting out. She smiled. "Perhaps if I wait for you outside."

"That won't be necessary."

"But . . ."

"Rachel!" His arm shot out when she tried to skim around him. "Stay here." He spoke firmly and meant every word he said.

As they entered the Cherokee town earlier this afternoon she turned to him, her expression apprehensive. "You mustn't go anyplace without me," she said. "I . . . I feel there is something amiss."

He scoffed at her concern then, as he did now. Perhaps he shouldn't have.

"Ostenaco has returned from Kaintukee."

Logan sat across the ceremonial fire from the Adawehis and glanced up only to look away again. The Cherokee didn't turn their eyes toward those they spoke to, and were often suspicious of those who did. But Logan hadn't expected the news Adawehis imparted . . . even with Rachel's dire warning. And he wasn't pleased by it either.

"There are those who remember his deeds," Logan said, knowing he was one of them.

"And there would be many would wish to take their satisfaction. But this is the season of the *Ah,tawh,hung,-nah*."

"The chance to begin anew," Logan translated instinctively.

"Yes." Lone Dove's somber face bore the marks of many years. "It is our custom to forgive."

"I do not think Ostenaco will forgive . . . or forget."

The Cherokee's eyes did meet Logan's then, briefly. "We must hope you are wrong." His body seemed to settle more deeply into the robes draped about his shoulders. "You have brought the *Adan'ta* woman?"

Logan couldn't help it. He studied the holy man through the haze of smoke drifting up from the fire. His knowledge of the Cherokee language was imperfect though he could carry on a rudimentary conversation. And he knew Rachel was being referred to as the soul woman. He leaned forward, resting elbows on knees. "I don't know what she told you . . ."

"She told me nothing my spirit could not see for itself."

"I don't want you to tell her that Ostenaco is here."

"Why is that? She may be able to persuade him to let the past lie only in our memory."

"Rachel?" For God's sake, what did she do to convince the Adawehis that she had powers beyond mere mortals? Ostenaco would chew her up and spit her out if she ever tried to reason with him. Just as surely as a bear—Logan paused in mid-thought, a vision of the bear looming over him, of Rachel rushing forward. He tried to swallow and couldn't.

"It will be as you say. She is your woman."

Which she most certainly was not. But this didn't seem the time to convince the Adawehis of that. Even if it did mean he might be spared the frustration of sharing a cabin with her. His fingers nearly ached with the desire to touch her again. It would be a long week till he could take her back to MacLaughlin's Mill, and leave her for good.

Logan walked back across the common area. Though the dancing wouldn't start until tonight, there was already a sense of anticipation in the air.

Ah,tawh,hung,nah was a much heralded ceremony among the Cherokee. They looked forward all year for the opportunity to begin anew. Everything from their homes to the village square was swept clean. They burned old clothing and possessions, and danced, purged themselves, and forgave old trespasses.

At least that was the theory.

"There's something wrong!"

Logan no sooner stepped into the cabin he shared with her before Rachel was on her feet, staring intently at him and seemingly reading his mind. He shook his head to dislodge that perplexing notion and to convince her she was wrong. "I was only thinking of the coming ceremony. I doubt it's to your liking."

"Why do you say that?" She approached him, her head tilted, her expression contemplative. "From the Adawehis's description it sounds quite interesting."

"Did he mention the black drink?"

She paused, folding her arms and clamping her mouth shut as Logan continued. "It's a physic. One of the most powerful." He thought he noted the blood draining from her cheeks and continued. "The purpose is to—"

"I am aware of what a physic is used for."

"Ah." Logan shut the door and leaned back against it. "Then I suppose there is no need of me to describe it to you, Your Highness."

"None at all." Rachel let her gaze travel slowly from the casually crossed ankles, clad in deerskin moccasins, up to the confident turn of his sensual lips. "What you may explain is why you are all of a sudden so anxious for me to be gone from this place."

His mouth thinned, the dimples deepened. "I don't wish . . ." He pushed his shoulders away from the door. "The hell with it. I was only trying to save you some unpleasantness."

She didn't doubt him there, but Rachel wasn't sure he referred to drinking a physic. Which she had to admit didn't sound appealing. But for some reason she knew this was where she must be.

"Lone Dove wishes to see you." Logan realized there was no sense prolonging the inevitable. The Adawehis had requested a visit from her and if Logan didn't send her someone would be knocking on the door soon. Besides, with her safely ensconced with the old man discussing . . . whatever it was they discussed . . . he could find Ostenaco.

She gave her hair a pat, which did little to tame the curls escaping from her braid, and opened the door, only to glance back, her expression pensive. "You will be all right, won't you?"

"Damnation, woman . . ." Logan began, holding up his palm when she opened her mouth. "Do not tell me again how you were sent to save me. Just go off and visit with the Adawehis."

Rachel was settled on a mat exchanging pleasant-ries with the Cherokee holy man before she realized Logan hadn't answered her question.

Ostenaco was not to be found. He'd gone with several warriors on a hunt.

So, their meeting was to be postponed. Logan strode through the village, the dog at his heels, hop-ing he could return to the cabin before Rachel. He would just as soon not have to explain where he'd been. Not that he owed her any explanation, but it would just be easier if he could be lounging on a bearskin rug when she returned.

His luck was not holding today.

When Logan pushed through the door she whirled around, a frown marring the sweet perfection of her face. Their eyes met and Logan was annoyed that he was the first to look away.

"You didn't find him then."

That brought his gaze back to clash with hers. "What in the hell are you talking—" He cut his denial short. "Lone Dove said he wouldn't tell you." Logan let out his breath. "I didn't want you to worry for no reason."

Rachel moved forward until she was close enough to touch him. The tips of her fingers whispered across his cheek. "But I do worry about you." Rachel pulled back her hand and turned away when she realized what she was doing and why. For that instant it had been Logan MacQuaid, not herself, that she cared about. Which was ridiculous. Keeping him alive was her way to return to her own life, to leave this misera-ble existence she was forced to endure.

She slanted him a look over her shoulder. "And you needn't be angry with the Adawehis. He didn't tell me."

"Then how did you find out?" Logan's hands rested on narrow hips. "And don't tell me some madness about talking to the dog."

"Fine." She whirled around to face him. "I shan't." Besides, Henry didn't tell her, though she had suggested the dog stay close by Logan to help protect him. Rachel had simply known. She paused a moment. "Are you going to tell me why he wants to hurt you?"

Logan leaned back against the door. "What? No magic potion to conjure up the answer for you?"

Rachel folded her arms in imitation of his stance. "I'm not a witch, Logan."

"Ah, that's right. You are a lady-in-waiting to a queen . . . and an angel."

Her chin notched higher. "It is not necessary for you to believe me." She paused and tilted her head slightly. "At least I don't think it is." Giving her head a shake she continued. "I don't think I'm really an angel. I don't feel like an angel. But I was sent here to save you and I can't return home until I do."

"To London?"

"Yes."

"And the queen?"

Rachel didn't bother to answer. Those green eyes glittered with amusement. And it wasn't difficult to understand she was the object. With an exasperated sigh she looked heavenward, hoping for some sign of what she was to do with him.

But, of course, there was none.

It wasn't till later that evening that she broached the subject again. They had eaten a simple repast of cornmeal and rabbit, nicely scorched by Rachel who didn't realize the mixture needed to be stirred at regular intervals. They'd barely spoken. Not even when the dinner proved disastrous. Now they lay on separate mats pretending to sleep. At least Rachel was. And by the amount of turning and "humphing" Logan did she assumed he was in the same predicament.

"I really should know whatever it is you're trying to keep from me."

At first her words brought only silence. Then Rachel heard the telltale rustle of the blankets. It was dark in the cabin, with only the soft glow of dying embers to light the room. But when she turned her head Rachel could see the outline of his upper body as he leaned on his elbow.

"What makes you think there is anything?"

Because I can feel your thoughts, she wanted to say but didn't. And obviously she couldn't "feel" him that well, for as much as she lay there and tried, nothing clear came to her. "If you do not wish to tell me that is one thing, but do not pretend with me."

She knew he was looking at her lying there, though it was too dark to see his eyes. He was watching her and thinking of what to say.

"There's a man here who has sworn to kill me."

"Oh my heavens!" Rachel shot up and gasped, letting the bearskin slide down to her lap.

"Now, you see. This is exactly why I didn't tell you before." Logan sat up too but only to calm her as she came scurrying across the packed earth floor toward him.

"We must leave immediately. I'm sure the Adawehis will understand." She paused as his hands came around her upper arms. "Or do you suppose we should stay and fight? I don't know which would be best."

"Neither." His fingers tightened. "Listen to me, Rachel." He gave her a shake. "Are you listening?"

"Oh . . . yes," she said in a way that made him know she hadn't been.

"This has nothing to do with you and you are to stay away from this man." Another pause. "Do you understand?"

"Who is it? What is his name?"

"Rachel! Have you heard a word I said?"

"What? Of course. I'm hardly deaf. But how shall I know to stay clear of him if I don't know who he is?"

"That's the only reason you wish to know?"

He sounded skeptical. Even if she lied it was doubtful he'd believe her. And Rachel could hardly blame him. But she couldn't stand by and let anything happen to him. She just couldn't.

Her palms pressed against the hard muscles of his chest. Rachel could feel the steady beat of his heart as she looked directly into his eyes. "What is it between you and this man?"

"A warrior's code of revenge." Logan's hands slid down her shift sleeves. "Hell, I shouldn't blame it on the Cherokee's creed, our own Bible states as much. 'An eye for an eye. A tooth for a tooth.'"

"What happened between you and him?" His hands cupped her elbows. She could feel his warmth through the lace.

"I killed his brother." She lowered her gaze and Logan leaned back so he could see her face. "What, nothing to say? That's not like you, Your Highness."

"You must have had a reason."

"Do I detect a note of doubt in my champion's voice?"

Her head jerked up. "Not at all." She let out her breath. "That doesn't mean I don't wish to know the entire story."

"Well, you won't hear it tonight. I'm tired and the dawn will come too soon as it is."

"But—"

"You do realize you will be expected to bathe in the stream with the women, don't you?"

"Yes, Lone Dove explained the ceremonies to me and you're changing the subject."

"Aye, that I am." Logan twisted away from her and lay on his side, pulling the blanket over his shoulders. Perhaps if she moved away from him quickly he'd be able to keep from pulling her down beside him and making love to her until the sun rose above the mountaintops. "Good night, Your Highness."

"I shall have the truth from you."

"Sleep well." Which was more than he would do. Her innocent touch ignited a fire in him that only the morning's plunge into the river would abate.

She held her ground a moment longer, waiting for him to turn back toward her. But he didn't and finally Rachel stood and returned to her mat. Yet she couldn't sleep for the longest time. It was as if she could still feel the rhythm of his heart pulsing through her body. It was disconcerting. It was overwhelming. And it made her want to creep back to his mat and lie by his side.

To feel his heat again. To feel his body on hers.

Her moan sounded loud in her ears and Rachel clamped a hand over her mouth. She must stop thinking of him in that way. She was here to save him. To save him so she could return. So she could have her revenge.

"Mr. MacQuaid."

"Oh, hell."

Rachel ignored his grumbled reply. "There is someone I intend to kill." She heard him turn over.

"Damnation, woman, what are you prattling on about?"

"When I return to London, I plan to kill Lord Bingham." She let her head loll to the side so she could see the outline of his shape. "I shall have my revenge. He murdered my friend and her lover . . . and inadvertently me."

"Christ." How could he allow himself to forget just how insane she was?

The ceremony of *Ah,tawh,hung,nah* involved work!

Why should that surprise her? It seemed everything in this life did. Still, Rachel couldn't help sighing, her hands akimbo when Logan described what she was to do.

"Why is this *my* task?"

"You're the woman of this house."

How could she find his smile so appealing when she was so angry with him? Rachel took a deep breath. "But this isn't my cabin."

"You are the temporary resident."

"As are you," she was quick to point out.

"Aye." The dimples beside his mouth deepened. "But I'm a man."

Something he hardly needed to tell her, although Rachel had no intention of letting it end there. But apparently Logan did. He started for the door, only stopping when her hand closed over his arm. "What are you going to be doing while I sweep out this . . . this house?"

"Having a talk with the Adawehis."

"Talking, but—"

His finger touched the tip of her aristocratic nose. "You best get busy, Your Highness."

Rachel looked down at the broom he handed her as if it might suddenly sprout wings and fly away . . . as she was wont to do. But neither she nor the thatch of straw bound to a stick with a leather thong seemed capable of such a magical feat. The only special powers she seemed to have were possibly understanding with her heart and the dubious distinction of communicating with animals.

Her eyes closed only to pop open when she heard the garbled snore behind her. She found a use for the broom. "Wake up you worthless excuse for a watchdog." She swatted the bristles—not too hard—across the spaniel's rump.

The animal gave a surprised yelp, then settled two mournful eyes on Rachel. But she refused to feel sorry for him. "I don't care if you were dreaming of chasing the largest and fastest rabbit you'd ever seen . . . and gaining on it. Logan has gone off by himself and here you are snoozing as if his arch enemy couldn't appear at any moment and murder him . . . and any chance I have of returning to England."

After the dog left, with a contemptuous expression Rachel didn't need heightened understanding to analyze, she studied the broom. Sweeping was the one chore Logan never requested she do . . . perhaps because he knew nothing of it himself. Memories of his dust-encrusted cabin surfaced and Rachel smiled. Mayhap she would clean his cabin a bit before she left him.

It didn't take long for that charitable thought to disappear in a fit of dust-induced coughing.

Her *cleaning* seemed to have the opposite effect. Not only was the fresh feeling from her morning dip in the bone-chilling river gone, but the cabin seemed even grimier than before she started. Rachel backhanded her streaming eyes, smearing grit as she did, then glanced around to where a pair of Cherokee women stood staring at her. They must have entered when she was coughing, for she hadn't heard them.

And now she wished her annoyance with Henry hadn't kept her from shutting the door. Rachel found it embarrassing for them to see how inept she was. She sniffed, then scrubbed at her still streaming eyes.

"I—" She opened her mouth to give some excuse and stopped, biting her lip before admitting. "I don't know how to do this. If you could show me, I'd be most grateful."

There was a moment when in unison they stopped staring at her and turned toward each other, saying something in the same language Logan had used with Swift Fox. Of course they didn't understand English, Rachel thought. How foolish she was.

But before she could dwell on that the two women stepped forward, one reaching for the broom, the other taking Rachel's hand. She couldn't understand their words, but their tone was kind. They waited till the dancing motes of dust settled, then showed her where to begin and how to sweep without stirring the dirt. The older of the two handed the broom back to Rachel, smiling to reveal a gap where her front teeth should be and Rachel smiled back.

The women stayed with her, offering direction and words of encouragement and it wasn't until they left and the cabin was reasonably clean that the reality of what happened hit Rachel.

She understood them.

Not their language, of course. It wasn't as if she suddenly learned the Cherokee way of speaking or that they began verbalizing in the king's fine English. They'd communicated through their spirits.

Just as Lone Dove said she must do with Logan.

Rachel couldn't keep from bouncing on her toes at the idea that she'd actually done it. Oh, there were times when she caught a glimpse of what was in Logan's spirit, in his heart. But never for any extended length of time. And it was never enough. But now she knew how . . . or at least had done it.

She was so excited she rushed from the cabin toward the Town House, ignoring the people who were dabbing the outside curved walls with white mud. It took a moment for her eyes to adjust to the dim light inside. But when they did, Rachel knew she'd done something wrong. She imagined King George's expression would be as scandalized if she burst into the throne room while he met with his ministers.

Logan sprang to his feet and Rachel had visions of him tossing her across his naked shoulder and hauling her from the building. But before he could do more than take a single step toward her, the Adawehis spoke.

"It is all right if the Adan'ta woman joins us."

Tension seemed to drift away like the mountain mist. The circle of brightly painted warriors settled back on their bottoms and Rachel couldn't help the smirk that crossed her face as she glanced toward Logan. Which she regretted immediately for his expression told her no matter what the Adawehis said, she would answer to him for her disruptive behavior.

There would be dancing that night. And a ball game of some sort the next day.

Rachel learned that much from Lone Dove before she was kindly asked if there was something she wanted. Her eyes darted toward Logan, but he stared at the small, smokeless fire burning in the center of the Town House.

"No, I merely came to report that I'd finished the task he gave me this morning." This did bring his gaze clashing with hers. And she suddenly became aware of how she must appear to him, her hair tangled and layered with dust as if her maid had sprayed it with powder. Her face streaked with grime and her gown nearly in shreds.

Of course he looked no better, his long, dark hair unbound, dressed like a heathen with nothing covering his hard body but a scrap of leather about his waist. Rachel's mouth went dry and she turned her head, trying to follow what the Adawehis was saying to her.

"The *asi*?"

"Yes, Adan'ta Woman, it is most kind of you to clean the cabin and the *asi*, winter home, for your host family."

"The winter home?" What did he mean? This time when Rachel's eyes sought Logan's they were pleading. And his, if not kind, were understanding. He said nothing, but somehow she knew. "Oh, the circular building beside the cabin. Yes, well, I . . ." she sputtered, not knowing exactly how to say she hadn't entered, let alone cleaned, the *asi*.

But it wasn't necessary that she say anything. The Adawehis spoke again. "We are readying ourselves for the game tomorrow, 'the little brother to war.' "

"War?"

"It is but a figure of speech, Your Highness."

Rachel's lips thinned and she refused to look back at Logan.

"It is like my friend says, merely a game. But it is for men only and we must prepare our bodies and spirits."

"I understand." Rachel backed toward the small door. Her gaze swept over the dozen or so other warriors who sat on the benches that circled the fire, but none so much as twitched a muscle her way. Rachel wished she could be as invisible as they seemed to find her. But of course she couldn't just disappear. She had to make her way slowly and ungainly in her broken shoe. Just before she left, Rachel gave Logan a parting look. Finding his gaze on her, she lifted her chin and stared at him down the length of her dust-powdered nose.

The inside of the dirt-covered *asi* made the cabin appear sparkling clean in contrast. The winter house was used only in cold weather and was small and conically shaped, with a high pointed roof. Unlike the main house which was made of wood, the *asi* appeared to be constructed of a lattice work of saplings strengthened by mud. It was windowless, dark and dreary, and obviously hadn't been inhabited for months.

Filthy.

Thank goodness she now knew how to clean . . . or at least sweep.

When she finished Rachel imagined she bore a strong resemblance to a blackamore. The thought made her chuckle and she slid down the outside wall of the *asi*, too tired to go back to the cabin and sit on the bench.

She was sprawled there, her feet thrust out when she noticed the two women who helped her earlier. The older one reached down, grabbing Rachel's hand and pulling her up. Though she didn't feel like going anyplace, Rachel followed, giving a sigh of relief when she saw the river. They led her downstream to where she and the other females of the village bathed this morning.

The women stood as if guarding her while Rachel stripped out of her clothes. Garbed in nothing but her diamonds she stepped into the swirling current. Even though the day had warmed, the water still held the chill of mountain streams and Rachel shivered as the liquid lapped about her thighs. She should have jumped squealing onto shore, or at least hurried to be through with this experience, but she didn't. For there was something about standing in the river that was not at all unpleasant.

She moved toward deeper water feeling the sensual pull as the liquid inched higher, across her stomach, then to cover her breasts. It was like the tingle that overpowered her body when Logan touched her. Rachel closed her eyes and imagined what it would be like if he were standing there in the current with her.

As naked as she.

The ache that raced through her body made her gasp. She plunged beneath the surface, only to shoot up again and start to briskly wash the dirt from her flesh. Once clean she hurried to shore, accepting the toweling handed to her by one of the women and wrapping it around herself.

She dressed quickly in shift and petticoats. Her corset no longer seemed necessary. So she simply fastened her bodice and added the tattered lace of her overskirt.

The clocked stockings were also a thing of the past, burned and worn into nothing but loosely connected holes. Rachel settled on a flat rock to slip on her shoes, but before she could one of the women touched her hand. When she glanced up the Cherokee held out a pair of soft hide shoes. There were several holes punched in the overlapping tops with a thong woven through.

They looked comfortable and warm, and Rachel wasn't certain until the woman nudged them closer that they were for her. Then she opened her heart, feeling the woman's love . . . returning it.

"They're lovely." Rachel's eyes strayed to the blue satin slippers with their silver threads and buckles and

knew a stab of regret. They were once so beautiful. It
was hard to believe they were now as useless as her
life had been.

Rachel paused, her fingers splayed above her new
shoes. What was in her mind to think of her life as
worthless. She who was nearly betrothed to Prince
William . . . the king's brother, for heaven's sake.

Yet she couldn't help what silliness flew into her
head.

Rachel hurriedly pulled on the moccasins, parad-
ing around with her skirts lifted to show them off for
the two women. They *were* comfortable.

Rachel ate alone that evening, if you didn't count
Henry who gobbled up Logan's share of the meal.
"You needn't act as if it's the best thing you've eaten
in a sennight." Rachel stared hard at the dog who
chose to push the pottery dish around on the floor
rather than comment.

"Oh, perhaps it is good." Rachel took a bite of a
stew thickened with corn. "But I did ask the woman
to show me how to make it." The Cherokee didn't
seem to have a certain time to break their fast or sup.
They simply ate from a pot always filled with hearty
food whenever they were hungry. Rachel didn't think
she could get used to that concept, but she was grateful that her new friend took pity on her and offered
something from her pot.

Especially since Logan was fasting.

And seemed intent upon keeping his distance from
her.

She only saw him once after she burst into the
Town House. He stopped by after she returned from
her bath. Her hair was still damp, the curls only beginning to frizz around her face.

Rachel had turned to him, excited about her new
shoes only to have him announce he would not be
staying in the cabin with her tonight.

"But why?"

"After the dancing we must prepare ourselves for tomorrow's games." He looked at her sheepishly. " 'Tis the custom of the Cherokee and as their guest. . . ."

"Of course, you must do as they suggest."

"You will be all right, then?"

"Yes." Rachel smiled though she didn't really feel like it. "The question is, will you?"

"I think I can manage to stay alive for one night."

Rachel thought back over his words. He'd been teasing her. She knew he didn't believe anything she told him. With a sigh she scraped the remainder of her stew into Henry's bowl.

She did her best to comb through her hair, then braided the length of it and twisted it up . . . all without the aid of a mirror. Then she wandered outside, Henry at her heels, to watch the dancing.

The sun was setting behind the village with a splash of orange and mauve. Already a bonfire burned in the center of town, in front of the Town House. Most of the Cherokee were gathered about, sitting on benches under the covered sheds that surrounded the common area.

Rachel looked, but could not find Logan. She did see her two friends and hurried toward them, thankful she wouldn't have to be alone. Rachel tried to communicate with the women, asking what was going to happen, but she had to wait until it actually did.

A hush fell over the assemblage when the Adawehis came out of the Council House. He was dressed in his long cape of turkey feathers, looking much as he had the first time Rachel saw him. He spoke in a strong, low voice, continuing on for a very long time about Rachel knew not what. When she tried to open her heart to him she only managed to gather something about how important the coming games were.

When the musicians started, Rachel sat up straighter. There was a large drum, which appeared to be made from a hollowed-out log and covered with animal skin. The sides, stained red with designs, were as colorful as the warrior pounding it. Another man shook a painted rattle.

They had just begun playing when a line of young women, all clothed in decorated white dresses, danced out. Their long black hair shone in the firelight. They sang, their voices pure and sweet as they circled the musicians, their bodies moving in a slow sensual rhythm.

Watching them, their dark, innocent beauty was almost hypnotic. But the spell was broken when a group of warriors, skin glistening, leaped from the Council House. The men were painted, their near naked bodies decorated with silver gorgets and bracelets wrapped around their upper arms.

Rachel's breath caught when she saw Logan. Except for the fact that he was taller than the Cherokee and had those mesmerizing green eyes, he looked like the other warriors. He danced as they did, no civilized quadrille or even lively folkdance, but a gyration of movements so masculine, so primitive, that Rachel couldn't look away if she'd wanted to.

She tried to swallow and couldn't as the pounding drum and the dancer's feet . . . Logan's feet stirred her blood. Her heart seemed to catch the beat, quickening as she watched him, watched his body. And then the young women lined up with the warriors, swaying, a feminine counterpoint to the savage beauty of the males.

And jealousy swept over Rachel so intense there was no mistaking it.

She wanted to leap to her feet. To push aside the woman who dared undulate her nubile body in front of Logan and take her place. To show him that she was woman to his man.

Rachel's nails dug crescents into her palm's soft flesh as she watched, as she forced herself to sit through the performance. And when she finally stumbled back to her cabin, alone in the darkness, it was to spend a sleepless night, thinking of him. Wondering if he thought of her.

Chapter Nine

"There is time when fear is good
It must keep its watchful place at the heart's
   controls
There is advantage in the wisdom of pain."
                                            —Aeschylus

Rachel woke with a start. Noise filtered through the closed door and it took her a moment to realize it wasn't the drums from the night before. Their memory still seemed to pound through her body, pulsing with every beat of her heart. With a groan she sat up, dropping her head into the welcoming cradle of her palms.

Her skin seemed afire, and an ache had settled deep in her body. With another groan the remnants of last night's dreams swamped over her.

"Oh, no." How could she even conceive of some of the things she imagined in her sleep? She glanced across the room to see if Logan was there. Would he know by looking at her what tempestuous, what passionate things she did to him in her dreams?

But he wasn't there. Giving herself a shake to dislodge the sensual haze enveloping her, Rachel pushed to her feet. Of course. This was the day of the games. The day everyone took a hiatus from work to watch two groups of men chase a small deerhide ball down a field of play.

Stretching, Rachel decided she didn't have time to do more than wash her face and hands and try to tame her wild curls. Even though it was no more than sport she probably should be there to cheer Logan on. If he didn't already have a champion in the doe-eyed girl from last night.

Her teeth clamped together so hard her jaw hurt. What did she care if Logan MacQuaid had a lover in the Cherokee village? It meant nothing whatsoever to her, or her mission. As long as the woman didn't plan to kill him, that is. And as often as Rachel herself thought it might be enjoyable to wrap her fingers around his throat and squeeze, she didn't think the girl last night felt the same. No, the Cherokee maid seemed quite taken by the strapping, sun-bronzed man.

"Blast Logan MacQuaid. Who cares what he does?" Rachel griped at Henry, who only lifted one lazy eyelid and stared at her a moment before settling back to sleep.

Grabbing her hair she quickly divided it into three sections and did her best to braid it. Her fingers stopped only once and that was when the idea hit her that the warriors might have spent the night with the beautiful girls. Perhaps they were the Cherokee version of courtesans, about which she was supposed to know nothing, but did all the same.

What if it was the women's job to entice the athletes and draw them into their beds before the big game? Rachel braided her hair with a vengeance, tying it off and tossing it over her shoulder before marching to the door. She threw it open.

And was immediately overcome by a feeling of impending doom. Of evil.

She hurried toward the throng of spectators who

stood about the open area, calling out cheers and taunts. Gone was her jealousy, her anger at Logan. She only knew she must find him. Save him.

Her feet gained speed as she reached the wall of people. As she tried to find a way past them. But the frenzy of the night before was still with them and they seemed to swell and sway with the action on the field. She heard a collective groan and her breathing quickened. But though she tried to push herself through the men and women she couldn't.

"Please." Her voice cracked. "Please, I must see what is happening." Frantically she searched the row, gasping when she noticed the Adawehis. He was more willing to allow her through and she elbowed her way ignoring his advanced age and lofty station.

"Where is he?" she asked, her eyes on a frenzied search for Logan. She spotted him just as another man swung a long webbed stick at him from behind. She screamed and flung herself forward only to be caught and yanked back by two strong hands.

"What are you doing Adan'ta Woman?"

"Let me go." Rachel squirmed, unable to believe that the frail old man was as strong as he was. "I have to save him." She jerked her head around to see Logan running the length of the field, his own webbed stick held high. Through a glaze of tears she saw a bleeding gash on his arm.

"He will not appreciate your interference."

"I don't care." Again Rachel tried to no avail to rid herself of his confining hands. "He will die and then . . ." She didn't finish her words or the thought because again an Indian was swinging his stick at Logan. It was the same man as before and though he was new to Rachel, she knew who he was. "That is the Cherokee who wants Logan dead." Rachel twisted around toward the Adawehis, trying to make him understand. But it was obvious he already did.

"Logan knows."

"But he will die."

"I don't think that will happen."

She couldn't watch.

Yet she couldn't look away.

The game was savage in its intensity. She knew now why Lone Dove had called it "'the little brother of war." Yet war asked for no spectators.

The men thundered down the field, urged on by the screaming fans. There must have been fifty on the field of play, and Rachel was told the other team was not from this village. The object it seemed was to hurl the small ball over goal posts planted at each end of the playing area. When that happened to the north of the field a huge cheer of noise swelled around her.

No one in the competition seemed immune to violence. It took only possession of the deerhide ball to make one a target. There was kicking and punching, tripping, without so much as a blinked eye from anyone who might be refereeing. But no one attacked as fiercely as Logan's enemy.

His long, webbed stick became his weapon of choice. And he didn't care if Logan had the ball or not.

Rachel tried to call out warnings, but she knew no one could hear her. The crowd was too noisy. They all appeared drawn up in a frenzy of excitement. The gentle people who she'd come to think of as warm and friendly were now caught up in the spirit of blood-letting. She spotted the two sweet ladies of the day before, and saw that they, too, were yelling, shaking their fists in the air at some real or imagined transgression.

Only the Adawehis remained calm. And his very
composure amid all the turmoil was disconcerting.
It was almost as if he knew what might happen and
was powerless to act.

And Rachel knew just how he felt.

She touched her face and realized tears streamed
unchecked down her cheeks. The warrior was pounding toward Logan, stick raised as if it were a club,
and she stood motionless on the sidelines, unable
to help. A scream was futile. The Adawehis's strong
fingers still dug into her shoulders. Nothing she could
do.

Logan.

It was as if energy flowed from her body. She actually felt it connect with him, knew that in the next
moment she would feel the pain as the webbed stick
crashed down over his head.

Except it didn't happen.

At the last moment Logan twisted about, ignoring
the play of the ball and facing his foe.

She heard the stick's clash and wondered briefly
why neither shattered as Logan blocked his assailant's
blow.

"Hit him. Hit him. Hit him." It wasn't until she
realized he didn't, that Rachel heard the litany she
sent Logan's way. Was the blood lust of the crowd
contagious? Or did she know that simply warding off
an attack would not be enough. The warrior would
only try again.

Rachel had no idea how long she stood there, surrounded by strangers, her eyes following every move
Logan made. Someone explained to her once in her
other life that knights in their armor needed someone
to watch their back. She was that someone for Logan.

When the "play" ended the throng surged onto
the field. Though she hadn't kept track of the score,
it was obvious the home team had won. In the confu-

sion she lost sight of Logan, and tried to jump into the melee to find him.

But the Adawehis still held her firmly. "Return to your cabin, Adan'ta Woman and he will come to you."

"But the warrior will not stop merely because the game ended."

"That is true. Ostenaco has a blood vengeance for our friend and even though he tried to tell me otherwise it is still strong."

"Then I must go to him."

"No. MacQuaid would not want that. Ostenaco will not act now. They are both sore and tired. It will not happen at this time."

She wanted to argue and scream, pound the old man's narrow chest and insist he do something. But irrational as his words seemed, Rachel believed them. She did as he said, fighting her way against the stream of joyous spectators to the cabin.

It seemed to take forever for him to come to her.

When he appeared in the doorway, soaking wet, Rachel ran to him. Her arms wrapped around his waist and she pressed her head to his chest, breathing in the scent of him. He held her a moment, clasping her to him, his body seeming to swell as he did. Then he dug his fingers through her hair, pulling her face away, looking into her eyes.

His kiss was rough, tasting of the victory he'd help win. For that moment in time Rachel lost her fear for him. She opened her mouth, kissing him back as she clung to his sleek flesh.

His tongue taunted hers and she responded in kind. Teasing, but not really. Joining the foray with an ardor she didn't know she possessed.

She could feel him, hard against her lower body, and she pressed against his manhood, gyrated her body in unison with his. All the sensations from her dreams flooded over her, but stronger, more powerful than she ever imagined they could be. She was being swept away and she didn't care. Possessed. Yet wanting nothing more.

And then her greedy hands slid down his ribs and she felt him stiffen in her arms. It was just for an instant, but she felt it, felt his pain.

Rachel tore her mouth from his. Her breath was ragged and she noticed when he bent his head to recapture her lips, his was as well.

"You're hurt."

" 'Tis nothing." His tongue burned a path along her jaw when she turned her cheek aside. Unbidden by her, her head lolled back, giving him greater access to her neck as he continued his delicious torment.

Her knees felt weak, as if at any moment she would sink to the floor and beg him to assuage the ache inside her. She sucked in her breath and flattened her palms against the hair-roughened skin of his chest. "No, please. Stop."

He did, immediately, as if he'd been drifting about in a fog and her words suddenly made everything crystal clear. His hands dropped to his side and he took a step back like he found being near her repugnant.

"I do beg your forgiveness, Your Highness."

"Stop it. Stop it this instant. I won't have you calling me that anymore. I'm not the queen, nor even a royal princess and you know it."

She never sounded or looked more like one, Logan thought, with her head held high and that haughty expression stamped on her beautiful features. But he kept his tongue. Partly because she now was leading him toward the bench. It was as if the heated exchange at the door never happened. Except he knew it had. His body was still hard from wanting her. And she knew it had, too. Logan would bet his soul on it.

But for now she acted the ministering nurse, tsking over a cut here, a bruise there.

"I can't believe you let that man do this to you." She gingerly touched a scraped spot on Logan's chest, pulling back quickly when he winced. Gritting her teeth she dipped a bit of cloth in water and brushed it across his skin.

"I didn't exactly 'let him.'"

"Certainly you knew who he was."

"Aye." Logan watched her through lowered lids. "The question is, how did you?"

She slanted him a look that spoke volumes, though Logan couldn't quite decipher it. "Is he going to come here after you?"

"I doubt it."

"Doubt?" Her voice grew shrill. "You doubt it." She tore a strip of petticoat—that she could ill afford to lose—with a vengeance. Then none too gently wrapped it around his chest.

"Ouch, damnit, Rachel. That hurts."

"It should hurt." She tied the strip off only to watch the bandage slip down his ribs to pool at his waist. He saw it, too, and when he raised his eyes to hers she was nearly in tears. Couldn't she do anything right?

Tossing the rag in the bowl of water, heedless of the diamondlike droplets that splashed up, Rachel jerked away. "Do you have any idea what I've been through trying to save you?" She looked back at him and this time her blue eyes were dry. "Do you?"

"How in the hell am I supposed to answer that? For God's sake, you plop into my life and nearly kill me in the process—"

"I saved you. You were going to jump."

"The hell I was. Though the way things are going it might have been easier than putting up with you constantly hovering about me."

He shocked her. Logan almost reached up to lift
her jaw—she kept her mouth open for so long. Then
it slammed shut into a tight, annoyed line. Finally
she lifted her freckle-dusted aristocratic nose, and
stared at him as if he was something his lazy dog
dragged in.

"I do not hover. I was sent here to protect you,
though why shall remain one of the great mysteries
of our time. And I shall continue to do it until . . ."
Her gaze seemed to search the cabin's rafters. "Until
my task is complete."

That said she folded her arms and, with a huff,
turned away.

Logan was quiet a moment, his gaze tracing the
outline of her outthrust chin and slender neck. He
could see the pulse beating beneath the delicate white
skin. "Aren't you going to finish ministering to my
wounds?"

"No, I am not."

With a shrug Logan reached for the cloth floating
in the bowl of water only to have her swirl around
and grab it from him. Without wringing it out she
pressed it to the bleeding cut on his shoulder.

"If it hurts it's only what you deserve, getting yourself into a game like that and with someone who wants
to kill you."

"Ostenaco didn't seriously want me dead. At least
he wasn't willing to do it with the entire town looking
on."

"That's not how I saw it. Oh, heavens, I can't get
it to stop bleeding."

"Press your hand against it." His covered hers.
"Aye. Like that."

"I think we should leave. Today. Right now."

"And miss the festival?"

"I'm frightened for you." She stepped closer, between the V of his muscled thighs. "Today I could do nothing. What if that happens again?"

Logan had to bend his head back to see her. She was looking down at him with genuine concern. Whatever her state of mind, she sincerely believed it was her duty to save his life.

The thought scared him.

She didn't like leaving him.

But a summons from the Adawehis was not to be ignored. At least that's what Logan told her when the young man appeared at the door.

"But I can't simply leave you here alone."

Logan had assured her she could, standing and nearly shooing her out of the cabin. She left, hurrying across the square where but a few hours ago the men had enjoyed their game.

Lone Dove was alone when she entered the Council House. He sat in his usual position near the small fire, his body seemingly shriveled beneath the weight of his turkey-feather robe. Rachel wondered again at the strength he demonstrated earlier, keeping her from running toward Logan. Looking at him now it would seem that a strong wind would knock him over.

"I see you have calmed yourself Adan'ta Woman."

Rachel settled onto the bench near him that he indicated. "To my mind I had reason to be upset." She still was.

"Perhaps you see with the eyes of a woman."

"I am a woman." When he simply stared at her with those dark, knowing eyes, Rachel lowered hers. "I am," she repeated, her voice low. She tried to take a deep breath and couldn't. Rachel knew he continued to stare at her, but it was her own state of mind that bothered her more.

What was happening to her?

She felt like a woman, like the person she was before in her other life. But it wasn't her other life, not really. It was her life, period. What was happening now, the emotions she felt, weren't real. For she wasn't real.

Yet her passions seemed to stir her more deeply than ever before.

Rachel swallowed, then lifted her lashes. "You told me I must seek with my heart."

"That is true. There is no understanding without compassion."

"And I am trying to understand." She reached toward him, taking his hands in hers. An old man's hands, frail, the skin withered and thin. Strong hands. "There are those I seem able to know. To really know. It is as you say, that I can see into their hearts. Two women who befriended me." Her shoulders rounded.

"But it is not so with the man you must save."

"Logan is complex." When she realized a smile curved her lips, Rachel sobered her expression. Her gaze flew up to meet his and she wondered if the Adawehis could read her thoughts. She hoped not.

Sharing memories of his kisses, of the heat of his embrace was not something she wished to do.

"I shall try harder," she finally said, only to watch him shake his grizzled head.

"It will be easy when it happens, Adan'ta Woman." He turned his hands, enveloping hers, giving them a squeeze before letting them go. His serious demeanor evaporated into a smile that made his face a maze of wrinkles. "I have asked you here to speak of the ceremony of *Ah,tawh,hung,nah.* It is the people's time of purifying ourselves and beginning anew."

"The black drink." Rachel grimaced. She hadn't

meant to say anything but concern over this aspect of the ritual hadn't strayed far from her thoughts.

"Who told you of the drink?"

"Logan. He said it was a . . . Well, he explained it to me."

"I do not believe you need take it."

"You don't?" Rachel's spirits brightened. "Oh, I shall if you wish me to, of course. But if you don't think I should, then that is fine, too. And you don't think I should." Rachel realized she rambled and clamped her mouth shut.

"There is one custom I think you have need of."

Before she could ask what he meant, the Adawehis called out. The two women from yesterday entered the Council House. They carried a garment made of animal skin.

"I think you could use a new dress, Adan'ta Woman."

Rachel glanced down at the gown she'd worn since the night she drowned. It was torn and burned in spots, dirty nearly beyond recognition. Yet she hesitated to give it up. It was a part of her other life. And it seemed as if she was slowly losing that life. It frightened her. She was going to have to save Logan MacQuaid quickly and return . . . before there was nothing left.

But common sense and an ingrained desire to look her best dictated she abandon the shredded ball gown. Rachel accepted the folded dress with a smile.

The leather was white, softer than the finest silk, and decorated with beads and quills. "It's lovely."

"Go Adan'ta Woman. Bathe in the river and put on your new gown. And tonight you will dance with the other women."

"But I don't know how." She was proficient at the minuet and the quadrille, but this . . . Visions of last

night, of the firelight illuminating the slender bodies
of the maidens as they moved to the pulsing drum-
beat, of Logan, flashed through her mind.

"Move with your heart, Adan'ta Woman," was all
the Adawehis said before she left.

Rachel felt like a new woman.

Perhaps what the Cherokee said about *Ah,tuwh,
hung,nah* was true. People did need to begin over
upon occasion. At any rate they needed new clothes.
But Rachel admitted the transformation she under-
went consisted of more than simply a Cherokee gown.

She had washed in the river and brushed her hair
dry until it shone. Her blond hair had always been
one of her best features but now it seemed almost
alive with golden color . . . sparkling near as bright
as the diamonds at her throat and ears. She couldn't
help wondering what Logan would think when he
saw her.

He seemed to have few ill effects from his earlier
game playing. Rachel saw him once that afternoon
carrying furnishings from one of the cabins. In the
village square he and several other men piled the
benches and chairs into a giant heap which they then
set ablaze.

This was another way the Cherokee celebrated starting life anew, Rachel was told. To burn your old
possessions meant to fully embrace your new life.

Rachel nodded her understanding when the old
woman explained it to her. But she did not burn her
blue and silver gown.

By the time darkness enveloped the town most of
the work associated with the festival was complete.
Houses and winter *asi* were swept clean, the furnishings burned and new ones set in place. The Council

House shone white in the firelight, boasting a fresh covering of clay.

It seemed many of the villagers had even partaken of the black drink, purifying their bodies inside as well as out. As a consequence not much emphasis was put on cooking for the day. Although Rachel did manage to make a few corn cakes without burning them. She ate one herself, gave three to Henry who followed his meal with a nap, and left the remaining three for Logan.

Then she went in search of her friends. That afternoon they taught her a few steps of the dances for tonight. The older woman was too ancient to dance, she said with a laugh, but the younger, Nakawisi, would. With the combination of signals and words they used to communicate, Nakawisi assured Rachel she would stay by her side.

Even so, Rachel was nervous when the drums began their hypnotic beat. Just as last night, a bonfire flamed in the center of the square, shooting ribbons of fire toward the heavens. The evening was cool, with a hint of winter in the breeze that ruffled the fringe on her dress. But there seemed to be a heat generated inside her that kept her skin warm and her face flushed.

There would be several dances tonight. The first representing The Beginning started when Rachel followed the other women to form a circle around the bonfire. Then the men joined the dancers.

But not Logan.

Rachel noticed his absence immediately. She imitated Nakawisi's steps and she searched the onlookers for him, finally spotting him near the edge of the group. Unlike most of the Cherokee who sat beneath the canopied shelters, he stood, arms folded, one ankle crossing the other. It was a casual stance, but there was nothing casual about his expression.

His green stare seemed to burn into her as she danced, swaying with the rhythm. He stayed, leaning against a supporting pole, not moving except for the eyes that followed her everywhere.

At first she found it disconcerting for him to watch her so intently. She looked toward her feet, trying to concentrate on the steps, only to lift her lashes and meet his gaze. Warmth flooded through her body.

Blood pounded in her ears.

The cadence changed, the dance steps quickened. This part portrayed Friendship. For a time Rachel was caught up in the complex weaving about she did. But each time she glanced around it was Logan she saw. He seemed to pull her toward him, an allure she couldn't understand. And didn't want to.

Her pulse raced.

Rachel knew what was coming. What the third dance would be. Her body felt fluid and sensual, like the Cherokee people. Their ideas were so different from hers yet at this moment she embraced them. She lifted her arms, sighing as the buttery soft leather skimmed down her skin.

The third dance was the Rounding.

Intimacy.

Rachel would have known what it depicted even if she hadn't been told. The dancers moved with a new energy, a new passion. There was a general pairing, a subtle shift that melded each man and woman into a single unit.

Except for Rachel.

She continued to move to the pulsating beat of the drums, the rattling gourds, but her attention was not on another dancer.

She only had eyes for Logan.

He stood, as immovable as before, but she could feel the music flow between them in an invisible stream. An indestructible stream. Rachel swayed, her

body undulating, stepping back and forth, as the crescendo built.

She danced for him.

Never before had she been more aware of herself
as a woman. Of him as a man. Hair brushed her
shoulders, swirling about her body and the sensation
was enticing. Her flesh quivered and her breasts
swelled. Rachel wet her suddenly dry lips and could
taste him.

And deep within her an ache began, built as steadily
as the tempo of the music.

She had flirted before, but never seduced.

Now she practiced that beguiling allure as if she
were created for it. As if the Sirens had taken control
of her body. From the heart, the Adawehis said, and
she complied.

She teased, she tantalized, she enticed. And
through it all, the force of her desire escalated.

A sheen of perspiration covered her skin and still
she danced, faster and faster as the pounding soared.
The pace was nearly frenzied now as she swayed toward him, imagined he swayed toward her.

And then it was over, ending abruptly as the drum-
mers ceased their beating and the dancers their movements.

She'd imagined his movement toward her before.
But not this time. With masculine grace he pushed
away from the pole and strode toward her. Rachel
could barely breathe as he reached for her, his long
fingers encircling her wrist.

He said nothing, but then the time for talking was
past. And they both knew it. She followed without a
backward glance as he led her toward the cabin.

Chapter Ten

"Take heed lest passions sway
The judgement to do aught, which else free will
Would not admit."

—Milton

His mouth covered hers before the door slammed shut.

Rachel thought she knew passion before but that was a poor substitute for the fire exploding through her now. Her hands shot around his neck, tangled with his hair, clutching compulsively. She couldn't stop trembling. It was as if her body suddenly grew too large for her skin and wanted out.

Wanted.

And oh, her skin. It burned and shivered at the same time.

"Rachel." He tore his lips from hers only long enough to breathe her name and then he was back, marauding, devouring, filling her with his tongue. His hands bracketed her face, holding her still for his onslaught. Deeper and deeper he plunged as the maelstrom in his blood pounded, flattening her against the door with the power of his body.

She couldn't stop squirming, rubbing herself along the length of him. Her breasts filled, stimulated by the feel of his hard chest. And deep within her an ache grew, blossoming outward till her entire body throbbed.

When his hands pressed down over her collarbone, she moaned. When they blazed lower, kneading her flesh, her knees folded. If not for the rough door behind and the power of his body she would have fallen to the floor.

And then he was yanking the deerskin dress up and over her head, tossing it aside with a flick of his strong wrist. Except for the jewels at her neck she stood naked before him, naked and unashamed, her body glowing in the soft, rosy glow of the logs in the hearth.

It struck Rachel suddenly that she had fed the fire before leaving the cabin and that she was glad. Without the light it offered she wouldn't have seen the smoldering appreciation as his eyes skimmed down her. Her flesh burned wherever he looked, wherever his gaze lingered. She seemed to pout toward him, her nipples puckered, her womanhood dewy with desire.

She expected him to touch her then, to skim his long fingers down her. She craved it with an intensity that frightened her. But it was not his hands but his moist mouth that forged a path of fire.

Rachel called out when he suckled the pebbly tip of her breast. Her fingers clawed into his muscled shoulders, finding the opening in his shirt, seeking the hot, slick skin beneath.

She could barely breathe, air coming in ragged gasps, as he attacked her other nipple, nipping and sucking, swirling his tongue over the straining tip. Rachel hadn't known there was such pleasure on earth; didn't think anything could surpass it. But then his mouth inched aggressively lower.

His stubble-roughened chin abraded the creamy

flesh of her stomach, and she quivered. When he dropped to his knees in front of her she pressed back, some dark recess of her brain realizing what he was about. But though the splintery wood was hard against her back she could not escape him.

And from the moment his tongue, wet and insistent, probed the secrets of her womanhood she had no desire to.

His strong hands clasped her thighs, supporting her, spreading her wide for his invasion.

He probed.

He plundered.

Attacking her with no mercy.

Rachel's fingers thrust into his hair, gripping the back of his head and holding him to her. She couldn't breathe. Couldn't think. Could only feel. The sensations so strong, so overpowering, it seemed she would die.

A pounding drummed through her head, beating louder and louder till she could no longer bear it. And still his tongue ravished.

"Logan!" His name escaped her lips on a scream as the whole of her seemed to shatter into a thousand shiny pieces. She soared, sailing above the confines of earth, to float in heavenly ecstasy.

For one brief moment lucid thought struggled to control her mind and she wondered if this was the way back, the trip of spiraling colors and dazzling light she'd longed to take. Was she on her way home, back to the place of angels or the palace in London? And why did the possibility hold such little appeal?

But when she opened her eyes it was Logan that she saw. His eyes that bore into her. He bent down, swooping her into his arms, holding her high against his chest. Her head fell against his shoulder and the thumping of his heart vibrated through her.

And then he was lowering her to the mat and his

gaze was searing her flesh and she reached for him and the wild abandon clutched her again.

Logan hesitated long enough to yank off his shirt and leggings. But even those simple tasks were interrupted by the need to touch her, to see her eyes flash with desire when he did. She tore at his loincloth, as eager as he for their joining.

He knelt above her, his muscles bunched, his desire bold.

"I'm on fire for you." Logan growled the words against her neck, as he lowered his body, settling into the cradle of hers.

His kiss was savage, complete in its ravishment of her mouth, and her passion equaled his. He slanted his head, devouring her, his tongue thrusting, hers countering.

He had never wanted a woman as he did her. From the moment he first saw her, the need to possess her had grown. Each attempt to fight the attraction seemed to make him want her more. When she'd danced for him, her sensual movements fanned the flames till he feared he would leap among the dancers and take her right there.

"Open for me."

His manhood pulsed against her stomach, near ready to explode. Her legs shifted and he slid down and thrust.

The cry of pain surprised him. He'd given no thought at all to her innocence.

But he was already buried deep inside, the barrier of her maidenhead, no barrier at all. Logan tried not to move, straining against the urge that he thought might surely kill him. Beads of sweat broke out on his upper lip and his heart pounded painfully against his ribs. But he remained still, waiting for her to grow used to him. Waiting for the fever of desire to sweep over her again.

When she started to writhe beneath him, he lost what little composure he had. Logan's body jerked, pulling out only to thrust back in, further, deeper. She raised her knees, opening for him, sending him along a frenzied path toward fulfillment.

She cried out again, clutching him, her limbs quivering, as he exploded, sending his seed shooting into her womb.

He collapsed, burying his face in a tangle of golden curls. Reality, that seemed so distant moments before, now came thundering back with unerring accuracy. Logan lifted his head, staring at her with narrowed eyes. She looked totally debauched, her lips red and swollen from his kisses, her cheeks rosy. He couldn't help brushing her mouth with his.

She was staring at him as if she didn't understand what had happened and Logan wished he could explain it to her. Instead he levered himself off and rolled to the side, gathering her into his arms as he did. The morning would be soon enough for questions.

At least that was his opinion.

Her heart was filled with him.

Rachel shut her eyes, breathing in his smell and rubbed her cheek against his shoulder. She could feel what he felt, knew what he knew. The power consumed her, freed her. Made her strong.

He thought of her. Of her beauty and sensual delights. Of how much he'd desired her . . . and still did. A smile tugged at her lips and she snuggled closer.

And then he thought of Mary.

Rachel's eyes popped open and she would have sat up if not for the imprisoning arm crossing beneath her breasts. She took a deep breath and tried to put aside her foolish jealousies. But she couldn't. She knew it was not a time for questions, for accusations, but her tongue seemed bent upon both.

"Who is Mary?" The words were from her mouth before she could stop them. She felt him stiffen. And lost the power to be one with him.

"How do you know of Mary?"

I don't know, which is why I'm asking."

"She's my wife . . . was my wife."

A chill swept over her that had naught to do with her naked state. "What happened to her?"

She knew before he answered. She remembered and she knew. Yet she listened as he told her, his voice flat, of the Indian raid that left her dead.

"There was a child, a girl, newborn who died with her," he said. "My child, though I never saw her."

"The Indians who killed her. Were they . . . ?"

"The Cherokee?" Logan let out his breath. "Aye. It was during the wars. I blamed them at one time." He shook his head. "But no more. Their grievances were many."

"Against your wife?" They were sitting now, Logan toward the foot of the mat, his back to her. Rachel couldn't remember exactly when he moved from her but she missed the feel of him.

"Nay, not Mary. She never hurt a soul. It was not in her nature. But those who attacked didn't know that, didn't know her. Not like I did."

His feelings were filtering through to her again, a jumbled quandary of guilt and sorrow. He speared ten fingers back through his hair and, pulling up a blanket, lay back down, urging her to do the same. But he didn't settle her in his embrace.

And he didn't stop thinking of his dead wife.

Rachel didn't wish to know his thoughts, his grief. Yet now that she had turned on the meeting of their

hearts she seemed unable to turn it off. He lay awake
for a long time, as did she. Rachel's only consolations
came when he finally slept.

He dreamed of her.

He was sitting on the bench, staring at her, when
Rachel awoke. He was dressed, hair combed back and
tied and there seemed to be a wall about him. A
wall she couldn't penetrate. She concentrated upon
opening her heart to him, but nothing happened.
Rachel pulled the blanket to her chin. "What is it?
What is wrong?" She glanced about. "Is it Ostenaco?"

"Nay." He leaned forward, elbows on knees. "I
said last night that we had to talk."

"Yes, you did." She wished he would open to her.
That there was some way to know what he was thinking. But she couldn't even seem to concentrate on
what he said. "I beg your pardon."

" 'Tis I who am begging yours."

He lowered his eyes, the shadow of dark lashes
fanning across his cheek, and Rachel wanted to go
to him . . . to have him come to her. "I don't understand."

"Last night." He looked up and she had a glimpse
of his torment. "I was wrong to seduce you."

She couldn't help smiling. "I thought it was more
the other way around."

He didn't seem to find her words amusing. From
his expression she'd have thought him a prude. Memories of the night before proved otherwise.

"As I was saying, it was wrong of me. You were an
innocent . . . are an innocent, and I—"

"Was Mary a virgin when you married her?" She
didn't want to know, not really. She didn't want him
to think about his dead wife again. Yet the question
blurted from her mouth, leaving him staring at her

in amazement. Rachel imagined him awake before dawn, dressing quickly, even shaving. Then sitting on that bench and planning what he would say to her. It was obvious he didn't expect or want remarks from her.

He was on his feet pacing the area in front of the hearth. Careful not to come near her. Blocking her out.

Shut out was not where she wanted to be. Swallowing, her hand trembling, Rachel pushed aside the blanket. She was on her feet and nearly upon him before he realized what she was about. The stricken expression on his face was amusing, but Rachel didn't laugh.

She did nothing until she stood before him. Her breasts puckered, whether from the sudden chill or memories of what he did to them last night, she wasn't sure. "Was she, Logan?"

"Rachel, I . . ." His voice was husky and Logan started again. "You don't realize what you're doing."

"But I do." She stepped closer as if to prove it. Her nipples nearly grazed the front of his linen shirt. A muscle jumped in his cheek and she longed to run her fingers along the curve of his jaw.

"Rachel." The word was a plea.

"Tell me, Logan."

"Hell, yes, she was a virgin. Mary was a kind, sweet woman."

"Who would never do what I'm doing now." Her resolve began to crumble, but she kept her shoulders back, her chin high. He didn't have to answer her. No one else would be as shameless as she. Certainly not the saintly Mary. As quickly as that thought entered her head she felt contrite. It was not Mary's fault that she was good, or that Rachel was showing herself to be shameless.

Unable to continue her charade of nerves any

longer, she turned. Would have walked away if not
for the hand on her shoulder. She trembled at his
touch.

"You must be sore." His words were gentle but
fraught with tension.

Her hair hung down her back and it covered his
hand when she looked over her shoulder. Her eyes
met his and held while the earth seemed to stand
still. Then slowly she shook her head.

His breath left him in a rush as he pulled her back
into his arms. Rachel closed her eyes, overcome with
how wonderful it felt to crack through the wall, if
only for a short time. His desire flowed through her,
igniting her own.

He held her tightly, pressing kisses to her forehead,
nudging the spiraling curls at her hairline aside with
his chin. His mouth slid down to her ear and he
nipped her lobe before dampening it with his tongue.

"Are you sure?" His words sent chills up her spine.
The feel of his hand as it slipped down to cover her
mound set her afire.

His fingers curled and Rachel bit her lip to keep
from crying out.

"I want you." His voice was a raspy whisper. "But
I was not gentle last night." His hand stilled as she
arched her hips forward. She saw the cords in his
neck tighten as he swallowed. "I can wait," he finally
said.

"Perhaps." Rachel wet her dry lips. "But I cannot."
Slowly she spread her thighs, angling her body toward
him, leaning her head back so she could see the
desire burning in his green eyes.

He ran his mouth down the curve of her neck,
tasting, closing his teeth gently over her skin. Her
breasts were full, the nipples swollen, so sensitive to
his touch that she jerked forward, the movement

sending his fingers deeper into the slick, wet secrets of her body.

She whimpered. The nearness of him was intoxicating and overwhelming and she couldn't seem to get enough of it. It was Rachel who led them back to the sleeping mat. Rachel who lifted the loose-fitting shirt over his head, who fumbled with the ties of his loincloth.

They knelt down together, the proof of his desire huge and throbbing between them. The kiss they shared was openmouthed and carnal. Rachel sighed as he covered her, drawing up her legs, wrapping them instinctively about his narrow hips.

He entered her slowly, inch by sensual inch. Hard, satin-sleeved silk sliding into her body. The pleasure was so intense Rachel didn't think she could bear it. When he was completely buried he let out his breath on a groan before pulling out again. His pace was excruciating. It was exquisite.

Rachel writhed, her head turning from side to side, her legs urging him on.

"Slowly, Rachel." His whisper rasped in her ear. "We shall take it slowly this day."

But the toll was too great and the next time she bucked, bringing her hips off the mat, her body shattering around him, Logan lost his own control.

Rachel tried to stay awake, to connect with his feelings. But they mirrored her own so closely she couldn't tell where one ended and the other began. And she was tired. Falling asleep in his arms seemed the most natural thing to do.

When she woke he was gone.

The scent of him lingered, on the sleeping mat, on her body. Rachel stretched, lifting her arms high above her head, feeling the twinges of discomfort where their bodies had joined. He was right about that then. No doubt he'd ask her again and she would be forced to tell the truth. Which would mean no—

Rachel sat up so quickly she felt light-headed. What was she doing, lying here, indulging in sensual memories and fantasies? She was here to save his life, not to satisfy his sexual whims. Forcing herself to be honest Rachel admitted it was more her own desires she had to bridle.

What was it about this man that seemed to dissolve any restraint she possessed? She might have flirted over her fan and allowed a gentleman to kiss her hand, but she was a basically virtuous woman. However, last night she acted like the "ladies" she and Liz were wont to gossip about. Like a courtesan. But kings and earls had courtesans. Not a simple man like Logan MacQuaid.

Yet in all honesty she had to admit he was more complex than she originally thought. And much more handsome.

She whipped off the blanket and jumped to her feet. If she didn't put such thoughts from her mind immediately she would forget her purpose here. He was off by himself. Rachel reached for the Cherokee dress, her fingers lingering on the smooth deerskin. The feel of it sent a shiver through her body as memories of the night before cascaded through her mind.

"Oh, no," she murmured. It was best if she bound herself up in her own clothes, no matter how threadbare. She dropped the white leather to gingerly pick up the blue silk. And dirty, she added.

She dressed quickly, wondering where he was and what he was up to. If he'd managed to get himself killed without her there to save him she would never forgive him. Didn't he know better than to go off without her? Rachel skimmed over the nagging worry that she would miss him if something did happen to him. Of course she would. He was a nice enough person . . . when he allowed someone to know him.

But her real concern should be for herself. If she didn't save him where would that leave her? Rachel didn't take the time to comb through her tangle of curls before rushing from the cabin. She couldn't let anything happen to him. She didn't want to live the rest of her life, or death, or whatever netherland she was in, as a guest in a Cherokee town.

He was in the Council House with the Adawehis. Rachel let out a sigh of relief. She nearly burst into the building to assure herself he was safe, but memories of her reception the day before kept her from it. Besides, the Adawehis knew why she was here, actually believed her. He wouldn't let any harm come to Logan.

Which gave Rachel time for a bath. It amazed her how she could now think of a dunking in a bone-chilling river as such. And even look forward to it. Wouldn't her maid, Ruth, who knew the exact temperature Rachel preferred her floral-scented water, and strove to please, be shocked if she knew.

Thoughts of Ruth's hazel eyes open wide in dismay made Rachel smile as she walked along the path to the area where the women bathed. She didn't see the Indian warrior till he stepped directly into her path. She didn't gasp until she recognized him.

Rachel's heart pounded but she tried not to show fear. After all, he could do nothing to her. "I suggest you remove yourself from my way."

He didn't say anything, only stared at her from his superior height. He had a hard face, tattooed skin taut over sharp bones. Odd, but she never considered the scarred countenances of her Cherokee friends fearsome. But this man's was. Perhaps it was his eyes that made him seem so formidable. They were dark and hard. Her courage began to fade.

"What do you want?" Though she tried not to, Rachel found herself taking a step back.

"You are MacQuaid's woman."

There was no question in his voice. Only a churlish quality that she would never abide in her other life. Or in this one either, she decided. Her chin lifted. "As you obviously speak English, then you had no trouble understanding my earlier request. I must insist that you—"

His hand snaked out, latching on to her jaw, wrenching her head to the side. Tears stung her eyes and she heard a pathetic whimpering sound, only realizing after a moment that it came from her.

"You do not *insist* with me, white woman."

Rachel tried to swallow and couldn't. His fingers bit into her skin; his dark eyes held hers.

"You will tell MacQuaid I have not forgotten." His hold tightened, then he released her chin. But his hand lingered. Rachel tried to pull away when she saw his gaze drop to the tattered ruffle of her décolletage. But those strong fingers tangled in her hair, before outlining the curve of her breast.

Her skin cringed, and a sob escaped. No one, *no one* ever treated her thus. Rachel wished someone would come along the trail. But the only sound she heard was her own ragged breathing juxtapositioned over the faint breeze rustling the dried oak leaves and the chatter of a blue jay.

"I shall scream."

Her words were cut off by his satanical laugh. "Scream all you wish, white woman. I want MacQuaid to know what I can do to you . . . whenever I wish. There is more than one way to die."

Rachel never knew whether he let her go, or if she broke away. One moment she was his prisoner, the next she raced back toward the town, her bare feet unmindful of the sharp stones in her path.

She never even looked around to see if he followed her. All Rachel knew was that she had to reach Logan. She had to tell him what Ostenaco did to her.

The Adawehis was alone in the Council House. He looked up, concern deepening the grooves in his forehead when Rachel threw open the door. "What is it Adan'ta woman?"

"Where is Logan?" It hurt so much to breathe she nearly doubled over.

"He is not here, but—"

Rachel didn't listen any further. Twirling around she headed for the cabin they shared. Logan held a stack of wood, which he dropped unceremoniously to the packed-dirt floor when she burst through the door.

He was cradling her shoulders before she could catch her breath. "What in the hell happened to you?" He gave her a shake when she didn't answer. "Are you hurt?" His voice sounded raw with concern.

"We . . . we have to leave. Today." Rachel gulped in air. "Right now."

"Rachel?"

She jerked away from his hold, pacing toward the fireplace, unable to stand still. "Didn't you hear what I said? We have to go."

"But why? Tell me what happened."

She opened her mouth to do just that, then clamped it shut. *I want MacQuaid to know what I can do to you.* Ostenaco's words came back to her. And with an insight she didn't know she possessed his reason for frightening her crystallized in her mind.

Logan would go after Ostenaco if he knew that the warrior touched her. And who among the Cherokee would fault Ostenaco for defending himself? For killing his attacker.

"Nothing happened." The denial left Rachel in a rush. "Nothing at all."

He didn't believe her. He folded his arms and looked at her through lowered lids, and she had to turn away from his doubting expression.

"I was on my way to the river when I saw a . . . a bear." Rachel slanted him a look but couldn't tell whether he accepted what she said. "It frightened me and I ran." She managed a self-effacing laugh. "Foolish of me, I know, but . . ." She let the rest of it fade away as she lifted her hands.

"Your lip is bleeding."

Was it? Had Ostenaco gripped her hard enough to cut her skin? Rachel licked it gingerly, wincing when her tongue encountered the wound. "I must have bitten it when I saw the bear."

"And this encounter with a bear made you decide we must leave?"

"Yes."

She held her ground as he stalked toward her. He stopped, when he was close enough to touch her. But he didn't. "Tell me what really happened, Rachel."

She swallowed. "I did." Rachel felt the pulse pounding at the base of her throat and wondered if he noticed. "May we leave?"

"Because of a bear? I think we'd be safer staying where we are, don't you?"

Before she could think of an answer, he turned. He was reaching for the door latch when her hand clamped onto his.

"Where are you going?"

"I have been challenged to a game of Chungke."

"Take me with you," she ordered, her eyes clashing with his.

"Still frightened of the *bear*, Your Highness?"

Rachel didn't deign to answer, but he did bow and usher her through the doorway.

Chungke was played on a cleared acreage to the west of town. To Rachel's delight, this game didn't appear to be as violent or potentially dangerous as the other she'd watched. There were only four players, counting Logan, but as many as two-score spectators lined the field.

Ostenaco was there. And Rachel had to stop herself from bolting toward Logan when she first noticed him.

There was much cheering and calling out of advice as the first player rolled the disc-shaped chungke stone. But Ostenaco said nothing, nor did he watch the action as the second player tried to hit the stone with his pole. The warrior's hard eyes never left Rachel. Even when she tried to ignore him, tried to follow the play of the game, she could feel the power of his evil boring into her.

The men raced about, trying to intercept each other's poles in flight, trying to perfect their aim, striking the chungke stone. Around her men and women wagered upon the outcome and moaned when their champion missed. But Rachel saw none of it. She watched only Logan.

"Your man did well to win."

Rachel jerked around at the sound of that hated voice. She didn't think he would approach her here, surrounded as she was by so many people.

"You did not give him my message."

"Yes . . . yes I did."

"Do not lie, white woman. MacQuaid would not leave you unattended if he knew what I plan for you."

"I shall tell the Adawehis. He shall have you expelled from the village."

"It will not matter, white woman."

She felt Logan's presence, his anger, before he reached her side. She turned, holding out her hand to stop him, but he ignored the gesture. "Is Ostenaco annoying you?" The words might be directed at her but his eyes never left the Cherokee warrior.

"No. Please, Logan, do not concern yourself. We spoke of the game only."

She could tell he didn't believe her. His jaw clenched till she could see the telltale quiver of a muscle. He faced the warrior chest out, ready for battle. But she couldn't be the cause of this fight.

Rachel touched his arm. "I beg you to take me back to the village. The Adawehis wishes to speak with me."

She watched as he relaxed his stance. His gaze dropped to hers and he nodded. It wasn't until they were walking away that Ostenaco spoke.

"Your new woman is beautiful, MacQuaid. You must take care not to lose her."

Chapter Eleven

"It is love, not reason, that is stronger than
    death."
                            —Thomas Mann
                            The Magic Mountain

They would not make love that night . . . and Rachel
was glad.

Memories of the day shattered her tranquility, making it nearly impossible for her to concentrate on
Logan. She had to remove him from the danger. She
knew that. But how?

When they first returned from the chungke field
she nagged at him to leave, but to no avail. He was
determined to stay till the end of *Ah,tawh,hung,nah.*
Which meant two more days. Two more days of unbearable tension, unbearable fear. How was she supposed to save his life when he wouldn't cooperate?

Rachel didn't realize it at first but she asked the
question in the form of a prayer. Eyes closed, head
bowed, hands clasped in supplication.

But it was not God's voice that answered her.

"Imploring the Lord to save you from bears?" His
tone was fraught with sarcasm.

Rachel turned her head, meeting his narrowed eyes
with her own. "Dull-witted men, actually."

They lay perhaps a rod apart, as distant from each other as they could get in the small cabin. Nearly an hour earlier they had bid each other good night and Logan rolled out the sleeping mats. Apparently neither found slumber easily.

Now they stared at each other, the glowing embers of the fire the only light. But she had no trouble reading his expression. It was hard and closed, showing no glimpse of the warmth he let her see before. And then suddenly he broke the bond, twisting his head till a faint flicker of flame catching in the hearth limned only his strong profile.

Rachel studied him, mesmerized by the depth of her feelings. Since her father died and she came to court she noticed that some men were pleasant to view and some were not. But she never encountered anyone like Logan MacQuaid. Someone who could infuriate her so completely and intrigue her at the same time.

What was it about the slant of his nose or the jut of his chin that captivated her so? Rachel shook her head. A sudden longing for her old life swept over her. She wanted . . . needed to return to things she understood. To things she could control.

"I want you to stay away from Ostenaco."

Logan's voice brought Rachel back from reminiscing about festive balls and cream-filled pastries. She took a deep breath. "I did not seek him out. But if you truly wish me not to be around him, don't you think we should leave?"

"Tell me what he said."

"I did," Rachel insisted, thinking that, even to her own ears it sounded a lie. She pushed up on her elbows. "Why does he hate you so?"

"I killed his brother. I told you as much."

"But you didn't tell me why."

He was quiet for so long Rachel thought he refused to tell her. Her mouth was open to argue her case when he spoke.

"Ostenaco had two brothers, Tal-ltsuska and Cwahwia. They both took part in the raid upon Seven Pines. The raid when my wife and child were slain."

Rachel's mouth went dry. "Did you ... did you have your revenge on both of them?"

"Nay. I was too late to punish Tal-ltsuska. My brother, Wolf did that."

"But you did kill Cwahwia."

"Aye. He bragged of his feat to me. Bragged of taking her scalp."

She could feel his pain, had to fight for it not to overpower her. Rachel wet her lips. "Surely if Ostenaco knew of this he would stop—"

"What was done is no secret. Ostenaco and his brothers hated the white man. The blood letting did not begin with Mary's death."

"Yes, but can't Ostenaco simply let it end?"

"The Cherokee are not a people to overlook the death of a relative. To restore harmony to their world they must retaliate. It is as much a part of them as breathing."

"Yet you insist upon staying here and pretend to think Ostenaco has forgotten because of some silly festival."

"I'd not let the Adewehis hear you call *Ah,tawh, hung,nah* such." Logan twisted to his side, resting on an elbow, his expression serious. "Of course I don't believe that Ostenaco wishes to follow the ancient laws and forgive transgressions. He does not wish to start anew ... to give up his hate. But I think it better to finish this business once and for all."

"And have him kill you?" Rachel was sitting now and nearly shrieking at him.

"Thank you, Your Highness, for the show of confidence." He flopped down onto his back. "Did it ever occur to you that it is *I* who might kill him?"

No, it hadn't. And though she knew him to be strong and apparently adept in the manly pursuits she also knew that some higher being felt he needed protection. And she was the one sent to give it to him.

Rachel also lay back down. "I would not trust Ostenaco to play this little game fairly," was all she said before pulling the blanket up to her chin and closing her eyes.

She woke to something wet and cold nosing at her arm and Logan gone. "For heaven's sake, Henry, haven't you something better to do?" Rachel yanked the blanket over her head only to shove it down again. "Where is he?"

Rachel jumped to her feet. "What do you mean you don't know? This is becoming so tiresome. Perhaps I should tie a rope to him." As she rambled on, Rachel pulled her blue and silver gown over her shift and headed for the door. "How can I be expected to save him if he forever rushes off without—"

The remaining word caught in her throat as she yanked open the door. Before she could scream a rough, dark hand clamped over her mouth.

Damnation.

Logan left the Council House more confused than ever. "You must be gentle with the Adan'ta Woman," the Adewehis said. As if Logan hadn't turned his entire life around for her.

Hell, the reason he went to the holy man this early in the morning was to tell him they were leaving.

Logan didn't know exactly what caused Rachel to suddenly beg him to leave, but he did know she was frightened. And not of a bear.

So he would take her away.

And not only from the Cherokee town. He was going to do what he should have the moment she showed up on his mountain. Before he listened to her foolishness about being sent to save his life. Before he tried to teach her a lesson for telling such giant lies. Before he made love to her. Logan's fingers tightened into a fist. Before she disrupted his entire life.

But it wasn't too late.

Hell, it couldn't be. He would take her somewhere . . . to Seven Pines. His sister-in-law would know what to do with her. Caroline was a sensible woman. If nothing else Rachel could be her companion. And if things got worse . . . Logan tightened his hand on the door latch. If Rachel's madness became too much for Caroline and Wolf to handle . . . Well, Logan knew there was a hospital in Philadelphia that might help her.

He took a deep breath, trying to fight the tightness in his chest. His hand still lingered on the latch but he hesitated to push open the door. Knowing what he would find. She would be lying on her mat, her breasts covered only by the threadbare fabric of her shift. Nearly bare before his eyes. It was the way he left her and just the sight of her then, her angel face framed by those wild curls, the rest of her body outlined by the thin blanket, was almost his undoing.

It took more willpower than he thought he had to turn away and head for the door. A part of him, a strong part, had teased in his ear. "Lie with her. She will have you. She will welcome you. And you can bury yourself deep in her body and wallow in the pleasures of the flesh. Taste again her rosy nipples, drink of the essence of her womanhood, and savor

the oblivion of her tight sheath. You will forget all
else.''

But it was the same voice that spoke to him of the
sweet surrender of rum. That urged him to swallow
one more drink. To forget.

And it was the same voice that taunted. That led
him more than once to the edge of the mountain.
That whispered, ''Take but one more step and you
will never be haunted by guilt again.''

But if she professed to be an angel then this voice
was the devil . . . he was the devil.

Logan shoved open the door . . . and his heart
stopped beating.

She was gone, her mat still unrolled, the blanket
tossed aside. But it was not that that concerned him.
It was the tomahawk savagely slashing the mat.

Ostenaco's tomahawk.

With a primal yell, Logan wrenched the weapon
from the woven straw and shoved it into his belt. If
he hurt her . . . Logan's fingers itched to squeeze the
life blood from Ostenaco. Pausing only long enough
to grab up his gun and snap at the dog to follow,
Logan exploded out the door.

There was a trail.

But then Logan knew there would be. Rachel was
not who Ostenaco wanted. He was. Not that the Cherokee warrior wasn't capable of doing unspeakable
things to her, of killing her. But in the end it was
Logan he wanted to pin beneath his scalping knife.

It had always been Logan.

He'd known that and yet he brought Rachel here,
when there was a chance, however remote, that Ostenaco would come also.

Just as he had wed Mary, bringing her to the frontier and leaving her to the mercy of an unforgiving
people. He lived with the weight of her death on his

We've got your authors!

If you seek out the latest historical romances by today's bestselling authors, our new reader's service, KENSINGTON CHOICE, is the club for you.

KENSINGTON CHOICE is the only club where you can find authors like Janelle Taylor, Shannon Drake, Rosanne Bittner, Sylvie Sommerfield, Penelope Neri and Phoebe Conn all in one place...

...and the only service that will deliver their romances direct to your home as soon as they are published—even before they reach the bookstores.

KENSINGTON CHOICE is also the only service that will give you a substantial guaranteed discount off the publisher's prices on every one of those romances.

That's right: Every month, the Editors at Zebra and Pinnacle select four of the newest novels by our bestselling authors and rush them straight to you, usually *before they reach the bookstores*. The publisher's prices for these romances range from $4.99 to $5.99—but they are always yours for the guaranteed low price of just $4.20!

That means you'll always save over 20% off the publisher's prices on every shipment you get from KENSINGTON CHOICE!

All books are sent on a 10-day free examination basis, and there is no minimum number of books to buy. (A postage and handling charge of $1.50 is added to each shipment.)

As your introduction to the convenience and value of this new service, we invite you to accept

4 BOOKS FREE

The 4 books, worth up to $23.96, are our welcoming gift. You pay only $1 to help cover postage and handling.

To start your subscription to KENSINGTON CHOICE and receive your introductory package of 4 FREE romances, detach and mail the card at right *today*.

We have 4 FREE BOOKS for you
as your introduction to
KENSINGTON CHOICE
To get your FREE BOOKS, worth
up to $23.96, mail the card below.

FREE BOOK CERTIFICATE

As my introduction to your new KENSINGTON CHOICE reader's service, please send me 4 FREE historical romances (worth up to $23.96), billing me just $1 to help cover postage and handling. As a KENSINGTON CHOICE subscriber, I will then receive 4 brand-new romances to preview each month for 10 days FREE. I can return any books I decide not to keep and owe nothing. The publisher's prices for the KENSINGTON CHOICE romances range from $4.99 to $5.99, but as a subscriber I will be entitled to get them for just $4.20 per book or $16.80 for all four titles. There is no minimum number of books to buy, and I can cancel my subscription at any time. A $1.50 postage and handling charge is added to each shipment.

Name _____

Address _____ Apt. _____

City _____ State _____ Zip _____

Telephone ( ) _____

Signature _____

(If under 18, parent or guardian must sign)

Subscription subject to acceptance. Terms and prices subject to change.

KC0595

shoulders. Logan didn't know if he could survive the burden of Rachel's.

He walked when he wanted to run. Forced himself to remain calm when he wanted nothing more than to scream to the heavens.

But Ostenaco did not make it simple for Logan to find him. There were false leads. A bit of holly branch bent that seemed to lead further into the spruce stand. Only after wasted steps and untold minutes did Logan realize it was nothing but a fool's trail, leading nowhere.

Ostenaco reveled in weaving him over and across the river, deeper into the mountains. He seemed to pick the hardest path, through brambles and over rocks. And he pulled Rachel with him—Logan hoped. He let his eyes stray as he tramped through the underbrush of moss and fern, wary of any clue that Ostenaco grew tired of dragging his hostage along.

When Logan saw her small bare footprint in the soft mud leading out of a stream he let out his breath and forged ahead with increased resolve. He had to get there before Ostenaco killed her. He simply had to.

The sun rose higher in the east and still Logan followed the carefully planted leads . . . alone. It took him till he crossed the river for the last time and headed up the mountain path to realize the lazy dog hadn't come with him. And to think, he had started buying into Rachel's notion that the spaniel should be called something noble like Henry. So much for her contention that she and the dog were friends. She probably gave him extra food when Logan wasn't around to inspire the animal's devotion. But obviously when it really counted, the dog didn't care.

Which simply showed how distraught his own mind was, if he could think about such foolishness as Rachel's relationship with his dog when she was in such mortal danger.

He should have told her everything about Ostenaco.

No, he should never have brought her here.

Logan climbed higher and higher, never looking back. Never looking down. He wasn't at all surprised that Ostenaco chose to bring her here, along what the Cherokee called the sky path. The rocky ledge twisted around the mountain, rising into the mist, wide enough for a division to march on at one point, narrowing to barely accommodate a man at another.

The Adawehis preached that it led to the world of spirits, a place comparable to the heaven of Logan's childhood memories. But to Logan the mountain and its torturous trail was another hell on earth.

And Ostenaco knew of his fear. Of the ofttimes immobilizing anguish that standing on the edge of a precipice caused him. Logan's father had laughed at his fear, chiding him with taunts that questioned his courage and manhood. Ostenaco, himself a young man, had been present at Seven Oaks, Logan's father's trading post, during one of those tirades.

As was the case with most Cherokee, Ostenaco loathed Robert MacQuaid, as did Logan. The warrior had been Logan's friend. He seemed to close his ears to Robert's tirade. But he heard and he remembered.

Gravel crunched beneath Logan's moccasined feet as he pressed forward. There were no more signs of Ostenaco's presence . . . of Rachel's. But Logan knew they were ahead of him. There was no other way down the mountain except over the edge. The path had narrowed, sheer rock to his left, nothingness to his right when Logan allowed himself a peek into the abyss.

He'd hoped years of living on his mountain, on the edge of another cliff would harden him. But the too familiar sweat broke out on his upper lip and he dragged first one, then the other hand down over his shirt to dry his palms.

The self-exile to his lonely mountain had been nothing more than the punishment he planned. The punishment he deserved.

Realizing how snug his body was pressed to the rock face, Logan forced himself away and hurried on. Wondering when Ostenaco would make his move. Wondering how Rachel was bearing up . . . if she was bearing up.

She might fantasize about being a friend of the queen and the like but she didn't know how to survive in the wilds. She was small and delicate and Logan cringed at the thought of Ostenaco's rough hands on her.

His mind was so inundated with thoughts and fears for her that when he first saw her standing on a flat rock jutting over the gorge below he hardly credited it. She seemed to float, the mist swirling about her ankles and the breeze catching the golden curls. For an instant, he believed she was an angel.

Then she screamed, her face a mask of despair. "Go away! Logan, don't let him kill you!"

He lurched toward her, only stopping when she stepped back toward the edge. "Rachel!" Fear for her lodged in his throat like bile, paralyzing him. "For God's sake!"

"The white woman would sacrifice herself for you."

Logan whirled around to see Ostenaco standing, his back to the quartz-veined rock. Like Logan he cradled a musket in his arms, a tomahawk and knife in his belt. Unlike Logan he had nothing to lose but his own life.

"Let her go, Ostenaco. She is nothing to you."

"But she is to you, white man." The last words

were spoken with such venom Logan knew Ostenaco would kill her if given the chance. There was no doubt.

"It is time we settled our differences." Logan spread his legs, claiming the ground between the warrior and Rachel, silently vowing to protect her with his life.

"The time is long overdue." Ostenacoe tossed his musket aside. "I will kill you, white man, and the soul of my brother will finally go to the darkening place."

Logan's gun fell to the rocky ground. Ostenaco stalked toward him, shifting his weight easily, his legs spread for balance. Logan shifted the tomahawk out to his side and raised to the balls of his feet. He'd practiced the Indian ways of fighting since he was young. He was a match for Ostenaco . . . if he concentrated. But his mind kept dancing to the woman behind him.

Then Ostenaco's tomahawk flashed in the sunlight, striking out toward him, and there was only the two of them and their fight to the death. A fight long overdue.

Feinting to the side, Logan escaped the first swipe. They were both crouched, Ostenaco moving lightly on his feet, trying to circle. But Logan wouldn't allow it. As much as he'd prefer to have the solid rock rather than a sheer drop to his back, he wouldn't let the warrior get between him and Rachel.

They each took tentative swipes as if they needed to test the mettle of their adversary. Methodically trying to force the other back . . . off balance. Then with a savage cry Ostenaco lunged, hacking down with the honed edge of steel. Logan's arm shot up to ward off the blow but the footing was uneven. The force of the attack sent them both stumbling to the ground.

Sweat poured off them as they rolled, Ostenaco on

top, then Logan. Straddling the Cherokee, Logan
strained, his fingers clamped around the wrist of his
opponent. Ostenaco's hand worked feverishly to keep
Logan's tomahawk from cleaving his skull.

They rolled again, toward the edge of the path,
twisting and turning, sleek muscles straining. Logan
was the first to draw blood, but it was a glancing blow,
more a victory of style than substance. And he quickly
lost any advantage he'd gained when he caught a
glimmer of blue and silver moving toward them from
the corner of his eye.

The break in concentration was infinitesimal, but
it was all Ostenaco needed. He broke free, leaping
to his feet, lunging toward Rachel. But Logan moved
faster, surging forward and tackling his foe, yelling
for Rachel to get the hell away.

The movement cost Logan his tomahawk, but he
managed to grab the knife from his leggings. They
grappled, dodging blows, snarling, their chests sucking air like bellows. Logan thrust with his knife, knew
it sliced through flesh. They twisted again and blood
dripped onto Logan's face. Ostenaco's blood.

And then they were at the edge . . . over the edge.
Logan's head hung over nothingness and Osentaco
was forcing him down. The old fear clawed at his
innards. Logan tried to take a deep breath, tried to
steady the hand that gripped his knife.

Logan barely saw the blur of blue before she was
on top of the Cherokee, pummeling his back.

"Rachel!" Logan's warning came too late as Ostenaco twisted about. Logan jumped to his feet but she
was already held prisoner, bound to the bleeding
warrior by his wounded arm.

"Let her go, Ostenaco." Logan's heart pounded
in his chest. "It is not a warrior's way to shield himself
with women."

Ostenaco's face was a mask of hatred as he stared

at Logan. Then suddenly he thrust Rachel from him and she stumbled, falling to the ground. Logan forced himself not to look. Both their lives depended upon him besting the Cherokee.

They went at each other with renewed vigor. Arms and bodies entangled, their ebb and flow again brought them precariously to the edge of the uneven rock shelf. And certain death below. They broke free of one another, staring with a blood lust that vowed defeat for one of them. Then as Logan grappled for footing the Indian attacked, tomahawk raised.

Logan held his ground, lifting his knife. Live or die. The next split second would decide.

And then Ostenaco swerved and Logan saw why. His heart stopped beating, then pounded with chest-shattering intensity. Rachel came at Ostenaco yet again, pounding his shoulder with her fists. The Cherokee swung around, catching her chin with his elbow, knocking her unconscious. She fell, slipping toward the edge as Logan's blade thrust deep into the warrior's gut.

Logan lunged for Rachel, catching her hand as she slipped off the ledge, barely noticing Ostenaco as he tumbled into the abyss.

Rachel dangled over the precipice, her only link to life the fingers that clasped hers. She was far from being a heavy woman, but his arms were weak from his struggle with the Indian, and she was dazed, unable to help herself. Logan inched forward, forcing himself to look down as he reached with his other hand, grasping her wrist.

"Hang on, sweetheart." He didn't think she heard him. Logan's breathing rasped in his ear as he strained to pull her up. His palms were slick with blood and sweat, and tendons stood out on his neck, straining as he felt her slide.

"Rachel." His first attempt at calling her name failed to elicit response. "Rachel! Grab on with your free hand and pull." He could feel his hold slipping. "Rachel!" He didn't dare move forward or the weight of their linked bodies would send them both plummeting to their deaths. His fingers tightened, digging into her flesh, struggling for purchase. He would go over the side before he let her go.

And then she looked up at him, her eyes as large as saucers. His own stung as he gulped in air. "Reach up," he ordered. "Reach up and latch on to my arm." Rachel struggled to do as he said, swinging her body as she did. He felt her hold on him as his on her hand slipped further.

"There. That's good. Now don't let go. Just hold on as I catch you under your arm. Aye, that's it." His muscles bulged as he labored to pull her up. When her upper body cleared the ledge she let loose her hold on his arm and clutched the rock, wriggling along as he pulled her the rest of the way.

After rolling them both away from the edge Logan lay as did she, on his back, his chest heaving with each breath. His head twisted to the side, staring at her and only then did all the fear he'd felt for her settle over him. Logan swooped over wrapping her in his arms and hugging her tightly against him.

Her sobs tore at his heart. "Did he hurt you? Tell me."

"No. I'm fine. Well, my jaw pains me a bit, but it's nothing really. I was just so frightened."

" 'Tis over now."

Rachel clung to him, her fingers digging into the soft animal skin of his shirt. He was safe. That was all that mattered. She'd saved his life. Then why wasn't she gone? Not that she wanted to leave just this moment. It felt too good, just holding him, knowing he was alive.

But in the next instant he sat up, grabbing her shoulders and thrusting her to arm's length. "What in the hell were you thinking coming at him like that? You could have been killed."

That was not very likely. But this didn't seem the time to point out that she had already died. "Well, so could you."

"Me?" He simply stared at her a long moment. "For God's sake, Rachel, I had a weapon at least. Ostenaco and I were closely matched. But you . . ." He couldn't continue. In his mind's eye he saw her again, coming at the Cherokee, being knocked aside, rolling toward the edge.

She didn't appear at all contrite though. "I was afraid he would kill you and I couldn't let that happen."

"My God." Logan's arms stiffened. "Does this have anything to do with your foolish notion that you are to save my life?" She didn't need to answer. He knew it did. What in the hell was he to do with her? She obviously was so committed to this crazy idea that she acted without thought to her own safety. If he wasn't careful there would be yet another woman feeding his guilt.

"Come on," he said, standing and pulling her to her feet. "Are you well enough to walk?"

"Of course, I am." She yanked her hands from his grip. She was tired of him making light of her predicament. She did everything she could, risking her own life—if she actually had one—for him. And this was the thanks she received.

Rachel took a step down the path only to stumble. If not for his strong hands clutching her elbows she would have fallen to her knees. She whimpered when he folded her into his embrace.

"I'm sorry." He smoothed curls back from her

forehead. "None of this was your doing. 'Twas mine. And that's where the fault lies."

"But you did nothing." Rachel looked up at him, her eyes brimming with unshed tears. "It . . . it was that man." Her gaze left his to stray toward the cliff's edge.

Logan shook his head. "I brought you here. Come on, lean on me and we'll get down off this mountain." He lifted her chin with his thumb. "He didn't force you . . . ?"

It was clear from the expression on his face, the way his green eyes looked at her, what he meant.

"He said things." She felt Logan's body stiffen. "But there was no time for him to do anything but drag me about. You came so quickly."

"I couldn't let him take you." He held her a moment longer before scooping up the tomahawk, jamming it into his belt, and retrieving his musket. Then he moved slowly toward the edge of the path, searching the rocks and underbrush below for Ostenaco's body.

"You should have, you know."

She was behind and slightly to the side of him. He couldn't tell whether she could see the grotesquely twisted form below or not. At any rate it wasn't something he wished to dwell on.

"Should have what?"

She just shook her head. There was no reason to make him angry. And telling him he should have let Ostenaco take her would do that. "I'm ready to leave now."

She sounded more like her old self and Logan couldn't help smiling as he offered his arm. "As you wish, Your Highness.

She gave him a look which clearly showed her displeasure and Logan nearly laughed. But his spirits sunk as they made their way down the mountain, for his thoughts kept straying to what might have happened if he hadn't found her in time. If he hadn't killed Ostenaco.

Whoever she was, Rachel Elliott didn't belong here.

Chapter Twelve

"The restraints we impose on ourselves to refrain from loving are often more cruel than the
severities of our beloved."

— La Rochefoucauld
Maxims

"I thought you refused to go East until spring."

"I've had a change of mind."

"Because of me?" Color blossomed in Rachel's
cheeks when he glanced up at her. Of course it was
because of her. She wasn't such a ninny that she
didn't know that.

He didn't answer, instead returning to his task of
tightly rolling several blankets together. She watched
him a moment longer. His hair was unbound and
fell forward, shadowing his face as he worked. She
wished he'd look up at her again. But no, that
wouldn't help.

Her ability to connect with his thoughts and feelings seemed to have disappeared.

Though she knew it wouldn't work, Rachel tried
to concentrate on him, but she sensed nothing. Yet
in this instance did she really need to read his mind
to know what he thought?

Restless, she pushed out of the chair . . . his chair

. . . and began pacing the cabin. They arrived back at his cabin yesterday, two days after leaving the Cherokee town of Cheoa. And they were leaving again tomorrow. For his brother's place at Seven Pines.

"I thought you were tired."

"I am," she insisted. At least that's one of the excuses she used when he told her they were leaving his mountain. It didn't help. He was adamant about leaving.

"Then perhaps you should lie down and rest." He tied off a rawhide thong and stood, raking fingers back through his hair. She saw him glance toward the jug on the shelf over the fireplace, then look away, his jaw tight.

He hadn't imbibed rum since they left for Cheoa, but it was apparent he wanted to now. A wave of desolation swept over her. She moved closer, standing between him and temptation. If anything his body grew more tense. Instinct had her reaching out to touch his shoulder. Pride halted her hand in midair.

Ever since the episode with Ostenaco on the mountain Logan avoided any contact with her. He was solicitous, but unfailingly distant. Never touching her unless absolutely necessary.

What would he do if she dared to dance for him?

Rachel could almost hear the drums pounding in her head, feel her blood heat. What *would* he do if she began swaying to unheard music, undulating her body against his? If she stripped from her gown and danced in the glow of the fire?

The urge to find out was near irresistible.

She wanted him to look at her as he had then. To hold her. To kiss her and fill her and make her forget everything but him.

But when his eyes met hers, they were hard as green glass. "You should get some sleep. We will leave early."

Without even waiting for a reply he turned away, continuing to scoop cornmeal into small leather sacks.

She wanted to scream at him, rail and pummel his chest with her fists, anything to break this wall he'd erected about himself. She didn't understand it. But then that wasn't all she didn't understand.

His life had been saved again. Perhaps it wasn't all her doing, but she had helped, had done all she could to keep him out of danger's path. And she was still here.

Though not for long. She knew he planned to take her to his brother and leave her. That much she was able to learn. And if he did she was doomed.

"Do you have any other mortal enemies?"

They were making their way along the path leading to MacLaughlin's Mill. As Logan promised last evening, they started their journey early this morning, waking and eating a bowl of scorched, lumpy porridge before the sun splintered light over the crest of the mountain.

Logan paused, staring back at her when she spoke. "I doubt we'll be attacked between here and Seven Pines, if that's what you mean."

"It isn't, and you know it."

He started walking before she finished speaking and Rachel hurried to catch up with him.

"Mind the cow," was all he said when she did.

Of course, the cow. He gave her the chore of urging her along the trail, herding her as if Rachel were some milkmaid. He even gave her a switch from a poplar to help with her task. Rachel considered using it on Logan, in the end deciding it wasn't one of her better ideas. Before twisting her head round to see what the cow was doing, she dropped the branch on the trail.

"Do come along, Mistress Ellen." she said, adding an encouraging, "That's a good girl. Yes, I know you're tired, but we shall rest soon," when the cow complied.

Logan pretended not to notice the exchange. No one could communicate with a cow. Or a dog either for that matter. He slanted a look at his dog . . . Henry, and shook his head.

"You didn't answer my question, you know."

"I know." He tramped on along the trail, finally glancing down at her and letting out a gust of air. "Nay, no more mortal enemies . . . that I'm aware of."

That was good . . . she guessed, though it left open the question of how she was going to save his life, yet another time. As if he read her mind his gaze caught hers. For the first time since Ostenaco captured her, Rachel saw a glimmer of humor in the emerald depths.

"You can consider your assignment complete."

He was teasing her. Rachel knew that. He didn't believe she was sent to save his life any more than she believed the job was finished. But talking to him— even enduring his bedevilment—was better than trudging along in silence. Or listening to Henry complain about missing his nap.

"Is your brother like you?"

Again he glanced at her, merriment showing about his eyes. There were even hints of the dimples on either side of his mouth. "How exactly do you mean that?"

"I wasn't asking if he was a taciturn hermit. You already mentioned he has a wife and children."

"I wouldn't call myself a hermit."

"Really?" She arched her brows as if to say he'd be wrong. "In any case tell me about you brother."

"He's the Indian agent for the area. Very dedicated

to his work. Equally dedicated to his wife and children.''

''He's interested in the Cherokee?''

''Aye, his mother was one.'' Logan motioned behind him with his chin.

Sighing, Rachel called out to the cow. ''You really must keep up, Mistress Ellen.'' She hesitated, then turned back to Logan. ''Do you think we could rest for a while?''

''Is that *your* request or the cow's?''

Her lips thinned but she didn't respond. With a shrug, Logan stepped off the trail into a small clearing where a slow-moving stream reflected the color of the surrounding hills. It was as good a time as any to take a break. They'd been walking for hours and he had to admit Her Highness hadn't complained . . . much.

''Is your brother's wife a Cherokee also?'' Rachel dabbed at her lips delicately after drinking from Logan's water pouch. She passed it back to him, glad to find out that it did contain water and not some of his rum.

''Caroline? Nay.'' He took a drink and backhanded his mouth. ''She's from England.''

''Really?'' Rachel sat straighter. ''Where in England?''

''I'm not sure.'' Logan pulled at a tuft of dried grass. ''I think Wolf told me her father was an earl.''

''An earl?'' Rachel leaned forward. ''What was his name?'' Perhaps Logan's sister-in-law would turn out to be someone she knew. The notion brought a wave of excitement. But Logan could only tell her the woman's name.

''Lady Caroline Simmons,'' Rachel repeated, tapping her finger against her chin. ''I don't believe I know her.''

"Hmm."

"What do you mean by that?"

"By what?"

Rachel crossed her arms. "I know what you think of me."

"Well, I'm glad you do, for I haven't a clue what to make of you." Logan pushed to his feet. "We need to get moving."

"You think I made up everything I've told you." Rachel scurried to stand, turning to brush debris from her skirt, deciding it wasn't worth the bother. "Well?" she continued when he said nothing. "Isn't that true?" She grabbed hold of his arm.

"Listen, Rachel. You tell me you're a friend of King George, and that you died in some lake in London, and that you . . ." He glanced toward the cow busily chewing her cud. "And you pretend to talk to dogs and cows, and want to save me from untold threats of death." He picked up the gun and turned on his heel.

"What do you want me to say? Would you prefer I made up some lie?"

He didn't answer, only stared pointedly at the animals who were her responsibility. Neither of them had moved. "Henry. Mistress Ellen," Rachel snapped. "I shan't want to tell you again."

Logan gritted his teeth when the dog and cow immediately ambled after them.

She shouldn't let him bother her so. Rachel stared at Logan's broad back and shook her head. What did it matter if he believed any of what she said? She should never have told him anything. Perhaps if she'd pretended to be a . . . what? What could she have been? Surely not someone used to living on the frontier. He would have seen through that ruse in an instant. Yet he wouldn't believe the truth.

Rachel sighed. In all fairness the truth was rather difficult to believe.

He must have mistaken her sigh of frustration for one of fatigue for he stopped in the middle of the path, turning to face her. " 'Tisn't long now till we reach MacLaughlin's Mill."

She knew that. Though this was only the third time she'd traveled this mountain trail, she was beginning to recognize some of the landmarks. The crystalline waterfall that plummeted over rocks smoothed by untold gallons of water. The noise from it reminded her of the constant cascading of the creek over rocks at Logan's cabin. At first she'd found the sound disturbing . . . annoying. But later the endless surge blended like threads of a tapestry with the chirping of birds and the whistle of the wind till it became almost soothing.

A slight frown curved her lips. Certainly she wasn't becoming maudlin, homesick for that ramshackle cabin. It was crowded and smoky, hardly large enough for one person, let alone two. At Queen's House such an eyesore wouldn't be allowed to remain standing.

She sucked in air, breathing in the tangy scent of fir. Nay, if she was homesick at all it was for the manicured gardens and lofty halls of her home . . . her real home.

The path twisted about, climbing sharply over an outcrop of rocks and Rachel accepted the hand Logan held out to her. Instantly her pulse quickened. She studied him from beneath the fringe of her lashes as he pulled her up onto the flat ledge. What was it about him that made her heart flutter? He was as rough and rugged as the ragged peaks of the surrounding hills. Hardly the type of man she found appealing.

Yet there was no denying what he did to her, the

sound of his deep voice, his touch, a flash of his moss-green eyes. He looked at her now with the same stirring sensuality as when she danced for him.

"Do you think . . . ?" Rachel let go of his hand. "Do you think Mistress Ellen can make it up?" Henry had already scaled the rise and loped down the other side amid a scattering of loose pebbles.

"I imagine so. How do you think she came to be up there in the first place?" He arched one dark brow as if to imply that the animal had a more plausible explanation than she did.

And of course after enduring the tough climb as she had, often with Logan's assistance, it was obvious why he questioned her initial appearance at his cabin.

By late afternoon they crossed the last ridge and peeked down into the gap. The buildings of MacLaughlin's Mill squatted at the far end beneath a canopy of chimney smoke. The harvested fields which were hacked from the pine and hardwood forest appeared like mismatched squares on a checkerboard.

Word of their arrival was out by the time they reached the outskirts of the small village. Angus, anxious to be home, left for the Mill day before yesterday, nearly as soon as Rachel and Logan crested the knoll behind his cabin. Now he ambled toward them, his gait seeming a bit lopsided by his missing arm.

"Hail to ye, Logan and Mistress Rachel," he called. "My mother and I expected you hours ago."

Logan grinned and Rachel was struck again by the easy relationship he had with the boy. He even reached out, ruffling the shock of coppery-colored hair. "Not all of us are as swift afoot as you Angus. Even when it is your ma's cooking waiting at the end of the trek."

The freckled face seemed to split open and a short chuckle erupted. Then he caught sight of the cow and his expression sobered. "You've brought Mistress Ellen."

She had the boy doing it, too. Calling the cow by that silly name. Logan wondered if she'd fed Angus any nonsense about talking to the witless animal. Or it talking back. Forcing that thought from his head, he tossed a glance over his shoulder. "Seems as though she followed us down the trail. She must have grown enamored of you."

Angus blotched red, then joined Logan in laughter. And Rachel stood as if rooted to the tangle of dried grass where she stood. Had Logan MacQuaid just uttered a humorous remark? True, it wasn't near as witty as some of her gentleman friends at court, but it did have a certain appeal. As did the reticent man who said it.

Penny seemed as glad to see them as before and Rachel had the feeling again of being surrounded by a soft down comforter. It was almost bedtime before they had a moment alone together. The men, along with Angus, were out checking the stock, which now included a certain cow.

"So you're off to Seven Pines, then." Penny sat by the fire, straining to see the stitches she made in a pair of breeches. She glanced up and smiled shyly. "You'll be liking Mistress Caroline."

"Do you know her?" Rachel leaned forward, resting her idle hands on the rocker's arms. "Logan tells me she's the daughter of an earl."

"Aw, I wouldn't know anything about that. But she is sweet and quite friendly. Beautiful, too, though not so radiant as you, I should think."

Warmth flooded into her cheeks and Rachel lowered her lashes. She, who'd heard more compliments about her appearance than she could possibly recall, was oddly moved by Penny's unjaded observance.

They sat for a moment in companionable silence. A log shifted in the hearth sending a spray of sparks up the chimney. The accompanying crackle seemed to snag Penny's attention for she glanced around, but then she focused again on Rachel.

"I had a talk with Malcolm, like you said."

Her expression was so serious, Rachel hesitated to insist that she had no idea what she meant. Had she suggested Penny speak with her husband about something?

"It seems we were both festering the notion that our boy's misfortune was our fault. Talking it out made us both feel a might better."

"I'm glad." Which of course she was. Rachel liked Penny, and though she didn't know her husband well, he appeared a decent sort. But she still didn't know why Angus's mother gave her any credit for doing anything.

"We come to realize it was like you said. Nothing could have changed what happened. And we're lucky to have our son. Lucky, too, that Logan MacQuaid happened by when he did."

Had *she* said that? Rachel settled back in the chair.

"We're both, Malcolm and me, grateful to you."

"I'm . . ." What? Her usual glib tongue was failing her. She was truly touched by Penny's words and still a bit confused by them. She remembered the story Penny told her about the Indian attack and their son's wound, but failed to recall that she did or said anything other than a few words of sympathy.

Rachel was spared making a reply by the return of the three men. Angus came first, pushing open the door with his shoulder, seemingly unaware that there was no arm attached. Then came his father, sweeping off his hat and stomping toward the fire. Finally, taller than the rest and meeting Rachel's eye for only a second, came Logan.

Rachel tried to pretend the shiver that raced through her body when he looked her way was caused by the flurry of chilled air that swept through the open portal. She knew better.

Her reaction to him was only one of the many mysteries she couldn't explain about her present life . . . as she'd come to think of it. But like all the puzzles, the ability to communicate with wild creatures, the way she could sometimes look into other's minds and hearts, she was certain her desire for Logan would vanish as soon as she accomplished her task. Whenever that might be.

Till then it seemed wiser to keep all her secrets just that. No one but the Adawehis believed her anyway. But as Rachel noticed Penny's knowing appraisal of her, Rachel realized the other woman had read her thoughts. With a smile she inclined her head slightly toward Logan who was stripping out of his buckskin jacket, and nodded.

Rachel would have to work harder at keeping her attraction to Logan hidden.

Over the next few days her new resolve was easy to keep. They met no one on the trail. And Logan was not at his most lovable.

That was the only thing easy about those days.

The constant walking—even wearing, as she was, her new moccasins—was exhausting. "Have you never heard of a coach and four?" she complained one afternoon when it seemed as if they'd been trodding up and down over foothills forever.

"Is that what you're used to Your Highness?"

He didn't even glance around when he said it, a fact that made Rachel square her shoulders and pick up her pace. He'd treated her like this, with a sarcastic aloofness, since they left the Cherokee town . . . since Ostenaco captured her. And she was tired of it. Perhaps the Adawehis did suggest that she refrain from referring to her "other life." But then he didn't have to contend with Logan MacQuaid.

Rachel grabbed his arm. Obviously surprised by her actions he whirled around. Facing her. Looking her straight in the eye.

"As a matter of fact that is the way I traveled. In a well-sprung coach with soft leather squabs and liveried footmen to see to my needs. I've even ridden in the king's royal coach, though admittedly not often. But there have been—"

"Shut up, Your Highness."

Rachel wasn't certain if it was his words or the feel of his fingers grasping her shoulders that made her gasp.

"I don't wish to hear any more of this foolishness. Do you hear me?" The question, if indeed that's what it was, was accompanied by a shake of his arms that freed more golden curls from her braid.

She imagined this was his attempt to intimidate her, but she didn't feel intimidated at all. She felt angry and frustrated, and tired of this prolonged farce.

"I will speak of what I wish." Her chin shot up. "Without the likes of you to gainsay me." His green eyes hardened, narrowing till they seemed no more than slits of green glass, but she continued. "I *am* Lady Rachel Elliott, ward of His Royal Highness, King George the third. And I *do* live at—"

The rest of her words were swallowed up as his mouth slammed down on hers. The kiss hurt. She could taste his anger. His frustration. *His*! As if his problems could possibly compare to hers.

Lifting her balled hands she prepared to push him away, to pummel him if necessary. And she would have to, if not for the faint whisper of a moan. She wasn't even sure which of them made the noise. But the sound brought with it a flash of memory. Of lying

in his arms, feeling the weight of his body on hers
. . . in hers.

Of their own volition her fingers uncurled. Before
she could even form a rational thought her hands
flung about his neck and her mouth slipped open.

He hadn't shaved since they left Cheoah and near
a sennight's worth of black whiskers roughened his
face, chafed hers. But she didn't care. He was kissing
her again, touching her as she'd longed for, dreamed
of since the night she danced for him.

Perhaps she hadn't realized what she longed for.
Perhaps she tried to smother the memory beneath
layers of annoyance. But there it was.

His lips were gentler now, though every whit as
insistent as they moved over hers. He tasted, prodding
with his tongue, catching hers between his teeth.

She felt his hand slide down her shoulder, then
mold her breast, making it fill and swell beneath his
touch. She quivered. She melted. Rachel's back bent
as her body arched toward him.

It was almost more than she could bear.

And then it . . . he . . . was gone.

Rachel stumbled back, nearly falling in the process.
He might have come to her assistance except that he
had already turned away. Had already started along
the path. She watched his stiff back crisscrossed with
his musket, powder horn, and their blankets in disbelief.

Unfulfilled desire strummed through her veins,
making her feel hot, though the day held a chill. But
that's not what made her run after him. What made
her shove him with both palms.

He was so large and solid, the blow affected her
more than him. But she did have the satisfaction of
seeing him turn, his face full of anger. "How dare
you," were the only words that came out.

His jaw clenched and he seemed to clamp down

on his fury. "I apologize." He whipped back toward the trail. "It shan't happen again."

For a moment she just stood, her mouth gaping open. He thought she was angry about the kiss. Rachel could barely keep from laughing. Silly, silly man.

Had he forgotten the way she danced for him . . . did her best to seduce him? Didn't he notice the zeal with which she kissed him back?

He didn't.

The thought came to her unbidden. Rachel closed her eyes and let herself feel. Let her heart feel.

He imagined he took advantage of her. That's what he was thinking. That she was confused and frightened and more than a bit daft and he should be able to control his desires.

Rachel smiled when she realized how much he did want her. His goal was to get her to his brother and her wife without compromising her again.

Rachel called behind her for Henry to wake up and come along. Then she started after Logan. The poor man was going to have a difficult time achieving that goal.

He could use a drink.

Logan sat near the small fire he made in a clearing on the banks of a splashing stream and wished he had a jug. A swallow of rum would go a long way toward calming his desires . . . or perhaps it wouldn't. Still . . .

He hadn't had a drink since they left for Cheoah. And there were times he missed it. Especially now.

"Do you want more?"

"What?" Logan stared over to where Rachel knelt beside the fire. She had done an admirable job of roasting the fish he caught earlier . . . at least they weren't burned beyond recognition. Now she gazed up at him through the wavery smoke. "Nay, I've had my fill."

Logan watched as she gave what was left of the trout to Henry, grimacing when he mentally thought of the dog by that name. Without even waiting for it to cool, the animal gulped it down, ignoring even Rachel's lament that he might burn himself. He folded his arms. She could no more talk to animals than he could. He shoved from his mind the sight of her explaining why she was leaving to the cow they left at the Campbells'. All that scene did was reinforce his fear that she was mad.

He glanced up to see her watching him, her head bent to one side. He shifted self-consciously, then looked away.

"I'm not, you know."

"Not what?"

She inched closer to him. "Ready for Bedlam. That is what you were thinking."

Logan started to deny it, then realized she hadn't worded it in the form of a question. And that was *exactly* what he was thinking.

"I realize it must seem strange to you . . . actually 'tis strange for me, too." She somehow managed to settle so close to him that he caught the sweet fragrance of her skin. "You really don't have anything to fear from me you know."

"I'm not afraid of you."

"Really? Then why are you moving away?" Rachel sighed. " 'Tis not as if we haven't made love already."

"That was a mistake."

"Because of what happened to Mary?"

Her brow wrinkled and Logan had the strangest feeling in the pit of his stomach. "Mary has nothing to do with this."

"Then why were you thinking of her?"

Logan scrambled to his feet so quickly that Rachel

who'd been leaning on his knee, fell forward. "What I'm thinking is that I'll keep watch. You get some sleep," was all he said before grabbing up the musket and disappearing into the darkness.

Which, of course, wasn't what he was thinking at all. Rachel wrapped her arms around bent knees. Her little ploy to confront him and his fears of her had failed miserably. He'd not only been convinced she was mad when he jumped up, but that he was, too.

In trying to get closer to him, she'd alienated the one human being she was destined to be around . . . at least for a while. Rachel stretched out on the blanket, groaning at how hard the ground was. Obviously the spirits who sent her to him were prone to mistakes. Not only was her own death an example, but their theory that she could do anything about Logan MacQuaid showed them to be true bunglers.

She was no closer to really saving his life now than when she arrived. And no closer to home.

Chapter Thirteen

"Yet many will not believe there is any such thing
as a sympathy of souls."

—Izaak Walton
Life of Dr. Donne

It took them four more days to reach his brother's
home and not once during that time was Rachel
called upon to save his life. They walked along in
near silence through pine forests and over hillocks,
following the trail that curved along beside a swift
running stream. No longer was she tempted to startle
him into accepting her power to read his thoughts.

For she no longer could.

It was as if again he'd built an invisible wall about
himself. One that not only kept her out, but him
locked inside. He didn't smile. He merely trudged.
And Rachel found herself missing his witty sarcasm.

Her nose angled higher with each mile, hoping
he'd call her "Your Highness" as he was prone to
do when she became haughty. But he didn't. He
barely spoke at all.

Rachel felt a great deal of relief and anticipation
when he announced Seven Pines was over the next
ridge. Despite her fatigue she almost ran to get her
first glimpse. Glad when she finally saw it that she
hadn't taken the trouble.

Seven Pines wasn't nearly as grand as she imagined it might be. Not that the compound was particularly small. The house, the first she'd seen in this life constructed of something other than rough logs, was painted white and had two stories. The glass in the windows sparkled in the late afternoon sun, giving them a jewellike appearance. Several outbuildings nestled about the main house and beyond them were fields.

Not a grand estate that befitted the daughter of an earl, of course, but it did appear to offer some semblance of civilization. Perhaps there was a bath and a bed. The very thought quickened her pace as she started down into the vale. It had been so long since she bathed in anything but a cold creek. And the thought of snuggling between soft sheets was enough to make her swoon with joy.

Before they were halfway across the clearing the front door opened. The tall dark man who stepped outside, cradling a long rifle in his arms looked fierce.

Only after instinctively stepping behind Logan did Rachel remember her task. She boldly moved in front of him, but by that time the tense moment was past. The man, who she now assumed was Logan's brother, walked toward them, his hand out in welcome.

"Logan." They pumped each other's hand, then Logan's brother reached out enveloping him in a bear hug. Rachel thought the dark eyes had an unnatural sheen when he called over his shoulder. "Caroline, look who has come home."

Rachel glanced toward the door as a young woman stepped out. She, too, held a gun which she leaned against the front wall before descending the three steps to the gravel walk. She shaded her eyes as she came forward. Then broke into an awkward run when she recognized her brother-in-law.

"Be careful, Caroline." Her husband placed a

steadying hand on her arm before she threw herself at Logan.

"Let me look at you." She pulled away enough to take his bristled face between her delicately shaped hands. "Too thin, just as I thought."

"I can hardly say the same of you, Caro."

Her refined laugh joined the hearty chuckle of the two men. "Hardly." She looked down at the curve of her stomach. "But what can you expect when I carry another child of Wolf's inside me."

"*Another* baby. I know I've been away awhile. Have I lost count? This is number three, is it not?"

"Four," corrected his brother, looking more like a proud father than a man called Wolf.

"You haven't been home in over three years," Caroline added. And Rachel thought her more saddened by her words than angry. But before she could reflect on the reason for this, Caroline turned, seemingly noticing her for the first time.

"I do apologize." She held out her hands toward Rachel. "Do forgive our rudeness. It's just been so long." Her gaze returned to linger on Logan for an instant before focusing on Rachel. "I'm Caroline MacQuaid and this is my husband, Raff, although he is also called Wolf."

"This is Rachel Elliott," Logan introduced. "She's a . . . an acquaintance of mine."

Rachel admired Caroline's inbred manners for she didn't blink an eye at Logan's awkward introduction. Nor did she seem to take note of the horrid condition of Rachel's gown. She simply linked her arm with Rachel's and headed toward the doorway, where two dark-eyed children stood.

"Do come inside. You must be exhausted and hungry. Children," she said, touching each of their heads as she passed. "We have a guest."

The boy bowed, the girl curtsied in a way that

brought tears of homesickness to Rachel's eyes. She blinked quickly, managed a nod and was bustled inside.

"I shall present them to you later after you've rested," Caroline said.

Sheets. The bed had sheets. Rachel had to fight the tears as she sat on the side of the mattress, running her hand along the stretch of white linen. She had been shown up a narrow stairway to this room by a Cherokee woman named Sadayi. Rachel assumed she was a servant but she seemed to be treated more like a member of the family by Caroline.

Containing a bed, dresser, and two winged chairs set at an angle beside the fireplace, the room was not large. But it was comfortable, even by Rachel's standards, and clean.

She almost hated to lie on the brightly colored quilt for fear of soiling it. The dust of the trail seemed ground into her skin. Rachel didn't have to look into the beveled mirror over the chest to prove that.

Rachel slid off the bed, nearly groaning as her tired feet hit the braided rug. She paced to the window, lifting the simple curtains to the side and peering out. Her view was of the trees and mountains behind the house. She caught a glimmer of water—the river whose churning lullaby was beginning to make her eyes droop.

But there was no sign of Logan.

She hated having him out of her sight like this. What if something happened to him? He could encounter all manner of dangers, and who would be there to save him?

Sighing, Rachel let the fabric slide through her fingers. There was nothing she could do now. Besides, at her last glimpse of him, he was accompanying his brother into a small room opposite the parlor. There seemed to be nothing but brotherly love between the two. Rachel slipped off her moccasins and climbed onto the bed. She yawned . . . loudly. He would be all right while she rested. Just for a moment.

Hours later Rachel's eyes sprang open, but she could see little except a rosy glow. She was comfortable and warm, lying on something as soft as a cloud and for a moment her senses convinced her she'd returned to the angels.

She was on her way home. They realized her task was done. She'd saved his life and now could get on with her own. Where she belonged. Without Logan MacQuaid.

Rachel let out her breath when she heard the soft tapping. Her limbs relaxed and she turned her head enough to see a sliver of moonlight reflected off the window panes. Of course, she was at Seven Pines.

The door creaked open and a small wedge of light flickered through. Rachel saw Caroline's face above the candle she held.

"Do come in." Rachel pushed to sit up. "I'm awake."

"Are you certain I'm not disturbing you?" Caroline opened the door a bit wider. "I only came to check if you were all right, and ask if you'd like something to eat."

Rachel's stomach growled at the thought of food. "Yes, a bite of something would be lovely."

Caroline turned and spoke in low tones to someone in the hall, then smiled at Rachel. "It won't take long." She began to close the door. "Good night then."

"Wait." Rachel whipped off the quilt. "I mean, do come in. Perhaps you would like to join me?"

Caroline hesitated a moment, then entered the room, cupping the flame to keep it from sputtering.

"I've already taken my evening meal. But I will keep you company if you like."

"I'd like that very much." Rachel's feet slid to the floor. She considered pulling on her moccasins but decided against it. The room was warm—someone must have tended the fire while she slept. A vision of Logan flashed through her mind.

"Everyone has eaten?" The question sounded innocent enough, she supposed, but Rachel was thinking of Logan. She looked down, shaking out what was left of her skirts to hide the color she felt flooding her cheeks. But she needn't have bothered. Caroline was turned away, placing the brass candlestick on the dresser.

"Yes, hours ago. I sent Sadayi up to wake you but she returned, saying you seemed so weary."

"I suppose I was. I don't even recall her presence." Rachel took one of the chairs angled before the fire, offering the other to Caroline. Caroline sat, grasping the check-covered chair arms and lowering herself awkwardly.

Her smile was self-effacing when she glanced up. "I doubt my confinement will last much longer. When the other children made me this uncomfortable they were born shortly after."

"How selfish of me. I didn't mean to keep you from your bed. Of course you must find a more agreeable position to—"

Caroline's laughter cut off her words. "Oh, do forgive me. I don't mean to make light of your suggestion. 'Tis simply that there *is* no agreeable position."

"Oh."

"Do not look so stricken. 'Tis not nearly so bad as that." She shifted, settling her feet upon a small stool. "As I said. This won't last much longer. And then I shall have another dark-eyed babe to present to my husband."

She said the last with such obvious love and devotion that Rachel felt as if she were eavesdropping on a private moment. Her lashes fluttered down, but when she looked up Caroline's expression had changed. She was studying Rachel with avid interest.

"Do forgive me for asking, but . . ." She sighed and clamped her lips shut. "Nay, 'tis as Wolf says, none of my business."

"You wonder what I am doing here. Dressed as I am." Rachel's fingers skimmed down the front of her tattered gown. "With your brother-in-law."

"W-ell." Caroline spread the word out. "It is a question that crossed my mind. Not your clothing," she added quickly. "Days on the trail would explain that easily enough."

"But my coming here with Logan is less easily unraveled?"

"Logan's appearance at all is a surprise . . . a pleasant one, I assure you, but . . ." Caroline's voice trailed off. "He keeps so to himself. We've only seen him once since he left."

"And you've been worried." Rachel wasn't sure if she read the other woman's thoughts or simply the concern in her delicate, cameo face.

"Oh yes. Wolf and I both are very concerned, though Wolf, perhaps because he is a man, hesitates to admit it. But I see him at times looking up toward the mountains, and I know what he's thinking . . . who he thinks about. Especially since he discovered James.

"James?"

"Of course, you wouldn't know of him, for Logan doesn't. Apparently everyone thought him dead, hanged before Robert brought Logan to the frontier."

Rachel blinked . . . confused. All of a sudden Caroline's thoughts were coming to her, quite easily. But so were her words. So used to Logan's reticence, to the wall he built around himself, Rachel found this plethora of information, both spoken and sensed, overwhelming.

Yet she didn't dare do anything to stem the flow.

With renewed determination Rachel focused her attention.

James was an older brother. Logan's older brother. And over two years ago, Caroline and Wolf discovered he was alive, married, and the owner of a shipping company in Charles Town.

"You must have been so excited, finding someone you thought was dead." Much as the queen and her court would be when Rachel reappeared.

"We were. For Wolf it was like finding a bit of himself."

Again Rachel's senses were flooded by the warm, loving feeling Caroline had for her husband.

"Though they never knew each other before, Wolf and James have become friends. Anne, his wife, and I have as well."

And they'd talked of finding Logan, of going into the mountains to search for him. But they didn't know where he was or even if he was still alive. Logan's life seemed to mean nothing to him. He even confided to Wolf that it might be best if he threw himself from the highest summit one day never to be heard from again.

"Are you all right?"

Rachel opened her eyes to find Caroline and the Cherokee woman Sadayi leaning over her. Caroline swished a handkerchief, stirring a flutter of air. "I rose to let Sadayi into the room and when I looked back you'd grown so pale and your eyes were closed." She moved to the side. "Perhaps I should wake Logan."

"No." Rachel grabbed for her hand. "Please

don't." She paused, her eyes locking with Caroline's. "Please."

Caroline didn't know what to do, and Rachel could hardly blame her.

"I think it's because I haven't eaten for so long." Rachel glanced toward the tray of food on the table beside her.

"I suppose that could be the problem."

Though she doubted it. Rachel picked up the cup of steaming tea in hopes of convincing her. She took a sip, then smiled. "I'm feeling better already."

Rachel watched as Caroline and the Sadayi woman shared a look. The latter shrugged her shoulders clad in a bright calico, and backed out of the room. *Her feet hurt and she was anxious to rest them. Who knew why the skinny white woman swooned.*

"I'll stay with you while you eat," Caroline said as she settled back into her chair. "Then you must get back in bed."

She was still toying with the notion of waking Logan to find out if Rachel had been ill. Luckily, her concern for her brother-in-law, who also was tired, overrode her curiosity.

Still, Caroline watched Rachel like a mother might watch her child as she bit into a piece of fresh white bread. Rachel ate quickly . . . hungrily, devouring every bit of fruit and cheese, along with the pastry of meat and the other slice of bread. She tried not to connect with Caroline's thoughts and she kept her own to herself.

Rachel allowed herself to be tucked beneath the covers when she finished, though it seemed more that she should be doing the favor rather than receiving it. It wasn't until Caroline closed the door behind her, taking the light of the candle with her, that Rachel allowed herself to dwell on what she learned by reading the other woman's thoughts.

Logan had contemplated throwing himself from the mountain, had considered killing himself. The idea chilled her more thoroughly than the quilt could counter.

Had she saved his life that morning when they first met? And if she had why was she still here?

But more importantly, why was he so overwrought by life that he thought his solution was to end it?

His head was going to explode.

Logan combed long, black hair from his face, wincing when his fingers caught in a wet tangle. God, why did he finish off the jug of rum after Wolf went to bed? Better, why did he begin drinking in the first place?

Logan pulled on his shirt, but rather than go back to the house, he slid his back down the length of an oak, finding the slight rise at the bottom an acceptable seat.

His brother woke him this morning to suggest they bathe in the river, a custom they started years ago when they both lived at Seven Pines ... one that Logan had continued alone on his mountain. Professing a need to check on Caroline who was still in bed when he left, Wolf hurried back, admonishing Logan not to miss breakfast.

As if he could eat.

What was it about this place that made him feel as if his body was too big for its skin?

Surely memories of his father, of Mary, should have faded by now. Yet when he came here, it was as if it were yesterday that he left his wife in the care of a man he hated. As if he could turn his head and still see her sweet face, smiling at him, her eyes searching for something she could never find.

Dried leaves crackled, and instinctively Logan twisted around. But it wasn't his dead wife he saw.

"You lied to me."

Logan lifted his brow and leaned back against the bark. "I trust you rested well, Your Highness."

She paid his insolence no heed, instead marching round to face him, hands planted firmly on hips. Her lips were thinned, her eyes narrowed . . . not one of her more endearing expressions. But Logan had to admit the rest of her looked fetching.

She wore a gown of blue silk, obviously Caroline's. The skirts were a tad too short, showing a peek of deerskin moccasin, and the bodice a bit too tight. Logan's gaze lingered on the enticing swell of creamy breast that showed.

"Why didn't you tell me you considered throwing yourself off the cliff before? I wouldn't be surprised if I did save your life the day I pulled you up."

"Wolf has a loose tongue."

"Don't blame your brother. He didn't tell me. And don't change the subject of our discussion. I—"

"As far as I can tell, we aren't having a discussion. And you did *not* save my life. You nearly cost it."

"But if you were preparing to jump, I—"

"I wasn't going to jump for God's sake!" Logan pushed to his feet and grabbed her shoulders. "Perhaps my mind flirted with the thought during a couple of brief moments of insanity . . ." He glanced away, his voice low. "Or when I was too drunk to know better. But I'd long ago decided against it."

He was looking at her now, his green eyes intense and she knew he was telling her the truth. But the question still remained. "Why?"

"Why did I abandon the idea?" His hands drifted down her shoulders and he turned away. "I haven't the vaguest idea."

"That's not what I meant, and you know it." Rachel followed him to the river's edge.

"Ah, I forgot. Your Highness can read my mind. Some special power you picked up in the afterlife. Perhaps you should tell me then."

"You aren't going to force me away with your sarcasm." Rachel almost said she was immune to that, but it would be a lie. But she also could not tell right now what he was thinking or feeling, other than pain. And it didn't take any special powers, as he put it, to figure that out. His stance was rigid as he stared across the waterway to the wall of pines beyond.

"You know I never could figure out why my father called this place Seven Pines. There are easily a hundred times that here."

Rachel stared at his broad back, at the *V* of dampness soaking into his shirt from his wet hair and wished she could break through the wall surrounding him. Wished she could touch him. She breathed in slowly. "He must have had his reasons."

The look he sent her over his shoulder sent chills up her spine. "My father had a reason for everything he did."

A quick stab of loneliness and despair . . . his despair . . . raced through Rachel before he spoke again. When he did, she understood.

"My mother killed herself. Nothing as dramatic as leaping off a mountain, but she killed herself all the same."

Blood. His thoughts . . . Rachel's thoughts were of blood. Everywhere. Of seeing his mother lying on crimson sheets, her lifeless face pale and calm, serene amidst the surrounding horror.

Rachel wanted to run away, to hide her own face and beg him to stop reliving the horror, to free her from the pain. But she couldn't. She'd wanted this. Wanted to know him.

Rachel stepped closer. Close enough to touch, yet she didn't. "It must have been horrible for you . . . to find her like that."

When he whirled toward her she wasn't prepared for the anger contorting his features. "Find her. I didn't find her. Hell, that would have been impossible seeing that he had locked her away." His voice sounded all the more ominous because of his unemotional delivery. "He took me to see her. He explained it to me while I stood there, afraid to look . . . afraid not to. She was mad, he said, driven insane by my brother's foolish actions . . . by my support for him."

"How old were you?" Tears ran, unheeded, down Rachel's cheeks.

"Twelve, I think." He shook his head as if trying to recall. "Nearly thirteen. 'Twas 1746. The year my older brother was hanged."

"But he wasn't hanged. He's not dead." Now Rachel did grab his arm, so hard he jerked his head around, a strand of dark, damp hair snagging on the black stubble covering his chin.

"What is this, more talk of angels and hereafter?" He obviously didn't appreciate her assertion.

"No, 'tis true. Caroline told me last night. He lives . . . his name is James, is it not?" At his nod, Rachel continued. "He is alive and living in Charles Town. With a wife and—"

With a sigh Rachel let her voice trail off. She was speaking to thin air anyway. Logan was stalking toward the house.

"I can't believe you didn't tell him."

"There was no chance." Wolf glanced up from his breakfast of cornbread and ham. His eyes met his wife's, then dropped back to his plate. "I wished to, but was unsure of how to broach the subject."

"You . . . ? Unsure?" Caroline sipped her tea, not even bothering to finish her thought. It was a rather ridiculous notion given Wolf's past and his current position as Commissioner of Indian Affairs.

Discussing difficult subjects such as unfair trade practices and treaty violations was what he did all the time. And he was contentious, some said brilliant, most agreed, outspoken. Surely delivering the good news that a brother long thought dead was alive and well should not have been formidable.

Pushing from his chair, Wolf went round to stand behind his wife's. Her stomach made it impossible for her to sit close to the table and he smiled before resting his chin on her moon-spun hair.

"You were right about the rum. I should never have offered him a drink."

"Oh, Wolf." Rachel twisted till she could look into his face. "Did he do anything?"

"No. But I could tell it wasn't a good idea—" Wolf's mouth clamped shut when he saw his brother standing in the doorway. Caroline smiled beseechingly when he glanced her way.

"I mentioned James to Rachel last night."

"Aye. And she told me." Logan strode toward the table. "Was she speaking the truth?"

"Yes. I should have told you as soon as you came. Caroline was just pointing that out to me." Wolf motioned toward an empty chair before resuming his seat, not surprised when Logan ignored the offer, choosing instead to pace the length of the dining room.

"He escaped from Scotland, and spent several years in the Caribbean."

"Did Father arrange it?" Logan hated to admit even to himself that something in him hoped that was the case. That the man who he'd grown to hate had at one time shown a spark of kindness toward one of his sons. But the expression in Wolf's dark eyes dashed that thought.

"It was other loyal supporters of Prince Charles, Logan." Caroline's voice was kind as she raised her bulk from the chair. "There are things that need my attention, if you gentlemen will excuse me."

They both nodded and she moved silently from the room, meeting Rachel as she entered the hallway.

"Is Logan in there?" Rachel pushed toward the dining room, pausing only when Caroline's hand came to rest on her arm.

"It would be best if we left them alone for a while, I think."

Rachel opened her mouth to argue, then clamped it shut again. Her breath left her in a rush. "Perhaps you're right." Her eyes focused on the paneled wood. "I don't know how to deal with him very well."

"And do you? Deal with him, I mean?" Caroline guided them toward the parlor, stopping only to give instructions to Sadayi before closing the door.

"I suppose I do. At least for the moment." She caught the knowing look Caroline passed her and shook her head so hard the caplet of curls came loose, several twisted locks falling down her back. " 'Tis not what you're thinking. Logan and I . . . well, I'm Lady Rachel Elliott, a ward of King George."

Caroline stared at her as if she'd suddenly grown a second head, and Rachel wished she could take back her words. She didn't need any advanced intuition to know what the other woman was thinking. And she hadn't even mentioned drowning and being put back on earth to save Logan's life . . . or the frustrating time she was having of it.

"Tell me about Logan's father." Rachel hadn't meant her question as a means of changing the subject, but it worked perfectly. Caroline's face drained of color and she fidgeted in her seat. Yet Rachel had to admire the other woman's courage as she met her gaze.

"Did you know he was my husband?"

"Yes, Logan mentioned it once, though I doubt he remembers he did."

Caroline nodded, then picked up her needlework from the small table to her right and began stitching. "My father's death left us . . ." She glanced up. "My younger brother Ned and I, penniless. So . . ." She jammed the needle through the cotton fabric. "I agreed to marry a gentleman from the New World. No," she sighed. "That's not exactly true. I was very grateful for Robert MacQuaid's offer of marriage. He promised to support Ned and care for me. What more was there to a marriage?" Her crystal-blue eyes met Rachel's deeper ones. "At least that's what I thought at the time." She squirmed in her seat again.

"But once you met him . . . ?"

"Actually, I knew differently before I met Robert." Her smile was soft and Rachel felt that now familiar surge of love. "You see, I met Wolf before his father."

Images flashed through Rachel's head, some endearing, some that made her blush. With effort she was able to dim the thoughts coming from Caroline and concentrate only on her words.

"I can't really describe to you what Robert was like. Cruel doesn't seem to do him justice." She gathered up her sewing and set it aside, not even pretending now to work on it. "He was hurtful." Caroline stood, pausing to rub the small of her back before moving toward the window. "Yes, I believe that would be a good word to describe Robert. He hurt Wolf and me, and, from what I understand, James." She turned to look at Rachel. "And yes, Logan."

"What of Mary? Did he hurt her?" Rachel hadn't planned to ask that. It just seemed to slip out. And she wished right away that it hadn't. Caroline's feelings came pouring through her. How sweet Mary was. How much she was loved by all. It seemed even Robert cared for her in his own way. At least he treated her with some respect.

"Did Logan love her? Did he love Mary as much as everyone else?" Rachel's hand flew to her mouth. "Please, don't answer that. 'Tis none of my business and I don't know why—"

"I think that's something you need to discuss with Logan."

"Which of course I won't." Rachel stood, shook out nonexistent wrinkles from her borrowed gown and headed for the door. Pity is what Caroline felt for her at this moment and Rachel could not bear it. "I really don't care one way or the other," she insisted before reaching for the knob. "It was simply—"

Rachel wasn't certain if she experienced the surge of discomfort or heard the small cry first, but when she whirled back toward Caroline she was grasping the windowsill, white brackets of pain framing her mouth.

"Caroline!" Rachel rushed toward her.

" 'Tis nothing . . . really. A mere twinge. Nothing to concern—Oh . . ." She allowed herself to be escorted to the chair by the hearth, but refused Rachel's offer to ring for tea.

"Do you suppose you could find Wolf?" Caroline asked, her voice breathless. "I believe he is to become a father again."

Chapter Fourteen

"It is said, and it is true, that just before we are
born a cavern angel puts his finger to our lips
and says, 'Hush, don't tell what you know.'"
——Roderick MacLeish
Prince Ombra

"Why is it taking so long?" she whispered when
her path took her near him.

"These things take time. Would Your Highness
kindly stop pacing the length of the parlor?"

Rachel shot him a scathing look before settling into
the chair opposite his. But before her skirts were
flared out to her satisfaction she realized Logan may
have called her by that deplorable name, but there
was none of the stinging sarcasm behind his words.

He was just as concerned as she was!

The thought hit her with unerring accuracy, chilling her so that Rachel wrapped her arms around
herself to ward off the sensation. Somehow her own
worry had seemed foolish. What did she know of the
birthing process? But Logan knew. Perhaps only from
the books he devoured, but he knew.

Yet somehow the fact that he sensed there was a
problem relieved her mind. She trusted him to do
something about it.

Her gaze drifted to Caroline's two older children.
They sat in a puddle of sunshine near the window
taking turns spinning a wooden top. Occasionally
they tired of trying to count the revolutions and took
to bedeviling Henry. The dog lay sprawled, vying for
the same patch of warmth glittering through the glass
panes. Three-year-old Mary, named no doubt for Logan's dead wife, also clutched a homemade doll with
a carved wooden head.

Rachel had been introduced to the children the
morning after she arrived and found them well-
behaved and amiable . . . and they thoroughly intimidated her. The girl especially seemed forever staring
at Rachel. But she seemed a sweet child, quite pretty
and soft-spoken, even at her tender age.

The boy, Kalanu, looked a miniature version of
his father, which held the promise he would grow
into a tall, handsome man. Being older, nearly six,
as he mentioned yesterday, he was obviously growing tired of entertaining his sister. The sound of
their most recent squabble drifted toward Rachel
and Logan.

Logan tossed Rachel a look as if she should do
something about the situation, which was returned
by a stare of utter shock. When he inclined his head
sharply toward the children, Rachel shook hers just
as vigorously.

His lips thinned. "I think perhaps the children
would enjoy a walk in the fresh air, Rachel."

"Then why don't you accompany them, Logan?"

"Because I thought I might see if there's something
I might do to help Caroline."

"Oh." Rachel felt thoroughly chastised. Of course
this was what she wanted him to do . . . had hoped
he would do. But the children . . .

With as much dignity as she could muster Rachel
stood and approached them. They looked up when

her shadow darkened their play area. "Shall we take a walk outside?"

They both seemed eager, scrambling to their feet, kicking Henry in the process. The dog protested by lifting his head and slitting open one eye.

"Can Henry come, too?"

Rachel smiled at the animal. "Yes, I think that would be an excellent idea. Now do get your cloaks, I think 'tis chilly out today."

The air was brisk, though the sky was an unfailing blue. Rachel took a deep breath, glad now that she was here. Glad for the chance to leave the house, where she'd been since Caroline began her confinement yesterday morning. Even if she was accompanied by two children.

"Is Baby Alkini sleeping?"

"Yes, she is." Wolf and Caroline's third child was still in leading strings. Rachel smiled down at Mary who immediately lifted two pudgy arms, one clutching her doll.

"She wants you to carry her," offered Kalanu. "She's such a baby."

"Am not," the little girl countered, yet she stood her ground, arms raised. They had barely stepped off the wide porch that fronted the house, so she could hardly be tired. But Rachel found no help for it but to lift the child into her arms. Settling her onto a hip seemed to help to ease the load.

They strolled toward the river, Kalanu dashing ahead at times and pretending to pull taut the string of a bow and arrow. "Papa promised to take me hunting with him this winter," he announced and Rachel nodded, trying not to meet Mary's eyes. The girl was using her perch to stare intently at Rachel's head.

Finally, unable to ignore the scrutiny any longer she drew in her breath. "Is my hair mussed, Mary?"

"No." But the wary stare continued. They reached the shore of the river before the little girl spoke again. "Is Mama going to die?"

"Of course not. I mean . . ." Was she? Was that what caused the uneasy feeling she had? Rachel shook her head. "Whatever made you ask such a thing?"

"We thought it might be so because you're here." Kalanu tossed a stone into the gurgling water. When he looked up his dark eyes shone with tears.

"Me? But why would you think—"

"Please don't take our mama away to heaven."

"Oh sweetheart." Rachel knelt with the distraught child, cuddling first her and then her brother into an embrace. "I won't take your mama away. I won't."

The sniffling stopped and tearful eyes stared into hers. "Promise?"

A chill ran through Rachel, so cold and so strong that she shuddered. "Yes, I promise," she breathed, unable to help herself from making that response.

The relief the two children exhibited was dramatic and frightening. What had she vowed? Only that she would not take their mother away. Which of course she wouldn't. But somehow, staring into their trusting faces, Rachel knew it was much more that she'd pledged.

She didn't know exactly what it was until she watched them play a bit later. Rachel sat on a tree stump, her eyes closed and covered by her palms, slowly counting to five and twenty. The children scurried about supposedly each finding a hiding place, though for the last three times Mary had insisted upon sharing her older brother's . . . much to his annoyance.

They were whispering and Rachel smiled, thinking how easy they'd be to find but how she would search about toward the house a bit before pouncing on them where they hid behind a holly bush. Then a word floated to her above the constant gurgling of the river.

"Angel."

Rachel shifted, turning her head to hear them better.

"Mama won't die," Mary said, her voice filled with relief. "And don't say she might. Angels don't lie. Mama said so."

Forgetting the game Rachel's hands dropped. She caught a glimpse of Mary's surprised expression before she ducked around behind her brother. Making no pretense to search elsewhere, Rachel hurried around the tree, dropping to her knees in front of the startled little girl.

"What do you mean, angels don't lie."

"They don't." Mary's eyes took up most of her face. "Mama told us how they came out of heaven to talk to the sheep."

"Shepherds. Can't you remember anything, Mary? Angels wouldn't talk to animals, baby," Kalanu declared.

"They might," the child insisted, turning toward her brother and stamping her foot. Then she focused back on Rachel. "Tell him they might talk to animals if they wanted."

"Your sister is correct," Rachel agreed before folding Mary's hands in hers. "But tell me what this has to do with you . . . and your mother."

"Mary thinks you're an angel," Kalanu said, adding under his breath. "She's only a silly baby."

"Am not." Mary pulled from Rachel's grasp, turning to face her older brother with her small chin thrust forward. "Besides, you said so, too."

"I said she looked like the picture in the book," he insisted, though he couldn't seem to meet Rachel's eye. "You're the one who thinks she sees the halo."

"I do see it. It's right there." One stubby finger

pointed to a spot over Rachel's head. Instinctively her hands reached up to feel . . . nothing.

"Children, I . . ." She what? Rachel could think of nothing to say. In the end she pretended the wind was too cold and bundled them into the house and up the stairs to the nursery, promising to return later to read them a story.

Rushing down the stairs she couldn't resist checking her reflection in the beveled mirror above the gateleg table in the hallway. There was nothing circling her golden curls. Shaking her head she hurried into the parlor, stopping short when she saw Logan . . . his fingers inches from the decanter of Madeira on the table by his chair.

He looked up, his expression unreadable. Rachel's gaze held his for a moment, her heart pounding faster. But when he looked down, the long dark lashes shadowing his eyes, her heart plummeted.

"Caroline isn't . . . ?" The lump of emotion in her throat wouldn't let her continue. All she could see was the sweet faces of Caroline's children. The calm belief that her word was true.

"Dead?"

His voice snapped Rachel out of her reverie.

"No." He took a deep breath. "But . . ."

"What?" Rachel was across the room, kneeling in front of him before he stopped shaking his head.

"The baby isn't coming as it should."

"Why not?" Rachel grabbed his hands.

"I don't know. Sadayi seems to think the child is too big."

"Well, what is Sadayi doing? Certainly there is—"

"She's given Caroline some herbs and called on the spirits to help." His voice was flat.

"She's given up on her then? They'll both die. Caroline and her baby." Rachel tried to meet his gaze but he would have none of it. "Where's Wolf?"

"With Caroline." He did glance up then. "She hasn't given up." Again he seemed to find the design in the carpet of interest. "Though she grows weaker."

"Then you must do something."

He did meet her eyes then, his shadowed in disbelief. "You're daft. I can do nothing."

"You can." Her gaze followed his as it slid toward the decanter. "I've seen you read your books."

"There's a huge difference between reading and doing, Your Highness."

"Perhaps not so huge. I also know of your surgery on the Campbell boy."

"Aye. 'Tis sawing off his arm, I did."

" 'Tis saving his life, you did."

He was frightened.

Logan's fear surged through her as surely as if it were her own. Rachel squeezed his hands, knowing again the joy of being one with him. She could even feel the magnetic pull of the Madeira and the power of the man sitting before her as he triumphed over the temptation.

"You will do your best for Caroline and her babe," Rachel whispered. Her fingers were white from the pressure of their bonding, and she knew when she released his much larger hands they would bear the imprint of hers.

Rachel was so sure of herself . . . of him . . . that even when he asked her to bring the wine she barely hesitated. "For Caroline," he explained, though she had asked for none.

But entering the bedroom on the first floor where Caroline lay shook all Rachel's confidence. It seemed as if the pall of death already hung over her. As if her soul already hovered between this life and the next.

Rachel expected Caroline to cry out in pain. She

was not present when Queen Charlotte delivered the young Prince George, but word about the court was that she'd bellowed quite loudly, calling out in her native tongue till the royal bedchamber echoed with German.

But Caroline lay still, barely whimpering when a spasm of pain rippled through her body. Her husband seemed in nearly as bad shape. The tall man Rachel thought so fierce hunched over beside the bed, his hand clutching his wife's as if he could imbue her with some of his own strength. He didn't even glance up when Rachel and Logan approached the bed. Nor did Sadayi cease her rhythmic chanting.

When Logan's hand settled on his brother's shoulder, Wolf finally tore his eyes away from his wife. His dark stare was so grief-stricken Rachel wanted to rush from the room. But she stood by Logan as he spoke, his voice a beacon of calm and reason.

"I want to help Caroline, but I must examine her first."

A shadow of puzzlement deepened the dark eyes and Rachel sank to the floor beside Wolf. He probably knew no more about his brother's knowledge of medicine than anyone else.

"Please let him. Please." On her knees, beseeching Caroline's husband, Rachel knew her plea sailed to a much higher authority. She let out her breath only when Wolf dropped his forehead onto the brightly colored quilt.

"Do what you can," he murmured.

As if those words brought *him* to life, Logan hurried to the foot of the bed. Before raising the coverlet he took a deep breath. "Rachel, perhaps you and Wolf should leave."

The emphatic, "No," came from them both at the same time. Wolf's fingers wove more tightly with his wife's as if he refused to leave her . . . ever.

From where she knelt beside the bed, Rachel could not see Logan's face. But she could hear his mutterings and prayed he knew what to do. When he finally stood, his expression seemed calm and determined.

"I need to turn the babe. Caroline, would you—"

"What are you doing?" Though he still held on to his wife, Wolf now grabbed Rachel with his other hand. "I can't let you hurt her further."

Sadayi seemed to agree with his words as she lowered her voice, giving the chant an unearthly ring, and stepped closer to the bed. She stopped, staring first at Logan, then Wolf. "I have called upon the spirits. It is in their hands."

"No." Rachel jumped to her feet, blocking the old woman's almost hypnotic stare from reaching Wolf. "The spirits have sent Logan to help." She turned toward Wolf. "We must let him."

For one tense moment Rachel could almost see the two cultures warring within the man. In the end it was concern and love for his wife that won out. "Do what you must to save her life."

He worked quickly and though Rachel knew what Logan did must be hurting Caroline, she hardly moved a muscle. When Logan stood again, he wiped blood, Caroline's blood, from his hands. "The babe is in position but Caroline needs to push and I don't know . . ." The rest of his words drifted off as his gaze fell upon the exhausted woman's pale face.

Of course she couldn't push. She'd been doing just that for nearly two days and her body could do no more. Except that it must.

Rushing around the foot of the bed—trying not to view the blood-soaked sheets, Rachel leaned toward Caroline's ear. "You must," she whispered. "You must try some more, Caroline." Rachel brushed damp, moonspun curls from her forehead. "For your new babe, Caroline, you must."

Blue eyes that were closed before, now opened, staring into Rachel's own. Tears clogged Rachel's throat as she touched Caroline's cheek.

"Do you understand what needs done?"

The nod was barely imperceptible, yet Rachel saw it. Saw Caroline's face contort as another wave rippled across her distended belly. This time though she didn't allow the torment to rule her. With a supreme force of will Caroline put the pain to use.

The tendons in her neck stood out in relief against her pale skin as she pushed.

"That's good, Caroline." Logan's voice held an air of excitement which infused Rachel.

"Did you hear what he said, Caroline? You're doing splendidly."

With the next contraction Caroline fumbled to push up and Rachel supported one of her shoulders, calling for Wolf to grab the other. He leaped at the chance to do something other than watch his wife expire before him.

Rachel didn't know how long this went on. Caroline seemed to gain strength with each of her efforts. Her face was covered with perspiration and between pains, Rachel wiped it with a linen towel. And she continued to talk to her. Words of encouragement. Words of support. They seemed to hang in the air, mingling with the Cherokee chants and Caroline's grunts of labor.

They all ceased when the baby's first cry filled the room. It sounded weak at first, then spiraled to a full crescendo as Logan lifted the slimy, blood-covered mass of humanity.

"You have a daughter," he announced to Caroline, before bundling the infant into linens and placing her on her mother's chest.

Tears streamed down Rachel's cheeks but she hadn't the wherewithal to wipe them away as she looked at Caroline staring at her newborn child. It was if she was trying to memorize the tiny puckered features . . . as if she feared there was little time to do so.

Wolf too seemed in awe of the tiny creature, and though he wasn't crying, his dark eyes were suspeciously bright.

Sadayi had taken over for Logan, finishing the birthing process while Logan poured water from the pitcher into the bowl and plunged his hands in to clean them.

There were so many emotions freely spiraling about the room that Rachel felt dizzy. They seemed to all assault her at once. The joy, the exuberance, the gratitude . . . the fear.

Rachel's eyes tore to Logan standing near the foot of the bed, staring down at Caroline. The fear was coming from him, and Rachel could sense that it was fear for Caroline.

But she'd delivered the child, with a great deal of effort, true, but surely now that she could rest all would be well. Except that as Rachel let her gaze stray back to the new mother, she could see the pallor of Caroline's skin. Her eyelids drifted shut. Now that she'd finished her task, the spurt of energy dissipated like a mist before the summer sun.

She was going to die.

Rachel had no doubt it would happen . . . was happening.

Unless . . .

Crouching down, her lips mere inches from Caroline's ear, Rachel began to talk. At first they were just words like she murmured earlier. Encouragement. And then it was as if it wasn't her talking at all, as someone or something else took control of her tongue.

"It is not your time," her mouth said, repeating

the words spoken to her. "You are to stay here and take care of your family. Your children need you. The newborn child needs you. Your husband needs you. Do you hear me, Caroline? You must come back. You must stay here on earth."

Rachel didn't notice the three sets of eyes staring in wonderment at her. It was only Caroline's she saw as the young woman opened her eyes. Her lips were dry, but her smile angelic when their gazes met.

Then Caroline was twisting her head, searching for her husband and the tense moment seemed forgotten. Except that Rachel felt as if she'd been wrung out like the shirts she tried to wash for Logan. Without another word she pushed to her feet and rushed from the room, then the house. She didn't know where she was going, but she had to get away.

There was a hill beyond the clearing in front of the house, and Rachel headed that way, breaking off the path and rushing into the shadowy curtain of trees. Fallen leaves crunched beneath her feet as she ran. Her breathing came in gasps and her hands fought at the limbs and tangling branches that seemed to claw at her gown, pull at her hair.

It wasn't until she reached an open meadow that she stopped, bending forward in exhaustion before dropping to her knees.

"What in the hell was that all about?"

At the sound of his voice Rachel jerked around. She hadn't heard anyone follow.

Logan came forward, his expression the antithesis of his sharp words. When he dropped down beside her, his arms came around her shoulders. His embrace seemed as natural as the way her head fell toward his shoulder.

"Why did you run away, Rachel?" His long fingers sifted leaves and twigs from her hair. "Didn't you hear me calling you?"

She could only shake her head.

"I was, you know." He lifted her chin with his thumb, smiling down into her upturned face. "Is it because you are afraid for Caroline?"

"She will live. I know that." Rachel twisted away from his hold even though staying there close to him, staring into his beautiful green eyes, was all she desired.

Perhaps this was the time to tell him again that she was not from this realm. He might believe her if she explained why she'd run . . . what she knew. But she couldn't. It was he who deserved the credit for saving Caroline's life. He who had fought his own demons and helped the babe enter the world.

Scrubbing the tears from her cheeks, Rachel told him as much. "I was so proud of you." She sat in a puddle of petticoats and skirt, reaching out for his hands to pull him down beside her. "You should do more than read your great books, you know. I think you would be a wonderful surgeon. Perhaps I could even secure you a post. Queen Charlotte keeps one close by at all times to watch over the heir—"

Rachel's mouth clamped shut. When would she remember to stop talking of her other life? As soon as she mentioned the queen, his expression turned from pleasure to disbelief . . . and sorrow.

She'd only wanted to show him what she could do. What he could be.

"Are you ready to go back now?" Logan pushed to his feet, offering Rachel his hand. With a sigh she took it. But when he pulled her up she slipped, falling forward, stopping only when her stomach flattened against the broad expanse of his chest.

They stood there a moment, hearts pounding in unison, gazes locked before Logan lowered his head. The kiss was all the sweeter for the anticipation.

What started as nearly chaste ignited, exploding over them like a firestorm. His arms swept around her, drawing her even closer. His mouth opened, consuming hers. Their tongues mated, dancing in the age-old ritual of desire.

Rachel clutched at his homespun shirt, feeling the corded muscle and sinew beneath. Reveling in the power of him, the raw masculinity. She wanted them gone. His clothes. Her clothes. She wanted to know again the magical joy of making love with him.

And Logan felt need and want. Such a burning want. It was all he could do to tear his lips from hers when he heard her name called.

"What is it?" Rachel asked. She looked as dazed as he felt.

"Sadayi. She must be looking for you."

"Oh no," Rachel said, her expression stricken. "You don't think something has gone awry with Caroline?"

Before he could answer Rachel was running back, leaving him to follow.

By early evening it seemed evident that Caroline was recovering. She leaned against a bolster of pillows smiling at her children as they viewed their baby sister for the first time.

"Rachel told us it was a girl, just as pretty as me," Mary said with pride. "Didn't you?" She glanced back toward Rachel who stood beside Logan near the hearth.

"I did," she agreed, smiling down at the little girl. It was Mary who had asked Sadayi to find her earlier. Who had interrupted Rachel and Logan. Rachel had forgotten all about her promise to visit the children and read to them. When Rachel hadn't come for so

long the children feared the worse. Rachel was glad
she could prove to them that she hadn't come from
heaven to fetch their mother.

"Well, she certainly has your smile, Mary." Caroline glanced toward her son. "And your eyes, Kalanu.
Don't you agree, Rachel?"

The only real glimpse she had of the baby was
immediately after her birth, when she appeared to
look like no one in particular. Even now Rachel
doubted she did, but dutifully moved to join the children as they peered into the carved cradle beside the
bed. As Rachel bent over, the baby let out a howl.

"I think she must want her mother," Wolf said
with a smile meant just for Caroline.

"Would you hand her to me please, Rachel?"

A simple enough request certainly, but for Rachel
who never held a baby in her life, and who seemed
to have some difficulty with everyday tasks. . . . So, it
was with a bit of trepidation that she scooped up the
child, blankets and all. It didn't help that the child
seemed to cry even louder.

But then all of a sudden she stopped. Her little
mouth closed to form a rosebud and her eyes tried
to focus. And Rachel almost dropped her.

"Elizabeth . . . Liz. It *is* you."

"Rachel?"

She was aware of Logan coming up behind her,
his arm curving down beneath the bundle of baby
and blanket. Summoning all her faculties, Rachel
tried to concentrate on what she was doing. But there
was no denying that this child had her friend's . . .
What? Spirit? Soul?

Rachel wasn't sure. But she did know it was there.

Of course the two looked nothing alike. Liz had
hair as dark as Logan's, while the child had only a
fuzzy cap of red hair. There was nothing about them
alike . . . yet they were.

She didn't know how long she was staring at the baby, communicating how happy she was to see her again, but when Caroline finally spoke, Rachel realized it had been awhile.

"What a perfect name, don't you agree, Wolf? Elizabeth." Caroline smiled when he nodded. "And we shall call her Liz, just as you did Rachel. How very perfect."

Perfect.

Rachel sat in her room later that night. She couldn't sleep, though her eyes felt gritty from lack of rest. Perfect, Caroline had said. Yet nothing was perfect.

She had saved Caroline's life . . . at least she had tried, yet she was still here. Of course, it wasn't Caroline she was sent to save. It was Logan.

But he seemed in no need of her.

And the rebirth of Liz reminded her of her need. Her need to return to her own life. To tell everyone of what Lord Bingham had done to his wife. To demand justice.

But she seemed as far from that goal as when she appeared on Logan's mountain over a month ago.

And the longer it went, the more difficult it would be to leave. Footfalls sounded in the hallway. Her heart beat faster as they paused before her door. She stood and walked forward cautiously, lifting her hand to the latch just as he opened the door.

Chapter Fifteen

"A guardian angel o'er his life presiding,
Doubling his pleasures, and his cares dividing."
—Samuel Rogers
"Human Life"

"You don't seem surprised to see me." Logan stepped into the room, closing the door behind him. His gaze drifted down her gown, his brow arching.

"I can't sleep either."

He merely nodded, appearing to accept her explanation of why he came. But there was more, much more . . . and they both knew it. The reasons simmered beneath the surface as she poked at the fire, sparking it to life before adding another log.

Rachel straightened, brushing bits of bark from her hands. "I'd offer you tea." Her head inclined toward the cup that sat on the chest of drawers. "But I fear 'tis cold as ice."

He shrugged his broad shoulders, then walked stiffly toward the fire, extending his hands toward the flames to warm them. "You've learned to build a good fire."

"Thank you." She stood primly to the side, watching him, wondering when he would reach for her. Unlike her, he seemed to have tried to rest. His hunting shirt hung open at the neck, revealing a *V* of curling black chest hair. The queue that tamed his long locks was gone. He looked unkempt and savage with a stubble of beard shadowing his jaw, and a smoldering desire lighting his eyes.

He stared at her, and Rachel wasn't sure if she knew of his needs because she was in touch with his thoughts or because they so closely mirrored her own. Yet when he wanted to reach for her, it was a question he posed instead.

"Why did you call the babe Liz?"

With a sigh Rachel settled into one of the winged chairs. " 'Tis a perfectly acceptable name."

"Aye. 'Tis also the name of your friend. The one you told me died when . . ."

"When I did?" Rachel cocked her head to the side in time to see his expression grow grim. "Did you think I'd forgotten?"

"Forgotten? Nay." He wanted to yell his frustration at her but feared waking the house . . . or not being able to stop once he began.

"I'm not insane, Logan. 'Tis what you think, I know."

"How do you know what I think?" His pent-up frustrations were near exploding. He paced the room doing his best to keep as far from her as possible.

"Logan, I—"

"What are you trying to do to me? I was perfectly content on my mountain till you came along." He speared fingers through his hair. "Hell, we both know that's not true." He looked at her then. "I drank too much . . . still want to at times. Like today." His gaze lowered. "I wanted . . ."

"But you didn't." Rachel stood. "And look at the marvelous thing you did because you were not hindered by drink. You saved Caroline's life, and her baby."

His long dark lashes lifted, revealing a stare that made Rachel's blood heat. " 'Tis not my only weakness."

She took a step toward him. Then another. "I think we share the weakness of which you speak." His skin was hot when she touched him. "And I'm not certain it isn't a strength."

Rachel was in his arms before she could say another word.

The kiss they shared was openmouthed and hungry. When his lips moved down her jaw, then rasped lower to the soft hollow of skin beneath her ear, his voice vibrated through her.

"I want you so much. I always want you."

She knew. Oh, how she knew. It was exactly how she felt. Rachel sighed as he scooped her into his strong arms. The room was small, the bed mere steps from where they stood, and he covered the space quickly. The rope springs groaned as he followed her down onto the mattress.

For a moment they lay there, side by side, bodies molded, eyes searching.

Then his hand lifted to brush a wisp of golden hair from her cheek. Such large hands, Rachel thought. Strong and callused, yet capable of the gentlest of touches. Of bringing a babe forth from a woman's womb.

A harsh stab of reality pierced the sensual haze of his stroke, for now his fingers drifted down the curve of her jaw. She would never know the joy of having him deliver her child. Of carrying his.

Some day she would return to her world. Never to see him again. Never to feel his touch again.

Rachel twisted her head, grabbing his strong wrist and and pressing a kiss into his palm. "Make love to me," she mouthed against his flesh. Then shifting her head on the pillow, begging him with her eyes, she asked again. "Make love to me."

There was no way he couldn't make love to her. Logan swallowed, tamping down the primal desire to tear at her clothing and his own. To mount her and take her; thrust himself into her soft flesh and let oblivion wash over him.

He made himself move slowly. A tender kiss. An angel wing caress. His hands trembled as he traced the petal softness of her neck.

The gown was plain but pretty, the narrow ruffle of her borrowed shift framing a modest display of gently mounded breasts. When Logan lowered his head, brushing his lips against her warmth she bucked toward him. Her fingers wove through his hair, cupping his scalp and drawing him closer. She smelled of heather and roses and the clean musky scent of the forest. Everything he'd ever loved or held dear. He rubbed his nose across her skin, breathing in her fragrance, tasting her.

His tongue dipped lower into the valley between her breasts and she moaned, a sound that seemed to come from deep within her soul.

"Oh Logan. Please. Please."

Her siren song plea broke through his resolve. Bundling Rachel to him his lips found hers, molding seamlessly together. Her mouth opened, offering Logan a tantalizing taste. The kiss deepened, his tongue probing all the secret, honeyed recesses, mating with hers.

And all the time their bodies wriggled, pressing closer, legs tangling with skirts and petticoats, striving for intimacy. Even through the layers of cotton Rachel could feel him hard and demanding.

Then he was above her, his hand driving up beneath her skirts. Rachel's legs spread and he sank down between them, sliding the layers of lace ever higher.

When his palm covered the nest of tight curls covering her womanhood Rachel gasped, pushing herself more firmly into the cup of his hand. His breathing was harsh, as was hers, as he tightened his grip. Pressing.

His face, shadowed by the curtain of dark hair, looked harsh in the light thrown off by the undulating flames dancing in the hearth. The skin was drawn tight across his sculpted cheekbones and his nostrils flared. He watched her, his green eyes searing, as she watched him. Anticipating.

Then slowly his finger curved, sliding sensually over the pearled nub of sensation, then deeper into her body. Rachel turned her head, muffling a cry into the heel of her palm.

Her arms flailed out, then reached up to find him . . . to touch him as he continued to work his magic. And then he pulled away. Rachel nearly followed him up but he reached down, sifting his fingers through the tight curls with one hand, tauntingly skimming down the dewy folds of her. The other hand yanked up his loincloth, uncovering his manhood. He was strong and thick, throbbing, and Rachel stared up at him, kneeling above her in all his savage power. Leggings still covered his muscled thighs, a loose-fitting shirt, most of his chest.

"Open for me, Rachel."

His words sang through her blood and she could do nothing else. Her legs spread further as he ran one finger tantalizingly from knee to inner thigh. Rachel moaned again, arching her hips to give him all of her.

And then he was thrusting inside, filling her completely. Driving. His hands lifted her bottom, sending her crashing over the edge of a great chasm. It was the same as before.

Another peek at heaven.

Rachel couldn't stop trembling. Her body seemed to milk his, sucking him in further as his hips gyrated against hers. Out of control.

His weight folded her deeper into the cornhusk mattress, His head slid down on the pillow beside hers and his chest crushed over her tingling breasts.

He was still inside her. She could feel the hot, hot pressure of him. Her heart pounded, her breathing rasped and she felt wonderful. How long they lay like that Rachel wasn't sure.

When he finally rolled away she gave a small whimper which he answered with a kiss. Then they were lying side by side. Rachel glanced toward him. His chest rose and fell with each ragged breath but she could see little of his expression. One muscled arm was thrown over his face. But then she didn't need to see him to know his thoughts.

"Please don't leave."

" 'Tis hardly where I should be found in the morn."

True enough, but not the real reason he wished to bolt from the bed. "You didn't take advantage of me, Logan. I wanted you as much . . . as desperately as you desired me."

He let out a long breath. "I doubt that possible." He shifted then, his arm lowering enough to leer sheepishly over his sleeve at her. Rachel rolled toward him, muffling her laugh in his shoulder.

"Next time perhaps we should lay wagers on it."

Of course she only meant her words as a jest, but they reminded him of what he did by coming to her room. Rachel could feel him withdrawing, though he didn't move a muscle. She wanted to gather him to her bosom and keep him close. To keep his heart open to her.

"Tell me about Mary."

He said nothing, only jerked his head around, glancing at her with questioning eyes before looking away.

"Caroline was very fond of her," Rachel prompted.

"They were friends."

"And Wolf? Was he her friend, too?"

"Aye. 'Twas difficult not to like Mary."

"I wish I could have known her."

"You're very different from her." Logan lowered his arm. "Perhaps that didn't sound as complimentary as it should."

"I know what you meant." At least she thought she did. When it came to Logan's feelings for his dead wife, Rachel could barely shift through the layers of emotions. He shut her out from the truth. And with an insight new to her, Rachel wondered if that was because the truth was locked so deeply inside him, that even he didn't know it. Or didn't want to accept it.

He wanted to leave . . . the bed . . . her. Rachel could feel his intentions so strongly that when he wrapped an arm around her shoulders, drawing her against his hard body, she was surprised.

"I care about you, Rachel."

The words filled her with warmth. If only she couldn't read his thoughts. Not that he lied. It was simply that he failed to tell her all.

He cared.

He desired.

He worried.

He feared her insane.

"I'm not, you know."

"Not what?" He tucked his chin to glance down into her upturned face.

" 'Tis of no matter." Rachel lifted her hand to touch his cheek. It was rough with stubble though she'd noticed he shaved before supper. She loved the feel of his warm flesh . . . wished she could simply luxuriate in him. With a sigh she prepared for him to pull away. "Why do you blame yourself for Mary's death?"

Even knowing it would happen, his withdrawal left Rachel bereft. "What makes you think I do?" Logan rolled to sitting, pushing his legs over the side of the bed. His elbows rested on his knees, his bent head in his palms.

It was all Rachel could bear not to wrap herself around his strong back. She lay still, watching him breathe. "It was the Cherokee. Caroline told me. It wasn't your fault."

"I should have been here."

"There was nothing you could do."

"Damnit, Rachel, we're speaking of my wife and child. Do you think Wolf would leave his family in danger?" He swung his head around but Rachel couldn't see his face in the shadowy camouflage of dark hair.

"You didn't know of the danger when you left to join the militia. The fighting was to the north. The Cherokee were considered allies." She paused. "And you didn't know of the child."

Now she could see his expression and almost wished she couldn't. "I see you've been talking with Caroline."

Rachel pushed to sitting, swiping a tumble of golden hair out of her face. "Yes, I have." Her chin notched up and she met his stare, hers defiant. "She told me everything."

"Then what do you want from me?"

"I want you to see, for heaven's sake, that this was not your fault. There's no need for you to carry this . . . this guilt inside you." Rachel realized her voice rose dangerously close to shouting and lowered it on the last word. She also let loose of the shirtsleeve she clutched.

He seemed unaffected by the outburst. "Did she also tell you that Mary asked me not to leave? That she wept, throwing herself into my arms and pleaded with me to stay or take her along. That I scoffed at her pleas telling her it was better this way. That the life of a camp follower was harsh."

"As it is, I'm sure."

He shook his head, his smile mirthless. "You still don't understand, do you?"

"I'm trying to." Rachel reached out to him with her heart.

"I didn't want her with me. Because I didn't love her." His words were filled with self-loathing. "She was sweetness and purity and 'twas not a soul who met her who didn't love her . . . except her husband." He sucked in his breath. "And because I selfishly left her behind, she's dead."

Before she could say anything Logan was on his feet. Straightening his loincloth as he went, he crossed the room. When he closed the door behind him, Rachel flopped back onto the pillow.

Why had she pushed him? There were obviously things he didn't want to admit . . . even to himself. Yet for some reason she kept forcing, chipping away at his protective wall as one might pick at a crusted-over wound. And for what reason? So it could bleed again?

Closing her eyes, Rachel took a deep breath. He didn't want to talk of his dead wife, or think of her. He wanted to forget. And she was supposed to be saving his life. Not make it miserable.

Just save his life.

It sounded so simple. But she was no closer now

to completing her task than when she first dropped onto his mountain. No closer to returning to her own life.

All she did was make him despise her. And though Rachel told herself she shouldn't care, she knew in her heart she did.

"Come in, Logan. I'm awake."

It was three days later and Caroline had improved so that she sat in the rocking chair by the hearth. Baby Liz slept peacefully in the cradle near the bed, her tiny rump sticking up.

Logan couldn't help thinking of his own daughter as he looked in on her. "The lass seems to grow longer every day."

"I know." Caroline's smile was full of pride. She nodded toward the winged chair to her right. "Can you sit with me awhile?"

For a moment, after he settled into the chair, spreading his long legging-clad legs toward the fire, neither spoke. Caroline kept her eyes lowered as she stitched the hem of a small hunting shirt. "For Kalanu," she finally said, holding the fabric up by the shoulders. "He's another of my brood that seems to sprout like a weed. 'Tis an endless task keeping him in clothing that fits."

Despite her words she folded the fabric in her lap, then looked up at him with her full attention. "I've wondered when you would come for a talk."

Logan blinked. "How did you know I would?" Hell, he hadn't even known until he found himself tapping on her bedroom door.

"Call it intuition." She shrugged. "Or perhaps 'tis because I've noticed how restless you are."

"I'm always restless."

"Then it must be the way you look at Rachel that made me think you might need someone to talk to. Where is she by the by?"

"With Kananu and Mary. They're playing with Al-kini. I fear she'll want to take your children with her when she leaves."

Her smile disappeared. "*Are* you leaving? Wolf and I hoped you might spend the winter at least. Or stay always. A third of Seven Pines belongs to you."

"I'd thought to go to Charles Town. To see James for myself."

" 'Tis that the only reason you're going?"

Somewhat surprised Logan glanced up from his study of the briskly burning logs. "Aye." He let out his breath. "Nay. I'd thought perhaps to talk with a physician while I was there."

She leaned forward, resting her fingers on his sleeve. "You aren't ill, are you?"

Logan patted her hand as he shook his head. She was a sweet woman, this wife of his brother. Even the first time he met her, when he was so drunk and torn up with guilt that he could barely stand, he'd thought her lovely. The years had only made her more so.

"Then what?"

"Rachel . . . says things." He leaned back, his head pressed into the chair. "Strange things."

"We've talked." He shifted, meeting her eyes as she continued. "About her . . . past."

"Then you know about the court of King George? And Queen Charlotte's wide mouth? And that the king's brother is enamored of her?

"Enamored of Rachel?" Caroline folded her hands. "She didn't mention that. But then, I don't suppose she would now."

"Now? Caroline, don't you know not a word of this is true? She couldn't possibly be all those things she said."

"Why not? 'Tis it so hard to comprehend that a woman of noble birth would come to the American frontier?" Her laugh was infectious.

"I haven't forgotten who you are, Your Ladyship."

"Was." Caroline patted the cotton of her apron. "Now I am the wife of an Indian agent and the mother of his children." She didn't say how content she was with her life. She didn't have to. Her face shone with it.

"Did Rachel tell you how she came to be on my mountain?"

"No." Caroline rocked back. "I don't believe she did. Is it an interesting story?"

"I haven't the vaguest notion."

"Well, tell me then and I'll decide."

"I don't *know* how she came to be there. One moment I was alone." He snapped his fingers. "The next she was there, pushing me off the edge."

When she said nothing, Logan sat up straighter. "I know what you're thinking. That it's me who's daft. That I'm imagining things because of the drink."

"Logan . . ."

"Don't think I didn't wonder the same thing. I was drunk when she showed up, true."

"I've always worried so about you." Her hand was on his arm again.

"I'm telling you, Caroline, 'twas not the rum. I've given it up . . . or at least I'm trying." Logan paused. "She says she's an angel. An angel come to save me. To save my life." There, he'd said it. He'd told another human being about Rachel, hoping for some sort of logical explanation. Or at least an idea of what he was to do.

That was what he wanted. What he got was an uneasy feeling that he'd betrayed Rachel. As if he'd shared something intimate meant only for the two of them. Even though it was Caroline, sweet, understanding Caroline, that he told, Logan regretted his admission.

Logan pushed out of his chair pacing toward the bed and back, feeling suddenly confined by the four walls. Wishing he were back atop his mountain, a jug of rum by his side.

"Forget I said anything." He faced her and shrugged. "That is if you can forget. As I said, you probably think 'tis me who's daft."

"I think no such thing. Logan, sit down, you're going to wake Liz."

"I better see if Wolf needs any help."

"He doesn't." Caroline reached up toward her brother-in-law. "Or if he does, 'tis not as important as listening to what I have to say. Which sounds very conceited on my part I admit, but do listen."

She took a deep breath when he finally lighted, albeit on the edge of the plaid cushion. "My brother Ned." She paused. "You met him at Fort Prince George, though you may not recall."

"I remember him." Hard drink hadn't washed everything from his mind.

"Good. Anyway, after that he returned to England to school. Later, when he came back to Carolina we spent a great deal of time together, talking. He told me of the gossip from England. Court gossip mostly. I was busy with Kananu and missing Wolf terribly and listening gave me something to occupy myself."

"You needn't apologize for gossiping, Caroline."

"No, I don't suppose I do." She laughed. "But sometimes it does seem a poor use of one's time. Though in this case I might make an exception."

"What are you trying to say?"

"Only that he told me about a Lady Rachel Elliott. Ned did. She was young and golden-haired and there had been a horrific scandal."

"With Rachel?"

"No. I don't recall all the details. I do wish Ned were here. But it was something to do with her parents . . . her mother. She'd run off with her lover I believe. Anyway, Ned said the daughter—Rachel—was the undisputed beauty of the court."

"But what would that woman be doing here . . . ?" Logan shook his head. "She could be anyone. Hell, Rachel could have heard the same stories your brother did."

"Perhaps, but if you want my opinion—"

"What is my wife trying to make you do?" Wolf pushed open the door, filling its frame with his tall body. The smile he gave his wife softened his words. Before she could answer he was across the room, pressing a kiss to her forehead. "How is our new baby daughter this fine day?"

"See for yourself, I hear her stirring." While her husband bent over the cradle, Caroline gave his brother a telling look.

Logan only shrugged.

When Wolf handed his now lustily crying child to her mother, Logan decided to take his leave, promising to think on what Caroline had said.

"What did you tell my brother?" Wolf bent forward to kiss the tip of her nose, then watched as Caroline loosened her shift. The hungry child latched on to her nipple as Wolf traced a line of pale blue veins on her breast.

" 'Twas nothing really." She smiled up at him. "Though I do believe your brother is in love."

Wolf folded his long frame into the seat Logan had used. "With Rachel, I presume."

"Why yes. And you needn't act so smug as if I told you something you already knew."

"Then I will not say it is so."

Caroline cupped Liz's small head, then glanced up to see her husband's sensual smile. "How did you know? Logan said he was but escorting her to Charles Town when they arrived. And they seem to barely speak to one another. How *did* you know."

"Because I have noted the way he looks at her when he thinks no one sees. I know that look well," he explained. "It is the way my eyes caress you."

Heat spread through her like sun-warmed honey. It was true what he said. Caroline felt Wolf's love every time he glanced her way. When she reached out her hand to him he left his seat, moving forward and kneeling in front of her.

"I do not think I could have lived had you died." His hands hugged her thighs while his head dropped to her lap.

Caroline choked down a sob. One hand fell to his head and she wove her fingers through the rough silk texture of his black hair. "You would survive Wolf because you are a strong man. Because your people need you. Our children need you."

His face lifted. "Do not ever leave me."

"I will be with you always, Wolf. As you are with me."

"What happened to the beautiful princess next, Rachel?"

"Oh." Rachel tore her eyes away from Logan and focused back on Mary. She was sitting in the parlor telling the children a story when she glanced up to see Logan watching her.

How long he'd been there she didn't know, but his presence was flustering. Especially when he'd done his best to make certain their paths didn't cross since the night they made love.

"Let me see. Oh, yes, she lived happily ever after."

"But you said she was given the task of saving the mean old giant's life. Did she do it?"

Rachel didn't dare look up at Logan. Leave it to Kananu to recall that her story had stopped suddenly and to remember what she had said. Rachel shot the boy an exasperated glance. He sat on the floor at her feet, Henry cuddled at his side while his younger sister wriggled into her seat of honor on Rachel's lap.

"Don't you remember, Rachel?" Mary piped in.

"Of course I do." She tried not to notice as Logan walked into the room, seating himself on one of the straight chairs by the window. "She saved his life when he . . . he fell into the creek. You see, the giant couldn't swim. He simply floundered about, unable to save himself, till the princess—"

"The beautiful Princess," Mary reminded.

"Yes, the beautiful Princess threw herself into the raging water."

"I thought perhaps she might toss him a rope."

Rachel did look at Logan when he spoke. Her lips thinned. "No, she dove into the rushing torrent."

"It would appear the Princess is brave as well as beautiful."

"She is."

Mary's head was turning from side to side as she tried to follow the conversation between Logan and Rachel. "Do you know this story too, Uncle Logan?"

"He thinks he does, Mary." Rachel smiled down at the child. "But he doesn't."

"Why don't you know it Uncle Logan?"

"Actually, I know more than the Princess gives me credit for."

"Who's the Princess?" Her dark eyes looked from one to the other.

"He means Rachel. You're such a baby."

"Am not."

"Are, too."

"Kananu. Mary. That will be enough," Rachel said firmly. "Perhaps you should both go upstairs for a while. Just don't wake Alkini."

"But you promised to tell us the story about the talking dog."

"And I shall." Rachel ignored Logan's groan. "After you rest for a bit."

"I'm too old for a nap."

"Then Kananu, you may read to your sister until she falls asleep."

After the children left the parlor, Logan stood. "Talking dogs, Your Highness. I thought you had more sense than to tell that to those children."

"They were stories, Logan."

"As I've known from the beginning."

Pushing from her chair Rachel strode to the door, pausing only when he called her Your Highness again. She whirled around. "I told you I am not a princess."

"Nevertheless, we are leaving in two days for Charles Town."

Chapter Sixteen

"As soon as you trust yourself you will know how to live."

—Johann Wolfgang von Goethe

She neither knew how to saddle a horse . . . or showed any inclination to learn.

Logan didn't know why that should surprise him. Getting any labor from her was a struggle from the start. She simply assumed someone else would do it for her.

Hardly the type of woman he would choose for a wife . . . even if he wished for one. Which he most certainly did not. Except . . . what was he going to do with her?

He glanced toward her as they rode along the path leading east from Fort William Henry . . . and caught her studying him, her blue eyes intent. It was morning. The air was cool. Frost still speckled the wild strawberries and yarrow.

"I don't know why you should be angry."

Logan simply arched a dark brow and looked away.

"How was I to know he was a friend of yours?" she persisted, though she knew it better to simply change the subject. Or continue on in silence as they had since leaving the fort.

His head jerked around, spearing her with his sea-green eyes. "What you're not to be doing is accosting everyone who approaches me."

"He had a gun." Rachel lifted her chin. "And I call crushing you in his arms more than simply approaching."

" 'Tis but a typical greeting for Simon."

Rachel sighed. She knew that now. She'd even been subjected to one of the mountain man's hugs after Logan introduced them. Which was after he peeled her off Simon's back. And made some awkward attempt to explain her actions.

Which weren't that outlandish at all, given the circumstances.

Rachel had stepped outside the cabin where she spent the night in time to see a huge blond man with a scar across his face rushing toward Logan. Perhaps if she hadn't been sent to save Logan's life she wouldn't have raced after the man . . . or leaped onto his back when it seemed his embrace could suffocate.

But she had. Rachel took a deep breath, the smell of pine strong, then urged her mount forward, even with his. "It wouldn't be so difficult if you would simply allow me to . . . to . . ."

"To what? Hover over me?" Logan reined in his horse, turning his head to stare at her when the animal sidestepped. "Disrupt my life? It seems you've already done that."

The words were out of his mouth but Logan came close to apologizing when he saw her face. For just a moment the proud woman who insisted she belonged in the king's court was gone. In her place was someone who simply tried to do the best she could. Someone who didn't realize how ill prepared she was to cope.

"We need be on our way," he mumbled, spurring

his horse forward. "Else we won't make the Grubers' cabin by nightfall."

As it happened they were far from the small settlement of Anderson Gap when the dusk of an autumn evening drifted about them. Rachel's horse went lame—at least she insisted the mare's right front hoof was sore. Logan could find nothing wrong when he grudgingly stopped to examine the horse. But the chestnut, after a few words from Rachel, refused to accept a mount.

Which meant they rode double, Rachel perched in front. And since Henry trotted along at his own pace, they rode slow. The result being it was quite late and a cold drizzle had begun to fall before they reached the Grubers' cabin—only to discover the Grubers didn't live there anymore.

"They done moved back to Charles Town, didn't they Pa?" the man who answered Logan's hail said.

The older of the two who stood in the doorway agreed. "That's what we was told."

The son was short and wiry with lank brown hair and pale blue eyes that seemed to bulge out when he stared . . . which Rachel thought he did too much. His father's most distinguishing feature was a mouth completely devoid of teeth. They were both dirty and their cabin made Logan's seem like a palace.

But it was relatively dry and for all their uncouth ways, they seemed to know how to treat a lady. Rachel was given the only chair, the only unchipped dish, and was asked by neither man to lift a finger.

Both father and son seemed starved for conversation and though Logan sat tight-lipped, his back against the side wall, Rachel obliged by answering their questions.

She didn't tell them who she really was. But by the time the stew was washed down with a bit of strong-tasting wine she was sharing anecdotes from her life at court.

"The king is very strict about observing the Sabbath, you know," she said, her voice only slightly slurred. Her head felt a bit muzzy so she took another sip, trying to clear it. "No gaming of any sort. Banned it, he did." The cracked cup came to her lips again. As she took a drink her eyes caught sight of Logan. His scowl grew deeper with each second. He'd pulled his mouth so flat she could see the indentations where his dimples should be.

She wished she could make him smile at her.

Rachel sighed, then took another drink. He was angry because she was telling the truth. He didn't like to hear it. But the two gentlemen . . . what were their names? Oh yes, Oscar and his charming son, Wallace. They believed her.

Putting the cup down, Rachel smiled at her engaged audience. Like Logan they sat on the floor. But they huddled close by her chair, leaning toward her a bit, their homely faces upturned in rapt attention.

One, Oscar, poured more liquid into her cup before she even realized it was empty. They treated her like the lady she was. Like a princess . . . Logan's princess. Rachel took another drink.

"He's very generous, you know. Well, perhaps you don't know, but 'tis true. The king showers Her Majesty with jewels . . . though she doesn't like to wear them much. Can you credit that?" From the corner of her eye, Rachel noticed Logan push to his feet. "Of course, I have stopped wearing mine." Caroline had helped her sew them into a pocket beneath her skirts. Rachel leaned forward toward her subjects. "The diamonds simply didn't seem appropriate on the frontier."

"I think a bit of fresh air might do you good, *wife*."

Rachel began to protest. She didn't want any fresh air, which if she recalled meant cold, wet air. And she certainly wasn't Logan's wife. But he hustled her out of her chair and toward the door so quickly that her head whirled . . . which caused the most unsettling sensation in her stomach.

She was out the door before she could open her mouth.

Which, as it turned out, was a good thing. For when she did, it was to empty her stomach, quite unladylike on the sodden ground.

"Oh . . ." she moaned. "I'm sick."

"You're not sick, Your Highness. You're drunk."

The voice came from very near, and Rachel realized with some embarrassment that she was bent forward and Logan was holding her up. He passed her a handkerchief, made wet from the icy needles of rain, and she used it to wipe her mouth. "Impossible," she mumbled when she could at last stand. "Ladies don't get drunk."

"Well, this one is. Now come on."

Rachel let out a whimper when he pulled on her arm. "I'm ill, I tell you. Don't." Then, "Where are we going?" as she realized he was hustling them away from the cabin.

"We're leaving," was all he said.

"But it's raining and dark." She could barely see her hand in front of her face, let alone him. But she felt his presence as he bent his face down close to hers.

"Listen to me, you little fool. Those men might not believe you part of King George's court but their greedy little eyes lit like torches when you mentioned jewels. And the younger one, hell, both of them, watched you as if you were a tasty morsel they couldn't wait to gobble up."

"Oh! How silly you are. Why those men are my—"

The word subjects died on her lips as the door to the cabin flew open.

Light spilled out, giving an eerie glow to the falling rain.

"Pa and I think ye need to come back inside."

Logan inched his hand back toward the musket he'd slung over his shoulder before dragging Rachel from the cabin until he remembered the wet powder would do no good. He tried to appear relaxed. "My wife insists we start off toward Charles Town tonight." With his left hand he gave her a shove, trying to push her out of the light. She resisted and before he could stop her, stepped toward the doorway.

"Actually, I wish to come in out of the rain."

Logan lunged for her the same time Wallace did. He would have had her, too, if the father hadn't leaped forward. The blade of his hunting knife glistened as it pressed toward her throat.

Logan heard Rachel's gasp; felt his own heart stop.

"Now get yourself in here." By this time the son had produced the ancient musket Logan noticed earlier leaning by the door. The notion struck him that he could probably disappear into the darkness before Wallace could get off a shot, but then he caught a glimpse of Rachel's stricken face as she was dragged inside.

"Come on with ye!" Oscar yelled. But the sound didn't drown out Rachel's fervent plea for Logan to run and save himself.

"Get in here, or I'll take a slice out of yer woman."

When Logan stepped through the doorway she seemed genuinely annoyed that he was there.

"Let her go." Logan tried not to flinch when Wallace shoved the barrel of the musket into his back.

"Now I don't think we will, will we, Pa?"

His father didn't answer. He stood behind Rachel, still holding the knife to her throat, but his free hand

began inching down her chest, his dirty finger juxtaposed grotesquely against her pale wet skin.

"Ye said I could have at her first, Pa," Wallace
complained.

The downward motion of his hand stopped mo-
mentarily. "Shut yer trap. We'll both have our turn.
Now get rid 'a that one."

"No!" Rachel's scream seemed to come from the
depths of her soul. "No, no. Don't kill him. You can't!
I was sent to save him." Tears ran down her face,
mingling with the icy rain. "You can't. I'm an angel.
An angel, do you hear me?"

"She's a mad woman."

Rachel's head twisted toward Logan. "I am not!
How dare you say that! I'm an angel, blast you, Logan
MacQuaid. An angel. Sent from heaven above."

She raised her hands, ignoring the knife held
threateningly close to her neck. Her face lifted toward
the smoke-darkened ceiling as if calling on all the
heavenly hosts. And in that moment, Logan wouldn't
have been surprised if the Lord God Almighty sent
lightning bolts flashing down to smite his enemies.

She was magnificent.

She was believable.

And Logan was not the only one thrown under her
spell.

Oscar stood transformed—Logan had a sudden
vision of him turned to a pillar of salt—his thick-
lipped mouth open, the knife dangling loosely by his
side. His son, too, though still aiming the musket
toward Logan, had eyes that bulged toward Rachel.

"Get down, Your Highness!"

Logan roared the command as he lurched toward
Wallace, chopping the gun from his hand with one
downward sweep of his arm. The musket clattered to
the packed dirt floor. He kicked it away, diving into
Wallace, fighting the overwhelming urge to look

around toward Rachel. Was she still alive or had the knife held so negligently by Oscar sliced through her delicate flesh?

Had his timing been off? Had he committed yet another mistake in a lifetime of them?

Wallace's bony fist connected with his jaw before Logan sent him sprawling, his nose billowing blood. He landed arms spread on top of the rickety table. It collapsed, sending the stub of candle flying into a pile of animal pelts.

Logan whirled around just as Oscar shoved Rachel to the ground. She fell hard, then didn't move, lying like a fallen angel.

Logan forced his eyes from her, though the vision remained, forcing his attention on Oscar, on the man who hurt her. Ignoring the the blade pointed toward him, Logan lunged. The older man croaked out a blast of air when Logan's head plowed into his stomach. He flew backward onto the dirt, Logan on top of him.

With one hand Logan searched for the knife and sucked in his breath when the blade found him instead. Blood poured from the slice in his ribs, but he ignored the pain as he grappled with Oscar.

From the corner of his eye Logan caught movement. Rachel. He saw her moving, groping to her feet. A swift surge of relief flashed through him that she was alive.

"Get the hell out of here!" he ordered.

The heavy smell of smoke, of burning fur, hung in the air. Someone coughed. Was it Rachel? He couldn't be sure. For the wiry man slashed again with the blade. This time Logan caught hold of his arm. Strong fingers manacled his wrist, slamming it toward the packed earth. Oscar gripped the bone-handled knife as if his life depended on it. Rising up, Logan straddled him, jerking the hand up and slapping it down once again . . . as hard as he could. This time the knife slipped from Oscar's limp fingers.

A backhand across the fleshy lips had Oscar begging for mercy. But Logan had none to give. Grabbing handfuls of grimy shirt he hauled him to his feet, jerking him around to face the yawning muzzle of the musket.

Wallace stepped forward, out of a cloud of smoke. "Let my pa go." Blood streamed from his matted hair into one eye. He blinked, lifting his shoulder to wipe it away, but kept the gun steady.

"Give me the musket, Wallace."

Before Logan could do more than shriek out a strangled, "Nay," Rachel issued her command and faced the son. She reached out when he shifted his aim from Logan to her.

"Stay back!" he yelled when she moved closer. "Stay away from me." Wallace's voice quivered.

"It won't do any good to shoot me. I told you I'm an—"

"Rachel, for God's sake."

The barrel jerked back toward Logan when he took a step, dragging the semiconscious father with him.

"Don't move, or I'll shoot. Damn if I won't."

"No you won't, Wallace. For if you do I shall see to it that you go straight to hell."

The bulging eyes, so like his father's, opened wider, and sweat mixed with the blood to flow down his cheek. Around him smoldering furs sent noxious smoke billowing into the air, looking enough like hell to give the threat credibility.

"You know about hell, don't you, Wallace?" Rachel inched closer. "It's burning fire and brimstone and the tortuous pain is constant. And there's no way out. Not for the rest of eternity."

"Shut up."

Logan stood tensed, ready to leap forward, ready

to push her aside. The weight of the father dragged down on his hands and Logan finally realized he still held Oscar up. Releasing the crumpled handhold of shirt the man fell to the floor like a sack of potatoes.

His son didn't seem to notice.

Wisps of smoke twisted up around him, but his eyes were fixed on Rachel. He didn't protest—though Logan did—when she took another step toward him. Then another.

"Rachel." Logan barely whispered the warning, afraid to startle the youth into doing what any true evil-hearted creature would do . . . should do. But even though she stood no more than a hair's breadth from the end of the muzzle, Wallace did not pull the trigger.

He only stared at Rachel, his skin pallid and sweaty, his hands shaking.

Her next step pressed the muzzle into her chest. She reached up, folding her soft, delicate fingers around the rusted iron, and Logan thought his head would explode. Blood pounded in his ears and he knew if he didn't take a breath soon he might pass out.

But he couldn't.

Not until Wallace let loose of the stock and wilted into a puddle of slobbering tears at Rachel's feet. He clung to her skirts wailing and blubbering about eternal damnation and repenting his list of myriad sins, some of which Logan was certain Rachel couldn't even begin to understand.

Logan leaped forward, snatching the musket, then feeling a bit foolish for his action. It was obvious the pitiful creature kneeling in the dirt had no use for it. He continued to clutch at Rachel, his dirty hands groping at her hem, but when Logan bent to drag him off her, she stayed him with a look.

"It's all right," she said, even deigning to let her

hand flutter to graze the greasy and no doubt vermin-infected head. Logan could only gape, his mouth open in disbelief as the force of Wallace's wailing diminished.

"Logan." Rachel said his name twice before his gaze met hers. She coughed, then wiped her streaming eyes. "Those furs are putting out a good bit of smoke. Do you suppose you could do something?"

"Oh, aye." He felt foolish for not thinking of it before. Now, as quickly as he could . . . and still keeping a wary eye on Wallace, he jerked open the door, barely sidestepping Henry as he bounded into the cabin. The dog was soaked, his black and white fur matted and he appeared primed for action, his teeth bared, a low growl rumbling through his body. Henry skidded to a stop. Seemed to assess the situation, then to Logan's amazement trotted toward the hearth and, after turning about a few times to pick his spot, plopped down.

Logan dragged the smoldering pelts out into the rain, leaving the door open to air out the cabin. In the small barn he found enough rope to tie father and son and hurried back to Rachel. He found her hunched over, adding more split wood to the fire. She glanced around and smiled and Logan felt warm inside, despite the icy rain that soaked through his clothing.

He blinked, then let out his breath, relieved to see the radiant circlet he thought he saw hovering above her head was gone. A trick of the freshly caught flames, he assured himself.

The woman wasn't really an angel.

Angels didn't exist. At least not in Logan Mac-Quaid's life.

Besides, if he hadn't believed in her madness before, this incident proved it. Logan's blood ran cold when he thought of her facing down an armed man.

A crazed armed man. Hell, if she didn't belong in Bedlam, he didn't know who did.

And to make matters worse, it was obvious she believed every word she told the man who still sat huddled and sniveling on the floor.

Logan jerked Wallace to his feet, receiving no resistance at all. He made no attempt to be gentle as he twisted Wallace's hands behind his back. When he was securely tied, Logan did the same to his father who, sputtering, was regaining consciousness. Without a word, Logan dragged both men from the cabin.

When he returned the cabin was aired out enough to shut the door. Rachel had found a piece of toweling and was leaning toward the hearth calmly drying her hair. Golden curls escaped from the linen, shimmering in the oscillating light when she turned toward him.

"What did you do with them?"

"They're tied in the barn . . . which is better than they deserve," he said defiantly.

"I suppose you're right." Rachel sighed. "I do feel a bit sorry for Wallace though."

"Because he was feebleminded enough to swallow your angel story?"

Her eyes narrowed and she shot him a harsh look before turning back to her task. At that moment she appeared anything but angelic. But that didn't keep Logan from regretting his words. She merely shrugged when he apologized.

" 'Tis of no matter. I do feel that Wallace was truly remorseful, though."

"Perhaps." Logan moved to the hearth more drawn by her than the roaring fire. "But only after you reminded him of the rewards the devil had waiting for him." Logan couldn't help it. A grin deepened his dimples. "Did you see his face when you spoke of the fire and brimstone?"

Rachel giggled, slanting him a look from under her lashes. "It was rather wan, wasn't it?"

"Aye, 'tis a wonder he didn't drop over dead right then and there."

Rachel nodded, then tossed her hair back over her shoulder. "I think I shall put in a good word for him."

Logan turned to warm his backside. "I doubt the authorities in Charles Town will care to do anything about father and son one way or the other."

"Oh, I didn't mean here." Rachel considered keeping the rest of her thought to herself. It wasn't as if she didn't know how annoyed he would be. But then she wasn't too pleased with his comment about feeble-minded Wallace believing her an angel. Rachel met his eyes, a guileless expression on her face. "I meant when I return to heaven."

What in the hell was wrong with him that he kept forgetting how daft she was? How many times did the fact have to slap him in the face before he accepted it? Was he so blinded by a comely face and form that he couldn't recall the lessons of his mother?

Illnesses of the mind were something he knew not how to handle. It wasn't like a fever or inflammation. No amount of purging or bloodletting would heal it.

Logan glanced at her as she dipped a cloth into the kettle of warm water. She insisted upon tending his wound, though he insisted it 'twas nothing. She smiled as she came toward him. Beautiful and serene. How very deceptive.

He closed his eyes as she bent toward him. Moments before he stripped out of his shirt and now she made a soft soothing sound with her mouth as she touched the cloth to his wound.

" 'Tis a wonder he didn't gut you, given the size of his knife."

"I dare say he tried. But as I said before 'tis but a flesh wound. The bleeding is already stopped."

She leaned down, a lock of her hair whispering across his belly and Logan sucked in his breath. His flesh quivered, and beneath his loincloth the proof of his desire thrust forward.

"Does that pain you over much?" Her eyes were very blue when she gazed up at him.

"Nay." He couldn't feel the cut at all. And when she looked at him like that the part of his mind that knew her insane couldn't seem to function.

He only knew how smooth her skin was, like fine porcelain. And her spun gold hair. And the scent of her, soft and wild as the heather growing on the hills. She drew him with all his senses. He wanted her. And as she stared into his eyes he knew the same carnal need that strummed through him, wove invisible threads about her.

Her fingers stilled as Logan's gaze lowered to her mouth. Her lips were soft and pink and as he watched, her tongue peeked out to moisten them. Logan nearly moaned.

His hands seemed to reach up, cupping her shoulders of their own accord. He pulled her toward him, wanting . . . needing . . . to taste those trembling lips. She came willingly, draping across his thighs as he sat on the side of the bed.

"Logan." Her breath drifted over him.

The force of his kiss had her melding against him. Her arms wove about his neck, her fingers tangling with his hair. Logan's tongue filled her mouth, thrusting and retreating with long, silken strokes.

He rolled them over without breaking the seal of their lips, no mean feat considering he was also reaching beneath her petticoats, searching for the velvet-smooth skin of her thighs.

She moaned when his fingers followed the curve of her leg, found the sensitive flesh beyond her thigh. He rubbed in circles, teasing at first, then, as if he could not control himself any longer, with more pressure.

"Oh, Logan, please."

Rachel groaned as he pulled away. Her body hummed, so close to that special place, that special feeling. He loomed above her, balancing his weight on outstretched arms, watching her, his skin stretched taut across his cheekbones. Her breasts raised and lowered, with each ragged breath she took. "Come back to me," she wanted to say. But before he could he was pulling her over, turning them both so that she straddled him.

Now it was she who loomed above him. Ruffles and silk were thrust aside as ruthlessly as his loincloth. And then his manhood, steel swathed in satin, penetrated the dewy lips of her sex. He held her, his large hands gripping her hips beneath the layers of frothy lace, controlling her, keeping her from sliding down the long, hard length of him.

Then he let her go and with one deep thrust had her gasping for breath. Rachel's head lolled back, her hair streaming around her shoulders as he arched his hips, sending his staff deeper. Her knees tightened, his fingers dug into her buttocks and the rhythm increased, the tension growing higher . . . higher.

She could feel him straining inside her, feel the pressure as he grew, expanded with each powerful thrust. He was a part of her, and she of him. She was so akin to him she knew not where his pleasure ended and hers began. They knew the soaring, spiraling rapture as one.

His thoughts were only of her, of the pleasure she gave him, as hers were flooded with him. It was all they knew. The cabin, the rough bedstead, the world outside themselves disappeared, leaving only the two of them. The one entity they'd become.

Their bodies moved now without thought, ruled by sensation. By the need to share the most intimate of ecstasies. Rachel plunged and writhed. Logan thrust deep, spinning them both out of control.

Whirling them off toward the heavens.

She fell asleep almost at once, nestled in the co-cooning embrace of his arms. But Logan could not. He was tired and spent and the slash across his ribs was beginning to smart. But slumber was beyond him.

The woman he cradled was warm and inviting and he cared for her . . . more than he ever had any woman. More than he wished to admit.

But she needed help, protection, which he obviously couldn't provide. She thought she was an angel. She thought she was sent to save him. And because of that, she was dangerous . . . to others . . . to herself. Because of him, she almost was killed.

His arms tightened and she sighed, mumbling in her sleep. He had to do something with her. And soon. He had no doubt of that now.

The only question was what.

Chapter Seventeen

"Angels are spirits, but it is not because they are spirits that they are angels. They become angels when they are sent."

—Saint Augustine

The city had changed since he was last in Charles Town.

Logan leaned forward, patting his horse's sleek neck, wondering if the animal felt as skittish as he did surrounded by all these people. Not that the hustle and bustle really bothered him. It had just been so long.

He didn't realize how . . . content wasn't the word. How settled into his life in the mountains he'd become. How much he'd divorced himself from everything, from everyone.

At the time, those years on the mountain, he hadn't thought of himself as lonely . . . simply alone. He told himself it was best that way. Because of his father. Because of Mary. Because of the drink. He had needed solitude. The mountain was his sanctuary.

A sign swung overhead, caught in the breeze drifting off the bay, and Logan read the ornately painted lettering. THE SIGN OF BACCHUS.

He was tired, and hungry. And the thought of a

soothing mug of rum was tempting. With a squeeze
of his thighs, Logan urged the stallion forward.

Glancing around to see if Rachel was as awed as
he by the people and activity, Logan stared. She sat
on her horse, her back straight, her head high, that
arrogant little chin lifted just enough to make her
appear a princess. Even though she wore a borrowed
gown and a cape made of patched-together buckskin,
she looked regal. Which was a silly thing to think.

But then no sillier than the sensation he felt in the
pit of his stomach when she caught his eyes on her
and smiled.

"Do you know where your brother lives?" she
asked, sidling her horse closer to his. They were on
Queen Street, near the New Theater, and all around
them the sounds of sawing and hammering filled the
humid air.

"Aye, but Wolf seemed to think it more likely to
find him on his wharf this time of day." Which was
where they were heading. Logan still had trouble
believing the brother he idolized as a lad was really
alive. He could remember so vividly, almost as if it
was happening now, how he felt when his father told
him of James's death.

He was in the library of MacQuaid House . . . to
his father's everlasting displeasure, Logan's favorite
room in the drafty old structure. He often thanked
Providence that though his father cared little for the
written word, some faceless ancestor did. The paneled
room was lined with leather-bound volumes covering
such diverse topics as husbandry and ancient poetry.

But Logan's favorite reading centered on philoso-
phy and studies of the mind. Books such as Descartes's
Les Passions de l'Ame and Berkeley's *New Theory of Vision*
along with an occasional foray into a medical book
kept him occupied for hours. He was contemplating

Hobbes's theory that all action is preceded by thought or idea when his father stormed into the room.

Guiltily Logan slammed the book shut, sending a cloud of dust motes dancing in the stream of sunshine pouring through the mullioned window. But for once Robert MacQuaid didn't appear to notice his son's choice of reading material or his unease. He simply strode to the mantel, slapping his palm rhythmically with a riding quirt.

Logan tried not to flinch as the hard leather snapped against his father's palm . . . tried not to remember the feel of it against his own flesh. His father stood a moment staring into the flames, then turned. Logan wondered if the unhealthy red hue of his father's skin was caused only by the fire's reflection.

"You are heir now," he announced, his tone steeped in disappointment.

At first 'twas that disappointment that wedged its way into Logan's consciousness. At twelve he had already constructed a wall around his emotions where his father was concerned. But it seemed no matter how thick he made it, there was always a tiny crack in the mortar. A crack his father found with unerring accuracy.

James always told him to ignore "the old bastard." "He only needles because he knows 'twill upset ye," his older brother said. But at seventeen James was bigger and stronger, with an outgoing charm, that even Robert found difficult to resist.

Thoughts of his brother brought Logan back to concentrate on his father's words. *You are heir now.*

Logan swallowed, his narrow shoulders stiffening. James left home months ago, inflamed with zeal for the young prince, determined to fight by his side all the way to London to help place him on his rightful throne.

There were rumors the fighting was not going well for the Scots. Logan actually heard very little, for his father had forbidden discussion of the subject in the house. Apolitical himself, a man who aligned himself with the winning side whenever possible, Robert's anger with James knew no bounds.

Yet Logan could not believe even Robert would disown the son he usually considered a worthy heir . . . especially compared to his bookish second offspring.

Stepping forward, steeling himself for the older man's anger, Logan cleared his throat. "I don't understand, sir."

By the sharp look Robert tossed his way, 'twas obvious he'd forgotten Logan's presence. His lips thinned. "He was hanged."

"James?" Logan felt bile rise in his throat. "Not James?" Not the brother he loved, the only living soul other than his mother, who cared for him at all. "No." He shook his head as if the very motion could make the words a lie.

But he knew they weren't. His father was raging on about how foolish James was. Of how he'd been warned repeatedly about his actions. Of how the entire family would suffer for his selfishness.

"He isn't selfish," Logan lashed out. "He believed in the cause of the rightful heir and he fought for it. James is a hero!" Logan had begged James to take him along, to let him know too the joy of doing something brave and wonderful. To be like his brother. But James refused, slapping him on the shoulder and promising that next time, when Logan was older, he could go.

Tears stung Logan's eyes, but not from the pain of the quirt slapping across his upper arm. His hand flew up, an involuntary reaction to his father's whipping.

"Never! Do you hear me? Never are you to mention

his name again." Another swat with the leather. "He was not a hero. He died a coward. Aye, a coward's death."

The blows were steady now, but Logan didn't seem to notice. He simply stared straight ahead and thought of his tall, dashing brother riding at the head of a glorious army.

"Logan. Logan, are you all right?"

The touch of a hand, soft and gentle, on his sleeve made Logan twist his head to the side. Rachel stared at him, her expression bewildered.

"Is this the right wharf or not?" She tilted her head in that way she had of looking indifferent. The touch of her fingers as they slid down to his hand showed that stance false.

Logan took a deep breath, trying to wash away the ghosts of the past—he hadn't allowed himself to think of that day for years—and glanced around him. They had reached the Cooper River. The smell of salt and pluff mud mingled with tar and pitch. The forest of masts they'd spied from a distance now loomed before them, bobbing schooners and brigs lining the wharves.

The sounds of building were evident here, too, and it was obvious some of the large warehouses lining the quay were new, their wood sides freshly painted. Over the door of the one to their right, the largest in the immediate area, were the words "MacQuaid Shipping and Transport."

" 'Tis just where Wolf said 'twould be," Logan said as he dismounted.

When he reached up to help Rachel from her side-saddle she eyed him curiously. "I would have sworn you didn't know where you were headed by the look on your face. You appeared to be a thousand miles away."

Her hands on his shoulders, she slipped down in

front of him. Logan was tempted to ignore her comment . . . he'd certainly become a man of few words
over the years. And she'd posed no question. But
something in the way she looked at him made him
answer anyway.

"I was thinking of my brother . . . of the day I heard
he died."

"It was terrible for you."

"Aye." His hands still rested on her waist. "More
than I can ever say."

"You don't have to." She knew how he felt about
his brother, how he felt about his death. As they'd
ridden through the streets of Charles Town, Rachel
could tell he was thinking of something; she assumed
it was his brother. After all, in moments he would see
for the first time in over twenty years the brother he
thought was dead.

But it wasn't until he told her as much that his
inner thoughts flowed through her. It was like after
they made love, when they were cuddled close. When
she could feel what he felt, touch his thoughts in
that special way. But they weren't making love. They
weren't even standing any closer than manners dictated. His hands rested lightly at her waist, hers on
his shoulders.

But they were as one.

Rachel took a deep breath. "You can never forget
the past." She shook her head. "Trying to only buries
the pain in a fool's cloak of gossamer threads." Rachel's laugh was self-effacing. "I'm hardly the philoso-
pher, but I do think it true. You must face your
demons before you can defeat them."

It was too much for her.

The piercing quality of his eyes as he stared at her.
The deep forging bond surging between them. His
thoughts were hers, and though he was certainly no

angel, she felt that he shared hers as well. It was intoxicating. It was compelling. It was overpowering.

Rachel had the unsettling feeling this force between them could consume her like the flames of a wild fire if she allowed it.

She was sent to save his life. No more.

Letting her fingers drift down his strong arms, Rachel turned away, to study the building. Anything to quell the near uncontrollable urge to throw herself at him. To profess undying love. For how could she . . . someone already dead . . . declare such a thing?

Toward the river, two large doors were spread wide, allowing a group of blackamoors to unload crates from a wagon. Even though the weather was cool, their faces were shiny with sweat. Logan tied the horses and, offering his arm, headed in that direction.

He was nervous about this meeting. Rachel slanted him a look from beneath her lashes as they walked. They had stayed at a planter's house last night and when Rachel saw Logan this morning she could hardly believe her eyes. His clothing was not fine compared to the court of St. James, but there were no animal skins today.

Logan wore a suit of dark green wool. The breeches molded well over his thighs, and she could attest that no padding was needed to shape the white stockings covering his lower legs. The snowy stock contrasted with his sun-darkened skin and black hair. The breeze caught a lock and he quickly swiped it back into the neat queue.

"You look very handsome." The words were meant to reassure him. But when he twisted his head to stare at her she felt heated color rise to her cheeks. "I only meant . . . I mean in your new clothes. Your brother will be most impressed."

She missed whatever response he might have to

that stumbling explanation—and from one of the wittiest of court belles—for at that moment a man with sun-streaked golden hair stepped from the warehouse onto the quay. Rachel felt Logan's muscles tense through the fabric of his coat.

The man carried a ledger and as each crate was carried inside he made an entry with a stub of a quill.

"Is that him?" There really was no doubt in Rachel's mind. The two men were of the same height and build, and though the color of their hair differed, their eyes were nearly the same, except that Logan's were a purer green.

Rachel hung back, letting her fingers slip from his sleeve as Logan moved forward. He didn't seem to notice. He had taken perhaps half a dozen steps before the other man looked up.

"May I—"

The question seemed to freeze in mid-sentence, as his blue-green eyes narrowed. Rachel let out her breath as he thrust the ledger toward a startled blackamoor and bounded forward, catching Logan in a hug.

When they separated Rachel quickly dabbed at her eyes, but she needn't have worried. Neither man looked her way.

"Wolf told me ye were in the colonies." Jamie held his younger brother at arm's length. "Living in the hills he said, though he didn't know where exactly." His voice sounded breathless. "I had it in my mind to take off and look for ye." He bit his bottom lip and swung an arm around Logan's shoulder. "Hell and damnation, ye don't know how often I thought about ye over the years, wondered what became of ye. How ye fared."

As yet Logan said nothing. He returned the embrace, the smile, but seemed incapable of speech. Rachel stepped forward wondering if she should say something, do something. And not having the faintest notion what. She glanced down toward Henry for some inspiration but as usual the lazy dog had found himself a puddle of sunlight in which to snooze.

But she really needn't have worried about the silence. For all that Logan was taciturn, it appeared his brother was not. He continued to talk excitedly about his wife chancing upon Wolf's wife, and his surprise at discovering another brother. His surprise at learning Logan was near.

"I—I thought you dead." Logan's voice sounded rusty. He gripped James' elbows as if he still couldn't believe what he was seeing.

And memories were surging over him in overwhelming waves.

Rachel knew, for they ripped through her as well. She spread her feet to counteract the dizziness these bombarding incidents of his life caused. She had no foundation to cement them to. They simply hurled around her a few fond, most frightening and emotionally charged.

A man, his father, anger turning his face the color of Her Majesty's royal cloak, coming at Logan, a riding quirt raised above his head.

A dazzling smile—James—as he took his leave, promising to return. Then an instant later the flash of teeth disappearing as he leaned down from his horse. "Stay clear of him, little brother. After Prince Charles becomes king I shall have my share of riches, and we shall set up our own household. With your mother, too, if she'll leave him."

A silent scream raged through her head as Rachel relived through Logan's mind his terror at being dragged in to see his mother, covered in blood.

". . . your wife?"

Rachel snapped out of her reverie—or perhaps it was Logan who stopped thinking—when Jamie turned toward her. She didn't know what the begin-

ning of his sentence was, but apparently Logan did
for he stumbled over his words while trying to explain
her to his brother.

"She is a friend . . . I mean I'm accompanying her
to Charles Town. I mean . . ." He took a deep breath
and squared his shoulders. "May I present Rachel
Elliott? Mistress Elliott, my brother James Mac-
Quiad."

It certainly wasn't the most courtly of introduc-
tions—especially as he'd eliminated her title—but
James didn't seem to notice. He bowed over her hand,
flashing her a grin that showed dimples ran in the
family.

There seemed to be no question that they would
both accompany him to his home on Tradd Street.
Rachel woke Henry, who was quite annoyed at the
prospect of trotting along behind the horses through
the busy streets. Though he did stop grumbling when
Rachel promised a juicy bone at the end of the trip.

She straightened to find both brothers staring at
her, their handsome faces registering different expressions. James appeared surprised and slightly
amused that she would converse at such great length
with a dog. Logan's dark brows were drawn together
in annoyance.

Rachel simply brushed a nonexistent wrinkle from
her skirt and, straightening her shoulders, pretended
she was standing beside the queen, hearing the peti-
tion of some undeserving underling.

Neither brother said a thing.

The house on Tradd Street was large compared to
Logan's cabin, small in relation to Queen's House.
But Rachel admitted it was lovely in the simplicity of
its design. Three stories of light-painted walls faced
the street. Each window was framed by black shutters,
some of them closed. A high fence, covered with the
same stuccolike material as the house, surrounded

the grounds, which were much more extensive than Rachel at first realized.

Logan helped her dismount and her horse's reins were immediately grabbed up by a small towheaded boy who James called Luke.

Before the boy could scurry toward the stables, pulling the three horses, James halted him. "See what you can do about finding a juicy bone for the dog, if you please." He glanced toward Rachel with a twinkle in his blue-green eyes. "His name is Henry, I believe."

The central hallway was wide and airy, smelling of beeswax and woodsmoke. They were met at the door by a tall imposing black man with tattoos liberally canvassing his wide face. Without really intending to Rachel cowered behind Logan.

But though his countenance was fierce, his voice, when he greeted them, was well modulated, with an accent Rachel didn't recognize. At first she thought him the butler, but at Jamie's greeting wasn't sure.

"Keena, ye will never believe who this is?"

The black man lifted his brows. "On first glance I would say the gentleman is your long-lost brother."

Jamie's grimace gave way to a chuckle. "Will ye never allow me a surprise? Where's Anne?" he said, moving further into the hallway.

"Upstairs in the nursery, I believe."

Before the words were out of his mouth Jamie was taking the wide central stairs two at a time, alternating calls to his wife with demands that Logan and Rachel follow.

"Anne. Anne!"

As Rachel neared the first landing she spotted a small woman with brown hair and large dark eyes rush from a room near the end of the long hall. She closed the door, then started toward Jamie. "What is it, husband?"

The last word deteriorated into a giggle as she was lifted into strong arms and whirled around. A smacking kiss followed, which may have developed into something a bit more intimate had not the woman, Anne, noticed they were not alone.

"Jamie." Her voice was breathless as she pushed at his chest. "We have guests."

"And who do you think they be, wife?" He turned her round, keeping an arm draped over her narrow shoulders.

"Well, I don't know, but I'm sure—" She hesitated, her pretty eyes moving from Logan to Rachel, then back to Logan, where they rested . . . studied.

Without another word she left her husband's embrace and moved toward the other man. Taking both his hands in hers she smiled, her brown eyes shimmering with unshed tears. "I'm so happy to finally meet you, Logan. Jamie speaks of you so often. He's missed you terribly." Then she took another step, wrapping her arms around Logan's waist.

Rachel saw Logan hesitate a moment before folding his around her shoulders. He glanced toward her, and Rachel smiled.

"This, as you may have guessed by now Logan, is my wife, Anne. And yes, either everyone in my household is suddenly imbued with mystical abilities or we must favor each other a great deal."

"I'd say the latter is true, Jamie," Anne said as she clasped first one brother's hand, then the other. "And 'tis all the more amazing for the difference in coloring."

After a few more pleasantries three pairs of eyes turned on Rachel. There was another awkward moment as she was introduced, this time as Lady Rachel Elliott. Rachel didn't have time to decide if Logan meant to do it or if it was merely a slip of his tongue before Anne took her hand, leading her toward a room where she could freshen up.

Painted in sunny yellow with a woven grass mat on the floor and canopy bed hung with crewel, the room was pleasant. Shortly after as Rachel sank into a tub filled by a servant with warm, perfumed water, she had to admit to being surrounded by more opulence than she'd known since her death.

Why couldn't she simply relax and enjoy it?

Let the water drift around her and push Logan MacQuaid from her mind. He was safe in the bosom of his family. Obviously she wasn't needed to save his life at the moment. And it had been so very long since she'd enjoyed anything close to luxury. Granted, Wolf and Caroline's home was pleasant enough, with comforts imported from England, and she did enjoy a bath there. But certainly not with a maid popping in and out of the room, building up the fire and offering scented soaps.

She was accustomed to such pampering, considered it part of her due, in her other life, but now she grew restless with the process. She wanted to talk with Logan. Be with him.

But though she hurried through her bath and toilette, allowing the maid, Jenny, to dress her hair in a style reminiscent of the English court, she did not see Logan. Not until she went to the second floor parlor to find the two brothers deep in conversation and Anne sitting by the hearth, her hands busy with needle and thread.

It was a homey scene, full of love and warmth. And Rachel hesitated in the doorway, feeling every bit the stranger she was.

"There ye be." Jamie stood and with his wife came toward her, their faces wreathed in smiles of welcome.

Rachel returned their greeting, accepting their in-

vitation to join them. But it was Logan she watched
as she moved across the room. He stood, one elbow
resting on the marble mantel, his ankles crossed. And
he stared at her, his gaze steady. But there was something in his eyes . . . a recognition . . . an acceptance
. . . that unnerved her.

She wanted to talk with him, but they exchanged
only the barest of greetings. To know his thoughts,
but the wall was in place once more. To hold him,
but he merely lifted the hand she offered in greeting
brushing it with his lips before turning away.

Her flesh felt hot and the pressure of his mouth
stayed with her as she settled onto the chinoiserie-
style settee. Her eyes sought his again and in that
moment she knew he wasn't as unaffected by her
as he pretended. Those light green eyes that had
beguiled her from the start flashed with passion and
desire.

"Logan tells us you're recently from England."

"I beg your pardon? Oh, yes, I am." Rachel shifted
her attention to Anne, returning the other woman's
smile.

"How does the weather blow there about the Stamp
Act?"

"Now Jamie, I don't think we should be troubling
our guest with our views on that," Anne scolded with
a telling look toward her husband.

Rachel could tell he wanted to pursue the subject,
but to his credit he settled back with a sheepish grin.

Anne leaned toward Rachel after the two brothers
resumed their conversation. "Please don't be of-
fended. Jamie is rather passionate about the colonies'
rights. We had a bit of defiance, I suppose you could
call it, last year when a consignment of stamps arrived
from England. There were riots and for days mobs
ran free through the streets."

"How horrifying."

"Yes, it was rather. Mob rule is never a pretty thing to behold. And believe me, James was as opposed to that as anyone. But in the end the governor decided not to enforce the Stamp Act."

"Goodness, I don't suppose George was too happy about that."

"George? Oh, you mean the king. No, I don't suppose he was." Anne tucked her needle into the fabric. "At any rate, James can talk on for hours about it."

As it turned out there were other guests for dinner. Anne apologized, saying she wished it could be just the family tonight. Which Rachel was certain wasn't meant to imply that she wasn't part of the family . . . which of course she wasn't. But they treated her as such. She couldn't help wondering what Logan had told them about her.

Dr. Quincy and his wife arrived shortly after. Mistress Quincy was a stout woman with powdered hair who did a great deal of preening when Rachel was introduced to her. Rachel supposed she did appear rather grand tonight in her borrowed gown and diamonds, and the woman's reaction was more what she'd expect at court. But Rachel found she preferred the doctor's attitude when she was introduced as Lady Rachel Elliott. He bowed quickly over her hand and told her she appeared to be a very healthy young woman.

Dinner was a delightful affair, most elegant. Three complete courses were served by servants dressed in livery. Certainly a far cry from the fare served at Logan's cabin. Rachel lifted a fork of savory rice and peeked at Logan. He sat opposite her, beside the talkative Mistress Quincy who seemed to be doing her best to impart all of Charles Town's gossip.

Rachel couldn't help smiling when he glanced up. He met her expression with a scowl that slowly softened until he, too, was smiling.

It was hard to believe this was the same man she found standing on the precipice of the cliff. Now he was clean shaven, his dark hair brushed, his clothing that of a gentleman. A very handsome gentleman. Though no one could deny there was still something compellingly wild about him, it was the subtle hint of savagery that would send female hearts fluttering in any drawing room in England, including the king's court. Her own pulse quickened as it always did of late when she looked at him.

But the changes in him were not only in his appearance. His eyes, light green and hauntingly sensual framed by long, dark lashes and sun-bronzed skin, danced with spirit. His head was held high, his broad shoulders squared. And he hadn't even sipped the wine sparkling amber in the crystal goblet.

"I see you're not eating your food." Dr. Quincy's comment drew Rachel's attention. She held a silver fork partway to her mouth, and wondered how long she sat thus entranced by Logan's gaze. "Are you perhaps suffering from a sour stomach?"

"No." Rachel felt a blush spread into her cheeks. "I feel quite well."

"Good, good. So many find this clime a trial for the system. Especially during the summer months. Though even now the days are warmer than I'd like. Charles Town, I fear, ofttimes needs every doctor it can find."

Perhaps it was because he was so much on her mind that the next words slipped out. "Logan's a doctor . . . of sorts."

Though to this moment everyone at the table seemed engrossed in conversation, all talk seemed to stop after she spoke. Everyone looked at her, then Logan.

As if on cue everyone spoke at once.

"Ye didn't tell me that Logan."

"I'm certain you're a wonderful physician."

"Perhaps you could advise me on a problem I'm having with my foot. Wait till I tell the ladies at St. Philip's we have a charming new doctor in town."

"Where did you study medicine?"

It was Dr. Quincy's question that Logan answered. "I'm afraid Lady Rachel exaggerates." His eyes found hers and held. "I have attended no university and am *not* a doctor."

She wasn't sure what spurred her on, but she did know he wasn't going to intimidate her. Slanting a flirtatious smile at the doctor she cooed, "Logan is much too modest. He has more books than I can count and he reads them all the time."

"Which hardly makes me a physician," Logan pointed out, grinding each word between his teeth.

Rachel shrugged her delicate shoulders, aware of the effect it had on men. "True, though the way he treated my fever was impressive. Why I've had no better diagnosis and care from the king's own surgeon." Perhaps a subject better not mentioned. "And he delivered Caroline's baby." She turned toward Anne who sat wide-eyed at the end of the table. "I did mention the newborn, did I not?"

"Yes, and you said the birth was a difficult one."

Rachel wished she had told Anne more about Caroline's confinement when she visited the nursery earlier in the day to see Anne and Jamie's two children. But Rachel had such a delightful time admiring the twin boys that she dwelled only on the pleasant details of Caroline's family. She decided to catch her up on the news now.

"They would have died if not for Logan. Caroline and her daughter." Rachel's gaze swept the table, finally resting on Dr. Quincy. "You should have seen him. It was magnificent."

"Rachel."

She didn't think she'd ever heard her name imbued with such hypnotic power. She couldn't help but look Logan's way despite knowing what his expression would be. If not for Dr. Quincy's next words she might have retracted all she said, even though she genuinely believed every word.

"I've always considered ability and knowledge equal to university, though I think some courses there are necessary to test one's skill."

"I agree completely." Logan's response was for the good doctor, though he never tore his eyes from Rachel. He almost feared what she might say if he did.

"That's why I think if you're serious about healing people." The doctor stopped and rubbed his chin. "Yes, I could write a letter, and if you're as knowledgeable as this young lady seems to think you could study where I did, at the University of Pennsylvania."

"I don't think—" Logan began, but he was no match for Dr. Quincy's enthusiasm.

"Yes, yes. That's what we shall do. The doctors there are marvelous. Come round to see me as soon as you can, and we shall talk of this more. Perhaps I have discovered a medical genius."

It took the doctor's wife to cut off his ramblings. Apparently she was thrilled by the prospect of spreading the word about a handsome new physician, but she could only curb her gossipy tongue for so long. Listening to her husband couldn't compare to telling tales. When Dr. Quincy stopped for a breath she jumped into the silence.

"I heard you mention the king's physician. Have you been to court Lady Rachel?"

Ignoring the subtle shake of Logan's head, Rachel smiled. "Yes, I have."

"Then it's too bad you weren't here a sennight

ago. Charles Town had the honor of entertaining one of the king's own emissaries.''

"Spies ye mean. The man was sent to see how the wind blows.''

"You mean because of that dreadful Stamp Tax affair.'' The woman seemed to dismiss the riots and ultimate victory of the rebels with a sweep of her pudgy fingers. "I doubt His Majesty would send a duke on such an errand.''

"Whatever his reason for coming, he'll find no better reaction to his visit in Williamsburg than he did here,'' Jamie insisted, though Rachel noticed he lowered his voice a bit after a look from his wife.

Anne signaled to a servant who pulled out her chair as she rose. "Perhaps this would be a good time for us to leave the gentlemen to their brandy and talk of politics.''

Even as she stood, Mistress Quincy spoke of the duke who spent a fortnight in the city. "You surely should have been here, Lady Rachel. Even though 'twas not the season at all, there were balls and fetes nearly every night. And was he not splendid in his attire? Rumor had it that the duke was a widower and the single ladies of Charles Town nearly tripped over themselves to impress him. I suppose becoming the next Duchess of Bingham was—''

Rachel stopped so suddenly Mistress Quincy who was following her from the dining room bumped into her back. She was straightening her wig when Rachel turned on her, grabbing her plump shoulders. "What did you say?''

"I said—'' Mistress Quincy's face contorted. "Would you cease shaking me?''

Rachel grew aware that Logan stood and started toward her. She could also feel hands, Anne's, resting on her arm. But she didn't loosen her hold on the

older woman. "Was it Lord Bingham? Was he the
duke who visited Charles Town?"

"Yes, yes, Lord Bingham."

Rachel was vaguely aware of Logan calling her
name as she raced from the room.

Chapter Eighteen

"Every angel is terrifying."
—Rainer Maria Rilke
Duino Elegies

When she opened her eyes only a few slanting streams of silvery light laced the darkness. At first Rachel could remember nothing. Not where she was or why . . . barely even who. Then a short snuffling noise sounded and she turned her head to see Logan. His large frame sprawled in a chair pulled up beside the bed where she lay. He obviously was watching her when he fell asleep.

And all the events of the evening came hurtling back at her.

The discovery that Elizabeth and Geoffrey's murderer was near. Her insistence that she leave immediately to find him. Logan's eyes as she acted in what Dr. Quincy called "a highly agitated and irresponsible manner."

"And who wouldn't be agitated," she'd yelled at the pompous old man. "Lord Bingham killed my dearest friend and her lover. Me," she added. "He killed me as well."

That was when Logan bundled her off to her room, away from the startled faces of Anne and Jamie. The uncharacteristically still tongue of Mistress Quincy. And the shaking head and medical jargon uttered by the doctor.

The last thing Rachel heard the doctor ask as Logan hustled her toward the landing was, "Is there any history of madness?"

"I'm not insane," she insisted, whirling out of Logan's grip and turning to stare back at the group. "I'm not."

When Logan closed the bedroom door behind them she expected a lecture on watching her tongue. There was none. Somehow his reaction, close-mouthed but gentle as he played the lady's maid, frightened her more than any tirade he could give.

"He did kill them," she said, as he loosened the stays of her corset. "And I must avenge them."

By the time Anne knocked at the door, offering a tray with teapot and cup, Rachel was trying to redress in a borrowed riding habit.

"I've no need of tea," she said when Logan offered her the delicate china cup.

"It will calm you."

"I don't need to be calmed. I need to find Bingham."

"We shall discuss it further in the morning."

"There's nothing to discuss." She flipped golden hair from her face and stared at him as defiantly as she could while fumbling with the petticoat tabs.

"Just a sip," he coaxed, and to please him, to try and show him that she wasn't mad, she complied.

After that she remembered nothing till her eyelids lifted moments ago.

She swallowed, her mouth dry, and called out his name. Logan lurched forward immediately, taking her hand as it lay on the coverlet.

"How are you feeling?"

"Like I've been drugged," she said and watched

as his lashes drifted down to cover his light eyes. "I suppose 'twas Dr. Quincy's idea."

"Aye. But that's not to say I didn't agree. You were wanting to run off in the night chasing some English duke you say killed your friend."

"He *did* kill my friend. And at the risk of being called mad, I shall repeat what I've told you from the beginning. He—"

Two fingers covered her lips, staying her speech. "Please, say it no more."

His gentle breath waft across her cheek. He slipped his hand away, then sealed his lips to hers in the softest of kisses. When he pulled away his eyes were closed and his head dropped to the pillow beside hers. A strand of dark hair fell, tangling with the tumble of golden curls. She thought she heard him beg again for her to stop.

Rachel reached up to touch him, the rough stubble of his beard, the raw silk of hair. She wished she could please him. At this moment she wanted more than anything to be what he wanted. To never think of Lord Bingham. To care nothing that he'd killed her friend. To forget that her own existence on earth was tenuous.

She heard his breathing, felt the pain he suffered because of her, and wished it would be no more. But there was nothing she could do to change what had to be.

She *was* Lady Rachel Elliott. She *had* witnessed Lord Bingham shoot two people. And she *was* an angel.

Rachel wasn't certain how long she lay there, her fingers drifting through his hair, caressing his cheek. He still sat on the chair, but his upper body leaned over the bed and his face nestled close to hers.

She must have drifted off to sleep . . . he certainly did. For when she woke again the palest pewter showed through the wedge between the curtains.

As carefully as she could Rachel slipped from beneath the arm draped protectively beneath her breasts and crawled off the bed. She didn't want to leave him. Rachel stood a moment, the clothing she gathered bunched in her arms, and looked down on him. His hair was loose, strands falling across his cheek, catching on dark stubble. He appeared ruggedly male, yet vulnerable in a way that tore at Rachel's heart.

She reached out, to touch, to feel his power, but paused, inches from contact. He would be safe here in the bosom of his family until she returned. Without another backward glance Rachel crept to the door.

It closed behind her with a soft metallic click.

Damnation! When he caught that woman he would . . . Logan paused in mid-thought as he spurred his mount on, following the post road north from Charles Town. What in the hell was he to do with her?

Dr. Quincy's suggestion had merit. He spoke of the hospital in Philadelphia. Of the section devoted entirely to patients with diseased minds. Logan gripped the reins tighter.

Was that what Rachel needed? Certainly her actions last night seemed to indicate such. He had never seen such single-minded determination, such an insistence that she needed to follow the Englishmen.

Logan could close his eyes and see again the expression on her face when she declared to all and sundry that the duke killed her friend . . . and her.

'Twas no wonder Dr. Quincy laced the tea with laudanum. Without the drug's calming effects, she might never have quieted. But Logan didn't agree with the doctor's assessment that she be sent away to an asylum . . . couldn't bring himself to agree.

Rachel didn't belong locked away in a dingy cell. He'd sooner believe she was Lady Rachel Elliott, darling of King George.

Which was exactly what James's wife Anne believed. Caroline, too, if truth be told. Even after witnessing Rachel's temperament of last night. After knowing she fled, alone, in pursuit of the enigmatic duke, Anne seemed convinced Rachel was exactly who she claimed to be.

"I haven't time to listen," Logan insisted this morning after he woke to find her gone. Acting very much a madman himself, he pounded on every door in the household, waking Anne and James, setting the young twins to crying, stirring the servants, demanding of all if they'd seen Rachel.

No one had, though James, stomping into boots, insisted upon helping Logan look. Anne was the one pleading for calm. "She can't have gone far. And I don't agree with you that she doesn't know what she's about. I think she knows exactly what she's doing. Logan, please calm down."

"You don't seem to understand—"

"I understand more than you think I do. You're in love with her, and she with you, I wager. And you're torn between believing what appears to be true, and what in your heart you fear might be the real truth."

He'd pulled away from her restraining hand, insisting that he must leave, insisting that he would go alone. Trying not to think on what Anne had said.

Logan had found Rachel's trail easy enough. She'd traded her diamond necklace for a seat on the post stage. At least she hadn't ridden off by herself, for the land was marshy with wide rivers to cross and dangers lurking in the heavy woods.

She was safe enough till he caught up with her, he supposed. But was he? Safe from the thoughts he tried to quell.

Was Anne right? Did he love Rachel? Did he fear she told him the truth?

As he rounded a bend in the road, Logan spotted the lumbering coach ahead, and dug his heels into the stallion's flank. There was time enough to ponder his feelings once he had her safely in his arms.

The driver, a surly fellow with a gaping hole where his front teeth should be, was reluctant to rein in the horses. But his companion seemed to think it a good chance to step to the side of the path and relieve himself.

"I need a word with one of your passengers," Logan said as he dismounted.

"Only got one."

"She'll do." Logan swung open the door, coming face-to-face with an irate Rachel.

"What are you doing here?"

"I should think that obvious." He pushed inside, flopping down on the seat opposite her. "To me a better question would be where in the hell you think you're going."

The way she crossed her arms and stuck her pretty chin in the air was hellish annoying. And Logan told her.

"'Tis something I must do," she finally said. "But you needn't have concerned yourself." She leveled her blue eyes on him. "I'm not deserting you. Obviously, though I have tried—and done so repeatedly— my task of saving your life is not complete. I was coming back to you."

"That be a relief."

She didn't care for his sarcastic tone. "If you are so inclined to be rid of me, then why did you follow?"

"Because, I feel responsible, damnit." Logan heard the two fellows grumbling between themselves on the road and lowered his voice. "I can't have you running around like a . . . a . . ."

"Madwoman?" She arched a delicate brow. " 'Tis what you think, I know. It's what that silly doctor thinks, too, else why would he have drugged me?"

"He's concerned only for your well-being." Logan remembered the man's insistence that Rachel be locked in an asylum, and questioned his own words.

"Logan." She sighed and leaned forward. "I know how . . . how this must sound to you. But I'm not in any danger. I can't die a—"

"I'm coming with you."

"What?"

"You heard me. If you insist upon this trip, foolish as it is, I shall accompany you."

"But—"

"There be nothing more to say on the matter." With that Logan leaped from the coach and tied his horse behind. A few words and a bit of coin assured the driver's cooperation, if not his pleasure.

After settling into his seat Logan held up his hand to stave off whatever she planned to say. "It seems that I'm tired. 'Tis perhaps caused by lack of sleep and rude awakenings." He tucked his whiskered chin onto his chest and closed his eyes. Moments later one popped open.

"I'm assuming you are content not to run away from me?"

"Why would I do that?"

"Why indeed," was all he mumbled before drifting off to sleep.

It took them three days—three days of torrential rains—to catch up with the ducal party. And they were only able to do that because the river was so high the ferryman at Negro Head Point refused to take the coach across. So the nearby inn was packed with travelers waiting to cross to Wilmington.

Actually, the inn would not have been crowded if not for the need to accommodate the duke with a sitting room and sleeping chamber, as well as providing rooms for his staff of servants.

As soon as the post stage pulled into the stable yard and Rachel spotted the shiny black coach with its coat of arms painted on the side, she lunged for the door. If not for Logan's hand clamped around her arm she would have swung to the ground before the steps were lowered.

"Let me go. He's here," she said, twisting round to glare at him.

"And *we* shall see him."

"There's no need for you to be there. I've told you what Lord Bingham is capable of."

"Which is exactly why I do need to be there." Logan had listened patiently as she told him the story again of her friend and her lover. Of the fateful night near the lake. He'd sat, fingers steepled as her story continued. Her death. The light. The angels.

And he believed . . . believed that she believed every word was true.

"I don't wish to wait till I've eaten."

"Nay, I don't imagine you do. But we shall anyway." Logan ordered them both a stew of rice and ham, then leaned back against the smoke-darkened paneled walls of the inn.

"I wouldn't have allowed you to accompany me, if I'd realized what a despot you were going to become." Rachel crossed her arms with a huff, turning so he could only see her profile. Looking back quickly when she heard his laugh. "I fail to understand what you find amusing."

"I beg your pardon," he said, though there was nothing apologetic in the amused grin he flashed her, the dimples deepening beside his mouth. " 'Tis just your portrayal of *me* as the despot."

"And why shouldn't I?" Rachel's eyes widened innocently. "Surely you don't mean that *I* . . . ?"

Rachel didn't finish her thought for at that moment there was a flutter of activity near the stairs. Before Logan could push out from his bench against the wall, Rachel was on her feet, heading in the direction of the chaos.

"Hell and damnation." Logan rushed after her, catching only a glimpse of her blue gown as she wriggled between two burly men.

It wasn't difficult to pick out the duke. He stood on a step looking as arrogant and pompous as Logan imagined he would. His voice was low and raspy as he called out orders. Apparently he had it in mind to do a bit of hunting while the break in the weather held. ". . . to relieve the tedious boredom of this disgusting hovel," he announced to the taproom in general. At any rate he was garbed in some richly embroidered riding coat, his powdered wig immaculate beneath a feather-trimmed hat.

And he barely lifted a brow when a feminine voice yelled, "Murderer!"

By this time Logan had managed to wrestle through the congregation of servants and guards to grab Rachel's arm. She twisted, trying to pull away and screamed the charge again. This time the duke did take notice. He stared down his long nose, his gray eyes glacier.

"Yes, Lord Alfred Bingham, 'tis you that I charge with murder. You killed Elizabeth, your wife. And Sir Geoffrey. And though it possibly wasn't part of your plan you also caused the death of Lady Rachel Elliott."

"Who among this rabble speaks so to the Duke of Bingham?"

Rachel stepped forward, and, after taking a deep breath, so did Logan. "I do, Your *Lordship*." Rachel lifted her chin. "Yes, take a good look and know who I am. And that I shall not allow your deed to go unpunished."

There was but the flame from one hanging lantern to light the stairs, but Logan could swear he noticed a flicker of recognition in those hard flint eyes. But if it was there at all, within a blink it was gone, to be replaced by steely contempt.

"Be gone with you, woman, and bother your betters no more."

" 'Tis Lady Rachel Elliott to whom you speak with you knavish tongue. And 'tis the king himself who will hear my tale before all is done." She took another step till she stood at the foot of the stairs. "You will not escape me."

"Out of my way, wench." The duke lifted his arm, but the force of the blow he intended for Rachel never came as Logan blocked the thrust.

After that everything seemed to happen at once.

Logan, whose only thought was to protect Rachel, suddenly found himself the target of three hefty fellows bent on making stew meat of his face. His arms were pulled roughly behind his back, keeping him from defending himself. He yelled once for Rachel to get away just before a hamlike fist flattened into the side of his jaw.

"Logan! Oh, my God, Logan!" Rachel tried to reach him but someone had grasped her around the waist and was dragging her screaming and kicking toward the door. She saw a giant of a man slam an elbow into Logan's stomach and winced.

He was being killed!

This was it, she was certain. This was the moment she was supposed to save his life and she could do nothing. She had been wrong to come here, wrong to risk Logan's life. With the brave determination of a mother bear protecting her cub, Rachel lashed out. She clawed. She bit. She tried everything she could think of, but her captor seemed not to notice. He simply continued backing toward the door, her in tow.

Water splashed up like the fountains at Vauxeax as she landed unceremoniously on her backside in the middle of a giant mud puddle. Her mouth opened in outrage. She, Lady Rachel Elliot, had been tossed in the mud . . . *the mud!*

But her indignation lasted a mere moment as she scurried to find footing, her sodden, mud-clogged gown seemingly sucking her down. Logan was more important than her dignity.

She'd managed to stand before the inn door opened again. This time three of the duke's guards surged through, shoving Logan before them. Rachel reached out to him as he came toward her, the momentum of his weight sending them both sprawling in the muck.

Instinctively her arms wrapped around him as the duke and his entourage stepped from the inn. Lord Bingham kept his head high, his gaze forward as he left the courtyard. He paused briefly when she called out Elizabeth's name.

"For God's sake, Rachel."

She looked down at Logan, who, despite her earlier fears, was not dead. He was however bloody . . . and muddy . . . and sporting a cut beneath his left eye. She could also see several scrapes on his chest where his linen shirt was hanging in shreds.

Her fingers reached out, gingerly touching his cheek, wincing when he did. "I'm so sorry. It was never my intention to . . ." She bit her bottom lip. "Does it hurt much?"

"Only when I breathe," he answered, pushing to

his feet. To his surprise his legs only wobbled a little as he reached down to help her up.

"You needn't sound so sarcastic. It's hardly my fault the duke is a bully . . . and a murderer."

He turned, holding up a finger, his stance only slightly less intimidating for the slim dripping of it. "That is exactly the kind of talk that landed us . . ." His eyes swept toward the ground. "Here," he finally ground out.

The innkeeper rather indignantly suggested they find lodging elsewhere. But Logan refused to budge. For one thing there was no "elsewhere." For another, he'd paid in advance. Ignoring the man's bluster Logan tossed down a few more coins, requesting a tub and hot water be sent to their room.

"I can't believe he denied even knowing me," Rachel said the moment the bedroom door closed behind them.

Logan said nothing, merely leaned against the mantel, hooking the heel of one boot with the other. The boot came loose with a sucking sound.

"He is so arrogant and cruel." Rapidly drying mud rained down as Rachel paced the length of the room, thankfully skirting the bed. "Bingham may think he has quieted me, but I assure you he has not."

"Is your goal, Your Highness, to give him only one alternative?"

She stopped making muddy tracks. "What do you mean? And don't call me Your Highness." She had liked it so much better when he used her name.

The other boot flew off. "I mean, *Rachel* that if you continue accusing the duke of murdering his wife, he'll only have one way of silencing you."

"You mean killing me as he did his wife and lover?" Rachel folded her arms staring at him down her mud-streaked nose.

"You seem convinced he's capable of such actions.'' Logan flexed his shoulders. "And I can attest to the fact that he's not against using violence."

Rachel's haughty expression melted as she rushed toward Logan. "How could I have forgotten how those men beat you? Are you badly hurt? Let me help you with your shirt."

"I'm not after your sympathy." Though he had to admit a purely erotic pleasure shot through him as she stripped off his shirt. "I only wish you would think before speaking."

"He can't hurt me," she tossed over her shoulder before answering the pounding at the door.

"Rachel." Logan leaped forward only to step back as two maids tugged a cut-off barrel into the room. Several others followed, carrying pails of steaming water.

"We requested a tub."

One of the women, a buxom wench with a pock-marked face and sweating upper lip stared at Rachel like she'd been dragged in by the barn cat. "We ain't got but one and his High and mighty Lordship needs that'un." She herded the other women from the room, mumbling something about a dunking in the river being what was needed.

Rachel took a deep breath, then looked back at the barrel with its measly supply of water. "You may go first."

"Not fancy enough for you, Your Highness?"

"Would you stop it? My offer had nothing to do with . . . with . . ." Rachel's bottom lip trembled. For a moment she tried to blink back the tears welling in her eyes, finally giving in and letting them plump down her cheeks, streaking the dried dirt.

Before Logan could say anything she was across the room, her arms wrapped tightly about his middle, mumbling something into the hair that arrowed down his chest.

"Your Highness?" He gently pried her loose, tipping her chin up with his thumb. "Tears?"

"Of course tears, you big dolt. I thought they were going to kill you. I thought . . ." Again her words were unintelligible as she pressed kisses across his flesh.

When her lips skimmed across the hard nub of his male nipple Logan sucked in his breath.

"Oh, did I hurt you? I never wanted for you to be hurt."

"Nay, if truth be known what you're about is making me forget there's any pain at all."

"Truly?" Rachel peeked up, a quivering smile teasing her lips.

In reply Logan's mouth closed in on hers, catching her sigh. His tongue filled her mouth, weakening her knees so that she had to hold on to him tighter.

"Oh, God, Your Highness." His hands tangled in her hair, pulling her nearer. His lips skimmed across her jaw after she said something against his mouth he couldn't understand. "What?"

"I'm not a Highness you know." Her words were breathless as she sought again the mindless ecstasy of his kiss.

"You seem like one to me. A sweet, sweet princess from a faraway fairy land."

Logan tugged at her skirts. She tugged at his breeches. Neither knew where the giant splat of mud came from. But it had them pulling away and looking at each other in laughter.

Logan's eyes skittered to the barrel and back. "You know, I think the tub is big enough for two."

Rachel blushed. "I think you're right." She reached up to unfasten her stomacher. "Then there'd be question of who should bathe first."

"Aye, but you're a smart one, Princess." Logan's

fingers closed over hers, the heel of his palm rubbing her nipple as he worked at the tabs.

Rachel moaned, reaching for the placket at the front of his breeches. The hard pressure of his staff and the anxious fumbling of her fingers made the buttons difficult to loosen.

"Perhaps," she said, her voice little more than a whisper, "we should each undress ourselves."

So for a moment they did, tossing aside mud-laden stockings and petticoats, stopping at regular intervals to view the other's progress. When she was down to her shift, he to his breeches, Logan grabbed her toward him, unable to resist any longer the feel of her skin.

He skimmed the ruffled yoke off her shoulders, his breath catching as the soft cotton fabric held tenuously on pearled nipples before drifting to the floor. Logan traced a smudge of dirt along the curve of her collarbone.

"I never knew mud to be so erotic."

Her own fingers followed a streak to where his breeches yawned open to reveal a thatch of dark, curly hair. "Nor did I."

Logan swung her up into his arms, then stepped into the barrel. The water, though hot enough to send billowy steam into the cooler air, felt chilly against his fevered skin. Slowly he lowered her till her feet barely skimmed the water's surface. His hips ground against hers, his sex against the soft cushion of hers.

"Oh, Rachel." He lowered her further then bent down, scooping a handful of water and pouring it over her shoulder. He followed the crystal droplets as they rolled down her body, tracing the path with his tongue. "Anne says I love you." He paused, licking the underside of her breast before straightening to face her. To see her expression.

"Do you?" It seemed strange to be standing here with him, both naked and aroused, yet embarrassed by words.

He played with a strand of mud-encrusted hair, meeting her eyes reluctantly. "I'm not sure I know how to." He gathered more water, watching her head fall back as he let the warm liquid drip over her breasts. "I know I want you. That every time we're together 'tis like the skies open and I see a bit of heaven."

This time he didn't stop as the droplets flowed downward. He followed them over the plane of her stomach, the warmth of his breath turning her legs to jelly. Then lower till he dropped to his knees, splashing water around the legs.

His tongue played her, dipping and lathing, teasing and sending her senses spiraling. She tried to keep some hold on reality. But the effort seemed beyond her. She wasn't even sure how she ended up sitting on his legs, hers spread round his hips. But his mouth drank of hers, hungry and carnal and she didn't care.

Hard and thick, his rod pressed against her spread womanhood. Water surged and swelled, seemed to boil around their hips as they both writhed, doing their best to assuage the desire that enveloped them as surely as the steam.

"I want to be inside you." His words vibrated against her neck, heated her blood till she was mad with want . . . with need.

Logan's hands bracketed her hips, lifting, sliding her up along the pulsing length of him. "Twist your legs around if you can. Aye, like that."

The last was slurred as his tongue speared into her mouth. The next moment Rachel sank down over the slick rounded tip. Her moan of pleasure mingled with his as slowly, sensually his flesh impaled hers.

She was tight and moist as a mouth and her sheath

gripped, massaged. Logan tore his lips from hers. His breathing was harsh, a raw panting, as he fought for control.

"Don't move," he rasped as his fingers dug into the soft flesh of her bottom.

"Can't stop. Oh Logan, please. Please . . ." She jerked, twisting, begging with each ragged breath she took. Her breasts, hard and so sensitive she could scream, tangled with the moist curls on his chest. Water churned, pumping round where their bodies joined.

Then one hand slid down between her legs, touching her so sensually, so privately. She cried out, unable to stop herself, not caring to. The tremors convulsed through her body, shaking her to the core. She could feel his explosion, savored the feel of his seed spewing into her. The feeling of oneness with him. With him.

It was like this whenever they made love. The barriers crumbled. Their thoughts joined. Their feelings melded.

Rachel collapsed onto his hard chest, relishing the intimacy, wondering if it was as it seemed, that their hearts beat in perfect unison.

How long they remained like that, joined and at peace, Rachel wasn't sure, but when they finally moved her legs were stiff and the water chilled.

They started quickly washing each other, sharing the small sliver of soap. Logan leaped from the tub, moving the extra pails of water close to the fire before turning back toward the tub. Rachel crouched low in the water, her hair a stiff pile of grayish bubbles, her eyes a smoldering, smoky blue as she watched him.

Logan covered the distance between them in three strides, pulling her to standing and slanting his mouth over hers. She tasted slightly of soap but he didn't care. "God Rachel, I can't get enough of you."

They took turns pouring the warmed water over sudsy slick bodies, rinsing away the rest of the mud. Logan lifted her from the barrel, carrying her to stand before the hearth, kissing her till their desire burned hotter than the flickering flames.

His attempt to dry her with the thin scrap of linen was more caress. But he patiently sat on the braided rug, finger combing her hair till it was merely damp before guiding them both toward the bed.

This time their coupling was slow, exquisite, satiating. Afterward Logan lay on his back, Rachel's cheek cradled on his shoulder.

"I do, you know."

Rachel nestled closer. "Do what?" The bond between them vibrated with what he felt . . . what he was going to say. But Rachel turned from the knowledge. She wanted to hear it from his own lips.

"Love you," he whispered. "I love you."

Chapter Nineteen

"Angels, as 'tis seldom they appear,
So neither do they make long stay;
They do but visit and away."
  —John Norris
    "To the Memory of His Niece"

Two strong fingers pressed to her lips, keeping them shut when she would have responded to what he said. The room was deep in shadows, the candle by the bedside sputtering in a pool of foul-smelling tallow, the logs nearly spent, sifting through the iron grate. Rachel studied Logan's face, trying to make out his expression in the grainy light.

"I didn't tell you of my love to force you to answer in kind." One finger traced the moist seam, skimming inside her mouth. " 'Tis just such a new emotion for me. Though with you I think 'twas growing from the start."

"Yet you don't know what to do with me." She couldn't help it. His thoughts were hers. She could not block them out.

He twisted, turning to face her more squarely. "I shall protect you Rachel. With my life, I shall make certain no one hurts you . . . ever."

Rachel touched the discoloration under his eye.

He feared her mad, and still he loved. Swore to himself that no one would ever take her away. Locking her arm round his neck, she wished it could be so. Wished she could forget her past, the life she had known. To stay with him, cocooned in his arms.

Wished it enough to promise Logan she would let him talk with Lord Bingham on the morrow. "Mayhaps we can discuss this and . . ."

And what? Logan didn't know. But he was willing to try for her.

Much later Rachel crept from the bed. Logan slept, his body turned toward her, his hair, tumbling across his cheek. Unable to sleep she'd watched him for hours, till her eyes strained in the darkness. Memorizing every angle and plane of his face. Breathing in his scent. Letting her fingertips skim across his muscled shoulder.

As quietly as she could Rachel built up the fire . . . as he'd taught her. Then she gathered up their mud-laden clothes and dipped them in the icy water in the barrel. She swished and washed as best she could, rinsing and wringing out his shirt, draping it across the chair back. She took less time with her petticoat and gown, only bothering at all because they belonged to Caroline.

Building his fire, washing his clothes, Rachel could pretend, could almost believe things were as he wished them. That she was his woman, and he her man. That the Fates hadn't played such a dastardly trick on them.

When everything was hung by the hearth to dry, Rachel slipped into the other shift and gown Caroline lent her, then searched through Logan's knapsack for his knife.

The dull clank of metal sounded loud to her ears but when she cast a nervous glance over her shoulder Logan still slept. His words this night had proved one thing to her. He would do what he must to keep her safe. And in doing so would endanger himself.

She could never allow that.

And protecting Logan had little to do with concern for returning to her former life. She cared about him . . . deeply. As she crept along the dark hallway toward the Duke of Bingham's rooms, she finally accepted that. Today, when she thought the guards would kill him, her own fate never entered her mind.

It was Logan she worried about.

Him she cared about.

And he was the reason she tiptoed past the guard, whose thick lips flapped open with each gurgling snore. Lord Bingham would never have stood for such slothlike servants in England. The wretch didn't even awake when she slipped the key from his coat pocket.

Inside, the only light came from the banked fire. But she could see enough to tell that Lord Bingham's servants had decorated the sitting room with many of his belongings, candlesticks and tapestries, armchairs and a small writing desk. Vestiges of his wealth and position, that he carried with him.

Which would all amount to nothing soon, Rachel thought as she inched open the door to his bedroom. Bringing a taper from the other room, she lit a branch of candles on the bedside commode, then bent down toward him. He didn't come immediately awake. Not even with the knife blade resting a heartbeat away from his neck. It took her gentle whispering of his name to bring him from sleep's embrace.

His strangled cry was quickly quieted by the slightest pressure of her blade. She could see the whites of his eyes as he stared up at her. Could feel his panic and relished it, remembering all too well the expression on Elizabeth's face moments before Bingham's ball exploded through her body.

"Lady Rachel." His voice cracked as he tried to swallow and found the honed edge of the knife.

"Ah, so you do remember me after all. Earlier I could swear you had no recall of me . . . or of the night you killed your wife."

"How did you survive? I saw you fall into the lake."

"And rushed to my rescue, too, I'll wager." Rachel tightened her grip on the ivory handle. She had to force herself not to slice through his neck immediately. To remember how she wished for him to squirm and beg for mercy first.

"Actually, Lord Bingham, as in the case of Elizabeth and Geoffrey, I did not escape the death you gave me."

"But . . . but . . ."

"Yes, I know. I do seem very much alive. Assuredly I look and feel as I did before you ended my life. But it is all an illusion. You see, I am an angel."

"Who lands in mud puddles and plays with knives?"

"I'm not playing Bingham. What I have in mind for you is no game."

"I never meant for you to be hurt, you know. You weren't supposed to be there. Only Liz and her damn cuckolding lover were to die. I honestly felt remorse when I saw you by the lake."

"Unfortunately, I won't be able to return the emotion."

The knife slipped lower. "Know that this is for Liz. Because you saw fit to snuff out her life, I shall do the same to you."

He lay there, vulnerable, his throat white and exposed. She hated him, for what he'd done to Liz and Geoffrey. For what he'd done to her. Her knuckles hurt from the death grip she held on the carved bone handle. And still she could not bring herself to thrust downward through his flesh.

Then her chance was gone.

From behind someone grabbed her arms. Rachel screamed and watched helplessly as the knife clattered to the floor. She yanked, doing her best to break free of the iron grip, but her efforts proved futile.

She was held immobile, tears of frustration swimming in her eyes as Bingham scurried to the far side of the bed.

"It took you damn long enough to come to my rescue," he yelled, bunching up the blanket to cover the wet spot on his nightshirt. "I could have been slain by this madwoman."

The guard mumbled something in explanation, which Rachel couldn't understand and doubted Bingham could either. But the duke seemed more interested in hiding the fact that he'd wet himself and dismissed the hapless guard with a sweep of his hand.

"What should I do with her?"

"Kill her," came his lordship's exploding reply. But he must have thought better of the order, for he twisted around to impale Rachel with a icy stare. "No. I don't think we shall. Not at this moment at least. The ferryman said the river should be down enough to cross today. Roust him. We shall take the madwoman with us." He stepped closer and Rachel could smell the stench of urine. "Mayhaps I can think of a more fitting punishment for one so fair."

Damp, black-trunked pines stood skeletal against the pearling sky as they left the inn. For one so vain about his appearance, it surprised Rachel how quickly the duke could manage his toilette. It seemed hardly any time after she was tied, gagged, wrapped in one of his voluminous capes, and bundled off to the coach, until he joined her.

The shades were drawn as they were ferried across toward Wilmington. Rachel could not see or be seen . . . except by Bingham. His cold eyes never left her face as the coach dipped and swayed with the current.

Once on dry land, he stretched across the space separating them and roughly yanked away the strip of silk covering her mouth. His fingers gentled as he brushed a strand of hair off her cheek. There was a light in his eyes that turned Rachel's stomach. She was pleased to extinguish it.

He jerked back against the soft leather squab, wiping spittle from his face with a lace-trimmed handkerchief. His expression was a study in rage, though it didn't take long for the cool facade to resurface. He stretched out his long legs, kicking hers aside in the process.

"Now Lady Rachel, that wasn't very . . . angelic."

"You obviously aren't familiar with avenging angels."

"Obviously not. However, I'd be willing to wager that you are no more saintly than I."

"My conscience isn't blotted by murder," Rachel said, her chin rising.

"No?" Bingham's fingers steepled and he smiled slightly, a gesture that made Rachel's skin prickle. "But then you were stopped before you had the chance." One finger strayed from formation to point her way. "It would be interesting to see if you had the nerve to actually kill someone."

"Return my knife and I shall be glad to satisfy your curiosity."

His chuckle was unnerving. "Ah, Rachel. My beautiful, clever Rachel. Would things have been different if I'd followed my . . . shall we say baser instincts and wed you instead of your cousin?"

"I would never have married you."

"Now, now, never say never. As I recall you were

tilting your skirts around Prince William. The king's brother to be certain, but hardly more influential or wealthy than I. And certainly less able to pleasure you.''

She tried to hold his gaze, but thoughts of him touching her, of doing with him what she did with Logan, made her physically ill. But he wouldn't allow her even the smallest courtesy of looking away. His fingers clamped over her jaw, forcing her to meet his eyes.

"You're under my power now Rachel.''

"I'll never be under your power.''

He sat back, his narrow face pensive. "We shall see. We shall see.''

As they rode on in silence Rachel tried to formulate some plan. Her hands were still tied, and though she tried her best to wriggle them free, she couldn't. At least not without drawing attention to herself. There was nothing she could do until her hands were free, and even then . . . The only thing she was thankful for was that Logan was not here.

"I am puzzled.''

Rachel was thinking of Logan, lost in memories of the previous night when Bingham spoke again.

"How *did* you manage to escape those waters? I'm quite certain I saw you go under.''

"I found the same escape you shall.''

His smile deepened. "Ah Rachel, we would have made a good pair. 'Tis a pity I chose Elizabeth and her fortune. And her cuckolding ways.''

"I daresay most anyone would be tempted to forget their vows of fidelity married to you.''

"Then they would suffer the same consequences as Elizabeth and her lover.'' His expression hardened. "Though next time I would not allow a chit of a girl to muddy my punishment. You caused me quite a bit of unpleasantness, Rachel.''

"Oh." Her brows lifted.

"Yes, it appears before you ran off to warn Elizabeth of my anger, you mentioned it to Lady Sophia who in turn caught the ear of our charming German pig of a queen. When you turned up missing along with my dear wife and her lover, no amount of public grieving on my part could allay the king's suspicion of me."

" 'Tis a pity he didn't hang you."

"I'm certain that's what he wished. But remember, I am a man not without influential friends, and a considerable amount of power myself." Bingham leaned back studying her beneath lowered lids. "No matter how often Charlotte prattled in his ear, George had no proof."

His mouth thinned. "But he exacted his punishment all the same by sending me on this ridiculous journey through the backwoods of hell."

"You aren't enamored of the New World?"

"I prefer the old, thank you. Which is where I shall head as soon as we reach Philadelphia."

"Is that where we're going?"

"Well, I am. You, my dear Rachel, shall have a much shorter trip." He reached across, draping his finger down across her breast. " 'Tis such a shame too. I would love to have shown you some of the pastimes that Elizabeth found so entertaining."

"Take your hands off me." Rachel tried to squirm as far into the corner as she could, but she couldn't escape his punishing grip. Tears of pain blurred her vision though she tried to blink them away. "I shall see that you burn in hell for what you've done."

"Lofty words for one forced to roam around the countryside garbed in the clothing of servants." With one final pinch he shoved back onto his own seat. "I think I shall have to fancy even you up a bit before you'll inspire my lust."

They rode on for hours. Rachel could see none of the countryside, could barely tell that it was day. Bingham sat across from her, his glacier eyes fixed on her, his expression stony. And she tried her best to disappear into the leather cushions.

When the coach finally rumbled to a stop, a footman opened the door and Rachel caught a glimpse of a large pink brick house before Bingham climbed down the lowered steps. "Take care of her," he ordered the man in bright red livery before moving out of her view.

The door was slammed shut and after a moment the carriage started again. Within minutes they stopped, the door flew open, and another burly man pushed inside. Ignoring her struggles he wrapped a gag around her mouth, then bundled her out. Covered from head to toe with the cloak she could do nothing when he tossed her over his shoulder like a bag of potatoes.

Dizzying visions swirled about—a stone drive, polished steps, an Aubusson rug—before she was deposited back on her feet. Before she could move he left, locking the door behind him.

Rachel glanced around at the richly appointed room, trying to think of something to do. Her hands were tied, her mouth gagged, and there seemed to be nothing to use to change it.

Then the door opened and the guard appeared again, this time leading two servant girls who carried frilly, ruffled petticoats and gowns.

The man relocked the door, then drew his pistol from a leather belt. Pointing it toward Rachel he nodded toward the older woman who'd deposited the clothing on the bed.

As soon as the gag was removed Rachel begged for help. But her pleas seemed to fall on deaf ears. Except for the guard's. And he merely warned that if she persisted, he would shoot first one servant, then the other.

After that Rachel kept quiet. Even when they removed the ropes binding her hands.

More servants entered, dragging a copper tub, and while the guard kept watch she was stripped and forced into the perfumed water. They scrubbed her hair and body, then made her stand still while they dried her off.

With the exception of the armed bully she was pampered and dressed much the same as when she was in England. The clothes they draped over her body were of the finest silks, the softest cotton. And though they didn't fit her perfectly, the maids were able to stitch tiny darts to make it appear as if they did.

Her hair was brushed dry, then dressed in curls, and all the while Rachel was thinking, her eyes searching the room for anything she could use as a weapon, wondering where she was.

When she was garbed near as splendidly as for an evening at court, the servants left the room. For the first time she was alone with her hands free and she wasted no time searching the room. In the desk she found a letter opener, barely sharp, but at least pointed. No pockets were tied beneath her skirts so she stuck the opener in her garter.

Rachel was straightening her gown over the wide side hoops when the door opened.

"His Grace will receive you now." The words seemed strange coming from the burly ruffian.

Rachel took a deep breath and held her head high. She would remember who she was. She was Lady Rachel Elliott. And though she might be held captive at the moment, it was imperative that she best Bingham. For her real purpose on earth was to save Logan's life. As she walked from the room she could only be thankful that he was safely out of the duke's clutches.

The staircase and center hallway were more splendid even than James's house. Rachel followed the guard across the parqueted floor to the double doors that led into the parlor. She paused as her escort knocked, then threw open the doors to announce, "Lady Rachel Elliott."

Rachel stepped into the room, her skirts swaying, her expression full of contempt.

And then she saw Logan.

Her eyes grew large and the blood drained from her face. Her first impulse was to rush toward him where he sat tied to a straight-back chair. The bruise under his eye was darker and he had a new bleeding wound near his right temple. She felt faint from the pain.

"As you can see one of your friends came inquiring about you."

Rachel forced her attention toward the duke. He lounged against the marble mantel, a pinch of snuff held under one nostril. She watched while he sniffed delicately, then sneezed into his handkerchief.

"What are you going to do with him?"

He lifted a shoulder. "I hadn't thought about it. What would you suggest?"

Rachel prayed her voice would remain steady. "I don't really care. He's of no importance to me."

"Really?" The duke pushed away from the hearth. "And here I thought differently."

Logan squirmed in his chair, his yell muffled by the gag when Bingham grabbed Rachel's arm.

"Don't play games with me, Rachel. We already know what the outcome will be." He let her go with such force she stumbled. "You *are* quite attractive

though. I just may keep your friend alive to insure
your . . . shall we say willingness this evening." His
fingers clutched her wrist. "Come, I believe dinner
is ready."

The last look Logan had of Rachel was as she
glanced back at him, her eyes full of regret, just before
the door slammed shut.

"You don't seem to be enjoying your duck."

Rachel toyed with her fork, then tossed it on the
plate with a clunk. "Where are we?"

Bingham touched the napkin to his lips. "Your
conversation skills have deteriorated since coming to
this godforsaken place." He motioned to a servant
who pulled out his chair. "I had hoped this might
be an interesting evening, but I can see that was a
foolish presumption. Your company grows wearing."
With no pretense of gentlemanly behavior, his Grace
latched on to Rachel's arm as he stormed past her
chair. She nearly stumbled to the rug trying to stand
and retrieve the letter opener at the same time. The
etched silver handle eluded her grasp.

"What are you doing?" Rachel struggled as he
dragged her down the hallway.

"Questions, questions. You are beginning to bore
me." He flung open the door to the drawing room,
shoving her inside. "Prepare yourself, Rachel. I've a
desire to take you before an audience."

Bingham paused briefly to summon one of the
guards. Rachel's heart stopped when the burly man
handed his pistols to the duke. Though she expected
no answer, Rachel couldn't keep the question from
escaping her lips.

"What are you going to do?"

"The ultimate experience my dear Lady Rachel,"
was all he said before shoving her back into the salon.

He didn't struggle.

At first Rachel feared that Logan was dead. He didn't look up when they entered the room. His chin fell forward onto his chest, his large body straining against the arms bound behind the chair.

Then she felt the powerful life force emanating from him. For a moment, till Bingham swung her around toward him, Rachel nearly forgot the duke. Even as Bingham shoved her back across a small table Rachel tried to reach Logan's mind with her own. "I love you." The message she sent seemed so real to her Rachel wasn't certain she didn't voice the thought.

She also wasn't sure he understood her.

Then the hot breath of the duke wafted across her cheek as he leaned over her. "Now I shall determine if my fantasies of you have any basis in reality."

His weight was suffocating.

Rachel squirmed, struggling to draw breath. To evade the bruising grasp of his hands. His palms flattened over her breast, then squeezed so hard, tears sprang to her eyes.

She gasped, trying to turn her face from his as she clawed at her skirts, searching for the silver letter opener. Her fingers slipped over the smooth metal just as the duke's weight disappeared.

Blood splattered as Logan's fist slammed into the aristocratic nose. The duke stumbled back, the expression of shock on his face grotesque.

But Rachel wasn't looking at Bingham. She pushed up, her eyes on Logan. He rushed toward the duke, though somehow it didn't seem as if he were moving quickly. As Bingham yanked the pistol from his belt it appeared to Rachel as if the whole world moved in slow motion. She could almost imagine the tall case clock near the mantel, measuring its ticks as they dragged by, droning through the protracted time.

She saw it clearly. Logan moving toward the duke.

The aimed pistol. And she was filled with such love, such an overpowering devotion, that her actions required no thought at all.

Rachel stepped in front of Logan just as the explosion vibrated through the air. The noise seemed to shatter the surreal world that existed moments before. But it was more the tortured shout that tore from Logan that she heard.

"Rachel!"

The bastard shot her at point-blank range.

She's dead. Rachel's dead!

The thought exploded through his mind as Logan fell on top of Bingham. She'd taken the ball meant for him. He tightened his fist. Pounding. Not feeling the duke's attempts to harm him. Knowing only the need to hurt.

"Logan. Logan, stop."

He didn't know how long it took for the words to permeate the haze of sadness clouding his brain. Logan felt her hands on his arm, pulling. But couldn't accept it was she till his head jerked around and she was there.

Rachel.

Looking at him, her angel eyes wide.

"Are you all right?" She melted into his arms as Logan stood, clinging to her, touching her back as if to assure himself that she wasn't an apparition.

"I was so frightened for you. He's evil." Logan felt her head turn against his chest and he knew she was staring down at the duke as she spoke. "I know what he can do."

"He can't hurt you anymore." Logan's arms tightened around her. "I won't let anything hurt you . . . ever." Reluctantly he pushed her away enough to look down into her face. "We need to get out of here. The guards . . ." He left the rest of his concerns

unstated. He was holding her. Watching as each
breath lifted her chest, as the pulse fluttered in her
neck. She was warm and vibrant.

He couldn't understand for an instant how that
was possible.

And he didn't care.

She nodded, then tilted her head to the side. "Is
he dead?"

"Nay. Come on." Noticing the letter opener for
the first time, Logan pried it from her fingers, then
took her hand and headed toward one of the tall
windows that lined the room. He was lifting the sash
when the shuffling noise from across the room
snagged his attention. Turning, Logan saw the duke
struggling to prop himself on one elbow. His face
was a mask of hatred and determination. And the
second pistol was aimed toward Rachel.

Instinct made Logan fling the letter opener
through the air. Like a knife it flipped end over end,
stabbing through the duke's brocade waistcoat and
into his chest with a soft whooshing sound.

Logan's hand on Rachel's arm kept her from rushing across the room. "We don't have time," he said
before opening the window. Logan helped Rachel
out into the cool night air, then followed.

The innkeeper seemed more relaxed than the last
time Logan saw him. Without a duke to consume his
time he lounged on the rough-hewn bench by the
fireplace, a tankard of ale resting by his hand. He
didn't seem interested in stirring himself until Logan
helped him from his seat with a well-placed hand on
his fleshy arm.

It had been a long, hard ride from the country
house where the Duke of Bingham had taken up

temporary residence. It was dark and unfamiliar, and for most of the time a steady drizzle had made the road a quagmire of mud. They'd managed to "liberate" two horses from the stable but the only knife Logan found was more adept at slicing through harness leather than defending two lone travelers.

All in all, Logan was glad to find shelter, especially for Rachel. Except that as soon as they ate and changed into dry clothing there would be nothing to keep them from discussing the events of the last few days. And how they affected them.

A vision of the pistol exploding, aimed at Rachel, swam before his eyes. There was no way the duke could have missed. No way at all. There was no explanation for why Rachel was still alive.

What if she isn't? a small, nagging voice seemed to say. *What if she never was? What if she told you the truth from the beginning?*

"Oh Logan, look at that poor man."

Rachel's hand on his sleeve drew Logan's attention from telling the innkeeper to send supper up to their room. He glanced around to follow her gaze and saw an elderly man with long white hair that hung unkempt and dirty about his hunched shoulders. His clothing was ragged, his shoes cracked, and several of the tavern's patrons seemed to find his attempts to scavenge food annoying.

"Don't be minding him," the innkeeper said. His eyes lit up as Logan tossed several coins across the bar. "That be Ol Eb." He raised a dirt-encrusted finger to tap his head. "He's a bit touched, that one."

Logan fished in his pocket for another coin to buy the old man a decent meal. When he turned to tell Rachel, she was no longer standing at his elbow. Across the tavern he saw her help the old man to a seat.

* * *

"Bless you, child. These old bones don't hold me as well as I'd like. But then we can't always choose, can we?"

"No, I don't suppose we can." Rachel settled down in the seat next to the man. She clutched her diamond earrings, her last material possession of any worth.

"Please, take these. I don't need them and they may help you." But as she reached across the food-smeared table to press the jewels into his withered hand, something in his expression made her pause. Rachel swallowed. "Do I know you?"

The old man's smile, though toothless, had a beauty and benevolence all its own. His eyes, dark as the midnight sky seemed to peer through her. "Perhaps you do child. It's not for me to say."

"No. No, of course it isn't. I didn't mean to pry. It's just that—"

"Rachel? Are you all right?"

"Yes." Rachel realized she blurted the word out as she turned toward Logan who'd come up to stand by her seat. He seemed concerned and she could hardly blame him. Her breathing was rapid and Rachel wondered if everyone could hear the pounding beat of her heart. Her free hand grabbed Logan's and she squeezed his fingers.

"I am fine. This gentleman and I were just discussing . . ." She was at a loss as to what to say.

"The meaning of life," the old man supplied with nary a pause. "We were discussing the meaning of life." He opened his gnarled fingers to stare down at the glittering gems sparkling in the hollow of his palm. When his eyes again met hers, the fire from the diamonds seemed to light up his face. "I think we have all learned our lessons well."

Rachel sat motionless as he stood with Logan's help. She didn't even realize he was gone till Logan touched her shoulder. When she glanced around he dropped to his knees, grabbing her hands in his own.

"What is it, sweetheart?" His thumb traced the path of a single crystal tear. "What did he say to make you so sad?"

"Nothing." Rachel bit her lip as she watched the old man close the door behind him. "Oh Logan, he didn't say anything bad. Ebenezer wouldn't do that." It wasn't until she said his name aloud that Rachel knew exactly who the old man was. She gave Logan a watery smile. "May we go to our room now?"

He needed to talk, but he needed her love, the passion of her body, more.

The door no sooner closed, sealing them in the safe haven of the room, than Logan's arms were around her. His kiss was long and deep . . . possessive. He wanted to hold her to him. To never let her go.

And she was as frantic to be with him. Her hands pushed at the hunting shirt, shoving it over his broad shoulders, skimming over his smooth skin. She followed the V of the shirt down, forging her fingers through the curls of dark hair, trying to absorb the feel of his hot damp flesh.

He was life and love and passion. More than she could ever hope to have. But for this moment in time he was hers.

"I love you." The words vibrated against her neck as Logan's lips skimmed up to nibble her ear. "I love you." An admission, a litany, he could do naught but repeat and repeat as his body pressed hers to the door.

He bunched up her skirts, causing them both to laugh as he cursed at the plethora of petticoats.

"Damn frills."

"I can't stand not to touch you." Her fingers worked feverishly, tugging his shirt, skimming down over the strong rack of ribs, then lower. The flap front of his breeches strained against his manhood. He shifted; she plucked at the buttons, sighing when his hot flesh surged into her hand.

"God, Rachel. I want you so much." His hands molded her bottom, clutching, separating. "Wrap your legs around me."

How could she not? Her knees were so weak she sagged against the door, barely able to stand. He lifted her. Slowly. Rachel moaned as her mound slid along the pulsing power of his rod. Then he impaled her and she melted around him, knowing she was home.

The trembling started immediately. First her breasts tightened till the feel of her nipples rubbing the cotton shift was near unbearable. Then her thighs tightened and the shudders wracked her body.

"Logan. Logan." Rachel could only call his name and cling to him as his fingers dug into her hips. As her body convulsed around him. Her lashes lifted and she stared at him, her eyes dark with desire as the power of their coupling shook through her. It was heaven, she knew. The wonders and glory of life beyond the restraints of earth. Heaven she felt. And Logan she saw.

Later, after a shared bath and meal, after the passion of another joining left them satiated and replete, they lay on the bed in each other's arms. Rachel knew what he was thinking, but she liked to hear his voice as he whispered words of love. She closed her eyes as his fingers sifted through her curls, then trailed down the side of her neck, and wished it could be.

But Ebenezer had been a reminder.

Rachel knew it as surely as she knew she didn't

want to leave Logan. But she wouldn't leave yet. Surely not. There was still his life to save.

"Are you asleep?" Logan tucked his chin, catching a glimpse of her thick, golden-tipped lashes as she glanced up at him and smiled.

Rachel cuddled up closer. She didn't want to talk about it. Logan's mind was replaying the way she survived Bingham's pistol ball. He was confused and beginning to wonder . . . wonder so many things. And how could she blame him? But she didn't want to talk about it. She didn't want to waste any time they had left together. So knowing full well what she was about, Rachel propped herself up and began raining kisses down across his chest.

His stomach muscles tightened and his moan vibrated against her ear. His reaction made her bold, made her dip her head lower.

"Do you know what you've done to me?"

Rachel let her tongue slip across his smooth tip. When she lifted her face, blowing a strand of hair aside, mischief was sparkling in her eyes. "I think I do."

Logan laughed, reaching down to pull her atop him. "Before you came to me my world was black. You brought the light." His palm curved about her cheek, touching the corner of her smile with his thumb. "You taught me to love. Made me believe in myself." He paused. "Saved my life."

Saved my life.

The words echoed though her head, draining all the warmth from her body. Rachel tried to catch her breath, to stop the shivers coursing through her, but it was useless.

"Rachel, what's wrong?" Logan's arms tightened about her. "You're so cold."

"I am. Oh Logan, I can't stop trembling." Rachel burrowed beneath the blanket he tucked about her.

"No, don't leave me. Where are you going?" She felt strange, so strange, as if his arms were her only link to life. As if she might slip away if he didn't hold her.

Logan kissed her forehead. "Let me build up the fire."

"But—"

"I'll be right over here." Logan tossed several slabs of wood on the fire, stoking it till the flames danced in the grate. When she called his name he looked around.

And found her gone.

"Rachel? Rachel!" Logan strode back, then felt beneath the blanket, though he knew she couldn't be there. Turning this way and that. Seeing the locked door, the closed window.

Knowing that a person didn't just disappear. Any more than they survived a pistol's deadly shot. Any more than they simply appeared on your mountain.

It was impossible. Logan yanked open the door, knowing she wouldn't be there. She wouldn't be anywhere. She was gone, as she'd come. "Rachel." Logan sank into the chair by the hearth. His head fell back against the cushion, and his eyes closed.

What was he to do now?

Chapter Twenty

> "How many angels are there?
> One—who transforms our life is plenty."
> —Traditional saying

"Impossible."

"That seems a strange word, coming from you."

"Nonetheless, I believe we've given you all the special consideration we can."

"But it was your fault in the first place. I mean, I wasn't supposed to die."

"She has a point there."

"Oh, do be quiet, Ebenezer."

Rachel listened none too patiently as the two spirits quibbled among themselves. If she'd had a foot, she would be tapping it now. She was back among the angels, the darkness calming, the light, a beacon in the distance. But it wasn't the light that drew her.

"All I want is a peek. Just to assure myself that he is all right," she said during a moment of silence.

"You had your chance with him."

"And I did as you asked. I saved his life. He told me so."

"Which is why you are back with us." Ebenezer didn't sound too pleased by the idea.

"He's correct . . . for once. You must forget about this man and get back to your life. Your real life."

Which was what she'd wanted from the beginning. To return to court. The gowns, the jewels, the finery. There were no discomforts at the court of King George. No work. Servants were everywhere. She had but to lift her finger.

There was no hunger. No rustic setting. No fear of the unknown.

No Logan.

Rachel tried a different tact. "He may need my help again."

"In which case his guardian angel will intervene."

"Logan has a guardian angel?" The thought was intriguing . . . and comforting.

"Everyone does."

"Even me? I mean, when I wasn't one myself."

"Of course. Why do you think Ebenezer looked after you so well?"

"Ebenezer?" Rachel felt herself being smiled at. "I recognized you as the elderly man, but—"

"Such an uncomfortable persona to assume. My bones ached and the filth . . . I think I preferred living the life of a dog, though that was a bit trying, too. All those silly rabbits to chase and fleas. Not to mention—"

"Henry? You were Henry?"

"Having to answer to any stupid name someone decides to call me."

Rachel thought Henry a fine name but decided not to argue the point. This aspect of heaven surprised her, though given Logan's dog's penchant for complaining Rachel realized she should have known all along. But all this discussion—of sorts—was not what she cared about. "I only need a little time with him. Just to assure myself that—"

"It would never be enough."

"That's not true. I just want—"

"Rachel, I have been at this business a very long

time, and I know of what I speak. You say it is only a moment you wish, to discover if your charge is all right. But he is human. He will always have problems."

"Which is exactly why I should go to him."

"No, Rachel. That is not a good enough reason."

"But—" Rachel felt the warmth of the spirit as it touched her.

"You taught Logan to love. To believe in himself. You gave him all he needs to survive."

"May we get on with this now?" Ebenezer interrupted. "I've arranged for you to turn up in a small gardener's cabin on the grounds of Queen's House. 'Tis not far from the lake, so there should be no question of how you got there after your near drowning. I thought a loss of memory would explain the time you were absent rather well. That always works nicely if I do say so myself."

Ebenezer rambled on, obviously quite proud of his idea to restore her life. And on some level Rachel had to admit it was an excellent plan. She was certain Her Highness and the king would welcome her back, dote on her. Her life would be the same as before. Queen Charlotte would insist her private physician check Rachel over. The queen might even expect her to stay abed a few days, but then it would be over.

And all would be as it was.

Before Logan.

Before she showed him the meaning of life.

Before she discovered it herself.

"I don't wish to return to England."

"I beg your pardon?"

"You see what I have to deal with. I told you she was trouble."

Rachel ignored Ebenezer's remark and the other spirit's surprise. She had no idea how this might work, or even if it would. But she knew what she wanted—

needed—for her life to be complete. And it wasn't to live in a palace smothered in jewels and costly silks.

"If you force me to return to my old life I shall get to Logan somehow. By coach, then ship. I will find a way."

"And she will, too. Haven't I told you how obstinate she can be?"

"Determined is more the word I would use."

"I don't care which you call it." Rachel's being seemed to tremble with an excitement that not even the soothing effects of her surroundings could subdue. She finally, finally knew. "My life is nothing without him. Without his love."

Very little had changed since he left.

It was simply the way he saw things.

The cabin was still roughly built, untidy, with a crooked chimney that smoked more than heated. The view from the top of the knob was still breathtaking, the vista a wide expanse of valleys and hills peeking through the gossamer veils of mist. He still felt a bit of discomfort standing too near the edge.

But the urge to take one more step and end it all was gone. As was the desire to drown his troubles in drink.

One of the first things Logan did when he returned to his mountain on the frontier was pour out every last drop of rum he'd squirreled away over the years. At first he was frantic to smash the jugs . . . until he realized there was no reason for his concern. He had no compelling need to drink. Not like before. Not like before Rachel.

Logan sank to his haunches, facing out over the world below. He smiled as he always did when he thought of her. Of her beauty. Of the light she brought to his life. Of the love.

Beside him the dog ... Henry ... lolled on his back and Logan absently rubbed the spaniel's spotted stomach. He still had a hard time seeing the animal as anything but rather lazy, but Rachel said he was different, so Logan tried.

"I miss her, Henry." Logan took a deep breath. He didn't expect any response, despite what Rachel said about the dog communicating with her. Not that he didn't believe it possible.

After Rachel, he believed anything possible.

The night she disappeared he searched the inn and surrounding area. He roused people from their beds, questioning them like a madman. Knowing in his heart that she was no longer there. Knowing everything she told him was true.

He'd held an angel in his arms. A bit of heaven in his heart. And thanks to her it was still there.

With a final pat to the warm stomach Logan pushed to his feet.

"For heaven's sake don't jump. Not when I've worked so hard to come back to you!"

Gravel slipped beneath Logan's feet as he jerked around. But her arms were there, reaching out to him, and there was no danger of falling.

Logan held her as tightly as he could, relishing the solid feel of her, bones and smooth, smooth flesh. His Rachel that he would never let go. Would never allow to leave him again. The wild thoughts ricocheted through his mind, slamming into reality.

There was nothing he could do to keep her, if it was not meant to be.

Slowly, he released her till it was only his hands cupping her shoulder that held her captive. Her face—wide angelic blue eyes and sweet mouth—looked up at him. He could barely resist swooping her into his arms and carrying her away.

"Is it really you?"

Her smile widened. "Oh yes, I've come back to you . . ." She hesitated. "That is if you want me."

"Want you? God, Rachel, I've always wanted you. Always loved you, I think, though I may not have realized it."

"And I love you, too." Rachel's admission won her a kiss, one that curled her toes and made her dizzy enough to pull them both away from the edge of the mountain. "Love you," she repeated, as he tongued the side of her neck. She moaned when the warmth of his mouth disappeared and she once more was held at arm's length.

She was more than willing to postpone any discussion of the whys and hows till later, till they'd made love and dozed only to awaken and enjoy each other again. But she supposed there were questions that needed to be answered. And by the quizzical expression in his light-green eyes, she knew he deserved an explanation.

"I chose to come back," she said simply, knowing there was no "simply" about it. "To be with you."

"But what of the king . . . his brother?" Was he truly arguing against his own happiness? Logan clamped his mouth shut, but only for an instant. Her happiness was more important to him than his own. And she'd seemed so anxious to return to her old life before. "Rachel, you were a Lady. You lived in a palace." His eyes swept back toward the dilapidated cabin. "I can give you nothing like that."

"Oh, but you can." Her hand curved up around his cheek. He'd shaved this morning but there was still a rasp of stubble that sent shivers down her spine. "You . . . your love are worth more to me than all the treasures of this world." Her fingers tightened. "I have seen the other side, and I know. Love is the only important thing."

His kiss was gentle. When he looked down into her

eyes again, his were searching. "Is this where you want to live?"

"Why do you ask?" There was no more reading his thoughts, yet she still knew there was something on his mind . . . something beyond worry about his lowly cabin.

"When you left, my heart broke, but I knew it was as it had to be." He fingered a curl behind her ear. "I also knew 'twasn't as it should be me living up here alone. When I was in Charles Town I spoke with Dr. Quincy again, and he told me of the work done with mental patients by a doctor in Williamsburg. I thought perhaps—"

The pressure of her lips cut off the rest of his words. "That's a wonderful idea. You have so much to offer the world. So much to offer me."

Rachel leaned into him, her head nestled on his broad shoulder. Together they looked out over the beauty of the mountains. The sun rose slowly, burning off the vapors that misted the valleys, unveiling the land's secrets.

A breathtaking sight. But in her heart Rachel knew the best secret of them all. The one she'd shared with Logan.

Love was the only thing that mattered.

To My Readers

I hope you enjoyed *My Heavenly Heart*. Writing it for you was such a special treat. Since I was a little girl I've believed in angels. And since I first saw *It's A Wonderful Life* I've wanted to help an angel earn his wings. If you listened carefully with your heart as you read *My Heavenly Heart* perhaps you heard a tiny bell tinkle. I know I did.

The story of Logan MacQuaid and his angel, Rachel Elliott, completes the MacQuaid Brothers Trilogy. Thanks to all of you who helped make *My Savage Heart* and *My Seaswept Heart* so successful. All these books are special to me and I hope to you, too.

So what's next? How can I top a book with an angel of a heroine?

Well, I've always loved fairy tales—tales like Cinderella and Snow White, like Sleeping Beauty and Rapunzel. Stories of queens, and sorcerers, and handsome heroes who save the day. Look for *Splendor*, a fairy tale romance, in February 1996. But don't be surprised if in this fairy tale the handsome hero receives a bit of help from the beautiful queen as he saves the day.

For those brave souls who aren't afraid of a little scare, be sure to watch for *Déjà Vu*, my novella in *Under His Spell*, Zebra's newest Halloween Anthology, to be published in October 1995.

And how could I close without thanking you all for

your wonderful letters. I love writing books like *My Heavenly Heart*. *Your* kind words are "icing on the cake." For a newsletter please write me care of:

Kensington Publishing Corp.
850 Third Avenue
New York, NY 10022–6222

SASE appreciated.

To Happy Endings,

Christine Dorsey

Please turn the page for an
exciting sneak preview of
Jo Goodman's
ALWAYS IN MY DREAMS
to be published by Zebra Books in
June 1995

Chapter one

New York City, Winter 1881

"You want me to *spy* for you?" Mary Schyler Dennehy was incredulous. Her wide eyes and raised brows complemented her tone. Even her jaw remained a trifle slack as she stared in wonderment at her father.

"Don't be so melodramatic," Jay Mac said dismissively. "Spying is not a word I would use."

Skye cut a sideways glance at her mother. Moira offered dryly, "It's certainly the word *I* would use." A sweet Irish brogue took the sting from her sarcasm. "I don't think I like the sound of this, Jay Mac. It's dangerous."

Skye's mobile and expressive mouth closed and flattened. She snorted a bit indelicately. "I don't care *this* for danger," she announced, snapping her fingers to emphasize her point. "It's just that I can't believe Jay Mac is asking me to be a spy."

On anyone's list of the rich and powerful, whether in New York or in the country, John Mackenzie Worth's name was always placed prominently. He was the founder of Northeast Rail, a transportation system that had long outgrown its name and expanded west beyond the Mississippi to California, Nevada, and Colorado, following the trail of gold and silver discoveries. He owned prime real estate around Central Park,

an investment that was returning itself one hundred—
fold as those who could afford it bought land and
built their brown and gray stone mansions uptown.
He sat on some of the most influential boards in
the city, counted among his friends six senators, five
congressmen, and a president, got away with his very
public feud with the mayor, and was often consulted
by other men of industry. Even more frequently Jay
Mac was sought as a financial backer by those with
interests in science, art, and politics. He gave gener-
ously to worthy causes, which generally left out all
things political.

With rare exception John MacKenzie Worth,
known simply as Jay Mac to most of the country,
was regarded with respect and something akin to
reverence.

The rare exception took place in the stone palace
he had built on the corner of Fiftieth and Broadway.
Behind the spiked iron gate and manicured rose
bushes, he was also known as Jay Mac. But here, surrounded at various times by his five daughters and
their mother, the nickname elicited decidedly more
affection and amusement than awe.

Jay Mac's attention darted between his wife and his
youngest daughter. Moira was quite serious in her
objections, but Jay Mac was just arrogant enough to
think he could handle her. Skye, on the other hand,
for all that she looked appalled by his suggestion, was
clearly intrigued. He knew how to interpret the glint
in her bright green eyes and the hint of a dimple on
either side of her wide mouth.

"This is *not* dangerous," he said to both of them.

Moira remained uncertain, but wanting to be convinced. Mary Schyler was trying to hide her disappointment. Jay Mac believed his confidence was well
founded. He had them both. The trick was to allay

the fears of one while making it an adventure for the other.

He rose from the dining table and went to the sideboard. While he was pouring himself a tumbler of scotch Mrs. Cavanaugh entered the room to judge the success of the meal. He heard his wife commend the cook for her special attention to the fish. Skye commented on the pineapple sorbet and asked politely if they could never have it again. Moira admonished her daughter's distressing lack of tact while Mrs. Cavanaugh merely chuckled. There was something comfortable about the scene that had just been played out behind his back, something reassuring in his daughter's cheerful directness, his wife's gentle scolding, the cook's laughter, and his own enjoyment. For an instant he felt a pang of alarm at the thought of sending Skye off. She was the last of his daughters, the only one of his five darling Marys still at home. What would it be like without her?

He quelled the momentary rush of fear by asking if anyone wanted a drink. Moira and Skye refused, taking tea instead.

"What do you call it if it's not spying?" Skye asked when her father returned to the table. She absently tucked a wisp of flame-red hair behind her ear. It slipped out again almost immediately.

"Investigating?"

Moira looked at her husband sternly over the rim of her teacup. "Are you telling or asking? I'm not certain I know by your tone."

"Investigating," he said more firmly. He took off his spectacles and rubbed the bridge of his nose between his thumb and forefinger, a gesture that was meant to convey that he was slightly annoyed at Moira's inability to grasp the difference. "Skye would be investigating the whereabouts of the invention. I thought I had already explained myself in that regard.''

''I'm certain you thought you did,'' Moira said with a touch of asperity. ''But you can see that Skye thinks it's spying and I don't disagree with her.''

Before Jay Mac could counter, Skye broke in. ''Please, Mama, I want to hear Jay Mac out.'' For a moment it looked as if Moira would object, and although her eyes remained worried, she gave in with a brief nod. Skye thanked her with a wide, dimpled smile, then turned to her father. ''Tell me about the invention.''

''It's an engine, or more precisely a particular part of an engine.''

Skye asked innocently, ''What part? The wheel, the cow catcher, the smoke stack?''

Jay Mac returned his spectacles to his face and gave his daughter a hard look, wondering if she was pulling his leg. ''I mean the motor,'' he said. ''The engine of the engine.''

''Oh,'' she said, her voice small. ''Sorry.''

Behind her cup, Moira permitted herself a smile. For a moment it looked as if Jay Mac regretted broaching the subject at all. ''What's so special about this engine?''

''The fuel it uses. The inventor swears it won't be powered by steam. It's going to use a petroleum by-product. Something similar to kerosene. It will be incredibly powerful, lighter and faster than anything in use today. It could change the way we all think of transportation. You can't imagine the application possibilities.'' Jay Mac's voice rose slightly as his excitement grew. ''This is something scientists are working on around the world, not just in this country. There's a push to develop some kind of steam turbine engine, not the lumbering impractical ones that exist today, but something streamlined and efficient. The impact of that invention would be enormous and yet I can honestly say that it pales in comparison to what would be possible with the engine this inventor has proposed.''

Jay Mac paused to let his words sink in. Skye was impressed. Moira looked interested in spite of herself. When he spoke again his tone was quiet, grave, and hinted at things he would not share with just anyone. ''Rockefeller's interested. You can imagine the implications for a company like Standard Oil. John D.'s already made one fortune on kerosene. Think of his profit if he's able to use products that he's now virtually throwing away.''

''Westinghouse?'' asked Skye. She saw her father was surprised that she knew the name. It was hard to know whether to be insulted or pleased. She had generally worked hard at giving the impression that she was mostly frivolous. She conceded now that perhaps she had worked *too* hard. ''Air brakes,'' she added to make sure Jay Mac knew it was no fluke. ''I may not know what Rennie knows about them, but I would have had to have been deaf not to know it was an exciting time for Northeast Rail.''

At the mention of Rennie's name, both Jay Mac and Moira smiled. Mary Renee must have been about seventeen, they recollected, when George Westinghouse had patented his air brakes. For Skye's sister, who had wanted to be part of Jay Mac's empire from the inside, and had realized that dream, the invention of the automatic railroad air brake was a milestone.

''Rennie did go on about it,'' Moira said wistfully. She turned her thoughtful gaze to her husband. ''I imagine you've shared this latest news with Rennie and Jarret.''

Jay Mac shook his head. ''Very little, actually. They've been in Colorado and Nevada since this came about and it isn't something I've wanted to trust to the telegraphers. In fact, I haven't wanted to put much about it in writing. There's a lot at stake, too much perhaps to include even the most trusted men in my employ."

Moira frowned. She smoothed back the temples of her dark red hair, not because there was a strand out of place, but because she needed to do something with her hands. She remembered very well what had happened only a few years earlier: Jay Mac had been the target of a murder plot that would have wrested control of Northeast Rail out of the family's hands. How could he say this wasn't a dangerous business? Her sigh, as well as the militant look in her eyes, expressed the words she would not say aloud.

Once again Skye managed to head her mother off. She was leaning forward in her chair, the perfect oval of her face animated with excitement. "Do you want me to steal this invention for you?" she asked with more eagerness than was either ladylike or strictly moral. Out of the corner of her eye she saw that her mother was appalled. Skye made a half-hearted attempt to appear abashed. It didn't fool anyone. In front of her eyes Jay Mac's hair seemed to take on a more grayish cast.

"I don't want you to *steal* anything," he said, just managing to swallow his drink without choking. "I want you to bring it back to me."

Confused, Skye merely stared at her father. Moira's comment underlined her own confusion. "You'll have to pardon me if I fail to distinguish the difference."

Jay Mac set his tumbler on the table. A damp ring of water beaded on the polished surface. "You can't steal something that already belongs to you," he explained patiently.

"You *own* this engine?" asked Skye.

He nodded slowly. "Bought and paid for every part of its development."

"Then why don't you have it?"

"I fully expected to get reports from the inventor on his progress. This is by no means a finished product. It has never tested reliably, but my early information has always led me to believe he was on the right track and getting closer. I've asked for the current status but I get little in return that's straightforward." Jay Mac shifted in his chair. "I'm concerned that he's backing out of the project, or worse, that he may even have thoughts of selling the idea elsewhere. That's forbidden in my contract with him. I want you to find out if my fears are founded. And if you can get the plans, or the engine, all the better."

Moira simply sank back into her chair and crossed herself. "Dear God," she said quietly. "I can't have heard any of this correctly. This is something you should be sending one of your men on, Jay Mac, not your youngest daughter.

Skye bristled. "Mama, how could you?" she asked, wounded. Her mother had always been supportive of whatever her daughters wanted to do. Traditionally, it had been Jay Mac who was the fly in the ointment.

He had been fiercely protective of all his children, planning, prodding, pushing, usually in directions they didn't want to go. He opposed his oldest daughter's decision to enter a convent but Mary Francis held her ground and did as she wanted. He tried to guide Mary Michael's career as a newspaper woman when he realized she would be a reporter with or without his support. When he attempted to buy her a job on the *Herald*, she promptly accepted a position with the *New York Chronicle*. Mary Renee had to prove herself twice over to gain a position as an engineer with Northeast Rail, and Mary Margaret was going to medical school because of her husband's support, not her father's.

He had been just as iron-handed in his machinations to see them married and settled. Mary Francis had slipped away from him but Michael, Rennie, and Maggie had given him some frustrating moments as they tried to avoid his openly manipulative touch.

Skye's ambition was vastly different from her sisters. Thus far it had kept her out of her father's sites. She had no desire to serve God, inform the public, build bridges, or care for the sick. Skye wanted to be an adventuress.

Not precisely a lofty goal, it was nonetheless one for which she felt eminently suited. Indeed, in her own manner Skye was just as single-minded in her approach to realizing her dreams as any of the Marys before her. She had decided long ago what skills were most needed for adventuring and had set about mastering them. Skye Dennehy was an excellent horsewoman and a crack whip. She rode sidesaddle in public and astride in private. In her phaeton she was completely at ease leading a high-spirited team on a rollicking ride over farmland just north of the city, or keeping them tightly in check on a crowded city street. People remarked that she had a passion for it. To Skye it was merely one means to an end.

Skye studied art and antiques and architecture. She devoured books on the history and geography of the places she wanted to go. Like riding astride, she did it outside the public eye. Even her family did not suspect the extent of her learning. Maggie had been the scholar. Skye was the scamp.

She was confident they would have encouraged her endeavors but found some way to discourage her plans to apply them. It was easy to be secretive about her accomplishments. She wasn't doing at all well in her final year at school. In fact she was failing most of her university classes and had no intention of returning in the spring.

It wasn't that she couldn't do the course work. Quite the opposite. With rare exception she found her private plan of learning had advanced her far beyond what was expected by her professors. With little to challenge her Skye avoided most of her classes and arranged tutoring in activities that interested her.

That was how she became proficient in the use of weapons. Skye was not only accurate with a bow, she could fence and was comfortable using a variety of guns. The advent of winter had curtailed her sailing lessons on the Hudson but she had recently found someone to teach her all about photography.

"Tell me about this inventor," Skye asked her father. "What sort of person is he?"

Jay Mac leaned back in his chair and picked up his drink. He rolled the tumbler casually between his palms, choosing his words carefully. "Serious," he said. "Yes, that rather describes him. It's difficult to know what the man is thinking. The plans he outlined to me were brilliant, though. Brilliant."

Boring. It was the word that came to Skye's mind. The man was boringly steady, dull, and probably too smart for his own good. She'd met a few men like that at social gatherings. Invariably they couldn't talk about the weather without describing what they intended to do about it. She practically yawned.

Moira said, "Now why in the world would a man like that want our Skye around?"

One corner of Skye's mouth kicked up. Her mother's question wasn't terribly complimentary but it was something Skye had been wanting to know.

Jay Mac sighed. "He doesn't want Skye around. He doesn't know her or anything about her. His social circles, such as they are, are vastly different than Mary Schyler's. What he needs is a housekeeper. Skye would be perfect."

Skye raised one brow. "As a housekeeper? I don't think so, Jay Mac." She stood, gracing both her parents with another innocently dimpled smile. "But I'd make a wonderful spy." Skirting the table, Skye dropped a light kiss on her father's cheek. "Let me think about it. Right now I have to be going. The ball's up in the park, the skating's wonderful, and I'm meeting Daniel in"—she glanced at the clock on the sideboard—"oh my, I'm already late." She quickly came around the table and gave her mother a kiss. "I should be home before ten, but don't give it a thought if I'm a little later." Skye didn't give anyone a chance to respond. She hurried out of the dining room, crisp petticoats rustling beneath her brushed wool skating skirt.

Jay Mac looked at his wife. "Your daughter's a flibberty-gibbet, ma'am, I'll never get used to it."

"*Our* daughter," Moira said, "is a breath of fresh air. You can't harness her."

"I'd be satisfied if she'd sit for ten minutes."

Moira ignored his attempt to sidetrack her. "I think you'd better tell me what's really going on. I won't have Skye exposed to any danger and I can't believe that you would either. There's something not quite right and I don't think it has anything to do with that inventor. You're hatching a scheme. I just know it."

"Scheme?" he asked with an exaggerated show of innocence. Chuckling, he took Moira's hand and bade her rise. He came to his own feet and casually rested his hands on either side of his wife's waist. He liked the way she automatically laid her palms on his arms and raised her face to him. After thirty years together, she only seemed more beautiful to him. "Let's go into the parlor."

Moira stood on tiptoe, kissed her husband on the mouth, and let herself be led out of the dining room. Under her breath she added, "Said the spider to the fly."

"What was that, darling?"

"Nothing, Jay Mac. Lead on."

"He wants you to be a *spy*?"

Skye continued to lace her skates, not bothering to spare a glance at her companion. "Don't be so melodramatic," she said, echoing her father's words. "This is Jay Mac we're talking about. My father, remember?"

Daniel Pendergrass shook his head. "I'm not likely to forget." He brushed a bit of crusted snow from the tip of one skate. "He hates me," he said forlornly.

"Now you're being ridiculous. He doesn't hate you. When you think about it, he hardly knows you." Skye looked up from her lacing and grinned at her friend. "He hates the idea *of* you." Daniel's forlorn look became morose. Skye laughed. "We wouldn't suit, Daniel. We both know that. We've known it since our very first kiss."

Daniel's pale cheeks flushed with color. "Do you have to bring that up? I didn't know what I was doing. I'm sure I'd do it better now."

Skye finished with her skates and thrust her hands into her ermine muff. "That's because you've been practicing with Evelyn Hardy," she said without a trace of jealously. She stood up. The park bench wasn't comfortable enough to linger in conversation. A cold wind was blowing across the pond. The skating party they were invited to join was circling on the far side of the ice. Skye could hear their laughter. "Come on, Daniel. Your friends are waiting."

Daniel watched Skye Dennehy step gingerly onto

the ice. By the time he came to his feet she was already
moving away, her sweep across the ice both confident
and graceful. He adjusted his hat over his fair hair
and tightened the scarf around his neck. Tall and
lanky at twenty-two, it seemed that he hadn't yet
grown into his skin. His course across the ice was
much less graceful than Skye's and infinitely less confident. But he was a good sport, amiable, and humor-
ously disparaging of his own shortcomings. Skye
assured him, in spite of the fact that she wasn't interested, he was also quite handsome. He grinned. Evelyn Hardy thought so, too.

When Daniel reached his group of friends, Skye
was skating by herself, intent upon cutting a perfect
circle in the ice. Daniel's easy grin faded. It was no
accident that she was alone. Skye's presence was
merely suffered by most of his friends, permitted because he invariably insisted upon it. She had chosen
her words deliberately earlier. The group of skaters
they were about to join were *his* friends, not hers.
Skye was skating at the pond at his invitation, not
theirs. It seemed incredible to him that anyone still
cared she was a bastard.

Skye looked up as Daniel approached and promptly
lost the line she had been tracing. "See what you
made me do?" she said. "You took your time getting
here." If she was hurt by her exclusion from the
others, she didn't show it. Her features were made
lovelier by her animated smile, the brightness in her
green eyes, and the color in her cheeks. Her hat was
set forward at a jaunty angle and a fringe of white
fur touched her forehead. Not far away, a bonfire on
the bank cast all the skaters within its circle of light
in a gold and orange glow. Where Skye's hair peeped
out beneath her hat and scarf it was like a flame.

He held out his elbow and waited for her to slip
her arm in his. He thought tonight she seemed to

grasp him more tightly, as if he had extended a life-
line. Daniel studied her face again. No, there wasn't
a hint that anything was wrong. Skye would never let
anyone see what she was feeling; she rarely let anyone
know what she was thinking.

"What happened?" he asked as they skated toward
his friends. Someone called out his name and he
raised a hand in recognition.

"Nothing happened."

"Skye."

"Nothing happened," she repeated. "Exactly that.
They cut me dead."

Daniel shook his head, hardly able to take it in.
His friends were not usually so deliberately cold to
Skye. He looked around as they joined the pairs of
skaters crossing the ice in a large circle. A band played
on the bank, loud enough for them to match their
movements to music, but not so loud that it interfered
with conversation. "Hi, Charlie. Alice." He cast a
quick smile over his shoulder so as not to misstep.
"You remember Skye Dennehy, don't you?"

Charlie looked distinctly uncomfortable. His Ad-
am's apple bobbed as he swallowed hard. Alice offered a wan smile. "Skye. It's a pleasure." They
offered their greeting in unison, and as if shocked
by the volume of it, they bent their heads and concentrated on their footwork.

Skye's laughter was bright and unfettered but she
leaned closer to Daniel. "I've known Alice Hobbs
since we were six," she whispered. "And just last week
Charlie confided in me that he intended to ask for
her hand." Behind them Charlie and Alice had left
the circle and were waiting to join it in another place.
"What's wrong with everyone?" she asked. She had
been snubbed before, in fact she took something of
a perverse pleasure in forcing people by the very act
of ignoring her to acknowledge her existence. This

was different. There was something almost vicious in
the way she was cut out tonight.

Daniel shrugged. "I'll be damned if I know," he
said. The band on shore struck up another tune. The
introduction of a banjo increased the tempo and
the skaters picked up their pace. There were bright
flashes of gold and crimson as the women whirled,
their skirts lifting to reveal white petticoats and flan-
nel leggings. Now it was Daniel who leaned into Skye
for support. She held him securely and made certain
their feet didn't cross paths. "I'll never understand
it. The circumstances of your birth are hardly your
fault."

Skye knew that Daniel meant well. In truth it made
no difference to him. She had sensed that from the
very beginning, which was why he probably knew her
better than anyone outside her own family. But he
was naive about it. She could have pointed out that his
parents had never invited her into his home although
they would have been pleased to have made Jay Mac's
acquaintance.

The circumstances of her birth, as Daniel referred
to them, had taken on a new twist in recent years
when John MacKenzie Worth had actually married
his mistress. It made some difference to New York's
elite social set that he had seen fit to make a match
after the death of his wife, although behind closed
doors they blamed him for her suicide. Prior to Nina's
death, Jay Mac had kept Moira Dennehy openly as
his mistress and raised five bastard daughters with
her.

Skye was no more accepted in the social circle of
her peers than her mother or sisters had been; Skye
merely worked harder at it. There was an awkward
transition when Jay Mac married Moira but by then
people were so used to cutting out the Dennehy
women no one knew quite how to stop. Then there

was the fact that Skye had not been moved to take Worth as her own surname. She had grown up as a Dennehy. She was not enamored of the idea of replacing it with something else.

That last thought brought Skye back to her earlier conversation with her father. "He's got some sort of plan up his sleeve, you know."

Daniel's light brows came together as he frowned. "Who? Charlie?"

"No, not Charlie. I don't care about Charlie or Alice or any of the others." Which was more or less the truth. "I'm talking about Jay Mac. This inventor business is just a bit suspicious. It's not like my—" Without warning Daniel's left foot slipped to the side and caught the blade on Skye's right skate. They wobbled, clutching one another, scrambling to hold their balance. Somewhat to Skye's amazement it was Daniel who managed to compensate, his lanky figure folding and unfolding like the pleats of an accordion. Skye went down with an unladylike "oooff" and sprawled across the ice on her stomach. Her face was protected by the ermine muff she had managed to raise at the last possible second. It cradled her head on the ice while she caught her breath.

She was vaguely aware that she and Daniel had become the center of some confusion and attention. A few couples had managed to avoid bumping into them as they had teetered on the ice, but two others not paying attention had gone down hard. Skye heard her name used like a curse. She smiled, closing her eyes as she took quick inventory of body parts. She sensed, rather than saw, Daniel hunkering down beside her and the beginnings of a crowd gathering around them both.

"Skye? Are you all right?" he asked, touching her temple. "Where do you hurt?"

She opened one eye and said dryly, "All over."

"Is anything broken?"

Skye was still taking inventory. She stretched her legs and rotated her ankles. "Nothing's broken."

"Do you think she'll lose the baby?" someone in the crowd whispered loud enough to be heard.

"She shouldn't have been skating," said another. "She probably wanted to be rid of it."

"I think she fainted," said a third.

The conversation around her was so absurd, so patently ridiculous that at first Skye had no idea she was the subject of the scandalous speculation. It was the stricken look on Daniel's face that made her take notice of the talk and eventually apply it to herself.

"It's happened before in her family," a voice whispered knowingly. The confidential tone was carried on the back of the wind to all parts of the gathering circle. "Her sisters, you know."

"Not all of them surely. Isn't one a nun?"

"Why do you think she went into the convent?" came a reply. It was said with the authority of gospel.

"My mother says this is the final straw," said a young woman. "I'm not allowed to accept any more invitations if *she'll* be there. It doesn't matter who her father is. My mother says it's what happens when a Protestant like Jay Mac takes up with a Catholic." There was a small pause, as if the speaker was shuddering. "If she knew about tonight . . ." She let her voice drift away allowing her friends to imagine the consequences she might suffer if her mother heard about this incident.

Skye was too angry to be mortified. Did they think she was deaf? She held out her hand to Daniel. "Will you help me up?"

He took her hand and her elbow and assisted her into a sitting position. "You're certain you're all right?"

"I will be as soon as you get me out of here." She hardly recognized her own voice. The words had been said through clenched teeth.

The crowd began to disperse as Daniel helped Skye to her feet. His own balance wasn't steady but no one offered to lend a hand. Looping his arm under Skye's, he supported her as they skated away from the party to the edge of the pond and the bench located on the perimeter. After she sat down he knelt in front of her and began loosening the laces on her skates.

"You shouldn't pay them any attention, Skye," he told her. "They were speaking without thinking."

Skye's low chuckle was humorless. "They were speaking *exactly* what they were thinking."

"They were showing their ignorance."

Skye had nothing to say to that. "How do these rumors start?"

He shrugged. "It seems as though there has to be someone to scapegoat."

"But this time it's me."

Daniel pulled off her skates and found Skye's shoes under the bench. "Put these on. I'll take you home." He sat down beside her and wrestled with his own laces.

"Remember the masquerade at the Bilroths' last month?" Skye asked.

"Of course I remember." He had had his share of attention as a buccaneer. Skye had had hers because she was one of two women to faint in the hot and crowded ballroom. The other was Mrs. Spencer, a matron in her sixties who was said to suffer a heart condition. Daniel supposed that was the origin of the rumors.

Skye saw by his changing expression that he understood. "I suppose it's easy for people to think the worst of me." She sighed. "Though, truth be known, there are a lot worse things than being pregnant."

Daniel blushed at her plain speaking. "Watch your voice," he cautioned her. "People will hear."

"So what if they do," she said recklessly. She raised her voice purposefully and repeated, "There are a lot worse things than being pregnant."

Daniel wanted to slink off the bench and into a nearby snowdrift. Skye's timing had been perfect. A lull in the music permitted her voice to carry across the pond unfettered. He saw several people in the skating party glance in their direction. "You've convinced them now."

"They were already convinced. They probably think"—she raised her voice again—"you're the father."

Daniel turned on her, yanking his scarf away from his face. "Skye! That's not amusing!"

She couldn't find it in herself to be contrite. "Would you be ashamed to be the father of my child?"

"Don't be ridiculous," he said, dismissing her.

Skye had expected a fervent denial from him, not some comment on the absurdity of her statement. "Daniel?" She turned toward him, studying his profile. "*Would* you be ashamed?" she asked softly. She watched the play of emotion on his face and heard in his hesitation an answer for which she wasn't prepared. "Oh, Daniel," she said sadly. "You, too."

He sat up a little straighter, defending himself. "You haven't let me answer."

"Yes, I have." She finished slipping on her shoes and picked up her muff. "It's all right. Don't give it another thought. I know I won't. It's not as if I wanted to have a child by you so I don't know why I'm disappointed. Perhaps it's just because I thought you were my friend."

"I *am* you friend."

"You wouldn't be ashamed." She stood, turned

her back on Daniel, and began walking away. He
called to her but he was tangled in his skate laces.
Skye didn't look back. When she heard him call again
she increased her pace. It was important to get away
from Daniel right now. What his friends thought only
touched her a little; Daniel's silent admission seemed
more like a complete betrayal.

Skye found one of the paths in the park and kept
to it. Where the snow hadn't been cleared it was
crusted and her leather boots made a crunching
sound as she hurried along. She concentrated on the
sound, trying to block out more intrusive thoughts,
but she was only marginally successful. In the silent
spaces she heard the condemning voices. She not
only heard what they had said, she imagined she
heard the reproachful things they had all been thinking.

In her mind she heard them call her mother an
Irish Catholic whore. The way they said it it was difficult to know which word carried the most disapproval.
Skye heard old, familiar phrases like ''the apple
doesn't fall far from the tree,'' and ''like mother, like
daughter.'' It didn't matter that Moira Dennehy and
Jay Mac Worth had been together for more than a
quarter of a century, that her mother had loved no
other man. She was a whore, her five daughters bas-
tards, and while Jay Mac's wealth and considerable
influence sometimes altered the way the Dennehys
were treated, it did little to change what anyone
thought of them.

The family had weathered scandals more damaging
than this little rumor, Skye thought, but it was the
first one that had touched her so personally. She
wondered if her father had heard the rumor. Was
that why he was offering her the opportunity to get
away?

It was something worth considering and Skye promised herself she'd confront her father directly on the matter. He'd scowl at her straight talking, probably waggle his finger at her for being impudent, but she'd be able to see through his bluster to his heart. She'd know if he was lying.

A sound behind her caught Skye's attention, stopped her musing, and halted her in her tracks. She felt the hair rise at the back of her neck as the crunching sound came again, this time closer. She had wanted to believe it had been her own feet making the noise, that the sound had been an echo of her own steps. She had to stop pretending that now.

Skye stepped off the path and moved into the shadowed area of some pines. The evergreen canopy sheltered her. She hugged the rough bark of one tree, making herself nearly invisible. She couldn't even say why she was suddenly wary, why she suspected it was someone other than Daniel sharing the path with her. Her breathing became light and shallow. She waited and watched.

The man who came along the path had established a pace that was both hurried and somehow restrained, as if he wanted to run but was holding himself back. Skye saw him pause not far from her grove of trees. He never once looked in her direction but cast a backward glance over his shoulder. It was then she realized she had never had anything to fear from him, that he wasn't following her, but that someone was following *him.*

His breath seemed to hang in the air a moment as he considered his options. He blew on his ungloved hands to warm them while his eyes darted around, looking for protection in the bushes and trees. Skye could hear another set of footsteps approaching, then realized it was at least two men, perhaps more. She almost called to the man on the path, beckoning him to join her, when she saw he had made his decision

not to hide or run. He was turning in the direction
of his pursuers, his fists clenching and unclenching
lightly at his sides.

His body crouched slightly, his lean frame coiled
in a way that made him seem powerfully wound. His
feet weren't planted, his shoulders weren't braced,
he held himself lightly and loosely, giving the impression of lithe, tensile strength. He wore neither a hat
nor a scarf. In the moonlight his hair only appeared
dark and overlong at the nape where it brushed the
collar of his coat. His profile was clean shaven and
stark, the lines of his face hard. He was so still that
he might have been a statue.

They came upon him suddenly. Two of them, Skye
saw, relieved there weren't more, though why she
should be favoring the lone stranger she couldn't say.
They were both burly and hard, muscular men with
shoulder spans that seemed as wide as they were tall.
They both wore wool caps that covered their hair and
ears. One cap appeared black, the other a lighter
color, probably yellow in daylight. Their faces were
broad and their cheeks were hidden by large side
whiskers. Their chins were bare.

"There he is!" Black Cap yelled. They charged
forward as if expecting their quarry to turn tail and
run. When he didn't they didn't stop to think what
it might mean.

Yellow Cap leaped first, throwing himself at his
prey to drag him to the ground. Skye pressed her
knuckles against her mouth to keep from shouting
a warning. As she watched, the man simply and gracefully pivoted to one side and Yellow Cap pitched forward, flailing at the air until he landed belly down
on the path. He grunted hard, the warm air spilling
from his body and misting in the moonlight.

Seeing what happened to his companion brought
Black Cap skidding to a halt. "You all right?" he

called. There was a muffled groan. Black Cap accepted it as a signal that no real harm was done. He gave his full attention to his quarry, circling slowly, elbows bent and gloved fists raised in a fighting posture.

Black Cap closed the circle, jabbing and thrusting with his right. The other man feinted, dodging and ducking the intended blows easily. A left hook sailed above his head. A right jab missed his ribs by inches. Skye saw Black Cap become frustrated and make his punches wilder and harder. Yellow Cap was on his knees, pushing himself upright. He staggered for a step or two, found his land legs, and threw himself into the fight.

With Black Cap and Yellow Cap both punching and jabbing, their victim had to watch his front and back. He was able to avoid their throws, bobbing and weaving, until both his assailants were fairly growling with anger. Without a word passing between the two of them, they closed in again. Then Black Cap managed a swing that connected. The stranger's head snapped back and he lost his footing for a moment, pushed backward by the force of the blow. Black Cap came at him again, this time aiming for his ribs, but his victim was already recovering.

From Skye's vantage point she thought the lone man's movements were so precise they almost seemed choreographed. He twisted and feinted with the powerful grace of a dancer, his hands and arms part of the same motion as his legs. He struck like a snake, coiled one moment, then unleashing a terrible fury in the next.

The stranger used his right hand like a cleaver, chopping Black Cap hard on the curve of his neck and shoulder. Black Cap's heavy coat wasn't enough padding to absorb the power behind that blow and his knees buckled under him. He groaned, as much in surprise by the attack as in pain.

Yellow Cap stepped back, confused by his victim's tactics. The distance he put between himself and his quarry prevented the stranger from using his arms. Yellow Cap couldn't have anticipated the stranger might use his legs.

Skye's eyes widened as she saw the stranger leap feet first. His right foot connected with Yellow Cap's midriff. Before Yellow Cap could take stock of what had happened, the stranger's left foot followed through, shoving Yellow Cap backward with enough force to push the breath from his lungs. Gasping for air, Yellow Cap dropped to his knees again, this time clutching his middle. When his head dropped forward, exposing the vulnerable back side of his neck, the stranger struck again, this time with the same cleaverlike chop he had used on Black Cap. Yellow Cap toppled sideways and lay groaning for a moment before his body jerked once, then was completely still.

Skye's gaze lifted from Yellow Cap's motionless body to his partner's. Black Cap charged the stranger from behind. She opened her mouth to yell a warning and in the next second realized it wasn't necessary. The stranger seemed to have an awareness beyond what his eyes could see. He pivoted and stepped out of the path of Black Cap's charge. At the same time he reached out to grab Black Cap by the scruff of the neck and the small of the back and pushed, using Black Cap's own considerable weight and speed to force him even further away.

Black Cap stumbled and fell forward, collapsing on all fours just a few feet from where Skye stood. She remained perfectly still in her hiding place, afraid to even draw a breath. Black Cap shook himself off, much like a shaggy, sopping wet dog after a bath, then he scrambled to his feet, turned, and charged again.

It seemed to Skye that the stranger waited until the last possible second to step out of the way. Black Cap was once again helped along in the direction he was already going. This time he skidded on the ground on his stomach and face, his broad chin pushing clumps of snow out of the way like a plow. For a moment he remained still and Skye thought he just might have the good sense not to get up. It wasn't to be. She winced as Black Cap pushed himself into a kneeling position, swiped at his icy chin with the back of his hand, and looked over his shoulder at the prey who had become the predator.

"You're a nasty bit of business, ain't you?" Black Cap muttered. "You afraid to face me with your fists?"

The stranger stood his ground, saying nothing.

"That's what I thought." He reached into pocket of his coat and pulled out a derringer, a deadly weapon in the right hands and at close range. "Then go up against this, you bastard."

The stranger didn't wait until Black Cap finished his sentence before he attacked. His lithe body was a blur of motion, spinning, flying, leaping. A single kick dislodged the gun from Black Cap's hand. His wrist, devoid of all feeling now, was trapped beneath the stranger's foot. A second solid kick to Black Cap's gut drove the breath from his lungs. Black Cap collapsed and never saw the blow that centered between his shoulder blades. His body shuddered once, then was as still as his partner's.

The stranger stepped back and paused, looking at his felled attackers. Skye thought he might be using the time to catch his breath but he wasn't winded in the least. He simply seemed to be indulging in a moment of detached curiosity.

Skye watched him take his fill. He shook his head back and forth slowly, as if he could not quite believe what had taken place, or at least that he couldn't comprehend the stupidity of his assailants. Though his back was to Skye, she imagined that she could see his mouth curved in an ironic sort of half smile.

"You were never in any danger, ma'am."

Skye started, blinking widely. She looked around, her eyes darting to shadows on the other side of the path. It didn't seem possible that he intended his comment for her.

"Or is it 'miss'?" he asked.

Mary Schyler inched away from the pine tree but not out from under its protective canopy. "Sure, and I'm thinkin' it's none of your concern," she said cheekily, affecting her mother's lilting Irish brogue.

He turned toward her and the moonshine on his face gave Skye slender evidence of a smile that was a bit menacing in its coolness. "You're right," he said. "You'd better be on your way."

Skye didn't want to leave the safety of the sheltering pines. She was merely a shadow to him and she wanted to remain that way. "You first." He ducked his head and she thought the action hid a more fulsome smile. She wished she could see him better, yet to do so would have compromised her own anonymity.

"I need to look after these men, don't you think?" he asked her.

Since both Black and Yellow Cap seemed to be perfectly unconscious, Skye could only imagine what his "looking after" might entail. "You're going to kill them?" she asked. "Right here in the park?" She thought she heard him chuckle. The low, husky, back-of-the-throat sound sent a shiver up her spine, yet she recognized it wasn't fear that she felt, but something just as elemental and infinitely more intimate.

"I'm going to tie them up."

Remembering what Black Cap had pulled out of his pocket after reaching inside, Skye held her breath as the stranger's hand slipped into his own overcoat. A normal rhythm resumed when he held out a length of rope and dangled it in front of her. "You were prepared," she said.

"I've learned to be."

She wondered what sort of man he was that he had anticipated a walk in the park to be so fraught with danger. It occurred to Skye that she didn't even know which side of the law he was on. "Why were they after you?" she asked.

"Sure, and I'm thinkin' it's none of your concern," he said, echoing her earlier words as well as her accent.

This time she heard the smile in his voice even if she couldn't see it. He was amused by her and that didn't set well with Skye. "I could scream," she told him, "and bring down the beat cops on your head."

"You could," he said. He knelt beside Black Cap, drew out a knife, and cut off a length of rope. In short order he had the man securely trussed, hands behind his back and one of his own gloves stuffed in his mouth.

Skye couldn't say why she was still standing around, except perhaps because it was the most exciting thing that had ever happened to her. It was practice of sorts, she supposed, for being an adventuress.

Out of the corner of her eye she saw that Yellow Cap was stirring. She started to call out a warning, then saw it was unnecessary. Once again the stranger seemed to have anticipated trouble. He turned on his haunches, saw Yellow Cap's struggle, and neatly clipped him on the chin with his fist. Yellow Cap's jaw cracked and his head struck the frozen ground with a thud. Skye winced.

"So you *can* fight with your fists," she said when

she recovered her voice. "Just like a Dublin street brawler."

The stranger merely shrugged and began tying Yellow Cap. When he was done he dragged the unconscious man toward Skye's hiding place.

She retreated quickly. "What are you doing?" she demanded. She wished her voice could have shown more anger and less fear.

"I'm moving him off the path," he said calmly. Even the exertion of dragging Yellow Cap's considerable bulk to the hiding place hadn't winded him. He came within a few feet of Skye but he didn't once turn in her direction. After leaning Yellow Cap against the rough trunk of an evergreen, he shifted his attention to Black Cap and repeated the procedure. He completed his activity by kicking up snow where it had been pressed flat from dragging the bodies. In less than a minute he had obscured the trail to the bodies.

When he was standing on the path again he glanced once in Skye's direction. "You'd better go before they come around and you're discovered with them."

Skye hesitated, waiting for the stranger to move on.

"I assure you they won't be half so gallant as I about a lady's welfare."

She blushed and her husky brogue deepened. "You do me credit, sir, callin' me a lady, but I'm not so fine as all that."

The stranger was quiet a moment, considering. "Then perhaps you'd agree to go somewhere with me. There'd be money in it for you."

"You mistook my meanin', sir, I said I wasn't so fine as a lady, but that doesn't mean I'm a whore."

The stranger was stunned into silence, then he chuckled lowly. "And *you* mistook *my* meaning. You could help me if—" He stopped. There was a shout of rowdy laughter somewhere along the path behind him. More than one person was part of the vocal fray. Someone called a name. A woman giggled in response. A joke was finished and there was more laughter.

"Go on," Skye urged him when the stranger hesitated, looking in her direction. "Get out of here." She would have repeated herself but he needed no second urging.

He vanished almost in front of her eyes.

RECEIVE
$1.00 REBATE
WITH PURCHASE OF
MY HEAVENLY HEART

To receive your rebate, enclose:
- ★ Proof of purchase symbol cut from below
- ★ Original cash register receipt with book price circled
- ★ Print information below and mail to:

ZEBRA
BOOKS

ZEBRA REACH FOR THE STARS REBATE
Post Office Box 1052-D, Grand Rapids, MN 55745-1052

Name_____

Address_____

City_____

State_____**Zip**_____

Store name_____

State_____**Zip**_____

This coupon must accompany your request. No duplicates accepted. Void where prohibited, taxed or restricted. Offer available to U.S. & Canadian residents only. Allow 6 weeks for mailing of your refund payable in U.S. funds. OFFER EXPIRES 7/30/95.

Reach for the Stars...
and always Reach for Romance
by these Zebra Superstars:

Coming in June 1995:

Always in My Dreams
by Jo Goodman

PROOF OF PURCHASE
0-8217-4930-7

TODAY'S HOTTEST READS
ARE TOMORROW'S SUPERSTARS

VICTORY'S WOMAN   (4484, $4.50)
by Gretchen Genet
Andrew—the carefree soldier who sought glory on the battlefield,
and returned a shattered man . . . Niall—the legendary frontiers-
man and a former Shawnee captive, tormented by his past . . .
Roger—the troubled youth, who would rise up to claim a shock-
ing legacy . . . and Clarice—the passionate beauty bound by one
man, and hopelessly in love with another. Set against the back-
drop of the American revolution, three men fight for their
heritage—and one woman is destined to change all their lives forever!

FORBIDDEN   (4488, $4.99)
by Jo Beverley
While fleeing from her brothers, who are attempting to sell her
into a loveless marriage, Serena Riverton accepts a carriage ride
from a stranger—who is the handsomest man she has ever seen.
Lord Middlethorpe, himself, is actually contemplating marriage
to a dull daughter of the aristocracy, when he encounters the
breathtaking Serena. She arouses him as no woman ever has. And
after a night of thrilling intimacy—a forbidden liaison—Serena
must choose between a lady's place and a woman's passion!

WINDS OF DESTINY   (4489, $4.99)
by Victoria Thompson
Becky Tate is a half-breed outcast—branded by her Comanche
heritage. Then she meets a rugged stranger who awakens her
heart to the magic and mystery of passion. Hiding a desperate
past, Texas Ranger Clint Masterson has ridden into cattle country
to bring peace to a divided land. But a greater battle rages inside
him when he dares to desire the beautiful Becky!

WILDEST HEART   (4456, $4.99)
by Virginia Brown
Maggie Malone had come to cattle country to forge her future as
a healer. Now she was faced by Devon Conrad, an outlaw
wounded body and soul by his shadowy past . . . whose eyes
blazed with fury even as his burning caress sent her spiraling with
desire. They came together in a Texas town about to explode in sin
and scandal. Danger was their destiny—and there was nothing
they wouldn't dare for love!

*Available wherever paperbacks are sold, or order direct from the
Publisher. Send cover price plus 50¢ per copy for mailing and
handling to Penguin USA, P.O. Box 999, c/o Dept. 17109,
Bergenfield, NJ 07621. Residents of New York and Tennessee
must include sales tax. DO NOT SEND CASH.*